THE *Ghosts* OF
ASHBURY HIGH

JACLYN MORIARTY

ARTHUR A. LEVINE BOOKS
An Imprint of Scholastic Inc.

Library of Congress Cataloging-in-Publication Data   Moriarty, Jaclyn.   The ghosts of Ashbury High / Jaclyn Moriarty. — 1st ed.   p. cm.   Summary: Student essays, scholarship committee members' notes, and other writings reveal interactions between a group of modern-day students at an exclusive New South Wales high school and their strange connection to a young Irishman transported to Australia in the early 1800s.   ISBN 978-0-545-06972-4 (hardcover : alk. paper)   [1. Interpersonal relations — Fiction.   2. High schools — Fiction. 3. Schools — Fiction.   4. New South Wales — Fiction.   5. Australia — History — 1788– 1851 — Fiction.]   I. Title.   PZ7.M826727Gho 2010   [Fic] — dc22   2009032651 • 10 9 8 7 6 5 4 3 2 1   10 11 12 13 14 15 • Printed in the U.S.A. 23 • First edition, June 2010 •

Book design by Elizabeth B. Parisi

To Liane

ALSO BY JACLYN MORIARTY

Feeling Sorry for Celia

The Year of Secret Assignments

The Murder of Bindy Mackenzie

The Spell Book of Listen Taylor

Note

Most of the following story takes place in an HSC English exam on the topic of gothic fiction.

The HSC (or Higher School Certificate) is a series of exams taken by students in New South Wales at the end of their final year of school. During that final year, students also complete "projects" and "assessment tasks," the results of which are combined with the HSC exam results to determine which university major the student may pursue.

Gothic fiction includes novels like *Wuthering Heights* and *Frankenstein*. In a gothic novel, you will often find mad people locked in attics, secret passageways, monsters, murderers, ghosts, and family curses. A beautiful young woman is likely to ride in a carriage through a bleak landscape, hear the toll of a distant bell, see a black crow, hear a rumble of ominous thunder, see drops of blood, hear haunting music, see a figure shrouded in mist, hear a bloodcurdling scream — and it will all make her prone to fainting several times a day.

PART ONE

Board of Studies

New South Wales

HIGHER SCHOOL CERTIFICATE
EXAMINATION

English Extension 3

General Instructions

- **Reading time — 5 minutes**
- **Writing time — 4 hours**
- **Write using black or blue pen**

Elective: Gothic Fiction

<u>Question 1</u>

Write a personal memoir which explores the dynamics of first impressions. In your response, draw on your knowledge of gothic fiction.

My first look at her was her name.

It was inky dark blue. On a note they'd left stuck to my backpack. *Knock on the second red door*, said the note. *Ask for Amelia.*

"Amelia, eh?" said I.

There's a lot you can do with a name like Amelia.

You can play with it, sure, is what you think I'm going to say. Make it cute (Amy), or cuter (Millie), complaining (Meelie), or French, I guess, like the movie (Amélie).

You can step right into that name, is what I mean, and walk around. Swim with it or spill it on your shirt. Whisper it over like a sad, soft ache, or bark it out loud like a mad, manic message: cam*ell*ia, come heee-re, a-million, ah murder you, ye-eah.

You can peel it off your backpack, fold it up safe, walk right past that second red door, or you can not.

This was a few years back. I was fourteen then.

I was still looking down at the name on the note, while I headed to the second red door and I stopped with a fist in the air.

And there she was.

You think you know what I'm about to say, don't you?

You think I'm going to say: *Amelia was just like her name.*

No. Amelia was a girl in a cute T-shirt nightie with a retro MS. PAC-MAN on the front, and the sexiest thigh-high boots I ever saw. If Jesus were a boot maker. And she looks at me with her eyes open wide and a face that says: Oh my God, I'm muckin' around in my sexy Jesus-boots, in my crazy dreamworld, and I've opened the door and let you in on my crazy dream-world and that's so embarrassing but, actually, who cares? because it's funny.

And then we're both laughing. There's this rope-length of laughter between us.

Funny thing is, even while I'm laughing, and falling in her eyes, a part of me knew she was a ghost.

The first time I saw her I knew that my Amelia was a ghost.

EMILY MELISSA-ANNE THOMPSON
Student No. 8233521

Lightning struck! There was a howling of wind, as if wolves roamed about, howlingly. Thunder crashed! Lightning struck again!

It was the first day of Year 12.

I had set out that morning with trepidation. I did not, in all honesty, see a crow, a raven, or any other black bird on the way to school that day.

And yet! I was trepidatious.

In part, of course, it was the Higher School Certificate looming like a monstrous entity at the end of the year. Not to forget the likewise looming of my future career in the law. (Or, anyway, the *degree* in law that awaited me at the wrought-iron gates of my future. A degree that could be locked in an attic like a crazed ex-wife if I did not do well in my HSC exams!!! But, by and by.)

But no, it was more than that! Something about the impending day struck me as ill. Perhaps it was the gathering dark clouds? (In all honesty, I don't think I actually noticed them because my dad's car has tinted windows and I always think there's a cloudy sky but it turns out to be the tint. So I've stopped bothering to look.)

But maybe my subconscious noticed!

At any rate, now it was lunch — and the storm had come!

And there I was on the green velveteen couch in the Year 12

common room at Ashbury High, which is in Castle Hill, forty minutes drive northwest of Sydney if you take the M2, while the thunder howled! And the lightning struck! And generally the weather rattled around, as if it had to carry gothic chains behind it!

I chatted with my friends Lydia and Cassie.

"There is a deep foreboding within me," I said (or words like that, not exactly that), "that my new shampoo doesn't actually bring out the honey highlights in my hair like it says it does!"

Lydia shook her head at me, slowly, cryptically.

It could be that she meant: "No, Em, don't worry. I see plenty of honey highlights."

But I doubt it.

Cass reassured me that the shampoo worked. *But she wasn't really looking at my hair!!* She changed the subject, saying that there'd been a snake in the doorway of the Music Rooms that morning. (A snake! Gothic.)

Lyd said she'd heard Ms. Wexford killed the snake with a saxophone.

"Seriously?" I cried.

Lyd gazed at me. "No," she said.

"It was already dead," Cass explained. "A kookaburra probably dropped it there."

Then Lyd spoke over my mild hysteria to say this: "Hey, did you hear there's two new people this year? A girl and a guy?"

TWO NEW PEOPLE THIS YEAR??!!

Strange time to be changing schools!! The final year? Why now?!

In all honesty I think my skin crawled a little. But it might have been the scratchiness of the velveteen couch.

"Seriously?" Cassie said. "Where from?"

"They're in my homeroom," Lyd commented (ignoring Cassie's question — why? *Why?!* Perhaps she did not know). "They're together."

"Together, you mean, like, together?"

"Yeah. Since they were fourteen or something."

Strange! Most highly strange.

Lydia told us several facts about the couple. She must have chatted with them at roll call! Unlike her! She is not shy, but she is suspicious and therefore a bit of a reservoir with strangers.

And yet, something was missing. What was it?

Of course.

"What's their names?" I said.

"Amelia and Riley," was my friend's reply.

(Did she tremble a little as she said that? I know not. Probably not.)

"Riley and Amelia." I swapped their names around. It seemed wrong, the order Lyd had chosen. There is always a correct order when you say a couple's names.

And yet — was *my* order right?

I think it was.

Riley and Amelia.

The names quivered before us.

At that moment, three things happened:

There was a roaring sound. (The rain was suddenly heavier, as if someone had held the volume down on the remote so that the room was now aghast with sound.)

There was a clanging of bells. (Our school bell ringing for the end of lunch.)

There was the creeeeeeaaaaking *of a door.* (The door to the common room opening.)

We turned as one, the three of us.

And I think that we felt chilled to the bones. (In all honesty, I myself did because the open door was letting in a draft.)

For there, in the doorway, they stood:

Riley and Amelia.

I knew, at once, that it was they.

There was the first time I saw this exam question.

It happened just now.

The "dynamics of first impressions," said the question.

"Are you serious?" I replied. (The supervisor frowned at me for talking out loud.)

My first impression of this question is that it sucks.

Nothing has happened so far to change my mind.

There was also the first time I saw them.

It happened in roll call, the first day of the year.

He had a pair of swimming goggles slung over his shoulder. She had bloodshot eyes. He sat on the window ledge, facing the room. She turned and pressed her forehead to the glass to look out.

They were talking to each other.

I remember he called her Ame. Like *aim*. Like a command. And I thought that her bloodshot eyes were looking out the window for a target.

I remember she called him Riley, like his name could not be touched.

They both had wet hair, only hers was brushed back into a long ponytail. From behind, I could see that the ponytail was leaking: Thin watershadows formed on her school shirt.

As I watched, he rubbed his hands over his head. He was friendly and rough with his head, as if it were a dog. Now his hair stood up in spikes.

And then something happened.

She reached a hand toward him and he reached his hand toward her, but his eyes found the eyes of strangers in the room. Their hands almost touched but did not.

I saw cobwebs in the slender, empty space between those hands.

Later, at lunch, I told my friends about them.

"There's two new people," I said — and a storm rattled the windows of the room.

I said they'd been together for years. I said they were swimmers. I said they trained every day, and that swimming was her passion but he went along just to swim beside her. I said she had a secret that was breaking his heart.

Everything I said was based on my impression of Amelia and Riley at the window in the classroom.

But nothing has happened so far to change my mind.

TOBIAS GEORGE MAZZERATI
Student No. 8233555

A blast of rain like a sudden loss of temper. Thunderclaps that feel personal. Hailstones the size of sheep.

Or practically that size.

It's a mad kind of weather that they have in this country, to be sure. I'm an Irish lad, been here in Castle Hill these past two years — and today, as the storm rages around me, I can feel a darkness looming.

Night terrors have haunted me lately. Strange, dreadful visions of spinning coins that turn into Maggie's face: She laughs and then her smile contorts into a scream.

Och, my Maggie, the sweetest, hottest girl you ever saw, and I left her behind.

When I said good-bye, I promised that I'd write once a day. Maggie said she'd write every hour.

Her eyes, I couldn't see them for the tears, as she swore she'd find a way to come here too. She'd find a leprechaun, she said, but she'd not take his gold coin, for it'd only turn to ashes in her hand.

"Ah well, then," I agreed. "Don't be taking that."

"I'll take his silver shilling instead," says she. "It's magic, the silver one, and returns to your purse each time you pay it."

Eventually, she'd have a stockpile of silver, and then she'd buy a ticket and come.

"Why go to the trouble," says I, "of finding the leprechaun? Just grow yourself a pair of wings and fly."

"Tom Kincaid," she says, and flicks my wrist, but it was good to see the spark behind her tears.

She's not written to me for almost a year now, but I keep writing.

I wrote about the snakes in Castle Hill the other day. *You can't walk anywhere,* I wrote, *but you'll fall over a snake.* (That was an exaggeration.) *They're not venomous,* I added next, so she wouldn't worry. (But the black or brown ones, they'll likely kill you.)

Do you remember, I wrote last week, *the day we lay side by side on the grass, and you told me your wee brother was learning to count? The little one would say,* "one, two," *and then* "six, seven" *and* "nine, twelve," *for he hadn't yet put it all together.*

"Imagine the world of numbers that way," you said. *"A great unfolding mystery is what they are, with chasms of wonder between."*

I laughed at you, but I knew what you meant, and I held your hand, and we looked at the sky and our thoughts flew together, the way that they do. Those clouds, *we thought,* are a great unfolding mystery, with chasms of wonder between. And the same, *we thought,* is our future.

And our hands tightened like to something fierce.

Today I wrote, *Dear Maggie* — and the thunder roared — *there are heat waves here so powerful that birds fall dead from the air. Days when the sky turns black with bats, driven in swarms by hot winds. They swoop down, these bats, crowd onto trees, and a constant, rhythmic thudding begins as they drop dead or dying to the ground.*

I tore that letter to shreds, and there it is now in the mud. For louder even than the crashing rain is the constant, rhythmic thudding of my heart. I know what is coming, and it's darkness.

I know that the future is gone.

Och, and when I think of how they shaved my head, clapped irons on my ankles, and sent me away to the ends of the earth for the rest of my God-given life — they got me for stealing a sheep — and when I think —

Not to mention, I have just noticed that the exam question asks for a personal memoir.

So you want to hear from me — Toby Mazzerati — not some Irish convict dude named Tom Kincaid who lived here in 1804.

Hence, please disregard the above, and I will start my answer now.

Thanks for your time.

The Committee for the Administration of the
K. L. Mason Patterson Trust Fund
THE K. L. MASON PATTERSON SCHOLARSHIP FILE

A Scholarship Enabling Two (2) Students to Attend Ashbury High for their Final Year of High School including Tuition Fees, Uniform Allowance, and Monthly Stipend. The Two (2) Students must demonstrate Financial Hardship and Outstanding Potential.

A Bonus of $25,000 each to be paid to the Two (2) Scholarship Winners upon the Completion of their Final Year of High School.

Memo

To: All Members of the K. L. Mason Patterson Trust Fund Committee

From: Chris Botherit and Roberto Garcia

Re: K. L. Mason Patterson Scholarship Short List

Dear Committee Members,

We're delighted to announce that we've narrowed the field to a tiny short list of FIVE applicants!!

The five students' names are:

David Peter Montgomery
Riley Terence Smith
Sura Eve Bajinksi
Xavier Paul Simeon
Amelia Grace Damaski

Supporting documentation for each student, including applicant essays, references, school records, etc., attached.

So! Next step is for the Committee to interview these five contenders. Look over the material, get back to us with your comments or questions, and we'll set up the interviews.

All the best,
Chris Botherit (English Coordinator, Ashbury High) with Rob Garcia (History Coordinator & Drama Teacher, Ashbury High)

P.S. Two of the applicants on this short list have clearly had some troubled times. As you will see from the attached, the troubles have manifested themselves in ways that are a bit startling! But you'll *also* see that they have lots of "potential" (in an unexpected area . . .), suffer great financial hardship, have very persuasive reference letters — and Roberto and I are keen to meet with them! So, they've made the cut!

(Sir Kendall Laurence) Mason Patterson Scholarship — Short list
Dear Mr. Botherit and Mr. Garcia,
Thank you for your memo.
To begin I'd like to quibble with your *tone*. Shouldn't we be more formal? This is, after all, the inaugural year of the K. L. Mason Patterson Scholarship. Does not the late Sir Kendall deserve

rather more respect? Phrases such as "narrowed the field" and "made the cut" have surely been lifted directly from the cinematographic films.

And, truly, are so many exclamation points quite the thing?

(As a dear friend of the late Sir Kendall, I can assure you there was little he loathed so much as the cinematographic film and the exclamation point.)

Now, I have studied the papers relating to the applicants David, Sura, and Xavier. What a marvelous little trio! Such diligent young things — and all seem to me to come from good, quiet, respectable stock. They are Ashbury through and through. Indeed, I can imagine each of them walking the corridors in my *own* glory days at Ashbury. I am sure they will enchant us at the interviews.

However, I am bewildered as to why you have included the students named Riley and Amelia. What I see here is not "manifestations of trouble," Mr. Botherit. It is *trouble*. Through and through. Either you are much less astute than I have been led to believe — and I say that with all the respect you are due — or you are making a sort of a "joke." If so, the joke is in very bad taste, and I assure you, Sir Kendall would *not* have laughed.

Yours faithfully,
Constance Milligan
(Associate Chair, Ashbury Alumni Association)

❖

Chris and Rob,

What are you on?

Riley Smith and Amelia Damaski?

Delete them from the short list and find another two, pronto.

Cheers,
Bill Ludovico
(Ashbury School Principal/Economics Teacher)

❖

Dear Mr. Botherit and Mr. Garcia,

Remind me how you talked me into joining this Committee.

I guess Sura and Xavier would be the obvious choices. They seem scarily smart. And desperately dull. I don't especially want to meet them. Do we really have to meet them?

Yours,
Patricia Aganovic
(Parent Representative 1)

❖

Chris and Rob,

My two cents' worth:

The one named Sura, now she sounds perfect. I can't tell you what an accomplished violinist like that would do for the school orchestra.

(Apparently, Riley has taught himself to play

the drums. A self-taught percussionist! So is my
two-year-old. Say no more.)

Kind regards,
Lucy Wexford
(Music Coordinator, Ashbury High)

Mr. Botherit and Mr. Garcia,
    Constance, once again.
    Forgive this scribbled "postscript" — but it occurs
to me that it would be the height of foolishness to
keep Riley and Amelia on our short list for a moment
longer. According to the Scholarship Charter, we are
obliged to interview all students on the short list.
Ergo, at present we have to interview them! *We will
have to be in the same room as them!* They will see
our faces!
    (No doubt, they will learn our names too, for good
manners will oblige us to introduce ourselves.)
    I urge you to remove them with haste.

Yours sincerely,
Constance Milligan

Mr. B and Mr. G,
    Guessing that Amelia and Riley are included for
humor value?
    David, Sura, and Xavier sound okay.
    Although, if any of those three come to Ashbury
their marks will be off the charts. My boy Toby's rank

will slip and, from what he tells me, if it slips any more it'll end up in pieces on the concrete.

Could you find a couple of "Applicants with Outstanding Potential" who aren't likely to live up to their Outstanding Potential for a few years yet?

Cheers,
Jacob Mazzerati
(Parent Representative 2)

Mr. Bothersome and Mr. Gracias,

I write with urgent haste. It is I, Constance, again — by my night-light — at midnight — for I have just awoken from a dreadful nightmare — dreadful! — and I have *no choice* but to write to you at once!

I have seen them! In my dream! It was those applicants, Riley and Amelia — oh, they were wicked, monstrous, *satanic* creatures — miscreants! — they had sprung, fully formed, from the loins of —

Please hearken to my words:

In the dream, we were interviewing them. Riley had taken the form of a great hairy ape, and Amelia was a little black viper. (She had wrapped herself around the back of that bright red chair, the one that dear Patricia Aganovic favors at our Committee meetings.) *And do you know what they did?* Why, *that ape and that viper, that pair of vicious repro-bates, they spent the entire interview STUDYING US ALL!* Oh, their quick, cunning eyes were busy staring and *staring at us*! (No doubt, they were valuing our jewelry and our clothes and the quality of our haircuts! And I myself, in this dream [and in real life, if you can credit it], had just got a new perm and rinse — it keeps my spirits up — AND I was wearing my good pearl necklace and my great-aunt's ruby rings!)

Quite reasonably, I asked a simple question: "What of your parents? What do they do?"

Well, they laughed and laughed and laughed.

Such hideous, horrible, howling laughter!

Then Riley, the ape, changed form and became a nasty little squirrel with bloodred eyes. And Amelia, the viper, turned into a sort of leaky fountain pen and spilled all over the floor, and there I was with my good mop and bucket, the expensive mop with the fancy handle that I use on the floorboards in my —

But that is incidental.

What is important is this! D'you not see it? The dream was a *WARNING.* And we MUST PAY HEED. If we interview these two, each of us will find ourselves secretly *WEIGHED* as a *potential target* for their wicked, scheming ways!

And worse, what do you suppose will happen, pray, when they miss out on the scholarship? Why, hell will have no fury —! The vengeance they will wreak — It is THEN that we will see their truly hideous — I can scarcely grasp this pen for —

For, do you not understand? They will have seen our faces. They will know our names.

Strike them from the short list at once.

Yours,
Constance Milligan

TOBIAS GEORGE MAZZERATI
STUDENT No. 8233555

If you could just ease your way out of the nineteenth century, and back to modern times?

Back, in your actual fact, to a couple of weeks before the summer holidays last year.

Cos that's when my dad had his tennis buddies 'round.

Thursday night and my feet're up, cold pizza, rain outside, TV bright like it's super-keen tonight, when a tennis shoe hits the back of my head.

I turn around and there's Frankenstein.

Laughing his arse off at me, on account of the direct hit to my head.

I kid you not: Frankenstein standing in my living room.

Couple of his monster buddies too. Big sweaty shadows in the twilight-fading room.

"Toby!" go the monster buddies. (That's their way of saying hi.)

"Tobias," says Frankenstein. (That's his way.)

You'd think his accent might have faded (like the twilight), cause he's been in this country twenty years, but no — "Tobias," says Frankenstein, accent smooth and sweet, "you still have leetle ping-pongs for balls?"

In one smooth move I had his shoe up off the floor and hurtling high speed toward his neck.

He took it from the air and let it drop.

"What happened to your tennis game?" I go.

All three monsters stand there looking at me. Sound of rain outside.

None of us blinked.

Next thing my dad's there, handing out beers. "I'm thinking a pasta," he says. "Whaddya say, boys?"

Skinny monster goes, "That one you do with the olives?"

Fat monster goes, "And the anchovy fillets?"

And Frankenstein: "You kick *ass*, my friend!"

Frankenstein's real name is Roberto Garcia.

Also known as a buddy of my dad. They met at this wine tasting course my parents did, back when my parents were an item. Roberto Garcia was running the course.

Turns out, by spooky chance, he's my History teacher now. Gets my dad onto school committees too. (He has Frankensteinesque powers of persuasion.)

Anyhow, this particular night, tennis rained out, big plates of pasta, monster glasses of red wine, hangin' with Dad's buddies, the stereo blasting out their favorite tunes — I played them some sets of my own — I'm a superstar DJ is what I am, in my spare time — and they started off ready to be full of mock and scorn but ended up kind of nodding along, eyebrows jumping with the beat, now and then making that face. Lips turned down, head tilted sideways: *Huh, who'd have thought it, this ain't bad.*

So I'm taking a break some point that night, nice and sleepy — Dad and his fat buddy shootin' some pool, skinny buddy frowning at the stereo (trying to replicate my DJ success) (no chance), when Frankenstein lands his big arse on the couch, shoving my legs to the floor at the same time, and gets me with a face full of garlic-red-wine breath.

Folks, he truly is one mother of a monster. Big acne-scarred face, nose like a landslide, hairiest arms and legs you ever saw so you'd think he was a mountain goat in his spare time, but — here if you forgive a bit of sentiment please — also the nicest guy in the world.

And this is the night when the story begins.

Let's just say, the short version is, Frankenstein recalled he was my History teacher.

"Tobias," he says, "Toby, my boy, you wish for an idea for your History Project — you wish maybe to start during this summer?"

I'll tell you what he meant:

He meant: Toby, my boy, your marks are running down the gutter to the sewers of the earth. Your future, my boy, is a flying fox strung up in electrical wires. Yes, you're a superstar DJ, my boy, but your future is a maggot in a chunk of rotting cheese.

That's what he meant.

But he's a nice guy like I said, so he didn't use those words.

"Roberto," I said, "I wish."

He'd been hangin' with his homeboys down at the local history club, he said. Some guy there had found some old papers in a termite-rotting blanket chest.

"The originals," says Roberto with that shrug he always does, like he thinks he's a South American sex god, when in fact he's a big ole ugly Frankenstein, "the originals, we give to the Mitchell Library, naturally. But I have copies. You can look at the —"

He gets a bunch of papers from his briefcase. They're the letters of a guy named Tom Kincaid. Once lived right here in Castle Hill. The letters tell a story, and it's true. That's the way of history I guess.

You're yawning, folks, I can see your drooping eyes.

You're thinking time lines, dates, import/export, sealing, whaling, sextant, compass, let me quietly die of boredom, let me slip so far in my chair that my chin smacks the edge of the desk and my teeth go through my tongue.

You'd prefer the names and sexual preferences of my cousins and their kids.

Or the tragic tale of my parents' splitting up a few years back.

Or the story of Riley and Amelia, scholarship kids who came to my school this last year.

Too bad.

By the time that Riley-and-Amelia started at my school, I was deep into the Tom-and-Maggie story.

It's blood, gore, betrayal, torture, murder — plenty of murder. And it's kind of a love story too.

Wake up and I'll tell you the story.

RILEY T. SMITH
Student No. 8233569

Three years later and my fist's in the air at the same door.

The fist hits a gust of moving red and rushing ponytail. The fist hits Amelia's voice: "What *was* that?"

"Forget it," I tell her.

My hands are on her chest. I'm moving her back into her room.

"Who were those people? What was that place?"

She means the new private school where we started that day.

"Soak it in bleach for half an hour."

I'm moving her into her room. My elbow juts back to slam the door.

Those wild, crazed eyes of hers can change to moonshine softness in a door slam.

Her skin is pale as watermelon sucked free of its juices.

That's the steel gray desk, that's the wardrobe, the bed, that's her giant stuffed cow, her guitar. Her bag spilling sheet music and water bottles. That's her hands, cheekbones, lips, that's the space behind her knees.

I love her bare legs from a distance. When she's standing by a pool. When she's facing the water, thinking. Her legs are white as watermelon rind, veined with blue from cold. There's that H shape behind her knees. The H that trembles softly with the swimming water cold.

Or when she swings in the park, when she sits on the swing in a short, short dress, and she pumps her bare legs, pumps all those muscles in her pale, slender legs. You watch from behind and you can see the long hair flying. She holds so tight that her knuckles turn dark pink.

She never wears makeup.

She wears this khaki cap sometimes, and the cap stays on her head even when she tips her face backward to the breeze. She puts her ponytail through the gap at the back. That's how it stays on. The ponytail flies free and holds the cap.

And there's that H behind her knees, stretching and contracting, stretching and contracting while she swings.

You know when somebody pushes you on a swing? The thud of their hands on the small of your back. You swing through the air then you spin back down and there's the thud of their hands pushing you higher. The hands are there to help you. They want to push you higher. They want to make you fly.

But there's the pressing of the hands on the small of your back, there's the force, there's the thud of their hands.

Don't ever push me.

EMILY MELISSA-ANNE THOMPSON
STUDENT No. 8233521

How did I know it was they?

This, I cannot explain.

Except to say that it must have been one of those previous sentiments of doom.

Anyhow, there they were! In the doorway of the Year 12 common room. At that *very* moment, the room lit up with lightning. And for a split end of time, I think I saw Riley and Amelia laugh! Their faces seemed to crack in two with laughter! Sudden, howling, shrieking, horrifying laughter! (No doubt it was also demonic.)

Perchance it was my imagination. I do have a hyperthyroid in my imagination so who knows. Anyway, before I could be sure, the lightning was gone and the room was dim again.

And there they stood. Riley and Amelia. Not laughing at all. Just looking calm.

Their eyes wandered the room.

They both put one foot forward and paused.

The air was silent. Every person in the room had stopped breathing.

In fact, the blood had stopped pumping in my veins. (Which was death-defying conduct on my part.)

There was an insufferable sense of *waiting*: a sense of *terrible suspense*. As if Riley and Amelia were lions, and we were a ménage à trois of lively, prancing deer.

The lions were stalking the deer. *Which of us would they devour?*

(Oh! Who could have predicted? If only I knew *then* what I know now!!)

Riley and Amelia did not enter. They turned at exactly the same moment — and they walked away. . . .

Why?

Was it that they knew, even then, that they did not belong? Did they sense the fear, and wish to torment a little longer?

Or was it simply that the bell had rung forth for the end of lunch. So they had to go to their next class or whatever. I suppose it might have been that.

Nonetheless!

I turned to my friends in amazement. Lydia raised a single eyebrow. Cassie raised both eyebrows and gave me one of her dimples-in-the-corner-of-her-mouth looks, which means she is trying not to laugh. I will say this about Cass: When a person is supposed to find something dramatic and mysterious, she will often find it funny.

I will also say this. That I wondered when I would see Riley and Amelia again.

I did not have to wonder long. It was four minutes later.

The girl (Amelia) was in History Extension 1 with Mr. Garcia. *And so was I!!*

But nothing of note happened in that class.

Plus, I couldn't see her. She was three seats behind me.

By the next day, I knew they were here on scholarships. In fact, Cassie's mother is on the committee that chose them! But she couldn't tell Cassie (or me) anything about their backgrounds, because it was "confidential." *Hmm*, I thought.

That day, Amelia was in English Extension 3 with Mr. Botherit . . . *and so was I!!!!!*

And so, normally, was Lydia. But she was not at school.

Now, I will here display two details which might seem shady now, but later? The bloodred moon will shine upon them.

First! Our English class took place in Room 27B in the Art Rooms across the oval.

The Art Rooms? Oh, you don't know how important that is! Hearken! I will tell you!

Well, the Art Rooms are not the Art Rooms anymore. Oh no! That building is now the K. L. Mason Patterson Center for the Arts. Because it turns out that a very rich man succumbed to death, and left a HUGE FORTUNE to our school.

A fortune which I could have taken off his hands with ease if he had only had the foreskin to ask me. But oh no, he had to go and waste it on our school.

Therefore, there is now a committee going mad, trying to think up ways to spend the money. I'm sure they have better reasons to go mad. But did KL think of that? No.

One thing they have spent the money on is, of course, scholarships. Another is the crazed renovation of the Art Rooms.

The Art Rooms were once the building where students slept, back in the olden days when our school was a boarding school! Anyhow, but then it became the Art Rooms, and now it has been renovated and includes conference rooms, drama theaters, auditoriums, art galleries, kitchens, and "state-of-the-art resource centers" (i.e., classrooms), and, furthermore, its name has grown so long you need mouthwash to loosen up the muscles of your teeth before you say it.

But we all still call it the Art Rooms.

Second! Mr. Botherit talked about the fact that English Extension 3 is a new subject this year, with an emphasis "on memoir," and therefore we had to write blogs.

I had a lot to say about this idea, but Amelia, who happened to be sitting five seats away from me (horizontally speaking) paid no heed to me.

She spoke to not a soul. She was silent as a chocolate bar.

Her posture was good. I'm not suggesting here that she hunched over or hid behind her hair or suchlike. Oh no. She was poised and clear-eyed and her posture was exquisite — *and her eyes followed the teacher every moment.*

He pranced around the room (as he responded to my many things to say), and Amelia's eyes followed so closely it was as if he had magnets in his face.

(I'm not suggesting here that Mr. B is hot.)

Eventually, Mr. B asked me to stop talking. He said he was going to give us topics for our blogs, and the first one was "My Journey Home."

And then I had a lot more to say.

Nevertheless, in the end, I wrote my blog. And as I typed, I heard the sound of Amelia typing. I looked across at her. Her long hair slid down her back like a waterfall. (I don't mean that it was wet; I'm being meteorological.) She would type very quickly and then she'd stop. There'd be a long, silent pause.

Her fingernails were the extreme short of someone who bites their nails overtly. And her fingers wandered across the keys, gently stroking them whenever she paused.

It was just as if we did not exist.

At the end of the lesson, she drifted back across the oval. A lot of the boys in our class stopped to watch her go. They'd been checking her out the whole lesson, both openly and stealthily. A mixture of both.

And then, at the other side of the oval, Amelia stopped. I looked in the direction of her gaze. It was Riley. He reached her. I did not see them speak. I did not see them touch. I simply saw the space between them close, and then I saw them gliding calmly onward.

The boys in our class uttered a silent, plaintive sigh.

LYDIA JAACKSON-OBERMAN
Student No. 8233410

The second day of term, I didn't see Amelia and Riley at all.

I stayed home from school.

Had to stay at home because my head exploded.

I was sweeping up the pieces of my head when my mum wandered into the room. She was half-asleep/hungover in her bathrobe. She'd been celebrating the night before — bought herself an independent record label just the other day. My mother picks up companies like other people pick up milk.

"Watch your feet," I said.

Her eyes flew open. Then she whimpered quietly: Opening her eyes had hurt her soul. She closed them fast.

"Seriously," I said, "there's broken head all over the place in here."

Mum sighed and drifted to the hallway. I could hear her telling Dad to stay out of the kitchen. I couldn't hear his answer, just his tone.

It was: *deep, low, hm, well, really, I'm too important a man to have to stay out of my own kitchen, aren't I?*

Mum replied with her own tone, which was: *huh, interesting. Are you?*

I finished sweeping up my head and then, for a laugh, picked out a couple of the bigger pieces, and juggled them.

That was funny. You should have seen our dog, Pumpernickel. He thought it was a game just for him — he was doing these frantic bounces, like, *spring! spring!* All the time getting closer, desperate to snatch one of the pieces of my head from the air. And I was shaking my head. I mean that literally. I'd put the rest of the head in a cocktail shaker and I was *shake, shake, shake.* And Pumpernickel —

Ah, just kidding.

My head didn't explode.

What, are you as stupid as my dog?

No, I stayed home because my mother asked me to let the roofing guys in. She had some appointment to take her hangover to, and Dad had to go rule the world! (That's what he does. He rules the world! Or, at least he judges it. He's a judge.)

Anyway, I needed a break.

Don't think I can't hear you, Exam Marking Person. This is what you're saying: "What?! She needed a break? Isn't it the second day after the summer holidays here? And she *already* needs a break? Isn't *that* just like her generation?! *I* don't know about the future when —"

Take it easy or you'll spill your herbal tea.

You're forgetting that you don't know everything.

Surprise!

You don't.

At the start of the summer holiday last year, my best friends, Em and Cass, flew away. (Em on a Canadian ski trip; Cass to voice training in Melbourne.)

While they were gone, my boyfriend and I broke up. And my dad moved out of the house. (Three weeks later, he moved back in.)

The summer disappeared.

Not a single drop of light. Pure darkness. An eclipse.

I'm much more sane than I sound. But this last year some kind of madness has found its way underneath my nails. This last year, I've made the worst mistakes of my life.

I'll get to the mistakes.

The point for now is this: At the start of the year — after that dark summer — I was not myself at all.

Or maybe I was. Maybe I'd been cut down to my essence.

www.myglasshouse.com/emthompson
Tuesday, February 5
My Journey Home
I journeyed home from school yesterday.

I have nothing more to say about that.

Who knew then that I would have to write about it today?

Nobody.

Not even me.

And therefore I didn't pay attention.

Now if Mr. B had given us *notice* that he was going to make us write *blogs* about our *journey*, well!

I would have paid attention. And then, now, I might have something to say.

I suppose I can say that Lydia was driving and Cass was in the backseat. I remember that. And I remember one time when Lyd put her foot down to get through an orange light and I breathed in sharply because she almost got us all annayialated. She's always doing that sort of thing when she's driving.

That's it, though. That's all I have to say about my journey home. The car drove along. The car stopped. I got out. The end.

And to be honest, I have neither the time nor the inclination to maintain a new blog. As I just now said to Mr. B, I'm already busy enough with MySpace and Facebook and constant IMing. Not forgetting homework and other extracurricular activities such as being a member of a family.

So, Lyd and Cass, where are you? Did you get my texts? You can comment now. I don't want to write any more. It's too hot, and I'm all used up because I've been lecturing Mr. Botherit.

And can someone tell me how to spell that word I used up there? Aniialate. Anayalate. I don't have a clue.

Great.

Thanks.

See ya. Em

41 comments

Lyd said . . . Hi, Em. Thanks for the urgent text telling me to read your unjustified attack on my driving.

Em said . . . Well, you know, Lyd, there is such a thing as RECKLESSNESS and I think you have it. And there is such a thing as DANGEROUS DRIVING and I think you have that too. And I just wonder. I really just wonder. Did you actually get your license?

Cass said . . . There was plenty of green left in that orange light, Em.

Em said . . . Great to see your voice, Cass, but listen, shut up, okay? You were looking out your window when Lyd drove through that light at a death-defying pace and

Cass said . . . Mr. Botherit is making you write blogs? He's the anti-technology man, right? Didn't he make us do that letter-writing exchange in Year 10, the one with Brookfield, cuz he wanted to bring back the "Joy of the Envelope"? Maybe he gets off on sniffing the glue on envelopes and that's why they're joyous to him.

Em said . . . Lyd, have you explained to your mum that she has to change the name of her new record company? "Distressed Weasel Records" makes me feel unwell. Actually, has it made you unwell? Cos why aren't you here? It's only the second day.

Em said . . . And I KNOW, Cass, don't get me started about Mr. B and his transportation of character. You should hear him go on about new technologies now!!! He wants us to spend all our time delivering content all over the place like we're bicycle couriers. He's disturbing me. You know how I feel about change. I told him that incontinence is a character flaw.

Lyd said . . . I'll be back at school tomorrow. You two can come over to my place tonight if you want. Do you mean inconsistency?

Cass said . . . OMFG.

Lyd said . . . What?

Cass said . . . Nothing. People never do online talking without saying OMFG at least once so now I've done it twice you two can stop worrying.

Em said . . . Okay but this isn't online talking. Mr. B said we can't do that in his class. I'm just, like, responding to comments on my blog, which is technically blogging.

Lyd said . . . There were leaks in our roof in the storm last night. So I told Mum I'd stay home to let the roofing guys in. And you know what?

Em said . . . What?

Lyd said . . . I didn't need to let them in. The roof is outside.

Em said . . . Can you believe the subject of the blog? Don't think for a minute that it was my idea. As you can see it has sapped all my imagination. And I said to Mr. B, excuse me? Our journey home from school? I said, well, no offense but is that really interesting? Is it, maybe, a little juvenile?

I said: You are new to technology, Mr. B, and so you are a naïve waif and do not know that it's a cutthroat world and if I write a blog about my journey home I am effectively inviting online stalkers to follow me home and cut my throat.

Cass said . . . What did he say?

Em said . . . He said we could just set up a profile with the highest level of privacy settings.

Em said . . . And he has this weird idea that he can teach without TEACHING. I mean, he says this is just like an exercise class in which we flex our writing muscles or something. And he's not going to read it, and I said you can't flex muscles without a personal trainer and he said — I don't know what he said. I got bored and stopped listening to him.

Lyd said . . . I think someone just fell through the roof. Gotta go.

Em said . . . And GUESS WHO'S IN THIS CLASS?

Cass said . . . Who?

Em said . . . AMELIA!!

Cass said . . . Who's that?

Em said . . . WHAT ARE YOU TALKING ABOUT?! *AMELIA!!!* The new girl! The one with the new guy named Riley! I can't BELIEVE you've forgotten those two already! We TALKED about them so MUCH yesterday afternoon!!! Or I did anyway.

Cass said . . . Just kidding. What's she like?

Em said . . . I think she's stupid.

Cass said . . . Okay.

Em said . . . And she's not SAYING anything or LOOKING at anybody. Isn't that weird? And she's even more beautiful in person.

Cass said . . . When have you seen her not in person?

Em said . . . I mean, close-up. I haven't seen her this close before and she's even more beautiful. I am LOOKING AT HER RIGHT NOW while I'm typing.

Cass said . . . What's she doing?

Em said . . . She's just sitting there. Okay, she's typing now. Now she's stopped. Now she's breathing. Okay, now I can't hear her breathing. No. She's breathing again. Really quietly though. Now she's typing again — no. She's stopped. Okay, she's typing.

Cass said . . . Lydia? Are you back yet?

Em said . . . Ha-ha. But come on, don't you think there's something kind of tranquilizing about her? Don't you want to know where she comes from and why she's here and what mysteries are trapped within the complicated confines of her mind?

Cass said . . . I thought you said she was stupid.

Em said . . . I have no basis for that.

Cass said . . . I think I have to go. My English class just walked past the library window and Ms. W looked right in at me. She's frowning to herself like she knows she's seen me somewhere before. What the f. are they doing walking around outside? See ya.

Lyd said . . . I'm back. It wasn't a person, it was a wrench. The roofing guy dropped his wrench through the skylight in the upstairs bathroom. Now the skylight has a hole shaped exactly like a dolphin. Gotta go again, though. Roofing guy looked so depressed about the skylight I had to invite him in for coffee. See ya tonight?

Em said . . . Okay. Mr. B. is saying some ridiculous things so I'm going to have to stop now anyway. Have fun. Pick me up from school if you want. Is the roofing guy hot?

Lyd said . . . I'll pick you up at 3:30. Annihilatingly hot.

Tuesday, February 5
My Journey Home
So this is me walking the bus shelter route with a
Kit Kat.
Lost Cockatoo on the telegraph pole.
Zombies faceup on the footpath.
Ledges of chocolate, Answers to Poppy.
Thinkin maybe I'll make me a Zombie.
Gar*Age* Sale at Undercliffe Street.
Maybe I'll buy me a *GA*rage.
And we miss her and please send her home.
Edges of ledges of chocolate.
And please send our Poppy back home.

So this is me thinking: not Undercliffe Street.
There's no effin 'e' at the end of the cliff.
How can you live in a street long enough
and not know the street by its name?
To get enough junk for a sale.
Thinkin Undercliff Street is a band name.
A lot of guitar and long hair.
The band is straight rock without angles.
The name's on an angle, the name's like a ledge,
like the ledge at the back of that moving truck now,
grenadine, lime juice, and Jamaican rum,
and please send our Poppy back home.

0 comments

5

EMILY MELISSA-ANNE THOMPSON
STUDENT No. 8233521

Anyway, the term tumbled onward like cobwebs swept from the staircase of a large, gothic mansion.

And everywhere I turned: Riley and Amelia.

I suppose this could have been because I was always following them around.

But still! *Why was I doing that?*

I know not.

I had never followed people around before! I mean, I'm a busy person with a life.

I guess it can only be explained using the dynamics of first impressions and drawing on my knowledge of gothic fiction. (*Sigh*)

But, listen! *The more I followed Riley and Amelia, the less I knew of they.*

Who were they? Whenceforward had they come? Why? Why not? What did they want with our school?

These and other questions gripped me like a stuffed toy in the claws of a shopping center skilltester machine.

And yet, what answers beheld me?

None. Three weeks passed, and all that I knew was this:

1. They were named Riley and Amelia, and they were here on scholarships.
2. They went swimming before school. (Lydia told me that.)
3. They were always together.
4. (Except when they were in different classes.) That's it.

When I say they were "always together" I don't mean in the way of other couples. Those couples who walk around making gurgling noises into the sides of each other's necks?

No.

Those couples are as disgusting as a gothic sewerage system.

Riley and Amelia had rhythm that matched and yet they were separate. Like bicycle wheels.

Sometimes they spoke and it's true that their voices were murmurs. But not the too-much-cheap-chocolate-weird-feeling-in-my-chin murmur of those *other* couples. It was more like the way my parents talked this one time when we went camping. It was late, and my brother and I were in our sleeping bags in the tent, and we could hear Mum and Dad by the campfire. Their low voices talked about strange, important things, and I couldn't really catch what they were saying. But it seemed to me to be all about how their kids were kind of stupid, but funny.

That's the kind of murmuring Riley and Amelia shared.

They never spoke to anybody else. Only to each other.

That is a lie.

They *did* speak to other people. Yet, confusingly, they spoke without *actually speaking*.

They were different in this way: Amelia did not look at anybody. Only at teachers and other inanimate objects. When spoken to, she answered in her murmuring voice, so people leaned in closer to hear. At that point she stopped talking and turned away, as if that was the end of it.

Riley, however, looked deep into the eyes for brief moments.

When that happened — when Riley's eyes looked deeply into yours — it made you feel as if a dragon was breathing fire in your chest.

And he chatted. He was a charmer. He spoke in friendly sentences. But *nobody could remember what he said*. I mean, once I saw him talking to someone and I said, "What was that about?" And the person looked confused, like, what did I mean?

So, you see, they spoke without actually speaking.

I tried to get close enough to hear what they said, but that was tricky. And it made me look ridiculous, e.g., the time I fell over Riley's foot and landed in Amelia's path. They were calm when I did that. They stopped and waited for me. I said, "Sorry, sorry," and they both half-smiled in a distant, patient way.

It was one of the low moments in my life, and I stopped following them around for a few days. For my dignity.

But then I started again.

And sometimes, I saw this: Riley and Amelia looking about them like lions. Just as they had at the doorway to the Year 12 common room that first day.

When they did this, they almost never *fixed* on anybody. They never seemed to choose amongst their prey. They simply moved their eyes in a steady, roaming way.

Here is the strangest thing: I wanted to hold their gaze.

I confess. That's what I wanted.

I was chilled, terrified, I wished to flee!

But when their predatory gaze began to wander, I wanted, more than anything, for Riley and Amelia to choose me.

Here, you will be pondering: Why not simply ask them some questions?

Or, in Lyd's words: "Em, would you talk to them already?"

Ah, that makes me laugh! Ha ha ha! You naïve waif! (I said to Lyd.) Do you not see the invisible barrier around them? (Like the gothic moat around a gothic castle.) *Nobody* approached Riley and Amelia.

"I don't get it," Cass said. "They're beautiful, but they're just, like, a girl and a guy. What's with the obsession?"

A girl and a guy! (I said to Cass.) They are aliens, ghosts, or vampires! They are former assassins in a witness protection program! They are undercover police officers! I don't know what they are, actually, but I *know* they are more than just a girl and a guy! I sense it.

"That's quite an imagination you've got there," said Mr. Ludovico, walking by like a swarm of wasps. He is my Economics teacher, and also became school principal last year. "It's not going to impress your clients," he called back over his shoulder, "if you *do* end up as a lawyer one day."

That "if you *do*" was like a wasp's sting to my heart.

"Spilled something on your tie," Lyd called, not even looking at him, and Mr. L frowned down at the stain on his tie.

But behold! The mystery of Amelia and Riley was about to take off.

It was the third week of term, and there came to be a Monday. (They oft happen, Mondays, and that is a gothic tragedy.)

I awoke with a paroxysm of terror in my soul.

Here's a funny thing about me: I *often* sense, via a paroxysm of terror, when I've got a new pimple.

And behold, there it was, a pimple of gothic proportions. I won't distress you by describing it, except to say that it was on my chin, where a witch will oft keep a wart.

I made the mistake of squeezing it and it turned into a volcano.

But things were about to get worse.

At the breakfast table, I beheld my younger brother in his winter school uniform. I was like, ha-ha, William, you lose, haven't you noticed the *temperature* outside, dude, it's like a million degrees, etc.

Making fun of him, but in a friendly, sisterly way.

And then my mother, who was listening to this while she peeled bananas for the blender — my mother said, "I guess you're supposed to be wearing the winter uniform too, aren't you, Em?"

And oh! Horror upon horrors! She was right. (And she had cruelly let me go on with the teasing of my brother before she said anything.)

It was school photograph day! (You wear the winter uniform that day.)

William kept on eating his crumpets with honey, and he hunches over the table to do this, so he hadn't looked up and seen my face, or he would have had plentiful material for his vengeance.

I went to school with all the makeup I owned on my chin. I was profoundly depressed. Maybe you think I am exaggerating and you are right, but the fact is: *This was going to be our last school photograph ever.*

(I don't think they do school photographs at uni, do they? No. And definitely not at work.)

So!! This would be the last time I would ever be an innocent schoolgirl standing on those metal seats, surrounded by all my friends, while a photographer tries to make us stand up straight and smile!

And it was going to be ruined by a zit.

Lyd and Cass were kind, and said they didn't think it would even show up in the photo. This proved to me that it was a monstrosity. Normally, Lyd would say, "Yeah, you've got a piece of rotten fruit growing on your face, Em; get over it, it'll pass."

Not in a cruel way, just because she believes in honesty, and in using opportunities for humor.

Yet, this day, she was gentle, so I knew the pimple was terminal.

Year 12 walked up to the oval to be photographed in front of the Art Rooms, as that's the oldest, most charismatic building of our school, and also is now the K. L. Mason Patterson Center for the Arts. So, two strikes and you're out. With one stone.

Every person in our year was laughing, messing around, making jokes — every single person except me.

I was so despondent I didn't even look out for Riley and Amelia!

Which was ironical, because guess what, after the teachers and photographer had rushed around getting us arranged, and finally we were ready, teetering and squished . . . I realized I was next to Amelia.

Right beside her.

I did not know what to do.

I decided I would turn to her, point to the giant pimple on my chin, and say, with humorous irony: "It's the little things, you know?"

Then I decided against that.

Then I was aghast at the idea that I had *almost* done that.

I began to hyperventilate, quietly.

On no account could she see the pimple. She was too beautiful and mysterious for the things of adolescence.

I started chatting with someone two rows behind me, as that gave me a reason to crane my neck so that my chin was the greatest distance possible from Amelia. And that's why I did not notice at first when the photographer called out: "Okay, could you just close that gap?"

He called this twice. Someone said, "Emily?"

I looked around and the photographer was pointing to a gap right beside me.

It was the space where Amelia had been.

She had vanished.

Leaving naught but a gap.

We pressed together and the photographer started snapping, and every chance I could, I searched about me. Yet Amelia had *simply gone*!!!

I could hardly concentrate on smiling, let alone smiling in a way that concealed my chin. For *I could not comprehend how she had done it.* We were crammed together like a chunk of frozen peas. I was in the middle of the third row back, people pressed behind, beside, and in front. That is to say, trapped.

Let's say *I'd* wanted to get off the bench? Say to go to the bathroom? I would have had to say, "Excuse me, excuse me," and half a row of people would have had to jump to the ground, complaining, talking, tripping — it would never have been worth it. I would have just had to hold on.

Yet Amelia had simply *faded away.*

It was impossible.

Moments later, when we were all climbing down, shaking our arms and legs, I saw her. Way across the oval. Slipping back into the main part of the school.

If that were not enough, the very next day was the swimming carnival.

The entire school was agog, but I will simply say this:

Amelia is the fastest swimmer in the history of water. (And Riley is pretty fast too.)

LYDIA JAACKSON-OBERMAN
STUDENT No. 8233410

Every day, the first few weeks of term, Amelia and Riley arrived late.

With wet hair, bloodshot eyes, and swimming goggles.

It was *really* such a stretch to think that they might — I don't know — do okay at the swimming carnival?

Turns out it was.

I was profoundly disappointed by humanity that day.

The shock! Everyone turning to everybody else: *"Did you know?"*

My friend Em was so astounded that her face fell right off her skull. Sewed it back on while she was busy shrieking out her disbelief.

And even Cass was kind of psyched. Time was, Cass didn't even know what house she was in. But this day, the three of us were sitting eating Pringles and watching the green crowd (Lawson) go wild. Cass was looking thoughtful. "So Amelia and Riley are in Lawson?" she said. "How'd you guess?" Em said. Another few moments of crunching went by. "I'm in Lawson too, aren't I?" Cass said, eventually. Then she reached over, tore the green cover off my notebook, and stuck it to her forehead with some gum.

Amelia and Riley entered every race they could.

They won every single one.

Riley's victories were solid. He was always maybe a swimmer's length or two in front.

But Amelia won by a pool's length.

To be honest, that was kind of a rush, even for me. Watching someone move that fast. It's mesmerizing. The strange thing was, she looked slow. From up in the stands it honestly seemed like the other swimmers were the fast ones: They were sprinting and thrashing through the water, while Amelia was out for a dip.

It was like she had a different way with water from everybody else.

No. It was more than that. It was like she had a different way with time.

She broke every Ashbury record, and they made her Champion of the Day.

So, they were swimmers. Great. I didn't let it make my head explode.

The thing that interested me was the trophy presentation. Amelia smiled but her eyes were searching. I thought she was searching for Riley, and I found him myself in the crowd. (Never seen so much pride in such a trace of a smile.)

Then I looked back at Amelia. She'd found Riley too; her eyes stayed on him a moment — and then they looked away and kept on searching.

Later that night, I was walking to my car from the 7-Eleven in Castle Hill. I remember I was eating a Magnum. Coming toward me in the summer dusk: a family. The woman was wearing jeans and a baseball cap. The man was carrying a baby in one of those pouches that you strap to your chest. The baby was facing forward, arms and legs hanging out.

I was looking at the baby. A bright light flashed from somewhere. I was in a bad mood. I cracked a piece of chocolate from the Magnum with my teeth. I was ready to stare the baby down. You know the way you smile at babies and they just look back with bland indifference? I was going to give this baby some indifference of my own. But as I got closer the baby gave an unexpected, wide-mouthed grin. I accidentally laughed aloud.

A light flashed again.

I looked up and realized that the man had a camera in his hands.

He'd taken a photograph of me.

I stopped. The flash was in my eyes and in my chest. I was ready with: How *dare* you take my —

Then a streetlight hit the faces of the couple and I realized who they were.

Amelia and Riley.

I kept walking.

RILEY T. SMITH
Student No. 8233569

Amelia's a tightly rolled newspaper, caught in a coil of rubber band.

Not usually.

Just in these situations: She's thinking of making spaghetti carbonara for dinner but she hasn't got any spaghetti; she hasn't had time to play her guitar for more than three days; someone asks her, in a nice, polite way, to stop doing something annoying like kicking the side of their chair.

It's the politeness she can't stand. They must be so pissed, she says, they're sitting in a café and she's kicking their chair, why are they being so sweet?

And competitive swimming.

It goes like this: She starts the day not caring, wins the first race, and realizes she cares too much. That makes her mad. And terrified she won't win again.

Not just win either: win in a way that causes frenzy.

The world presses in and that makes it worse. It's the frenzy that she wants but she can't stand it. After every race, she curls tighter.

Swimming carnival at our new private school. Sports teachers asking who her trainer is. Relay teams catching her in victory dances. (They could have waded down the pool — Amelia would still have won it for them.) Yearbook wanting her photograph. She never lets anybody photograph her. She knows she's a ghost and won't show up.

We had to be out late that night, starting 2 A.M.

The music helped — it helps us both. We're not musicians, we're average, but playing music makes us feel like gods.

But then she's on the dance floor, and Amelia's a newspaper that just got loose.

Pieces of her flying wild.

Flashes of her face, hands in the air, that piece of black string with the tiny white opal that she knots around her wrist.

At three, I find her by an exit door, some huge purple cocktail cold between her hands, a joint between her teeth, a beer held tight beneath her arm.

I'm thinking that I have to get her home.

Some guy is leaving. His hand hits the exit door just above Amelia's shoulder. There's a moment when he realizes: push the door, the girl will fall. He stops.

Then he looks sideways. "Amelia," he says. "Hey."

I see his mouth say this. Can't hear his voice over the noise.

Amelia stares back, breathes in through her nose. Her eyes give him a smile, like she likes the look of him.

"You were amazing today," says his mouth.

So he was at the swimming carnival. He's someone from our new private school.

I'm staring at his face, his clothes, his body language. He's a big guy. Looks okay.

We hit the exit door together, so I can find a taxi. He helps me look a moment, then he asks me where she lives. Says that's on his way.

I call her from the Goose and Thistle, half an hour later. She answers in her sleep.

The next day she's forgotten it all. I see the guy, point him out. He's running up a flight of stairs.

"Oh, yeah, him," she says. "I think he's in my History class. Why?"

"He drove you home last night."

And she laughs like she doesn't believe me.

That time in the café, she was kicking someone's chair and she didn't even realize she was doing it. She was sideways on her own chair, elbow on the table, sucking on a straw, talking to me, and one foot was doing this slam, slam, slam against the side of the chair at the next table. A middle-aged woman was sitting there. Didn't say a word until a kick so hard that the chair almost tipped to the floor.

TOBIAS GEORGE MAZZERATI
STUDENT NO. 8233555

It's just like with MapQuest. You've gotta zoom out sometimes.

Before I can give you Tom Kincaid's story, I'm going to have to give you the History of Australia. Starting from the point when England took it from the locals.

Sorry about that, but here it is.

Okay. Guy named Captain Cook was taking in the night sky in Tahiti, when he got a text message from back home:

> While U R down that way, pls check out the southern
> oceans for the Great Southern Land? Thx XX

So he packs up, sails around, and runs smack-bang into the right-hand side of the Great Southern Land. (One day to be named Australia.)

He sends a text back:

> Just arrived. They've got kangaroos ☺ ☺ Soil looks gr8.
> Let's take it.

He goes to write a check for the deposit, but then he remembers: It's 1770! You just take it! Feeling proud, he messages the king:

> George III! Word is U R about to lose America? War of
> Independence to start in 5 yrs? ☹ Sorry to hear it. But
> good news: have picked up gr8 new property for you: cld
> keep prisoners here? Sthrn exposure; gr8 beaches; plenty
> of flax. Spk soon. Luv Cptn Cook. XXX

That's why, twenty years on (more or less), you've got your English ships crammed full of convicts sailing down this way to get a country under way.

Shortly after arrival, they'd completely run out of clothes, shoes, and food, and they're running around starving and half-naked.

They're so cut off from the rest of the world, they don't even know that the French Revolution is on. (They're all just, "da dee da, hm, maybe I'll holiday in France next year? If only I weren't so hungry . . .")

The locals helped them out, and some ships arrived from home just in time to stop them dropping dead.

Anyhow, they got the convicts working, and started growing grains, greens, and potatoes. Got themselves some goats, hogs, poultry, sheep, and fruit trees. Threw together a town called Sydney, another smaller place out west (Parramatta), and some farms along a river called the Hawkesbury. (But that kept flooding.)

Next they started a huge farm that they called Town Gabbie. They let some super-evil dude run that. He had the convicts work from dawn until they fell down dead on the spot. There was a pit where they threw the corpses every day, and the native dogs gnawed on their bones through the night.

Couple of years later, super-evil dude had ruined Town Gabbie on account of double-cropping. So they started a new super-farm out west, toward the Blue Mountains, at a place they called Castle Hill.

That's it. The History of Australia. It all ends here in Castle Hill.
Now I'll let Tom take over — tell you how he got to Castle Hill, and why he sees the darkness coming. You might notice that my Irish accent is not exactly great, but you've gotta give me points for effort. Thanks.

6.

TOBIAS GEORGE MAZZERATI
STUDENT No. 8233555

June 26, 1800

Tom Kincaid, seventeen years old, and here I am on board a ship. The ship is named the *Anne*, 384 tons, 12 guns, 42 crew plus sundry others.

Just weighing anchor and setting sail as we speak.

Sure and you've got to keep your own spirits up, for there's no one else will do that for you! So here's my best efforts. It's a kind of a game:

True it is that they got me for stealing a sheep, but that were the eleventh sheep I'd taken, and they could have got me anytime before!

True that my papers say Life — but I hear that if you pay the right person enough you can get your papers changed!

Sure and I've not got a farthing to my name, so even if I knew who the right person was, all I could offer is my smile.

But I hear that it's a winner of a smile! That's what Maggie says at least.

Och, the thought of Maggie. It's enough to make my heart billow like sails! But it plunges me anchor-deep too, for I cannot spend another day without her. I cannot.

I'd best try again:

They've hardly scratched a corner of the land where we're headed, and who can tell what might be hidden there? It's a great unfolding mystery, it's the future! There could be monstrous creatures as big as the hills! Blue grass, purple trees, and little people! Nobody knows!

(There are natives, I suppose, who might know. But they'd be keeping it a secret.)

What else? They've stowed rations of biscuit, beef, pork, plum pudding, and peas! We're to get our own beds! I'll not know what to do with all that space! (At home I share my bed with three brothers.) What's more, they've given us two coarse linen jackets, two pairs of duck trousers, two shirts, two pairs of yarn stockings, two pairs of shoes, and a woollen cap! — all of them the ugliest things you ever saw, and I'd prefer to be stark naked than to wear them.

Ah, well. Perhaps I'll try that game another day.

June 30, 1800

Tonight, below deck, I was chatting with an errand boy from Dublin and a tinker from Galway. A shoemaker and a tobacco twister joined the conversation, and sure, it seemed to be a village square!

There's a crowd of Rebels aboard this ship too, and I'm wary of them. They think they're a class above us common thieves. I must tell them about the ten other sheep and they'll see I'm uncommon good.

July 2, 1800

The first mate, he's a right hostile fellow. Likes to press the heel of his boot into your foot. A girl, who reminds me of Maggie to look at, scalded her arm the other day, and that was the first mate's leering — it frightened her into carelessness.

July 12, 1800

I've made friends with one of the Rebels! He's a fellow named Phillip Cunningham, who doesn't put on the same airs. Maybe because he doesn't have to; the others respect him like he's something special. He's a stonemason from County Kerry; older than me but treats me like he hasn't noticed that. He's left a wife and two small children back home. You can see that he knows how to speak his mind, and he's already made me laugh twice.

July 29, 1800

A strange day. There was a fumigation below deck, and some of the Rebels used the distraction to try to take over the ship. Held a sword to the captain's throat. There was shouting, shoving, gunfire, and it was over.

Phillip knew it was planned, he says, but he hadn't mentioned it to me — which offends me a little. I thought we were friends. But he wasn't one of the ringleaders.

The ringleaders were punished. We had to watch that, up on deck.

August 15, 1800

Tonight, all convict hands were called on deck, and I saw the stars exploding in the sky. I said, *Look, Maggie, that's your eyes.* Such quiet eyes, such a soft, shy voice, but both of them brimming with something, exploding like stars. I don't even know what she's brimming with, my Maggie. Dreams maybe, magic, or fairies. (You must always call them "good people," she says.)

That sky made the future bright again.

September 4, 1800

The first mate broke one of his fingers today, trying to secure the longboat, which cheered us all a great deal.

October 1, 1800

At dusk today, a vessel was sailing at a distance and it had no canvas up, except the foretop sail, and that was all torn to pieces with the wind. The Captain steered toward her and the closer we got the clearer it was that *no person was alive on board that ship.* She was water-logged. The waves were washing over her, and every time the ship rose with the swell, the water came out her cabin windows.

We sailed on and left her be, a ship full of ghosts.

October 13, 1800

Some nights the darkness below deck frightens me. They pull up the ladder so you're trapped, and there's a barricade spiked with iron just above our heads, and the fierce smell of men all around me. Men are filthy creatures, and filthier the older they get. Mix their smells with that of foul water from the bottom of the ship below the pumps, and the rotting wood, and I'll tell you this, in a darkness such as that, the great unfolding mystery of the future, it doesn't seem so wondrous to me.

November 2, 1800

I think every moment of the last time I saw Maggie. I feel the touch of her fingertips on my cheek.

She talked of finding a leprechaun and taking its silver shilling so she could join me in Sydney Town.

Then she said she'd steal a ribbon or a watch. They'd catch her, she said, and transport her too.

I looked into her eyes and saw she meant it.

"You'll not be doing that," I said, and "Try to stop me," says she.

She's dreamy one moment, tough as nails the next, that's my Maggie.

"Don't be doing that," I said again.

"If I don't get caught," she said, "at least I'll have a ribbon or a watch."

December 15, 1800

Dreadful weather the last few days. Seas like mountains and the surf like smoke. Thunder that beats from somewhere deep in your chest; lightning that falls like rain; water that rushes into our quarters and washes us from our beds.

January 2, 1801

A child died today, the son of one of the female convicts. A sailmaker prepared a piece of canvas, and they folded the little one in it and tossed him to sea.

January 15, 1801

A whale swam alongside the ship a good half hour today, and turned on its back as if it wanted us to tickle its belly.

Phillip swears he saw shoals of the Merrow (or mermaids, as the English call them) swimming in the wake of the whale, but I didn't see a single one.

February 20, 1801

Och, and so the months have passed and tomorrow we sail into Sydney Cove!

It's been 240 days all up, which is unexpected long.

And let me tell you, if the smells were savage after just three weeks, you can imagine — no, you cannot — the smells after eight long months.

Twenty men have died on our passage.

Sure and I've seen things I never thought to see, and I've gathered Maggie into my mind so she could see them too! Flying fish, fog as thick as blankets, porpoises, and giant albatrosses!

But that strange day — the day that the Rebels tried to take over the ship — the punishments we had to watch on deck. One man they gave 250 lashes, and the other, a young man named Marcus, dark curls and a deep blush, a lot like a boy I was at school with — him, they executed by firing squad.

I turned to Maggie in my mind when it happened, and then I stopped and turned away. For I couldn't have her see the likes of that.

February 21, 1801

Boatloads rowing up beside us, shouting out greetings and welcome, and calling for friends and news — and my eye catches the glimpse of a skeleton, hanging from a tree on a tiny island in a bay.

Phillip tells me that the island's name is Pinchgut, and the skeleton belongs to a murderer.

"They strung him up there as a warning," says Phillip, and then he smiles and adds: "A warning and a welcome."

It's good, I suppose, that I saw that.

For sure and this is supposed to be a gothic tale.

LYDIA JAACKSON-OBERMAN
Student No. 8233410

Feet up on the leather couch, translation homework on my knees. The parents enter the room like stage directions.

Mum, from the left.

"How can you see in this light, Lydia!" She stops to press her shoulder to the wall switch. "Now, isn't *that* better?" My mother has invented electricity!

But I can see better in the dark.

Dad, from the right.

He drops himself onto the couch beside me. I bounce straight up and smack my head against the ceiling. Slip into a coma for a moment, then wake up. Dad doesn't notice. Flicks through the pages of my German.

Why?

He doesn't know either.

Drops it to the floor again. Leather creaks and squeals. He sniffs. Picks up a random paper instead. It's a note from my school. He's got it in both hands but he's gazing at the television screen.

"You always work with the TV on, Lyd?" Chatting now. He's curious. What's it like, this so-called *schoolgirl* life?

"Pasta on the stove, Lydia." Mum curls herself on the other couch. "Help yourself. What's this rubbish you're watching, Lyd?"

They have to keep saying my name: We're a soap opera family and need to remind the audience who I am.

Dad's still holding the note from school. Now he looks down.

Can he read?

"An optional Biology Excursion to Longneck Lagoon," he announces.

Turns out he can!

"Looks like it's not compulsory." He narrows his eyes at the note.

Now I'm truly breathless.

How can you be that smart and still be alive?

Dad's still studying the note. "They're really selling this excursion," he says. He gives a wry smile. "Focus on your schoolwork this year, eh, Lydia? Give the extracurricular stuff — optional stuff like Biology excursions — give them a miss."

"Oh, this is that race across the world thing." Mum has the remote control.

"*The Great Race*," Dad agrees. "No. That's not it. *The Amazing Race*."

"It's strangely compelling," muses Mum.

"Gotta go out," I say.

I don't even take Biology.

At the Caltex, I get myself a new set of parents. They're normally $45 but my shop-a-docket takes that down to forty. Got myself a bargain! And a Magnum too.

"Lyd."

That's a voice against the back of my neck.

It's Seb. He's my ex.

I wait while he pays for his petrol. We walk out the door together, stop by the dark-lit Customer Parking stripes.

"How's things?" he says.

I can't see his eyes in the shadows. He swipes suddenly, with his foot, at an empty water bottle on the ground. Kicks it fast against the wall. It thwacks and rolls away. He straightens up and faces me again.

"Fine," I say. "'Tsup with you?"

It's like we're talking in shrugs.

Then I remember my Magnum, tear off the paper, and offer him a bite. Now we're sharing a Magnum, so we can share sentences. I ask about his teachers and his Major Work for Art. He asks about my writing. Used to be, we planned to make books together. He'd do the pictures and I'd do the words.

There's quiet for a moment and he fills that up: "Hey," he says, "Riley and Amelia are at your school this year?"

"You know them?"

"They used to go to Brookfield."

That's Seb's school. The public school down the road from us.

"No." I shake my head at him. "They never went to Brookfield."

"Oh yeah." He nods thoughtfully. "You're right. They never did."

Now I'm half-laughing.

"They never," I say again. "They couldn't come from Brookfield."

He's still nodding slowly like he's made a mistake.

"Em's got this obsessive thing about them," I say. "Someone would've told her by now if they were just from Brookfield."

"Em." He grins, thinking of Em. "No, but" — he shakes his head — "Riley and Amelia went to my school."

"You're full of it," I tell him.

Now we're both laughing. He touches my arm, remembers, and takes his hand away.

"They were. But most Brookfielders don't know them coz they never came to classes."

"If that's true," I say, "how come *you* know them?"

"I don't," he says. "But I've seen them."

He saw them early one morning, he says, maybe a year and a half ago. He was on the Brookfield oval, early for soccer training, and he'd kicked the ball behind the equipment shed. He overheard the coach talking with a girl and a guy.

"They were kind of laughing around with him at first," Seb says. "They'd just turned up out of the blue, and they were going, 'Yeah you do, you do know us, we were here last year.' And the coach is going, 'Not ringing any bells,' and they go, 'We were on your swimming team — when we first came to Brookfield?' And the coach laughs then switches to his mean voice — the one he uses for fat kids or for kids who throw like girls — the one that used to make me lose it. He goes, 'You didn't actually think I'd forgotten you, did you? Best swimmers the team ever had and you bailed on us before you even got wet. What can I do for you today?'

"There's silence then. Sound of grass crunching: Amelia and Riley shifting around. Sound of the shed door creaking: Coach is leaning on it. Then they went ahead and asked for a favor anyway."

"What kind of a favor?"

A beat goes by. Seb blinks once.

"Saw them walking back across the oval a few minutes later," he says, like I haven't asked a question. "And then I never saw them again. But I heard the other day they're at your school now. Amelia still hot?"

The empty water bottle's on the ground. He sends it back and forth between his feet, but he's watching my face all the time.

I've had enough of drink-bottle soccer.

"Gotta go," I say.

Now we're separating, walking to our cars. We're watching each other as we walk. We've both got our strange smiles, the smiles that could be mean or could be funny. They could tip either way. It's like we're waiting to see how the other person's tips.

I'm buckling my seat belt when I hear his voice again.

He's standing by the side of my car.

"Stay away from Riley and Amelia, okay?" he says.

I wind down the window and grin like he's joking. But his own smile is gone. "Seriously, Lyd," he says. "They're trouble."

Amelia and Riley's swimming success meant that my strange interest in them finally made sense. It was not childish weirdness! (As I had secretly feared, and as Lyd and Cass had openly suggested.) It was my sixth sense.

I am a very intuitive girl, and I must have *sensed* that Amelia is the reincarnation of the Inuit sea goddess, Sedna. (I looked that up on the night of the carnival.)

No wonder I was so intrigued! I was in the presence of a goddess! And her boyfriend.

I felt oppressively excited. I went to school the day after the carnival in a bubbling state, sure that everyone else would bubble too.

And there *was* much exhalation about Riley and Amelia. Their Olympic chances and so forth.

Then. However. Well, it faded away. *Within a few days, everyone lost interest.*

I found this indescribably odd.

But then I remembered how celebrity works. It's always: Okay, great movie, but where's the next one? Show us what *else* you've got. And until you do, we'll forget about you.

From then on, I walked around with this expression on my face:

Well, I was trying to draw a picture, but never mind. It was an expression of admiration for Riley and Amelia, combined with contempt for humanity.

I don't think Riley and Amelia ever noticed. They didn't really look at me.

And now I must confess that I myself continued to look at them. Oft.

For my quest to discover who they were had reached epic proportions. It kept me awake at night! It consumed my every Toblerone!

Which is understandable. World champion swimmers join Ashbury in Year 12? I mean, come on.

Yet I alone, it seemed, was alone.

Nobody else seemed to care. Lyd and Cass humored me because they have to. They're my friends. But others? Well, I remember saying to one person, "Where do you think Riley and Amelia *came* from?" And that person immediately began to explain the mysteries of human reproduction. (I stopped him, of course.)

In English, I continued to watch Amelia while she continued to watch Mr. Botherit.

In History, I was unable to watch Amelia because she sat behind me. And she was exasperating in that she sometimes didn't come to class at all. And when she did, she never said a word and therefore did not give me an excuse to turn my head and look.

But one day, Amelia spoke.

It happened like this.

We had just written a deconstructive analysis of three different perspectives on a relevant historical event. That was teaching us what History is. (It's nothing. It doesn't exist. That's my conclusion.)

So, we had just done that and Mr. Garcia, our History teacher, was jumping around like a child who has eaten the whole box of Smarties. (Mr. Garcia is a lively man and hates having to be quiet for half an hour while people work.)

"So!" he exclaimed. "Everyone has written the analysis, I think?!"
At this, a sleepy, husky voice spoke.
"Does it count if you dreamed that you wrote it?" said the voice.
I turned around.
It was Amelia.
Oh, profound and beautiful mystery. What did she mean?
I gazed at her with fascination. She was blinking her sleepy eyes.
Mr. Garcia looked startled. Then he continued with his class.
(This was unexpected — usually he leaps on surprises and follows
them wherever they lead.)

Afterward, someone told me that Amelia had put her head on the
desk and fallen asleep at the start of the class.
She must have dreamed she wrote the analysis.
And yet, even this told me little about her. (Except that she was
tired and has mysterious dreams. Me too, sometimes, and so, I'm sure,
do you.)

And then! Pay heed, my gothic reader!
A couple of days after this, my dad drove me to school. I waved
absentmindedly to him as I wandered away from the car.
I was recalling to myself that this was the morning of the Zone
Swimming Carnival. I knew that Riley and Amelia would swim like
the wind but yet? Their fame would not be resuscitated. Oh, in the
next day or two there'd be an announcement at assembly — maybe
a note in the school newsletter — but amidst the students? Barely a
ripple. I knew that nobody else — not even Cass and Lydia — would
know that the Zones were on today.
Such is the nature of events outside school grounds. They mean
almost nothing to humanity.
Anyway, I was sunk in thoughtful melancholy about this, when
Lyd appeared beside me at the school gate.
We chatted as we walked, and then Lyd said, like an idling car:
"Oh yeah, and they're from Brookfield."

"Who?"

She looked sideways at me.

"Amelia and Riley?" I whispered. I stopped still.

"I ran into Seb at a petrol station last night," she explained, still walking, only more slowly so I could hear her from my frozenness. "He says they were enrolled at Brookfield but they never showed up."

I was shocked, confused, all manner of impossibilities — but you, dear reader, might just be confused. For you do not know this Brookfield!

Here please be patient and I will explain a background tale. If you are frustrated by this detour? Let me remind you that the great gothic novel *The Mysteries of Udolpho* is 704 pages, at least half of which pages are completely irrelevant descriptions of the weather.

So, I take you by the hand and lead you to a time two years ago. This was when we were in Year 10, and our English teacher, Mr. Botherit, compelled us to write letters to the public school down the road.

Brookfield is a den of iniquity, violence, vandalism, drug abuse, knife wars, and no doubt extensive gun possession. At the very least, it is a public school with students who dress badly.

My face took on a ghastly paleness when Mr. Botherit told us to write to it.

But I did as he commanded, and perchance! I met the only wonderful boy at Brookfield! His name was Charlie and he became my boyfriend.

Another perchance! Lydia wrote to the only other great guy at Brookfield. His name was Seb, and, although he was kind of a bad Brookfield boy himself, still, he had a golden heart, and you will guess that *Seb* became Lyd's boyfriend.

And you will be right.

Meanwhile, poor Cass wrote to the devil himself. But that is another gothic story.

Okay, so, let us hasten through times which need no analysis. Charlie and I decided to break up at the start of Year 11, so that we could stretch our legs and kiss other people. Or at least, so that I could. I didn't want him kissing anybody else, and I was quite frank about my preference that our break be one-dimensional. He gave me quite a look and it was many-splendored, that look. It meant that you can't have your bed and make it too. If you eat a cake, lie in it. Hm. You know what I mean.

Anyhow, Lyd's relationship with Seb rode the waves of Year 11.

But, at the *end* of Year 11? At the start of the summer holiday? A shock in the face for Lyd.

Seb broke up with her.

Now, this was a surprise for *all* of us because Lydia has always been the breaker-upper. She is the kind of girl who leaves behind a trail of shattered hearts. Nothing of this kind had befallen her!

So, but anyway, now it was the present day and Lydia had run into Seb at a petrol station! And *she had found out who Riley and Amelia were.*

They were from our very neighborhood! Regular public school students!

And yet, how could this *be*?!

Lydia was talking.

"I'm thinking maybe I'll *join* something this year," she was saying. "Like the yearbook committee or, I don't know, sign up for a school musical? Does our school even do musicals? I'm thinking it's time to participate."

Well, that was preposterous enough.

Lydia has never done anything participatory in her entire life. But far more preposterous was the idea that she could be trying to change the subject.

"They're from *Brookfield*?" I gasped.

And then, before my very eyes?

It was they.

We were walking by the teachers' parking lot at this point. Across the lot, I could see one of the sports teachers hurrying along — and Riley and Amelia were following. The teacher had her keys out, ready to open her car.

Lyd and I became silent. The trio across the parking lot were themselves eerily quiet. Their footsteps made a subdued *scuff-scuff* along the asphalt.

I felt a strange surge of emotion, watching them.

Could it be true? Were Amelia and Riley just Brookfielders: innocent, everyday, truanting, badly dressed Brookfielders?

"I give them six months," Lydia murmured.

At first, I thought she meant they would not last at Ashbury.

Then something made me turn a sharp eye. "You think they're going to break up?" I whispered.

Lyd didn't speak. We were almost upon them.

Within a moment, we were passing close by the passenger side of the car. The sports teacher was already behind the wheel, pulling on her seat belt. Riley was in the front passenger seat, and Amelia was directly behind him. Neither had yet closed their doors.

As we passed they both paused, hands on the door handles, and glanced at us.

I looked away quickly, ready to hurry on.

Then, behind me —

"Hey," said Lydia. "Good luck at the Zones."

She said it at just the right distance from the car. She said it in just the right way: cool, almost indifferent, yet genuine too.

And then she smiled her Lydia smile.

I cannot explain the Lydia smile, except to say that I love it.

It seems like a flash of something beautiful, cutting through to the truth. There's something ironic about it, an almost raising of her eyebrows at the rules that require us to smile. But at the same time it's a little shy. It's a warm, real, generous, and vulnerable smile, and it lets you straight into her heart — even as she's laughing at herself and at you and the world.

"Thanks," said Riley and Amelia. And I stared in wonder as they offered Lydia genuine, laughing, ironic smiles of their own.

RILEY T. SMITH
STUDENT No. 8233569

They're lined up, rigid, fervent, taut, and the starter gun signals: Attack.

Not Amelia.

She slides in like a mermaid. She picks up the water, she's polite, and she takes it for a stroll. Unfurls it behind her, stretching it, stretching — and the water sighs and relishes her touch.

The water loves her body; so do I.

Now she's treading water, wiping her nose with the back of her hand, waiting for the rest of the racers to finish, a vague, dazed look, then a brief, bright smile when she hears her time. It's another record or another personal best. She's all the winning swimmers in all the TV shots in all the swimming races of all time.

Now she's standing by the side of the pool, slick, wet, practically naked, facing away from me. The back of her knees are pale purple. (Press your foot to the back of the knees and they buckle.) I can't see her eyes but I can tell you this: She's staring at nothing now; she's looking for her past.

7

Progress Meeting — The Committee for the Administration of the K. L. Mason Patterson Trust Fund — Minutes

6:00 P.M. – 9:00 P.M., Wednesday, February 20

Conference Room 2B, the K. L. Mason Patterson Center for the Arts

Chair Roberto Garcia (History Coordinator, Drama Teacher, Ashbury High)
Secretary Christopher Botherit (English Coordinator, Ashbury High)

Participants

Constance Milligan (Ashbury Alumni Association)
Patricia Aganovic (Parent Representative 1)
Jacob Mazzerati (Parent Representative 2)
Lucy Wexford (Music Coordinator, Ashbury High)

Apologies

Bill Ludovico (Ashbury School Principal/Economics Teacher)

AGENDA ITEMS

Agenda Item 1: Preliminaries
Welcome back, Constance

The group welcomed back Constance Milligan (Ashbury Alumni Association).

Constance chose not to attend the interviews of our scholarship applicants, and therefore did not participate in the last meeting, when we chose the winners. Hence, we hadn't seen her for a while.

Constance said she had missed us. She was very touched to be "welcomed" and said it reminded her of the good old days when her cat, Lulu, was alive.

Minutes of the previous meeting

The minutes of the previous meeting were circulated for comment.

• Most of the comment came from Constance Milligan, who said that she was "bewildered and horrified" by our choice of the two scholarship winners, and seriously doubted if we had "our wits about us."

Agenda Item 2: Financial Report

Roberto Garcia (Chair) circulated the latest Financial and Audit Reports and invited comment.

• Everybody looked at the Reports for a while and there was a long period of quiet.
• Eventually, Patricia Aganovic (Parent Rep 1) said that it was a shame that Bill Ludovico (Ashbury School Principal/Economics Teacher) has stopped coming to meetings.

Action points

• Roberto Garcia will pass on our best to Bill, and tell him we really miss him.

Agenda Item 3: The K. L. Mason Patterson Center for the Arts: Progress Report

Chris Botherit (English Coordinator/Secretary/me) circulated a Progress Report on the K. L. Mason Patterson Center for the Arts.

• "We're *sitting* in the K. L. Mason Patterson Center for the Arts," said Lucy Wexford (Music Coordinator). "Why do we need a *Progress* Report on a building that is already finished?"

• Roberto Garcia said that nothing is ever truly finished. "Everything, all life," he mused, "is in progress. I am in progress! You are in progress! Even stars that seem fixed to the sky are in progress — a progress that only the future will see, a progress that took place in the past!"

• Lengthy discussion about the death of stars, black holes, the speed of light, space-time continuum, whether death is progress, whether progress per se is good/bad, the new parking lot at the local Woolworths, etc., etc.

• Chris Botherit interrupted in a smooth, firm voice to explain that: "Teachers and students are very pleased with the K. L. Mason Patterson Center for the Arts, especially the AV equipment, and the comfortable chairs."

• "However," Chris continued (sternly), "there are always hiccups when you rebuild an old building — and this is why we need a Progress Report." He tapped his finger on page 2 of the Report, which refers to cracks in the brickwork.

• Roberto Garcia said that he himself had noticed a crack in the brickwork as he came in tonight, and had thought: *Here is the fine, jagged line at which the past and the future meet. Here*, he thought, *is the NOW.*

• "That's all very well," said Lucy Wexford tartly, "but is this building safe?" Unexpectedly, a chill breeze wafted through the room and we all looked around uneasily.

• At that moment, the faintest cracking sounded in the distance. Patricia Aganovic (Parent Rep 1) inquired where the nearest exit was.

• Constance Milligan surprised everyone by exclaiming, "Why, you should have seen the antics of my chums and I, back when I boarded here! And what of the larrikinism they got up to in the boys' wing? Including, I might add, Sir Kendall Laurence himself! If it could cope with the hijinks of us girls and boys, it can cope with a couple of new wings!"

Action points

• Chris Botherit (Secretary) will contact the Structural Engineer to arrange an inspection of the cracks in the brickwork.

Agenda Item 4: Further Spending Proposals

Roberto Garcia (Chair) read through the contents of the "How should we spend the money in the K. L. Mason Patterson Fund? You tell us" Suggestion Box. The Box is kept in the Ashbury Upper Staff Room.

• There were several suggestions from the sports teachers about getting new sports equipment.
• Somebody pointed out that maybe it had been a mistake to have a Suggestion Box? It only reminded the other teachers that the fund existed, and then they felt irritable when money wasn't spent on their subjects.
• Chris Botherit said he'd been thinking of a joint drama production between Ashbury and the nearby public school, Brookfield High, to foster better relations between the schools, and as a kind of "community outreach" project — distributing some of our wealth to the much poorer Brookfield.
• Constance assured us that Sir Kendall never intended his wealth to be distributed. "He didn't even know what 'outreach' meant," she said, "and he certainly never gave a hoot about the poor."

Action points

• Chris Botherit (English) and Roberto Garcia (History/Drama) will put together a proposal for a Joint Ashbury-Brookfield Dramatic Production.

• When nobody is looking, Chris Botherit will remove the Suggestion Box from the Upper Staff Room.

Agenda Item 5: Scholarship Winners: Progress Report

Roberto Garcia (Chair) noted that the two scholarship winners, Amelia Damaski and Riley Smith, were now in their fourth week at Ashbury.

Roberto invited the teachers present to share any observations they had on the scholarship winners' progress.

• Constance interrupted to say that we should first discuss whether the scholarships could be withdrawn from Amelia and Riley at once.

• It was made clear to Constance that this was not possible.

• Constance repeated her assertion that she was "aghast" at our choice of winners.

• Jacob Mazzerati (Parent Rep 2) pointed out, carefully, that, as Constance wasn't there when we interviewed the applicants, maybe she wasn't in a position to judge?

• Constance said she had had no choice but to absent herself from the interviews, as her life had been at stake. (This had come to her in a dream.) Everyone was quiet and thoughtful.

• Lucy Wexford (Music Coordinator) interrupted the quiet to say that she was now inclined to think that maybe Constance was right, and that we *had* chosen the wrong scholarship winners.

• We reminded Lucy that she had agreed with our choice. Lucy said that, upon reflection, she could not understand why she had been so impressed by the winners. She now doubted whether "Outstanding

Potential" could mean *sporting* potential, although she admitted she had agreed at the time that it could. She thought she must have been "in some kind of a trance."

• Constance breathed in sharply and seemed about to speak, but:

• Roberto Garcia (Chair) suggested that we hear from the scholarship winners' teachers (including himself). He passed on a report from their Art teacher that their attendance at art classes had been perfect.

• Chris Botherit said that Amelia's attendance at his English class had been close to perfect.

• Lucy Wexford said that both Amelia and Riley were in her Music class and that, to date, their attendance had been abysmal. Also, when they did attend, neither of them said a word. Either to her, or, as far as she could see, to any other student.

• Chris Botherit here admitted that Amelia and Riley seemed to keep to themselves. "Perhaps," he suggested, "they have not integrated into the Ashbury community just yet?"

• "That," said Lucy Wexford, "is an understatement." She added that they both have the habit of watching her *extremely closely* while she talks. She finds this unnerving.

• Chris Botherit confessed that Amelia did focus on him to a considerable degree when he speaks. He worried that she was having trouble understanding what he was saying. Or that she thought it was more important than it actually was.

• Roberto Garcia said that Amelia is in his History class, and they are both in his Drama class. So far they have simply watched the other students with slightly bemused expressions. He does not blame them. He often feels exactly the same way when he walks into a room full of Ashbury students.

• Jacob Mazzerati (Parent Rep 2) suggested that if the dramatic co-production happens, Amelia and Riley could get involved. They might feel more relaxed with the Brookfielders around, and they are both taking Drama.

• Constance inquired how the pair were performing academically. (During the above discussion, she had exclaimed "A-hah!" at various points.)

• Chris Botherit said he has not yet seen any of Amelia's written work. Neither had Roberto — and so far, they had not performed in Drama. Lucy said she had invited Riley to perform a "drum solo," and he had politely declined. She had asked Amelia where her musical interests lay, and Amelia had smiled and wandered away, humming to herself. "It is sadly clear," said Lucy, "that there is nothing remotely musical about either of them."

• Roberto noted that neither Amelia nor Riley had chosen "performance" as their "individual projects" for Drama. It was legitimate, he said, for them to study the theory of both Drama and Music, without having practical talent in either field.

• Roberto said that, according to the Scholarship Charter, the next step will be for their subject teachers to provide written reports, followed by interviews with the winners themselves to discuss their progress.

• Constance pointed out that, once again, she would not be able to attend the interviews of Amelia and Riley, on the grounds of fearing for her life.

• Patricia Aganovic (Parent Rep 1) said, "How did they do at the Zones? My daughter, Cassie, told me —" and Jacob Mazzerati (Parent Rep 2) began, "Yeah, Toby tells me their swimming —"

• At this, there was an explosion of conversation, as all the teachers present exclaimed about Amelia and Riley's extraordinary success at the Zones. Much talk about the fact that they have *already* met the "Outstanding Potential" component of the scholarship, and that their swimming was even better than we'd expected.

• "Well, then," said Constance, serenely, "we will certainly not be spending any of Sir Kendall's money on sports equipment. That's what Amelia and Riley are, isn't it? Sports equipment."

• An uncomfortable silence.

Agenda Item 6: Any Other Business

• Jacob Mazzerati (Parent Rep 2) wanted to know why Patricia Aganovic (Parent Rep 1) was "Parent Rep 1" while he was "Parent Rep 2."

• Much discussion about this.

• Jacob eventually said he'd only meant the question as a joke.

• Roberto Garcia (Chair) said: "Let's go back to Jacob's and drink all the wine in his wine cellar."

Meeting Closed: 9 P.M.

<u>www.myglasshouse.com/shadowgirl</u>
Tuesday, March 4
My Journey Home
The woman approaches
with
Her tongue pushed so
pressed so
firmly
pressed so
tightly
into
Her cheek
That
For a moment
I think it's
a distortion of
Her face

Green leaves on the footpath
Such bright
Such translucent
Pressed so
Stamped so
Firmly into
The footpath
Stamped so
Rained so
Firmly into
The footpath

So
That now
They
Are
Like
Lime
glass

The woman —
or girl maybe —
As if I
Do not see
As if she does
Not see —
As if for a moment
She is
More
Alone
Than anyone has ever
The woman
Or is she a girl,
Relaxes her
Face
Relaxes
Her hands
Her shoulders
Her chest
Her hips
Her tongue
As if
She were
More
Than
Alone.

Relaxes even her
Hair
Even her hair
Which is

Then she sees me
and she sees
that her
hair is the exact
same color
as mine.

I remember
myself in
a graveyard,
wind blowing sideways,
smell of crushed
ants,
and here come
soldiers
on
horseback
in red,
so it's not a memory,
it's a dream,
and I get onto the bus.

A boy with
four bags
gathered at his feet says
Is this the bus to Central Station?
Well,
Why do you think

It says Railway Square on the front?

There's a mystery.

The cockatoos are eating my building,
says the man
in the seat behind.

Why do some things have so many names
Like Central Station is
Railway Square
An oblong is a rectangle
A biro is a pen
A woman is a girl

A cyclone is
A hurricane is
also
A typhoon

And Riley is
All three.

Look for
The woman
Or the
Girl
With the
Hair
But she
Is
Gone.

A small boy walks past
The window
instead
His hands around his
Throat
Choking himself
He sees me see him
Hesitates
Decides to see it through.

0 comments

www.myglasshouse.com/emthompson
Tuesday, March 4
My Journey Home
I journeyed home from school yesterday.

Wait a minute. Did someone say the words: déjà vu?

Yes. They did. Because we wrote this blog a month ago. *Our teacher has given us the exact same topic.*

Well, if Mr. B is trapped in the past, I for one, am not going to tell him.

I merely sigh.

And turn to my friends.

Farewell.

Much Love,

Emily

37 comments

Cass said . . . Ok. I'm here. 'Tsup? Whatcha doing?

Em said . . . I still can't believe nobody knew about Riley and Amelia.

Cass said . . . Knew what about them?

Em said . . . Ha-ha. But seriously, how could we not have known they were from Brookfield? It's, like, three minutes from here. What were we thinking?

Cass said . . . I wasn't thinking anything. This has been your own personal quest, Em.

Em said . . . That is a harsh yet fair attack. I failed in my quest.

Em said . . . But, to be fair to me, it's the people of Ashbury that failed me. I asked EVERYONE if they knew the story behind R and A, and I even turned to my contacts in power, i.e., teachers. They were as dumbfounded as me. And I talked to Bindy Mackenzie, who, as school captain, really has a responsibility to know everything about everyone, doesn't she? (And normally I think she does.) Bindy promised she'd raise the issue of Riley and Amelia's identity at the School Leaders' Conference in Canberra, but I don't think she ever intended to.

Cass said . . . Why would she not have? It's up there with greenhouse gas emissions, global financial meltdown, and all the other issues that high school leaders are gonna figure out for us in Canberra this year.

Cass said . . . Hey, is Lyd okay? Is she around? Is she really okay about seeing Seb the other day?

Em said . . . She's right beside me and she's writing her blog and ignoring me even though I keep telling her to cut it out and join this conversation.

Em said . . . And I know, I doubt she's okay about seeing Seb, even though she says she is, with her indifferent shrug. I would find it difficult to run into Charlie by chance, and we broke up a long time ago and in different circumstances! So. Of course she's not all right.

Em said . . . Although, I would also be stunned to run into Charlie because, guess what, I decided to get back together with him!

Cass said . . . I feel like something doesn't follow there, but anyway, really? You decided to get back with Charlie?

Em said . . . Yeah, I thought, well, this has gone on long enough, me not being with Charlie. Plus, if I'd had a contact at Brookfield (Charlie), he could have told me about Riley and Amelia long ago. Then I could have got on with my life.

Em said . . . But would Charlie have known R and A? Most other Brookfielders didn't know them. Hmm. Why didn't they? Seb told Lyd it's because they NEVER EVER went to any classes, but how can that be? Isn't that, I don't know, illegal?

Cass said . . . Em, you decided to get back with Charlie and then what?

Em said . . . Oh, yeah. Turns out he's in Singapore. So, no luck getting back together. That's why I'd be stunned if I ran into him. I'd be in Singapore. Which would be stunning.

Cass said . . . Why is Charlie in Singapore?

Em said . . . His mother got some job offer there. I called his home to announce my decision that we were together again, and one of his older brothers told me they were in Singapore. I was so MAD. But then I was weeping like a willow for an hour.

Cass said . . . You want to go into Castle Hill this arvo? To weep like a willow some more?

Em said . . . But they're still not regular folk really. They're *athletes*. I thought scholarship kids like that only existed in American movies. This is the first time I've met one.

Cass said . . . You still haven't technically met Amelia and Riley.

Em said . . . They must be out of their depths, treading water in the sophisticated halls of Ashbury, can't afford the bus fare home, etc. They'll be "flunking out of classes" and have to work hard or be "cut from the swim squad." Don't you think?

Cass said . . . I don't really know if I have anything else to say about A and R.

Em said . . . But you should have, because you should have found out they were from Brookfield from your mum. So, I totally withdraw my acceptance of failure of my quest. It's your fault.

Em said . . . Ha-ha, just kidding. Because I guess your mum was being confidential, but what's so confidential about them being Brookfielders? It should be the opposite. We should have been warned they were in our midst. They could have violent/criminal tendencies and distribute drugs and be on steroids. Or do you think not? I guess Charlie and Seb are great, and therefore not all Brookfielders are psychopaths, but technically, any of them could be.

Cass said . . . You betcha.

Em said . . . I think R and A are more sweet than psychopathic. What do you think?

Cass said . . .

Em said . . . Okay. Sorry. We can talk about something else.

Cass said . . . Is it just me or is skipping classes kind of a strange, flat thing these days? Ms. W actually came out of the library while I was coming in today, and she knows I'm in her English class, but she just said, "Casso!" in her weird, cowgirl way. It turns out you can do anything you want in Year 12, which is relaxing, but is it also depressing?

Lyd said . . . It's cuz we're equals now and they trust us to be responsible for our own academic futures and Ms. W knew you were going to the library to do intensive study.

Em said . . . Lydia, finally. Don't waste time typing your own blog like that again, will you? We need you in our conversation, e.g., when we were asking if you were all right about seeing Seb. You can talk about it now if you want.

Lyd said . . . Coupla things, Em. One, just read over your above conversation with Cass and you're not exhibiting any upper-middle-class conservative prejudices re: A and R or anything, oh no, don't worry about that. And two, I'm guessing you only let Cass and me have access to this blog? Cuz, if not, why aren't we doing this conversation the normal way? You get that the Internet's kind of like a public forum?

Em said . . . Don't even worry about it, Lyd. I didn't lock this blog down or anything, but seriously, nobody else will ever find it. Because, I mean, why would they? One thing I have learned in this tough, mysterious world is that the best way to hide is *not* to hide but to get out in the crowd. And that works even better online.

BindyMackenzie said . . . HELLO, EM, LYD, AND CASS! BINDY HERE. JUST SEARCHING THROUGH THE GLASSHOUSE ASHBURY BLOGS AND FOUND YOURS. AND I HAD TO STEP IN TO CORRECT YOUR DEFAMATION OF MY CHARACTER, EMILY! BECAUSE I *MEANT* MY PROMISE TO DO YOUR DETECTIVE WORK ABOUT AMELIA AND RILEY IN CANBERRA AT THE LEADERS' CONFERENCE! I don't make empty promises. Thank heavens, I finally figured out how to undo the caps lock, it was jammed.

Lyd said . . . What a relief.

9

TOBIAS GEORGE MAZZERATI
Student No. 8233555

March 7, 1802

I'm in Sydney Town now. It's pure madness and even the moon is topside turvy.

The weather, she's like an Irish jig, I mean, she's mischievous and you can never pin her down.

I'm living in a wooden shack with three other men: neither bars on the windows nor padlock on the door. I could slip down the cove and sail away! We talk of it, Phillip and I, of sailing home. (Phillip misses his wife and children with the fierceness of a wild cat.) We've even designed a boat with a stick in mud, and all we need is the materials.

And a little free time to build.

Or we could borrow a boat. Sure and that might be simpler.

In the meantime, I'm in the carpenters' gang. That'll help me with the building of the boat when the time comes. Phillip's the overseer of stonemasons, which makes me proud, how important he is. We'll not be needing stone on our boat, though; it'd sink.

You can't leave your property alone here, what with the thieves everywhere. And they've public floggings of men, and women too; and they shave the women's heads if they catch them having a good time.

The girls here have wild ways, crinkle-set eyes, sun-browned faces, and fine, long hair that they wear in braids down their backs. It's enough to tear your heart out, they're so pretty. And they're up for it too.

Sure and the people here have not done a bad job, so far as building a colony from scratch goes. It makes me strangely proud to be a man.

That men could start with nothing, and turn it into this. Five thousand people living under roofs, eating their breakfasts, and washing their clothes (or not washing them, if not inclined).

You know, all my life I've thought myself a country boy, and now it turns out not to be so? Lives exploding or anyway breathing all around me — some days, it's like I've fallen in love and want to kiss strangers and walls.

I'll never go back to the countryside or farming or it'll mean the death of me. I swear it on the good book and on all books ever opened or closed.

Maggie's letters fret that I must be miserable, surrounded by the English in an English colony. But my friends are Irish, and it brings us closer, makes us more Irish than we ever were at home, and, to be sure, I think I like that.

All in all, it's not so bad. Provided you keep out of trouble, make the overseer like you by cracking a joke, get enough grog, see enough pretty girls, and have enough laughs with the men —

And speaking of that, it'd make you laugh if it didn't make you cry — for what was I just saying about myself and farming life? Here and if it isn't Phillip telling me they've started a new government farm at a place they call Castle Hill.

There's talk he and I might be sent there.

They can't be sending me out to this farm, for haven't I just now sworn an oath?

EMILY MELISSA-ANNE THOMPSON
STUDENT NO. 8233521

I have mentioned Mr. Garcia, have I not?

He is a large and mountainous man, Mr. Garcia, with a voice — an accent — that belongs on television.

If only television were the radio.

How shall I put it delicately? Rugged and startling of appearance? A regular monstrosity to look upon? Yes. That will do.

Hearken, though! Mr. Garcia may be hideous to look at but he is kindhearted, funny, and he wears two hats.

Not literally. I mean, he teaches History but he also teaches Drama.

Now, near the end of Term 1, there came to be a History class, and Mr. Garcia, as is his wantonness, had led us astray from the school. We had walked to Castle Hill Heritage Park.

That is an immense and flowing park not far from our school where historical events of irrelevance took place.

So, this day, we were at the Park. It's just stretches of grass, distant patches of gum trees, paths that rise too steeply for my calf muscles, and a series of those historical signs, which, naturally enough, nobody reads.

Mr. Garcia was talking.

I said that he wears two hats? Well, oft he lets his Drama hat fall into his eyes when teaching History. That can be enchanting, but sometimes it's just, you know, please, you're giving me a headache. Especially when I'm feeling sleepy.

I can't recall exactly what he was talking about this day but it seemed that *he* at least had read those signs. The land we were standing on had once been a government farm where convicts worked. (Woo-hoo.) I remember he said that. And I remember he said: Look! Just behind him! It's the stone barracks where those convicts lived!

No.

Clearly not.

There were no convict barracks, just grass.

The barracks then became this country's first lunatic asylum! Mr. Garcia was saying. And then, look, it crumbled into nothing!

Yes. Exactly.

In disgust, my mind wandered, and so did my eyes.

And there I beheld Amelia on the very edge of our group. She was facing away from us, watching the trees.

She was standing very still, poised like an antelope.

Her long hair fell behind her.

Amelia's hair is soft and beautiful. It's the color of a gingerbread man, only without the white spots that gingerbread men often have, to indicate their eyes, nose, and buttons.

I was distracted by a kerfuffle. Mr. Garcia had stepped back, theatrically, and landed on Toby Mazzerati's toes. It seemed he had asked Toby to come forward but had immediately forgotten he was there and had stepped onto his toes. There were apologies, mild laughter, and then Mr. Garcia asked Toby to speak. Toby, it turned out, was doing a case study relating to this very park. So he had a *lot* to say.

I am fond of Toby, he's a friend of mine, but I had no need for his history.

I looked, once again, for Amelia.

And she had drifted even farther from the group.

She was almost lost amidst the trees, but once again was standing very still. Her head was tilted to the side now, almost as if she was listening.

Listening for what?

For the future?

Could she hear the amazing things that were just about to happen?

LYDIA JAACKSON-OBERMAN
STUDENT No. 8233410

Amazing things began to happen.

It started with Drama.

I don't do Drama, but I hear it was *amazing*.

At lunch one day, near the end of term, I saw Em walking into the school with her History class. She told me they'd just been to Castle Hill Heritage Park. She didn't know why.

Amelia is in the class. I saw Mr. Garcia, the History/Drama teacher, lean over and speak to her. I think he said, "We missed you in Drama yesterday. You coming today?"

As far as I could tell, Amelia didn't answer. Just looked into his eyes.

There was a flicker of something like uneasiness on Mr. Garcia's face. Or maybe I imagined that. But then he leaned closer and murmured something else I couldn't hear.

Turned out she did go to Drama that day.

And I hear it was *amazing*!!

Sorry if I sound cynical.

My mother is an actor. She used to be a soap star, got some endorsement deals, made some investments, and now she's got money growing in her ears where the wax used to be.

My father's an actor too. Of course, if you ask *him* what he does, he'll tell you he's a Justice of the Supreme Court of New South Wales.

My father, a Supreme Court Justice?

Don't make me laugh!

Ha-ha! Ha-ha!

Well. Okay. He is.

But only because he likes dressing up in a gown and wig and playing the role of Supreme Lord King High Commander of The World.

They act their way through their days and nights and my home is a television set.

So. You know. Forgive me if I think that acting's just a whole lot of deception.

Turned out Amelia and Riley could act.

Not just swim; also act.

The story was that all term long, they'd been silent in Drama class. Often they didn't turn up. The classes had been mainly theory, so no special reason for participating — but this day, Mr. Garcia started talking about IPs. (IPs are Individual Projects that you have to do for HSC Drama.)

Amelia said that she wanted to change her IP. She'd been doing costuming, she said, but now she'd decided on performance.

She didn't seem nervous when she spoke, people told me. That's what they found strange. She'd been silent all term, and when a silent person speaks the voice is often quiet. Faded and broken. Or accidentally loud: an unexpected clatter while a blush floods the silent person's face.

But Amelia's voice, they said, was perfect. Its edges curved smoothly; its tone was like cream.

Technically, Mr. Garcia told Amelia, it was not too late to switch her IP. The official choices hadn't yet been sent in. Did she have a monologue in mind?

At this point, *Riley* spoke.

Now, people *had* heard Riley's voice before — it had been there all along, but unobtrusive, part of the background noise, just some regular guy. Nobody seemed to remember what he had said.

These were the first real words. The first words that referred to *himself* as a human being.

"I'm thinking of switching to performance too."

He said he had an eight-minute monologue prepared, and then he looked at Amelia, who said she had one too.

There was an intense moment of suspense.

Mr. Garcia squinted thoughtfully, spoke in a quieter voice than usual, and asked if they wanted to perform.

They did.

One after the other, without a break.

Their monologues were independent, but also, and this is apparently unusual — they were interlinked.

Mr. Garcia shrugged when they were finished. "Not so bad, you know?" he said. "We can work on them." And moved to another topic.

But both of them — both were amazing.

RILEY T. SMITH
STUDENT No. 8233569

One day everything changed at our new private school.
Amelia said: Okay, it's time to —
I don't think she said: *Step it up.*
Or *take the next step*, or *step out from behind.*
I don't know what she said or
    what we said
        but what we meant was: *Here we are.*
(But we weren't.)

First time we'd ever done this. You'd think it would have been too late, but no. It was easy.
Her teacher made it happen.
He said — she said — he said into her ear: *You can be invisible.*
That's what he said.
"I know that's what you want," he said. "Okay, you've got it. But please, just come to class?"
It *was* what she wanted, to be invisible, but how did this guy know? It made her mad, him knowing. It changed everything. It tightened her — the newspaper rolling tighter all through lunch.
After lunch was this teacher's Drama class.
And we went.
After that was Art. We went there too.
We'd been before, of course, but not like this.
They liked our acting. They liked our art.

That night, we sat at the kitchen table and wrote our first English essays. That weekend, went to the library and researched our first History assignments.

Amelia and I were doing the same subjects: English (with different teachers), Drama, Art, and Music. The only difference was History — I'm Ancient and she's Modern.

In Music, we stayed quiet. We had no respect for that teacher. And that would not have fit into our plan.

But in everything else —

Also in those last few weeks of term, there was the Area Swimming. The next step up from Zones. I stopped getting places, but Amelia kept winning.

Then a week off to study for the half-yearly exams.

"Should we study?" she said.

"No." (I'd had enough now.)

But we studied anyway. On the floor of the Goose and Thistle before opening each night.

The exams were fine. And now there would be holidays.

This living in their world, we said, *it's easy.*

10

**The Committee for the Administration of the
K. L. Mason Patterson Trust Fund
THE K. L. MASON PATTERSON SCHOLARSHIP FILE**

Memo

To: All Members of the K. L. Mason Patterson
Trust Fund Committee

From: Chris Botherit and Roberto Garcia

Re: K. L. Mason Patterson Scholarship Teachers'
Progress Reports

PRIVATE AND CONFIDENTIAL

Dear Committee Members,

It is with great pleasure that we attach the first
ever K. L. Mason Patterson Scholarship Teachers'
Progress Reports!

With just one exception, the reports show
remarkable progress by our scholarship recipients.
You will recall that they had not demonstrated any
academic proficiency in the past? That their focus
was to be swimming? Well . . . some highlights:

• "Amelia's approach to essay writing is unique —
to say the least — but her imagination is quite
astonishing. She can also be perceptive and razor-
sharp. After a shaky beginning, she began handing
in all her overdue essays in the last few weeks of

term, and has now established herself as one of the top-ranked students in the year." (*Chris Botherit — English*)

• "At first I thought Riley was going to be a write-off — no participation, skipping classes, etc. — but in the last couple of weeks he's attended every class and made some interesting comments. He finally handed in an assignment last week and, to be honest, it blew my mind." (*Stephen Latimer — Ancient History and English*)

• "Have been teaching Drama for several years. Have seen plenty of talented performers. Am not exaggerating when I say that I have never, *never* seen performances like that of Riley and Amelia. They will participate in the Ashbury-Brookfield Dramatic Production or I will cut my own throat. Both of them! Am so filled with wonder and awe that I don't know where to put it. No font big enough to express it. Have been weeping, dancing, getting drunk on Jacob's wine. Seriously." (*Roberto Garcia — Drama and Modern History*)

• "I realize I'm not *technically* supposed to provide a report, since Amelia does not take PDHPE, but think it's important to get this on the record. Amelia should be swimming for her country. Riley is talented, but Amelia is astounding. *Yet she has never been properly trained and refuses to have a coach.* If she had been, I have no doubt she'd have been representing Australia three years ago. It may be too late — and it *will* be too late soon. Is there anything the Committee can do to persuade her? Sorry to be dramatic but this is a matter of life and death." (*Sarah McCabe — Personal Development, Health, and Physical Education*)

- "In recent weeks, Riley and Amelia have both revealed that they are talented artists: technically competent and with a sound knowledge of art history and theory. Riley, in particular, has a refreshing, original, and often startling approach — his work is a delight." (*Damian Carlton — Art*)
- "Neither Riley nor Amelia has impressed me in the slightest degree. They seem completely uninterested in music and have not handed in any work. So far are they from participating that I frequently don't realize, until near the end of a lesson, that *they simply are not there.* Ranked bottom of the class. Clearly have no knowledge of, nor aptitude for, music. Not sure why they've taken the subject. Disappointing." (*Lucy Wexford — Music*)

Of course, we will need to deal with the issue of their absences from class — particularly from Music. I do not mean to suggest that that is not a serious issue. However, I trust you are all proud and delighted!!! I think a celebration is in order — Roberto suggests cocktails at Jacob's place. Jacob?

Best wishes to all,
Chris Botherit

P.S. Just confirming that we'll be interviewing Riley and Amelia on Thursday, April 3 (last day of term), Conference Room 2B, the K. L. Mason Patterson Center. The interview will take the form of a casual chat during which we'll try to gauge their comfort levels/needs/etc. (and deal with that serious issue of absenteeism).

P.P.S. Also confirming that Constance has stated that she will *not* be at that interview — and is resolved never to be in the same room as Amelia and Riley — unless perhaps the attached reports have changed your mind, Constance?

EMILY MELISSA-ANNE THOMPSON
Student No. 8233521

You may recall that the first day of term was gothically stormy?

Now, come closer, let me chill you to the bone — for the last day of term?

It was ungothically bright.

I'm not kidding around here.

Golden sunshine and a blue, curvaceous sky — birds dancing — puddles asparkle — bits of glitter dazzling in the asphalt.

Such a reversal — such a strange twist in weather from the first day to the last.

What could it mean.

Perchance it was just, you know, the weather. It happens.

But I bethink me it was more than that. And, in honor of the strange, solemn mystery of it, I have not used a single exclamation mark.

But now I will begin exclaiming again! For that day, I naïvely saw the weather as a reward! I did not take it as imperative of doom!

You see, we had just completed our half-yearly exams and our fingers, our shoulders, our very *minds*, ached with confusion. Facts, figures, and formulae, exam times and places — all had been spilling from our sweat glands! (If I had any sweat glands. Which I doubt. Sweating is disgusting, plus I never do sport.)

And here it was, the morning of the final day and we were about to go home!

Who among us does not love the strange, cascading bliss of leaving the school grounds before noon on the last day of exams?! Who?! Show yourself!

Anyway.

Picture this: me and Cassie, standing near the front gate of the school. We were quiet for a moment, happily sleepy, allowing the clutter in our minds to drain away.

Probably, also, we were both thinking of the two-week holiday. Lydia's parents were about to go away, leaving Lydia alone in her fantastic house! (The parents would be gone not just for the holidays, by the way, but also for *all of Term 2.*)

SO MANY PARTIES WOULD BEFALL US!!

Tonight, there would be the first party at Lydia's place!

And looking up to the festive blue sky I saw a little white moon. It was pretending to be a cloud so it could stay in the sky through the day.

Oh, I laughed, a quiet, tender laugh. *Moon*, I thought, *you cannot fool anybody! You look exactly like yourself!*

Yet I also admired it, the moon, for its madcap bravery.

I include these details to give you a clear picture of the happy hilarity of my mood.

Beneath the moon was the oval — and here at last came Lydia. She was walking back from the Art Rooms — she'd just had German Listening over there. Cass and I brightened even further. Lydia waved from the distance. Her wave had the joyousness of one who has just finished her last exam.

And then, we saw them.

They had come from the direction of the school.

They were heading across the oval themselves, toward the Art Rooms.

Who do I mean?

Riley and Amelia, of course. Who else?

Here I must tell you something extraordinary. In the last few weeks of term, *the entire school had become me.*

I don't mean that literally. But *everyone was talking about Riley and Amelia.*

Their talents knew no gothic moats; their explosion of ability was beyond all shadow of reality! Swimming, acting, essay-writing — and the question went spinning through the school: *Who are these people?!*

Of course, it was now common knowledge that they were from Brookfield.

(Thanks to that information being on my blog, I guess. Blame Mr. B for that. Making us write blogs.)

But people wanted *more*. They wanted the *why*, the *how*, the other *how*, the *where*, and the *what*!!

Why had they chosen Ashbury? How had they hidden at Brookfield without news of their brilliance getting out? How was their existence humanly possible? Where would it end? And *what* would it take for Riley and Amelia to notice us?

That last question was key.

Truly, everyone was me, for *everyone* wanted to be noticed by them.

That, by the way, includes the teachers. I am not kidding when I say that teachers were dressing differently, and trying to liven up their classes. Students, meanwhile, were trying to be cooler, tougher, funnier, or more intriguing, just to make them blink.

You could see people changing as soon as Riley and Amelia walked into a room. Some would pretend they were *not* in the room. Everything became exaggerated. People moved in ways that were *slightly* slower than usual. Or slightly faster. Some people smiled more; others didn't smile at all. Girls would sit at their desks, eyes half-closed, pushing hair behind their ears with whimsical expressions that said: *I'm lost in a sort of sighing thought here.* And then their faces would exclaim: *I just remembered a really cool thing that I have to tell my close friend about!* And they'd swing around to the girl sitting behind them, prance their hands on that girl's desk, and say, "Guess what?"

Oft, the girl behind them would be a total stranger.

O, there were conversations! So many conversations! All to impress Riley and Amelia! I remember once walking into History and seeing a boy pick up a soccer ball and gently thunk another boy on the back of the head with it. At which the second boy turned around, breathed quickly out of his right nostril, and asked the first boy if he'd started his case study yet. At which the first boy gave a half grin and changed the subject to the demographics of democracy or some such. To show he was profound, possessing insights beyond a thunking football.

All of this, I guarantee, took place because Amelia was near them.

You see, we all wanted Riley and Amelia to think we were interesting. We wanted them to see us as languid people who simmered with interesting thoughts. We wanted them to *want* us as their friends!

(A lot of boys just wanted to have sex with Amelia.)

Some people actually believed they were cool enough for Riley and Amelia's attention. They invited them around. They said, "You guys want to come get coffee with us?" They tried to strike up conversations.

But every single time, they were thwarted.

Riley and Amelia listened. They concentrated even. A strange, kind of head-tilted concentration. As if the person was speaking a language they had heard once before in a jungle long, long ago.

Then, smoothly, politely, Riley and Amelia would block them. It was never exactly, *no thank you*. It was more often a mild joke, a brief change of topic, even sometimes a gentle laugh. And then they would wander away.

I watched this happen over and over. Always I would see the people left behind, blinking, confused, not sure what had happened — troubled, without knowing why.

As far as I could tell, not a single person had had a genuine conversation with them. Nobody had successfully invited them to a social event.

They did no extracurricular activities at school (besides swimming).

I saw Mr. Garcia fall to his knees, clasp his hands, and beg them to sign up for the Ashbury-Brookfield Dramatic Production.

I hoped they would agree. Lyd, Cass, and I had signed up. I joined because I knew Amelia and Riley were extreme actors so I thought they'd be in it, and I made Lyd and Cass join. (Lyd was in a strange phase of wanting to participate anyway, and Cass is an obligatory friend.)

But Riley and Amelia did not sign up at all.

They laughed mildly at Mr. Garcia on his knees, and then they helped him to his feet.

Nothing, it seemed, could break into their self-contained world.

Now, please follow me, gently, back to the school gate, on the last day of term.

There we were, Cass and me. There they were, Riley and Amelia, walking side by side, away from us. And there was Lydia, alone, walking toward us.

In a moment, their paths would cross.

I glanced quickly at Cass. She was also watching, with mild interest, this impending crossing of paths.

Now, a few paragraphs ago, I said that everybody at our school was intrigued by Riley and Amelia.

There was one exception: Lydia.

To her, they were just regular people. She remained *completely unchanged* when they were in the room. She scarcely glanced in their direction.

I was both exasperated and impressed. How could anybody be as cool as that? All I could think was that she had spent time around celebrities, since her mother used to be famous, and so was accustomed to it.

Cass, at least, was a human being and had learned the happiness of analyzing Riley and Amelia.

"There's something ethereal about them," I said. "Like gazelles. I wonder where they're going."

"I know where they're going," said Cass. "It's a scholarship thing — they're interviewing them in the Art Rooms today. My mum's over there now."

"It's wrong how strict your mum is about confidentiality," I said to Cass. "She should totally tell us everything."

"I know," said Cass.

"I would give anything," I said, "to see their scholarship file. I mean, what did they write on their application? Why did they want to come here?"

Cass was silent. We were quiet again, watching.

The distance between Lydia and Riley-and-Amelia was closing. Lyd did not seem to have noticed them. She was thinking about something; she was checking her watch; she was looking up at the sky and then over at us and doing a sudden, crazy face, which Cass and I could not quite understand. We held out our hands meaning, huh? And she just laughed. She looked our way again, and pulled another face. I thought to myself: *There is nobody else in this school who would be so free and easy — so much like themselves — with Riley and Amelia approaching.*

Nobody.

The distance was closing.

Lydia finally noticed who was heading her way. I thought: *What will she do?* Will she smile her Lydia smile?

I saw her manner calm slightly — I mean, the way you become more serious when you realize you're about to cross paths with somebody — you know, you don't want to bump into them or anything — she was watching them and walking.

And the distance closed,

And the distance closed,

And it closed.

Last day of term something brightened.

I finished my exam — German Listening — and walked out of the Art Rooms to a big, blue sky, and suddenly everything seemed brighter.

I'd been closing in, folding up, a chant in my head: *I am alone.* It was a statement, practical and flat. More a chat than a chant; more: *Of course, I kind of knew it all along.*

My parents were about to go away for four months. Taking the broken pieces of their marriage to Tuscany. ("Does Tuscany get a say in this?" I said. My parents turned toward me with their strained, pale, adult faces and then turned back to the brochures.)

I guess it kind of surprised me they would leave. I don't know why. I was seventeen years old, so. You know.

But the chanting started: *I am alone.*

Alone in my family, alone without Seb.

Anyway, this day, last day of term, the bright sky made me laugh at myself.

I was crossing the oval thinking, *I love the world, I love that stone wall, how it curves along the road, I love that tree and that broken hockey stick in the grass. I love that I'm young and smart and okay to look at, and soon I'll leave school and start life, and I think I'll be okay at life, and I love my friends —*

There they were by the gate: Emily and Cassie, waiting for me.

I thought: *They're beautiful; they're my best friends; they're not going anywhere.*

I pulled mad faces to show them it was true.

That's when I saw Amelia and Riley crossing toward me.

I felt sad for them. Before, they'd been ignored. Now they were celebrities and everybody wanted them as friends.

They were the ones who were alone.

The only person who'd seen them as special all along was Emily.

As we got closer, I smiled at Amelia and Riley. They smiled back.

Our paths crossed and I said: "People are coming to my place tonight if you want to come."

They paused, looked me right in the eye, didn't even glance at each other. Then both at once they said, "Yeah. Okay."

We kind of laughed, and I told them my address, and then kept walking.

Em and Cass were still waiting at the gate, watching me. They'd want to know what had just happened.

Most of all, I thought, *I love the expression that's about to burst onto Em's face.*

RILEY T. SMITH
STUDENT No. 8233569

We'd been watching them.

That's what you have to know.

We'd been watching everyone at our new private school.

And we'd chosen.

There were three girls, best friends: Emily Thompson, Cassie Aganovic, and Lydia Jaackson-Oberman. Em has a face that dimples madly when she smiles; Cass has a thin, sprinter's body; Lydia is gorgeous in a way that she doesn't dress up or paint over.

We couldn't help notice them. They were cool and they were hot, and from the first day there, Emily had followed us everywhere we went.

Lydia turned out to be exactly what we wanted.

Another thing you have to know.

Em was hysterical, melodramatic, and not very bright. Sheltered all her life, she'd stayed a little girl.

Cass was quiet, and essentially pointless.

And Lydia was one of those spoiled rich kids who know absolutely nothing, but put on a cool and cynical face because they think they know it all.

None of them was worth a thing. None of them was real.

Nothing about a private school is real. Those people are just playing roles; they're all playing at life.

Last day of Term 1, walking across the oval and there she was: Lydia.

She made it easy.

Asked us to a party at her place.

We said yes, of course.

PART TWO

English Extension 3
Assessment Task
Due Date: First Day of Term 3

Elective: Gothic Fiction

1. *The Ghost Story*
   The Ghost Story is a literary form that **always contains a ghost** — or at least the possibility of a ghost. Its objective is to **chill and terrify.**

2. *Your Task*
   Write the Story of Term 2 as a Ghost Story.
   Think back on the events of your life last term (Term 2). What happened to you? To the people around you? What "narrative" can you draw from your life in Term 2? Now reimagine that narrative as Ghost Story. *Write that Ghost Story.*

3. *Before You Panic . . .*
   Consider this: A ghost can be real, or it can be metaphoric. You may subscribe to, challenge, or subvert the "ghost story" genre. A ghost could be a memory, an idea, or a darkness. *You* might be a ghost. A close friend might be a ghost. . . . Look at your memories of Term 2 — and then look at them again. This time stretch the boundaries and study the shadows. This time find the ghost you never knew was there.

1.

Tobias Mazzerati
THE STORY OF TERM 2 AS A GHOST STORY

Once upon a time there was this guy named Toby (me) and also, once upon this exact same time, it was early on the morning of the first day of Term 2.

Term 2, Year 12, Ashbury High.

It's a snappy morning and here I am at the Blue Danish Café, warming my hands on my mug of cappuccino, and there's a ghost.

Right beside me. A ghost! Seriously. A purple, headless ghost!

. . .

Well. Okay. You got me. It's not a ghost. Just a fuzzy, purple cardigan hangin' on the back of the chair to my right, but the way I was holding my cappuccino mug, it curved off the edge of my vision for a second, and — for just that moment — a furry, purple guy was standing right beside me with no head.

Anyhow, this is my personal story of Term 2.

I've got myself a framework. Here it is: The term was ten weeks long.

Week 1
First day of Term 2, Blue Danish Café, warming my hands, cappuccino mug, etc.

Across the table from me, a woman in black pants. That's her purple cardigan hanging on the chair to my right. She took it off when she arrived.

She's eating a croissant and laughing at the flakes that keep floating to her clothes. Brushing them off. Laughing at herself.

But you can't blame yourself for croissant crumbs. They happen.

Every table in this café is full. There's a bunch of people from my school across the room, sitting by the window, including some buddies of mine.

"Oh, your dad, Toby. What can I say? He's kind of a black hole."

I don't exactly hear that.

I'm looking past her shoulder at my buddies over there. I'm thinkin': They've been up all night. They've partied hard and they've thrown on their uniforms and tripped their way here so they can burn something sharp into their brains before school.

I should have been at that party. I could be blending with them now: the way they're leaning, slumping, melting. Girls' hair falling, guys' faces shadowing, and I can't hear their words but I can tell that those words are melting into one another's words.

Sometimes the morning after is my favorite part.

"I still can't believe that movie last night."

Now I'm thinkin': *What am I thinking?* 'Cause I had fun last night.

Hangin' with my mum.

We didn't get trashed; we saw trash at the movies and we laughed until it hurt. Laughed some more when my mum fell asleep near the end. She's chronically unable to stay up past ten. Had to sleepwalk her over to the taxi home, and she was making dumb jokes, laughing in that half-asleep way. It was good, clean, pure, sober fun.

Whereas my buddies over there? They're hurting right now. Their brains are fried.

I can be stupid sometimes.

My mum lives in Brisbane, but she was down the last few days. Hangin' with me when she could. And now we're hangin' one last time before she flies.

She flips open her phone to show a coupla photos, then she notices the time and she says: "No."

She always says it like that, that definite, absolute way — like this time she point-blank refuses; *this* time it really can't be true; this time she's putting her foot down! — when she realizes she has to say goodbye to me again.

We share her taxi as far as my school: gives us five more minutes anyhow.

Folks, if you'll forgive me, I'm closing the curtains on the rest of this week. Leave me there at the Ashbury school gate, waving at a taxi.

'Cause that was a week of exam results.

Close the curtains now.

Week 2

Open the curtains!

Coz, second week of term I'm full of buzz and vim.

I'm thinkin': *I'll fix this situation.*

Ready with my sleeves rolled up, toolbox out, hammer and — anyhow, just being metaphorical here. Sleeves were in their regular place.

But I was concentrating *hard.*

Sometimes, you know, I get a surge like this.

I'm sitting on a couch in the Year 12 Common Room, binder on my lap. There's a piece of paper resting on the binder.

I draw a table. Three columns like this:

Subject	Mark	ACTION

List my subjects in the far left column, then the mark I got in the half-yearly exams.

No need to include them in this story. You can employ your powers of invention but keep those powers turned way down.

The third column is the wide one headed ACTION.

I look at that awhile.

Write down mind-blowing, earth-exploding thoughts like: "download practice exams" and "ask Bindy Mackenzie for her study notes."

Then my mind gets bored, and goes off on its own.

I think about the Friday before, how I went out and drank to the blackness of the curtains — they truly were a deep, dark black — and I guess I got home fairly late.

My dad was on the couch.

He was watching TV, and everything about him was curved. Slump enough and you can get that curved. Your shoulders, your face, your eyelashes, your elbows — all curving inward in the shadows of TV.

My first thought was: *I hear ya, Dad.*

Coz I felt the same way. Turns out alcohol does not erase exam marks.

My second thought was: *There should be disclaimers.* On the alcohol bottles, I meant.

So there I was, swaying to the humor of that thought — I was drunk so it was funny — still watching my dad — he hadn't seen me yet, just a curved-in shadow. And it came back to me, what my mum said in the café.

"What can I say?" she said. "He's kind of a black hole."

So my third thought that night was: *Yeah.*

Now in the Year 12 Common Room, I stop work on my Action table, and draw a circle farther down the page. Color it in with black ink. That takes a while, coloring it in. Now it's a black hole.

I'm staring at it hard when a friend lands on the couch by my side.

"Toby," she says, "there's a ghost in the Art Rooms."

"Yeah?" I say.

"But nobody believes me."

"I believe you," I say, and she gives a wise nod, like she knew I would.

"I believe you," I repeat, "but now I've gotta go."

Now she gets a tragic look, like she knew that too.

I did have to go. Had an appointment with Mr. Garcia to discuss my History Project.

"Roberto," I say, as I walk into his office — no disrespect, he's a buddy of mine and of my dad's — "Roberto, this is my action week. Everything changes this week."

I show him my Action table and he looks at the exam result column.

Now this is a remarkable man. He scans that column but his face doesn't so much as twitch.

Then he lights up.

"Design and Technology!" He points to the mark: the number 92, shining like a god. "At this, you are a *genius*!"

"But the rest," I say.

"The rest," he murmurs.

In fact, the number 92 makes the other numbers look like dead leaves. If they only had one another, they might have never realized there's a sky — might have been happy in the gutter.

"If you didn't have the number 92," Roberto says, "these other numbers would not look so bad."

Spooky. See that? The guy can read my mind.

"Maybe you should have left the 92 out of the table," he says. "No! What am I thinking? Keep the 92 and get rid of the rest!" And he starts scribbling out the other marks.

Now, another teacher doing this scribbling act would have had some agenda. Like, say they were a prick like Mr. Ludovico? They'd be being sarcastic. Or say they were up themselves, they'd be playing some ironic game. Or say they were the gentle, kindly uncle type of guy, they'd be doing this with a sparkle in their eye, watching to see if you were laughing — like cheering up a tearstained kid.

But not Garcia.

He's none of these types.

Garcia will do something mad and while he's doing it, he'll *mean* it — he'll make you think, for just that moment, *well, why not*? Maybe this *is* the solution?

"Except for History." He stops scribbling and draws a circle around the History mark, which is bad. "History, and Design and Technology. They are everything. Especially History. Now, let us take *action* in relation to History, and get this number higher! Get it as high as Design and Technology, why not?! Tell me about our friend named Tom. How is he doing?"

He's referring to my History Project.

And when he says Tom, he means Tom Kincaid.

Irish guy. He was seventeen years old when he stole a sheep and they shipped him out to Australia. Wrote letters home to his girl-friend, Maggie, and his mum, and now I've got copies of those letters. I'm going through them slowly now, filling in the details. Using, you know, History.

"Well," I say, "it's 1802, and he's right here in Castle Hill with his buddy Phillip."

"Ah, Phillip Cunningham." Roberto grins, like he's remembering the wild times he and Phil have had. "And what's going down at Castle Hill?"

"There's around three hundred men. They're clearing the land for wheat and living in your basic bark huts."

Roberto takes a deep, contented breath, like he's breathing in my facts. He's totally into History, that guy.

"And Tom is happy?" he says.

"Roberto," I say, carefully. "He's a convict."

"Yes. He is. And you think he's not happy because of this?"

Not a stupid man so he must want something else.

"He's happy sometimes," I try, "because he talks about his friend Phillip and the other guys, and like on Saint Patrick's Day, they all got trashed. And he likes seeing how the farm's, you know, shaping up."

Roberto gets an intense expression.

"But then again," I say, "he could be telling these happy stories to Maggie, so she doesn't worry. He could be keeping his darkest thoughts out of his letters."

Roberto makes a horse-snorting noise. I think he means it's a good point.

"He talks about how much he's missing Maggie," I say, "and he tells her it's too hot, and the colors are reds and golds but he wants the *green, green grass* of home."

"The colors, ah. And what else do you think he might miss about home, our Tom?"

I have a think about that.

I say, "Well, he'd be missing his mum. He'd be missing having her around to say good night each night."

Roberto's face gets a penetrating look, and I get a spooky feeling that he thinks I'm talking about my *own* mother.

I now have two things to say.

(1) I was not.

(2) I hate those TV shows where characters talk about one thing, such as their patient on the operating table (let's say they're a doctor), then you realize they're *actually* talking about themselves. The patient's open-heart surgery is nothing compared to their *own* messed-up heart, or whatever. It's selfish. And means they're not concentrating, which is medical negligence.

So, let me clear this up right now. Everything I say — you can take it at face value. Thanks.

The fact is, my mum moved away three years ago and I've just about forgotten how it was, having her around to say good night. Also, to the best of my recollection, she didn't say "good night." She said, "sleep well" or "sweet dreams" or "can you shut the computer down before you go to bed?" or "turn that down a *tiny* bit, would you? That's better, thanks," or "see you in the morning," etc. (I could go on). Never just a plain "good night."

So, you know: touché (is what you say to me) (I think).

And when Mum moved away she asked if I wanted to come. But I chose to stay with Dad. So, if anyone's got a right to a broken heart here, it's my mum.

Back to Roberto's office, with his eyes incorrectly in my head.

To get them out of there, I point to the blacked-in circle on my paper and say, "Do you reckon that my dad's a black hole?"

Roberto can be surprising.

"Tobias," he says. "What's a black hole?"

"A black hole," I go, "it's, you know, in space — one of those big black holes . . ."

Roberto's still looking.

"Yes," he says. "What is it?"

"It's, you know, if someone's a black hole it means they're in a really *black* mood, I mean, they're a real downer."

"That's what it means?" he says.

Turns out, I don't know for sure. I just assumed that.

"Okay," I go. "You got me. What's a black hole?"

Roberto gives his shrug and says, "You got me too."

Then he sends me away to research black holes.

Oh yeah, and the history of Ireland.

Week 3

Third week of term I did the research.

Both are straightforward.

BLACK HOLES

A black hole is a something that happens when you get so much stuff crammed together into one small place that the place can't handle it anymore so the place goes ballistic and turns into total, mad darkness.

History of Ireland

See definition of black holes.

Sometimes I wonder why I don't do better at school.

Thursday night of Week 3, Roberto's playing pool with my dad when I get home. Dad looks at his watch, and looks at Roberto, and they both raise eyebrows at each other. Then Dad chalks his pool cue and shoots.

It's not that late, just after one.

I tell them about black holes and the History of Ireland. I mean, I tell them the above.

They both laugh but Dad's drunk, and I see something in Roberto's eye, maybe disappointment, when I give my "history of Ireland." Just a flicker and I think, yeah, he's right. That was just: reductive, witty, ha-ha, aren't I clever, calling Ireland a black hole?

That's what I see in the flicker in Roberto's eye.

Or maybe it's just that Dad's cleaning up the table as I speak.

Whatever, I decide to tell them the real History of Ireland.

As I see it:

History of Ireland

Okay, so you've got your basic green and misty country with stone walls, sheep, and fairy folk. There's something kind of weird and tilted about it. The fairy folk are real, for a start, not imaginary. That's my understanding. Anyway, England goes: Now *that* country looks pretty — we might take it! (That was their way in those days.) So they took it. But, like I said, something tilted there, and so it slipped right out of England's hands. England went, huh, how did that happen? They took it back, it slipped again, they took it back, it slipped. And so on. Each time England held on tighter and Ireland tilted more.

Now, when I say that England held on tighter, I mean they tried various things, such as making it the *law* that Ireland was theirs; taking away the land from the locals; shipping in English people to own the land instead; massacres; asking nicely if they could have the country please. And so on.

I mean, they gave it their best shot.

So, in the end, they won! They got Ireland! (More or less.)

Meanwhile, in Ireland, a lot of unhappy people. Coz they didn't own their country. And they're all, like, poor, cold, hungry, you know, depressed. Like twenty people, no blankets, crammed together in a leaky mud hut. While the English owners lived in mansions and ate scones with jam and cream. And if the Irish people said, "Can I have a crumb from your scone?," the owner had them whipped and put a cap of burning pitch onto their head. More or less.

The Irish people didn't get on that well with each other either. The Protestants hated the Catholics, was the main issue, as I see it. You can't blame them for that. If I understand correctly, Catholics do not believe in contraception. So, you know, sex is not relaxing.

Anyhow, it was against the law for Catholics to own land, go to school, vote, join the army, or own a horse worth more than five pounds. Which was harsh.

In the end, the Irish people tried an uprising. Shot some English people, burned down their houses, and then the English people were super pissed so *they* shot Irish people, tortured them, burned them, hung them, and so on. And everything went to hell.

So, like I said, a lot of stuff, a lot of issues, crammed together into one small place and the place goes ballistic and turns into total, mad darkness.

And, in conclusion, that's the history of Ireland.

*   *   *

"That's my boy," says Dad. He leans over, sinks the eight ball, winning once again.

"More things probably happened, though," I say. "I stopped researching at 1799 when Tom came to Australia. I think things happened after that."

"Things might have happened after that," Roberto agrees, teeing up to start another game.

We played pool until four that night.

I remember a couple of things.

One was that Roberto talked Dad into a blind date with a woman he knows.

The other was I won the last five games. The booze always catches up with the old guys in the end.

Week 4

Athletics Carnival this week.

Everyone waiting to see Amelia and Riley's new superpowers.

Word on the street was they were going to (a) throw javelins to China, (b) run as fast as panthers, or (c) blitz the egg-and-spoon.

They didn't even show.

Coupla buddies of mine, Liz Clarry and Cassie Aganovic, cleaned up.

I was proud.

Other emotions I had this week included the opposite of pride.

I'm referring, in particular, to the Wednesday, the day that the Year 12 Report Cards were issued.

Closing the curtains on that day, and moving on.

On Thursday the emotion was terror.

A Tertiary Information Day was held in the Assembly Hall: presentations, booths, flyers, what have you.

The future stood in our Assembly Hall and let me know it wasn't mine. So. You know. Terrifying.

Anyway, Friday morning I felt what you might call intrigued.

Is intrigue an emotion? Why not.

Because everything was linked. (In my mind anyhow.)

Let me take you through it.

Well, for a start, I was half-asleep.

I should maybe have mentioned earlier that Term 2 was a party term. A girl in my year whose parents were away held parties on random nights at her mad mansion home. The parties were wild.

So Friday morning I was half-asleep.

I had a free period and was doing some reading for my History Project, and I came across a reference to an Irish prison called the Black Hole.

Spooky, right? Me and my new interest in black holes, and one shows up in my history research.

But it also made me realize that my definition might have missed something. See below.

BLACK HOLES

Stuff crammed together into one small, mad, ballistic darkness, *and be very, very careful of this darkness because if you go inside you NEVER GET OUT.*

'Cause a black hole is a prison.

In actual fact, those black holes in space were not even *named* Black Holes at first. I think they were called frozen stars. But then this guy suggested we name them black holes, thinking of a famous event called the Black Hole of Calcutta, which was when 146 people got locked up overnight in a small, crowded prison and the next day only twenty-three were left.

So, I guess black holes started out as hellish prisons.

Anyway, I'm thinking about this issue, and I'm thinking there's more links because you've got these poor Irish peasants all *crammed* together into their little leaking hovels with no windows and no chimneys, like poverty is their prison. They're going mad and they can't escape, so their houses are black holes. And then you've got people trying to escape by, you know, stealing sheep (like my Tom), or becoming super-cool rebels (like my Phillip). But they all got thrown into prison, so that's more black holes. Some got tossed from the prisons onto ships that were headed to Australia.

Such as the ship called the *Anne*. Crowds of murderers, drug lords, poor folk who stole to get their dinner, and super-hip rebels who had some way-cool secret handshakes — crowds of them — all crammed together in the deep, dark, dirty holds of ships. An iron grate dragged over their heads.

That's more black holes, see?

Not surprisingly, the last thought I had that morning as I fell asleep at the table in the library was about my dad. I was thinking: Is he a black hole? I mean, is he a prison? Did Mum mean she couldn't escape?

But she did escape. Ran away to Brisbane with a guy she met at work, and now they've got a two-year-old named Polly. And Mum's so happy she can't stop showing me photographs of Polly on her mobile, which is fair enough. The kid's cute: At least, her nose is cute. It's just like mine.

So maybe Mum meant that Dad's a black hole *now*. That he turned *in*to total-mad-dark prison-black-holeness *after* she left? (Which means it was kind of unfair — Mum, the one who made him a black hole, calling him on it like that.) And does that mean *I'm* the one who can't escape? Because I'm living with the black hole, my dad? Does Mum mean I should run away like she did, run to the sunlight up in Brisbane?

But then I'd miss my friends. Not to mention Dad. I mean, Mum's okay 'cause she's got the new guy and Polly, but Dad's got nobody but me.

*   *   *

So, anyway. That morning intrigued me right into my dreams. It was like there were links from Tom Kincaid to black holes to Irish peasants to the ships to Australia to black holes again to my dad and then to me. I felt like I could reach out and shake hands with Tom. Ride a black hole back in time.

But like I said, I was hungover.

Week 5
I found out something else about black holes this week.

BLACK HOLES
When you get trapped in a black hole you change. There's this super-powerful gravity dragging you in, and whatever part of you is closest to the black hole gets dragged in faster than the rest of you, so basically you arrive stretched out of shape. You never get back to normal. And this is called *spaghettification*.

That's another link between my dad and black holes: My dad makes some great spaghetti pastas.

Week 6
This week at my school there was a Shakespeare Festival and a cross-country race.

I know this because I just looked up the school's online calendar.

I have no memory of either event.

I do remember one helluva party at that mad mansion home I was mentioning.

The party was on a Wednesday night, and I remember it in pieces.

There's one piece where I'm in the living room chatting to my buddy Emily, and out of the corner of my eye I see Amelia and Riley. They'd just arrived, I think. Those two have the most intense gaze you ever saw. If this were a story about aliens, I'd say their eyes were artificially enhanced with built-in weapons. I shifted a bit, to see what it was that had attracted that laser-vision stare.

It was Lydia, on the couch.

She hadn't noticed them.

I don't know why, but something about that moment made the goose bumps rise up on the back of my neck.

Then I happened to see that Lyd was sitting next to her ex-boyfriend, Seb. A space between the two of them about the size of a plank of wood. Made me sad. Those two used to be the real thing. And that got me thinking about spaces between people who are meant to be together. From Amelia and Riley, watching from shadows, standing as close as two people can get without touching, to Lyd and Seb, a hand's width apart on the couch, to my mum and dad, a whole state apart — and then to Tom and Maggie, oceans, countries, hemispheres, destiny between them.

That piece of the party disappeared into a couple of beers.

One last piece: a conversation in a closet.

Maybe ten of us in that closet, trapped in the dark. (Don't ask.) Had a few bottles with us so we were fine. And at one point somebody, I think it was Amelia but it might have been Riley — those two are sometimes the same person — anyway, one of them started a conversation about shadows.

We talked about shadows for three hours.

I thought so hard and deep about shadows that night. I mean, a shadow is something that's there but *isn't* there. Your shadow is real, you can see it on the ground or on the wall, but it's actually nothing. It's only there because you're there — because of your *presence*. But, guess what, it's also only there because of *absence* — your shadow shows up because you're blocking out the light.

A shadow is the absence of light.

You remember the History of Ireland? I said that Ireland was a country of fairy folk, and as far as I could figure, the fairies were actually real?

Well, one of the "fairies" I read about was something spooky called the Fetch.

You know what the Fetch is? It's a shadow.

It's the shadow of any real person. You see the shadow wandering around without its person. It's like, there's your mum across the street, hi — but then you realize, no, it's not your mum, it's just her shadow. You go cold all over when you realize it. Then the phone rings in your pocket and it's somebody telling you your mum's just been in an accident and not sure if she'll make it — at which point you go even colder.

The Fetch is an absent presence: It comes to warn you someone's going to die.

So, I remembered the Fetch while I was sitting in that closet, and a chill ran straight from the base of my neck down my spine.

Then my mind bent in half and I got another link — you remember I said that a black hole is a prison and nothing can escape? That includes light. Light can't escape and that's why a black hole is black. *A black hole is the absence of light.*

Wait.

BLACK HOLES

A black hole is the absence of light.

So, a black hole is a shadow. A Fetch is a shadow. It was happening again: *black holes and Irish history slipping back and forth across my mind.*

And sitting in that closet, I realized that this was not intriguing.

It was horrific.

Why had I not seen it before? Those Irish fairies — bringing news of death; those black holes — sucking you in, stretching your limbs, locking you forever in a big, dark, silent absence. It's all part of one long chain of horror. Irish peasants getting hung, drawn, quartered, thrown onto ships, chained up in rotting black holes beneath the deck.

Then they arrive in Australia and it's a black hole of its own. They work all day, they can never escape, they do anything wrong they get whipped. Here's a couple of lines I found in a logbook of people who got flogged:

"William Hughes, refusing to work, 25 lashes, back much lacerated, but very little blood; appeared to suffer great pain during his punishment but did not cry out, having stuffed his shirt in his mouth."

That image — a guy stuffing his shirt into his mouth so he won't cry out while they thrash him — I can't get it out of my mind.

And somehow it all seems connected to my dad. Like this great dark shadow that no one can escape is sitting in my house and trapping him.

It's like *I* brought the shadow into my house with my research.

I realize that that makes no sense.

The timing is upside down. Dad's a black hole, according to Mum, and *then* I did the research.

But time, in that closet, was distorted. I knew for a fact that it was my fault that Dad was a black hole — I turned him into one by reading about Irish history, Irish fairies, and black holes.

I brought the shadow home.

Week 7

This week I remember stopping.

I mean, I got tired.

Went to school but not to any more parties. Took a break from schoolwork. Stayed home and watched my dad. (He was working from home this week.)

I watched him through windows. Watched him mow the lawn. Give the neighbor's car a jump start. Peel some old, wet junk mail from the bottom of the mailbox.

I watched him through doors. Frying garlic in the kitchen. Hunting down a tin of tennis balls from the closet. Carrying a cardboard box.

He looked fine.

I mean, he looked bored as hell mowing the lawn, but he joked around with the neighbor about jumper cables. Sang to himself while he cooked dinner. Told me a long and complicated story about that cardboard box. Something to do with a mistake at work and how Dad was going to fix it. It made him laugh his arse off: The mistake was not serious, but funny, apparently. I didn't really listen. I was watching him.

And, like I said, he looked fine.

Except for the shadow.

Even when he laughed, he was in shadow. Like a film where the lighting has gone wrong. You can't make out the characters' features.

Or was I imagining that? Because of my obsession with black holes? That's what I couldn't figure out.

So there I was, watching him carry that cardboard box — he'd stopped and was framed by the study door, the box under one arm (he's a big guy, my dad) — and he's telling his dumb-arse story about work while I squint my eyes to see his features — and a memory flashed into my mind.

Dad carrying boxes, three years ago.

See, he helped Mum when she moved out. He was telling stories then too, laughing at himself, taking heavy boxes right out of her arms so she wouldn't hurt her back. I remember Mum was so relieved and happy. She stepped onto the street to take a call from her boyfriend and I heard her say, "It's going much better than I thought. He's fine."

She's supposed to be the smart one in the family.

To me it was clear as day that this was just Dad's strategy. He was thinking, if I stay sweet and funny, even while she leaves me, if I help her carry boxes, it's dead certain that she'll change her mind. How could she leave a guy as great as that?

That's what he was thinking.

Right up to the moment when he pressed down on the boot of her car, testing it to make sure it was closed — right up to that moment, he thought she'd change her mind.

But I guess Mum must have missed that.

She drove away smiling in a sad, apologetic way, but smiling.

We stood on the curb and I looked at Dad's face and for as long as I live, I never want to see an expression like that again.

Anyhow, back to the present, and Dad had finished his funny story about work and was waiting for my laugh. I gave it my best shot. He went into the study, still chuckling himself, and I looked over at a print of purple flowers on the living room wall.

It belongs to my mum. (She's into purple.) She left it behind when she moved out that day.

In fact, she left a lot of stuff behind. Some of her favorite novels are lined up on our bookshelf. Humorous(ish) coffee mugs. Her CD collection (including a couple of great compilations that I made for her myself).

In the months after she left, I think it made Dad happy, noticing these things around the house. It meant that this was only temporary. She wouldn't have left *those* things behind for good. They were her home, we were her home, these were her warm, woolly slippers. She'd be back any day and slip back into them.

But the months went by and she didn't come back and put the slippers on.

I guess she didn't need them. Brisbane is warm. (Ha-ha.)

She didn't even *ask* us for the things. And that was a different kind of shock. Turned out she *really* must have wanted to escape. She'd sacrifice all that just to get away?

Dad and I didn't talk about it, though.

Just walked around amongst her things.

If you look at my house closely, even today, she's everywhere.

Family photographs on the sideboard. Magnet on the fridge listing the qualities of Capricorns (that's her star sign). The giant wooden M with hooks for keys that hangs in our front hallway (her name is Megan). She's even on our computer — a folder in the Inbox called "Meg."

It's like the past is still here. We live in it.

Which reminds me:

BLACK HOLES

They make time collapse. The faster you run toward the exit the farther you get from it. So your future falls back into your past. It's a curving of time.

(I don't get it either. Ask a science nerd.)

See, it's linked again. My dad's shoulders curving as he watches television — time curving inward, our future collapsing right into our past. It's all here in our house at the same time — all in this moment — our lives right now; our lives as a family with Mum, there's even the life of an Irish convict named Tom. It's all here, all at the same time.

Mum is everywhere. She's absent but she's present. She's a ghost in a way.

A presence that hasn't crossed over — an absent presence.

She's a shadow.

You know what? She's the black hole.

Week 8

Oh yeah, this week, on Monday night, Dad goes on the blind date with Roberto's friend. He brings her back home for the night.

This is not the first woman he's been with since Mum or anything. There's been quite a few. They all seem like nice, funny, sad, kind women to me. But the same thing always happens.

He forgets their names.

Seriously.

I mean, not in front of them, but later in the day. I ask what he thinks and he *never* remembers their names.

The other thing is, he's weird.

I have breakfast with the two of them on Tuesday morning, and I watch him talking to this woman. He talks like a freakin' *maniac*. He talks about himself, about work, about me, about goldfish, flying foxes, sugar cubes. Anything, I mean.

I sit still. I sit there staring straight at him thinking, *Who is this freak in my kitchen?*

Then, when the *woman* finally gets a chance to talk herself, for a moment or two, he looks down at the table, seems like he's concentrating hard, says "yeah, yeah." Then right away he gets agitated. Picks up the milk, nearly drops it, puts it back down. His "yeah, yeahs" keep coming but at all the wrong places, cutting right through her sentences. He looks up, his eyes flicker around the room. He picks up the cereal bowl, looks underneath it like he's checking where it was made. Next thing he's tipping piles of sugar onto the table, taking out his credit card, and using it to split up the sugar.

I got out of there as soon as I could.

Left the poor blind date sitting at the table watching him. As I reached the front door I heard her ask quite clearly, "Did you do a lot of drugs growing up?"

I don't think it was just the way he was cutting up the sugar like cocaine. It was the fact that he acts like his brains are fried.

I've said to him in the past, I've said, "Dad, you just have to listen. Women like you to listen to them."

And he's said to me, "Tobes, you're absolutely right."

But then he's exactly the same.

The funny thing is, he doesn't seem to need my advice. The women always like him anyway.

He's a big guy, like I said, and I get the impression that a certain kind of older woman likes a big guy. Maybe they think he's a bear that's going to keep them warm?

(I'm kind of a big guy myself but girls my age are not as turned on by this.)

(At least I know they'll like me when I'm forty.)

Fact is, the women give him their number, leave little notes with drawings of flowers, say they hope he'll call. He never does.

Still, it looked for a moment like things might end up different with this one.

Tuesday night, Dad and I are watching TV and an ad comes on for one of those antiperspirants that make women tear your clothes off.

"You reckon that really works?" Dad says.

I thought he was kidding around.

Wednesday night, he says, "You think I should dye my hair to cover up the gray?"

Once again, thought he was having a laugh.

Thursday, he came home from the chemist's with the antiperspirant in one hand and black hair dye in the other.

I kid you not.

He held them both out to me: "Whaddya say, Tobes, want to help me dye my hair?"

I felt bad. Would have stopped him wasting his cash if I'd realized he was serious.

Then late Thursday night he shut himself in his study with his phone and his new black hair. Couldn't hear what he was saying, just some low-voice talk and laughing.

That made my night. Thinking, finally my dad's found love! He's asking that blind date out again!

Woke up happy Friday morning.

School was a riot that day. You remember I mentioned a friend who said there was a ghost in the Art Rooms? But nobody believed her? Well, over the last few weeks, she'd been bringing them around. Now it was like everyone believed. Or was having fun pretending to.

And that day, I guess the ghost went wild. Something about a photo of the ghost. Anyhow, it was like someone had picked up a huge bag of popcorn, opened it, tipped it up, and started shaking hard. That's how fast the ghost sightings were coming. Everywhere I turned, people were running by with pale faces, or were telling breathless stories, or gasping. There was a lot of laughing. And a funny event at lunchtime with a party, and somebody's hair catching fire for a moment.

It was great.

Got home in a super mood. Walked in the front door.

And first thing I heard was Dad's voice on the phone sounding like low and distant thunder.

"The fact is" — I heard him say — thunder closer now — "he's your *son*. You —"

He stopped — silence — then a kinder tone, "I guess he didn't know so it won't —" paused, laughed. "Yeah, like *that's* going to happen" — laughed again — "take care," and hung up the phone.

Swung around and saw me.

"You weren't supposed to hear that," he said.

It turned out that Mum had been planning to fly down to surprise me tonight. Dad had kept it secret from me. He'd phoned her last night to finalize the details.

So that's who he was talking to on the phone last night — the low murmurs in the study — not the date at all, just Mum.

Anyhow, Mum had called just now to say she couldn't come; she had to work.

"She said she *might* make a late flight tonight," he said. "There's one at midnight, apparently."

"Yeah, like *that's* going to happen," I said, kind of echoing how he'd said it on the phone — making fun of him at the same time as showing he was right.

Mum would never stay up as late as midnight. She's one of those people who *turns into a pumpkin at ten*. (Her words.)

Have I mentioned this about black holes?

BLACK HOLES

They're impossible.

I mean, think about it, they're everything crammed into nothing, and they turn time upside down. So I'm pretty sure I'm being scientific when I say that they're impossible.

As impossible as Mum getting a midnight flight.

As impossible as Ireland getting out of England's grasp; as impossible as England holding on.

Or those Irish convicts escaping from their ships.

Or Tom ever seeing his girlfriend again.

As impossible as Tom's story changing, now that it's done.

Or of me reaching back in time to warn him.

As impossible as Dad getting Mum to come home, by changing the color of his hair.

Week 9

The final thing I'm going to say about black holes is:

BLACK HOLES

Who knows?

That's also scientific.

'Cause you know what I get from my reading?

Nobody actually *knows* what a black hole is or what it looks like or, you know, whether it's bad-tempered or sweet. It's all just guessing. 'Cause turns out nobody's been *inside*. I didn't realize this at first. Doing all this reading about what happens to you when you go into a black hole, and how you can't escape and so on, and I've gotta say, in the back of my head, there *was* this little voice going, "Hang on, something's not right here."

Eventually, I realized what it was. If you can't ever escape, how can you come back to tell us that you can't escape? See what I mean?

I thought maybe they took their mobile phones in with them, but no.

So, I thought, photographs? Those remote-control flying cameras. No again.

If a black hole is so strong even light cannot escape, well, you know, total darkness.

Black holes are technically invisible. Nobody can see them. Not even a camera.

Not the smartest scientist in the world. (Not that scientists have great eyesight. I'm thinkin': A lot of them wear glasses.)

Even if you could get a camera inside, it'd go all warped and never get back out.

The scientists even have a scientific name for this situation: *information paradox.*

Also known as, we don't have a freakin' clue.

Took me nine weeks of research about black holes before I realized this.

And between us, it made me feel good. Kind of powerful.

'Cause we live in a world where most things are all tied up. Everything's labeled and mapped. Nothing new to explore. Reading Tom's letters, I almost got jealous at first — there he was, back in time, all excited about the brand-new world.

It's like the afterlife, like ghosts, or the future — could be something wonderful, or could be pure hell. Either way, it's kind of fantastic that we don't know.

Makes me think of all those kids at school getting high on the idea of a ghost in the Art Rooms. Laughing because they know it isn't true, but also thinking: *Well, who knows?* You could see that in their eyes, that secret hope.

Ghosts could be real. We could have one at our school.

It's the horror and the beauty of the things that we don't know.

Until they pin it down, *I* could be right about black holes. Not likely, I know, but my guess could be better than a scientist's guess.

There could be dinosaurs or dragons. Those stars that disappear inside black holes, they might take on new personalities. Drive around in sports cars. Eat watermelon. Or teleport and turn into alligators, or newsprint, or water droplets. Or into the spark of understanding between a boy and a girl in a graveyard at two A.M. The girl's hair blowing sideways, eyes confused.

Week 10

According to the school's online calendar, this week (the last week of term) there was a meeting of the K. L. Mason Patterson Trust Fund Committee, and a Joint Ashbury-Brookfield Art Exhibition.

I know nothing about the Art Exhibition, but my dad is on the Trust Fund Committee. He's one of the two parent reps.

Roberto Garcia got him to join.

How?

See my most recent definition of black holes, a coupla pages back.

Anyhow, last week of term, Dad had to go to a committee meeting.

He was heading out into the cold, dark night and I was kicking back with the TV remote, when it occurred to me I should get back to work. You know, schoolwork. What with having taken a personal break the last couple of weeks. And there being only one more day before the school gave us an official break of its own. And this being the HSC year. And my future being on the line, and etc., etc.

"Dad," I go.

And I head out into the night by his side. (In the passenger seat of the car, I mean.)

Dad's committee meets in the Art Rooms, and that's where our school has its D&T facilities now. Seemed to me, a little woodwork might be a nice, smooth way to ease myself back into the scholarly life.

So I headed left and Dad headed up the stairs. I took a couple of corners, let myself into a dim, still, empty, warm room, and breathed it in.

No need for me to go on here about the smell of wood and how it soothes my soul like a long, slow hug, or how working with wood takes up a weirdly big piece of my heart? No need to tell stories of how Dad first taught me how to turn wood when I was seven. (I made a toilet roll holder that day.) Or how we worked together in his shed for years until I got so much better than him that he said, "The shed's yours."

No need for tales of Toby-the-carpenter here?

You get it, right?

I got right to work on my cabinet. The cabinet's my Major Design Project this year. Not so flash as the pool table last year — now a key feature in the lives of me and Dad (and Roberto Garcia, of course) — but I want this to be beautiful. Hauntingly beautiful. I don't know if I'll be able to pull it off; it's just what I'm hoping.

I got to work doing something quiet. No need to tell you how I disappear while I'm working, right?

Just that I do. Couple of hours passed. It must have been almost eleven, and I hadn't even heard my own thoughts.

So the scream was like a fire hose turned onto a fast-asleep face.

It was a long, loud, high-pitched, full-throttle scream.

Followed by a deep, black silence.

I had no idea where the scream had come from. Felt like somewhere just beneath my feet. Then I realized it had come from down the hall.

I'm ashamed to say, I couldn't move for a few moments. Heart was like a hyperactive jackhammer.

And the jackhammer kept on digging up streets as I walked to the door, opened it, and leaned out.

The corridor was empty. Building silent.

I remembered that the drama theater's two doors down the corridor.

They've been practicing for the Ashbury-Brookfield Production.

I think the theater's got good insulation but that scream was loud enough to break sound barriers.

That was a scream that could time travel.

I was dead relieved.

It was drama rehearsal!

Still, a good guy doesn't just assume that a scream's part of a play. Waited a few moments, to be sure.

Heard voices somewhere. Two people laughing — a girl and a guy. A door closing. Quiet again.

Decided I was right about the drama practice.

Headed back into the woodwork room, got out the power saw, and switched it on.

It can't have been more than half a minute later — there's this weird, creepy feeling in my shoulders, like something's not right with the world.

I switched off the power saw.

Something was fiercely wrong with the world.

It was a world of screaming, shouting, pounding footsteps, and slamming doors.

Once again, I'm ashamed to say, my first instinct was to drop to the floor and hide underneath the workbench.

I resisted the instinct, but did put both hands over my head for a moment.

And then, the silence again.

The clamor of noise can't have lasted for more than a few seconds, but the silence that followed was beyond terrifying.

Where was my dad and his committee? Hadn't they heard the noise too?

Got out my phone.

Decided the police would not respect me if I didn't at least open the door and check things out.

'Cause what if it was still just drama practice?

Who'd look like an idiot then?

Leaned into the corridor again. This time I was trembling all over. Still nothing.

And then, once again, the sound of laughter. Distant, murmuring laughter — a girl and a guy once again.

Must be one kick-arse drama they're working on, I thought. *Audience are going to need earplugs.*

Went back to work, but I've gotta say I didn't feel so peaceful. Also didn't use the power saw. Didn't want that clamor creeping up on me again.

Nothing happened — only the silence — and then it was time to go out front and meet my dad.

I have one more thing to report about this night.

As I headed to the exit, I remembered that the Art Rooms were haunted.

It was just a fleeting thought. Gave me a laugh. Kept walking.

Caught up with the committee members all heading out to their cars. Seemed they'd had a good meeting. All very buddy-like with one another. Dad was talking with the other parent rep on the committee. Roberto was off to the side on his own, hands in his pockets looking for his cigarettes.

First thing I said was, "How about that noise?"

Roberto looked around him at the still, starry night.

"What noise?"

I pointed to the building: "Bloodcurdling screams and pounding footsteps?"

Roberto grinned. Thought I was kidding: referring to the ghost stories.

Funny that I hadn't thought of ghosts myself right away.

"You telling me you couldn't hear that noise?" I said.

He lit his cigarette, smiled around it.

I remembered that the committee met way up on the third floor. Too far away maybe.

But something else — all the time I was talking to Roberto — something else was bothering me.

Then I remembered.

Roberto is director of the drama.

Can you have rehearsal without the director? Didn't have a clue how drama rehearsals worked. Maybe you could.

I looked back at the building. The windows deep in darkness. The building like a hulking pool of silence.

Looked out at the parking lot. A handful of cars. Committee members opening car doors.

"There was a drama rehearsal tonight, right?" I said.

Roberto wasn't paying much attention. He was searching through his pockets again. "No," he said. "No rehearsal tonight. What makes you ask?"

And that, as I mentioned, is the last thing I have to say about that night.

You can draw your own conclusions.

Last day of term, I had breakfast with my mother again.

Nice, poetic parallel, no?

Back in the Blue Danish Café. Mum down for work for the day.

I was telling her about the episode the night before. The screams and running footsteps, me thinking it was drama rehearsal, there not being a rehearsal, and so on. She was right into the story, believing the ghost theory, laughing at me for not.

But while she was talking, my mind started drifting.

I started thinking how, while I was talking to Roberto, I was half-watching Dad in the parking lot. He was talking to the other parent rep, like I said. She's a nice woman, the mother of my friend Cass. I know for a fact that this woman is single. Her husband died a few years back.

And she's talking to Dad, but he's doing his thing. Playing with his car keys. Almost dropping them. Catching them. Picking them up. Not looking at her. Talking through her talk. Saying, "yeah, yeah," "really?" Even from where I was standing I could see that his "yeahs" and his "reallys" were cutting through her words. Next thing he starts talking fast himself, and I see something fall in her face.

So now, here with Mum, I thought about black holes again. Thought about *too much stuff being crammed into one small space.* How the space implodes. How it *collapses under the weight of its own gravity.* How my dad never said a single angry word to Mum when she moved out. How he smiled and joked and carried cardboard boxes.

Having stuffed his shirt into his mouth.

I interrupted Mum.

I said, "You know how you said he was a black hole?"

"Who?"

"Dad."

Mum goes: "I said your dad was a black hole? I don't think so. No. I never said that. I wouldn't say a thing like that. He's not a black hole."

Then she reflected a minute: "He's more a ghost."

And here concludes my story.

For, if only my mother had said this on the first day of term — if only she had said that my dad was a ghost — well, I could have spent the term researching ghosts.

And this would be a ghost story.

As it is, it's not.

And this is where it ends.

Catch ya later.

2.

Lydia Jaackson-Oberman
THE STORY OF TERM 2 AS A GHOST STORY

[The following is a transcript of an actual exchange of correspondence.

The correspondents are myself (Lydia Jaackson-Oberman) and some other person/entity unknown.

The exchange commenced at approximately 11:35 P.M. last night, and concluded at 4:30 A.M. today.

It is important that I preface this transcript by saying that I am not, and never have been, a believer in ghosts. Nor, for that matter, do I believe in anything pertaining to the supernatural. I cannot emphasize this strongly enough. It is true that the opening letter was drafted by myself. (It was typed at the computer in my bedroom — I was home alone.) But it was written as an exercise in invention, designed for my own entertainment.

What happened next amazed me.

The exchange is set out below exactly as it occurred (annotated wherever I think helpful).

In the cold light of day, I have no doubt that there is a rational explanation for this exchange. I simply do not know what it is.]

The Exchange of Correspondence
To All Ghosts Reading Over My Shoulder Right Now,

BOO!!

Ha-ha.

Anyway, seriously.

The situation is, I have to write about what happened last term. And it has to be a ghost story. I'm thinking: That's too much for just one girl. I'm thinking: What if *I* do last term and someone else does the ghost? So then I'm thinking: Who? Who could do the ghost?

A ghost. It's gotta be a ghost.

That's obvious.

(Assuming I can get one at short notice. If not, maybe I'll ask my dog.)

So, if there are any ghosts in this room right now — well, first, I guess, how are you? nice to meet you! you sure haunt *quietly*; I appreciate that; never hear a sound! how's the afterlife treating you these days? (etc., etc.) — and second, I need a volunteer. Could one of you please step up and help? Here's how I think it could work: I write a letter in which I talk about last term, and you reply with a shriek.

Then I write some more about last term. You shriek straight back. More narrative. More shrieking. And so on, back and forth, until the term is done.

Here's something else. Every now and then, in response to a letter from me, you should be silent. Let the silence build and build. Every corner of this room should fill with silence. A great blank stare of it; the whole house should throb with it. Nothing but the escalating pounding of my heartbeat. Nothing. Nothing at all.

And then, suddenly?

BANG!

Break the silence with a bang. Like a window shutter crashing in the wind. That kind of bang.

That might be scary.

(After which we'd get right back to talking about last term.)

I know it's a lot to ask, but I'd be very grateful. And once I'm dead, I'll look you up and take you out for coffee.

Thanks,

And best wishes,

Lydia Jaackson-Oberman

❖

[After typing the above letter, I stood up, left the room, ran downstairs to the kitchen, stared at the fridge, decided I wasn't hungry, noticed the dog, remembered I hadn't fed him. Fed the dog. Ran back upstairs and sat at the computer. On the screen, directly below my letter, was the following.]

Dear Lydia!

I volunteer! Eagerly!

And are you not delighted with this GHOSTLY font? Certainly, I never so much as touched a "word processor" when I was in the living-being realm. But these last few years I try to practice whenever your house is living-being free. (Which is often!) (I do not count your parents amongst the living.) (No, neither your dog. Too small and fluffy.)

Well! To the point! Shall we begin? Pray tell. What sort of a term did you have? It was Term 2 of Year 12 for you, I take it. A time of much academic rigor! (Ha-ha! Ha-ha! Ha-haha! Hahahaha!)

Yours in Excited Anticipation (for rare it is that an opportunity presents itself for direct communion with living beings).

A Ghost

❖

[As you can imagine, as soon as I saw this letter — before I had read beyond its opening lines, in fact — I looked around and spoke aloud.

"Yeah, ha-ha," I said. "Where are you?"

Or something like that. There might have been stronger language.

Of course, my immediate assumption was that somebody — a friend of mine — was in the room. This friend must have emerged while I was downstairs, typed the above, and then hidden himself or herself again. I laughed as I called for this person, and yet I also felt annoyed — the privacy intrusion — and mildly uneasy. Just knowing that someone is in the room with you, without knowing where (or who), can be very disconcerting.

I walked away from the computer and began opening closet doors, looking under the bed, leaning out into the hallway, checking nearby rooms.

I searched the entire house.

Every door I opened, every ledge I peered beneath, every light switch I turned on — at each, I expected a tap on my shoulder. The cumulative, physical suspense of this became wearing. Small sounds took on startling significance. (And my dog, Pumpernickel, didn't help. His stomach kept gurgling weirdly. I should have fed him earlier.)

I returned to my room, searched it thoroughly again. Stood before the computer. Spoke in a voice that, in the hollow quiet of an empty house, seemed childish to my ears: "Okay. That's enough. Where are you?"

There followed a long stretch of silence.

I will replicate it here.

BANG!

My wireless keyboard had crashed from my desk to the floorboards.

It happened just as the silence had become too much — just as it was throbbing in my heartbeat, gathering me tightly in its clasp.

I stared at the keyboard on the floor while the BANG reverberated in my ears.

Then I picked it up and put it back.

I tried not to shake.

Objects often fall from furniture with no apparent cause. (Or sometimes, anyway.) Probably, the keyboard had been inching toward the edge of the desk for some time, so that it only took the slightest movement from me (as I stood, overcome by that silence) to shift the room's equilibrium and cause it to topple.

I looked at the keyboard, now back on my desk where it belonged.

It seemed so harmless.

And then — there is no way to say this other than simply to say it — the keys began to move.

The appearance, at first, was a sort of shivering, or jiggling — along with, most disturbingly, that busy clattering sound of a keyboard at work.

I moved closer. Keys were rapidly leaping up and down, the space bar jumping frequently.

Even as my mind rushed to explain this — some kind of defect in the keyboard, brought on by the fall to the floor — still, a terrible fear washed over me.

I could hardly lift my eyes; but I did.

I looked up at the screen.

And there it was.

Unfurling onto the screen in time with the clatter:]

Lydia!
Ahoy there! I'm still here! Still waiting for your reply! This truly is unexpected — you call upon a ghost and then, when one

replies, you rush around searching for a living being! As if an elaborate prank by a hidden friend were more likely than, well, a GHOST responding to your call for a GHOST!!

(When you hear the sound of galloping hooves, think HORSES, my girl, not zebras!) (Especially when you've whistled for a horse.)

Still, I hope I have not alarmed you. You seem horrible pale. Do you get enough spinach in your diet? No. You don't, actually. Never see you touch the stuff.

Anyhow, please! Do respond so we can get started!

Yours,
The Ghost

❖

[I felt pure terror. The clattering keyboard. Words melting onto the screen. My eyes washed over white with fear. Escalating horror at this vision . . . and then, suddenly, I laughed. My vision cleared. I understood. I laughed even harder. (I admit my laughter verged on hysteria for a few moments, but even that subsided.) I sat at my computer, thought for a few moments, and then I wrote:]

Dear Ghost,

Well, it's an honor to meet you.

You are my first ever ghost.

I have so many questions! What's your name? When did you come from? How did you d —

Wait.

I think that question might breach ghost etiquette.

Moving on smoothly:

What do you eat? Why? *Why* do you eat?

And most important of all: Why are you here?

I mean, why don't you just, you know, cross over?

GO TO THE LIGHT!

GO *INTO* THE LIGHT!!

THERE IS NOTHING HERE FOR YOU ANY LONGER!

YOU ARE DEAD AND HAVE NO PLACE AMONGST THE LIVING!!!

(No offense.)

Lots of love,
Lydia

❖

My Dearest Lydia,

What a *lively* letter! I feel as if a gust of wind had very nearly blown me from the room!

(I am rather insubstantial of form so gusts of wind do this all the time.)

My dear, I would be very glad to answer your questions — but is this the time? Do you really want to ask me questions when you should be working on your assessment task? Recall, you must narrate the tale of your life last term, and I must do my bit!

Do begin.

Fondly,
The Ghost

P.S. Near forgot! No standing on etiquette here! How did I die? I think that's the question you wished to ask. Well, they'll tell you I died of typhoid fever but, you know, it was a fish hook in the eye?

❖

Dear Ghost,

Hmm.

On the one hand, a unique opportunity to interrogate the afterlife about the mysteries of the universe and how it got a fish hook in the eye.

On the other hand, homework.

What's a girl to do?

I guess the homework is due tomorrow.

Life, eh? It's a balancing act. (Sorry. That reference to "life" was insensitive.)

Anyway, the story of last term. Well, here it is. Last term:

I met three different people who hated avocado.

Em got obsessed with a ghost haunting the Art Rooms.

I kicked my toe twice.

The weather was kick-arse cold.

I was here alone. I paid the household bills online.

I paid myself a generous management fee for paying the household bills online.

I went to school. Not all the days, but a generous number of days.

(Not on the days when it was kick-arse cold.)

I went to drama rehearsals.

There were a couple of parties here.

I drank a lot of coffee and ate a lot of dry roasted almonds, Magnums, and pecan cookies.

That's about it. My story of last term. Back to you, Ghost.

Love,
Lydia

❖

My Dear Lydia,
SHRIEK! SHRIEK! SHRIEK, SHRIEK, SHRIEK, SHRIEK, SHRIEK, SHRIEK, SHRIEK!
SHRIEK!
SHRIEK!!
SHRIEK.

Yours,
The Ghost

❖

Dear Ghost,
Huh.
Unexpected.
You just went ahead and obeyed me.
Well, I now feel all-powerful but I'm also thinking that my story could become repetitious. Maybe, if you feel like mixing it up a bit, you could howl sometimes instead of shrieking? And if you've got any chains? Clank them.

Love,
Lydia

P.S. You know what, even with howling and clanking, this story's going to end up unbalanced. Just go ahead and talk if you want.

❖

Dearest Lydia,
As you've released me from my former obligation (which I did not mind at all! Who amongst us does not love a little idle shriek-ing?) — but as I am now at liberty to speak my mind, I will!

And THAT's your story of last term?

Has it not occurred to you, Lydia, that *I was here?!!! That I witnessed it all!!* (Hence, my earlier manic, ghostly laughter at the idea of your "academic rigor.")

As a witness of your life in this house last term, I have one thing only to say. This is it — and here I am quoting from your "story of last term" —

"There were a couple of parties here."

There were a COUPLE of parties here????

Lydia? Are you, any longer, the ruthlessly HONEST girl I have come to know and love since I've been haunting you?

Much love,
The Ghost

P.S. I know the Ashbury ghost well, by the way — to be avoided, at all costs. You are all in danger — Em is the only one who sees this.

❖

Dear Ghost,

Okay. There were more than a couple of parties.

What do you want here? A woo-*hoo*-totally-cool-partygirl-look-my-parents-are-away-so-see-what-*wild*-times-I've-been-getting-up-to-when-I'm-supposed-to-be-*studying!!*-cos-I'm-in-Year-12 story?

"Party" isn't even the right word. People came around to my place sometimes.

That's it.

Lydia

❖

My Dear, Dear Lydia,

Your sharp tongue, I know it well.

I also know your generous heart.

And then, too, I know that, for an extremely honest girl, you sometimes speak a load of ballycock.

You think I was born yesterday, do you? My dear, I didn't even *die* yesterday.

I was here for every *party*, Lyd; there were three or four a week at least; and oh, my head (if I had a head) would have ached from the throb of the backbeat. I wonder how I could prod your memory? A catalogue of alcohol and drugs I saw consumed? The number of times the police were called? The destruction I beheld (furniture, walls, carpet, appliances, hearts, and self-esteem)?

I observed much! And heard more. (Your friends have powerful vocal chords.) And hence I know that a number of these parties spilled over from drama rehearsals.

Then, too, a number were started by Em on her "blog" without your knowledge. (It seems that Em's "blog" is some kind of a social hub for your year. I do not pretend to understand what a blog is but assume it is a kind of muddy hollow.)

There was that memorable occasion when you sat down to watch Season 5 of *The Sopranos* at ten o'clock one night, and found yourself growing afraid. (I was sitting on the couch beside you, and worried that my presence was what spooked you — but really, *The Sopranos* was a *menacing* show — it made my bones rattle! — so let's blame television.) Anyway, you messaged Em and Cass, asking them to come and watch the show with you. And ended up with 230 people in the house. (I counted.)

And yet, Lydia, the lion's share of last term's parties were initiated by *you*.

Why, Lydia, all the parties? Isn't that the question we should ask ourselves? If we want to find the heart of your Term 2?

Much love,
The Ghost

❖

Dear Ghost,
No.

Love,
Lydia

❖

Lydia the Lovely,
Very well, I shall swoop in a different direction. (How I love to swoop and dive around your house! You want a REAL party?! Try the afterlife!)

Where was I? Ah yes, a different direction. Perhaps you should consider the PEOPLE of Term 2. People are often the essence of an era.

(I myself was the essence of *my* era.)

Tell me, was there some one person who captured your every waking thought in Term 2?

Now, I DO remember seeing your dear friend Sebastian at a number of your parties. What a charming fellow he is! You used to be "together" but then he disappeared. Last term, however, he was back again — I heard he had joined the Ashbury-Brookfield Drama and so he came along to the spillover parties — but now he was "just a friend." Pray tell, how did this happen? What a grim tragedy! You seem so perfectly matched to me. I always see a spark and crackle in the air betwixt you!

(I mean that literally. Ghosts, being air, can see the air — I can see the essence of the air.)

So! Perhaps you would like to discourse upon Sebastian for the remainder of this assessment task?

Yours, in thoughtful anticipation,
The Ghost

❖

Dear Ghost,
    Seb? He's okay.
    Sweet guy.
    Talks about soccer way too much.
    Not quite as good at soccer as he thinks he is either.

Love,
Lydia

P.S. But his art is amazing.

❖

My Sweet Lydia!
    Surely you jest (about the soccer I mean). Why, oft have I seen young Seb on the grounds here at play with a soccer ball! How he tosses and spins it from foot to foot, whirls and twirls it faster than a blink, weaves it amongst the fairy-creature shrubs in your mother's topiary garden!
    He is at least as good as he thinks he is at soccer; most likely, better.

Moreover, he talks about all manner of things! I feel rather hurt on his behalf.

Yours,
The Ghost

P.S. Oh, and his art. Well, I think he does his best.

❖

Dear Ghost,
You know, if people are the essence of an era, then the essence of Term 2 was Amelia-and-Riley.

Their names drifted over us like snowflakes. Their names were passed around like something sweet and intoxicating. When people spoke their names, they held them on their tongues as if the words were fine liqueur chocolates.

And that's the real story of Term 2: What the f. was *wrong* with everybody?

Love,
Lydia

P.S. Sorry I've gone off the topic of Seb. You seem fond of him. Interesting. I wonder what that's about.

P.P.S. If you want to stay on Seb, tell me this: What does he know about Amelia and Riley? He told me a while back to stay away from them; he said they're trouble. And whenever he sees me talking to them, he gets that glint in his eye — the one he used to get when he lost his temper.

P.P.P.S. But he won't tell me why.

P.P.P.P.S. And I don't believe in secrets.

❖

Dear Lydia,
   Some warnings ought to be heeded.
   Some secrets need to be kept.

Love,
The Ghost

❖

Ghost,
   Secrets are darkness and shadows. You need light to live —
just like you need light in a painting, and I need to find the light
in the page when I try to write a story.
   You only get light from the truth. A secret's just another way of
lying.

Lyd

❖

Oh, now, Lydia,
   Here we go with the LIGHT again! What is it with you living
beings and light? If I had a farthing for every person who has
urged me to go into the *light*!! Don't you know it shows up my
wrinkles?
   We should all embrace the darkness and the shadows! (I suppose
embracing shadows is a predictable hobby for a ghost, but my other
hobby is mellowing out to Lionel Richie CDs in the small games
room downstairs and I'm the only ghost I know who does that.)

Back to the point: a little MYSTERY, now that's where it's at! Secrets, surprises, unexpected twists. Paintings and stories need *those* just as much as they need "truth"!

Much tender love,
The Ghost

❖

Dear Ghost,
   I'll tell you a secret I've never told anyone before.
   Earlier this year, I saw Amelia and Riley at Castle Hill one night. And Riley was carrying a baby.

Lydia

❖

No wonder you don't like secrets.
You don't understand them.
Riley was carrying a baby?!
Be still my beating heart! (If only it were beating still.)
   This doesn't even warrant the name of secret! Did they ASK you to keep it a secret? No? Then pffft! There are many reasons why A and R might have been out with a baby, most of them so mundane they make me drift into the ether. A brother or sister? A babysitting job? A niece or nephew? What — do you think they KIDNAPPED a baby? Is that why you see it as a secret?

Much Bemused Love,
The Ghost

❖

Dear Ghost,

Here's my story of Amelia and Riley.

They came to our school like a beautiful package of puzzles. Why did they stay so separate? Why were they always flicking past the corner of my eye? Sidestepping questions? Watching without blinking?

Then the surprises: Amelia could swim. They came from Brookfield but nobody at Brookfield knew them. They were actors. They were smart. Riley was an artist.

People decided that they were superhuman. I thought they were ordinary people.

Seb told me to stay away from them. I invited them to a party.

❖

All right, Lydia, my contrary friend, all making *perfect* sense.

And so . . .

❖

And so they came to the party.

I don't know why. Maybe they were tired of saying no.

I didn't see much of them that night. I noticed them drift apart soon after they arrived — join separate groups of people, drift together again. Like a regular couple at a party. I remember Amelia sipping something clear from a glass, chewing on a straw while she watched people dance. Once, I saw them standing close together by a painting in the billiards room. Riley was pointing something out in the painting. Amelia leaned forward to see it. They both smiled softly. They moved away again.

That's all I saw that night.

There were a few more parties during the holidays. They turned up to some, and it was more or less the same.

And then Term 2 began.

❖

And everything changed . . . ?

❖

No.

The only thing that changed was that I started paying attention.

Because as far as I could see, Amelia and Riley were ordinary people. But Seb had warned me about them.

And then Cass warned me too. She said she didn't trust them — she said they were watching me, and to be careful. Once, she said, she saw their shadows outside a window, looking in.

Seb and Cass are not the type to be spooked easily, and they were.

Meanwhile, everybody else hushed — or lit cigarettes, or changed position, or choked on ice cubes, or burst out laughing at imaginary jokes — whenever they walked into a room.

It reminded me of Dad's story about being in the same room as the President of the United States once. He said the President had an aura; something intrinsically *big* about him, separate from his physical size.

I thought that was total ballycock (as you would say).

I thought my dad was seeing him this way because he knew the guy was the President, and also, the guy probably had tricks that made him *seem* superhuman.

Okay, Amelia and Riley are beautiful and talented, but Ashbury is full of gorgeous-and-talented-kids-of-the-rich-and-famous.

There had to be more going on. Some trick or illusion. I wanted to know what it was. So I started watching them.

And these are the five things that I noticed:

1. Time

They always arrived late — usually around one or two in the morning.

They'd stay a few hours or all night.

Or they'd stay five minutes. When they did that, it never felt like a statement. Like: "This is boring, let's go someplace else," or "We're so cool we only make appearances." It was more like, "We were here, and now we're not."

It seemed to make perfect sense for them to leave at whatever moment they did, whether hours or minutes had passed.

Once, in a dream, it came to me that time was like a Slinky for them. You could stretch it out or stack it close together. Either way, it stayed a Slinky. (That seemed more profound in the dream.)

2. Standing and Sitting

They stood or sat differently from other people.

I think maybe they just had better posture.

3. Faces

They held their faces differently too. I mean, they seemed friendly or surprised at the right times — but the reaction appeared just a second too late. As if they had to *select* it first, rather than just feel it.

In a different dream, I was sitting next to Riley in a circus tent. I felt very conscious of his presence beside me because he seemed to be concentrating hard. I remember thinking, *Take it easy, Riley, it's just a juggling clown.* Then the clown tripped backward, and the audience burst out laughing.

I turned to look at Riley.

He had turned in his seat too, and was looking straight at me. I saw that he was holding a wooden picture frame. He watched me carefully, making sure I'd seen the frame. Then he pressed it up to his face. The top of it ridged along his forehead and the sides ran down and pinched his cheeks. Now he was looking at me through the frame. He straightened it a little, pressed it down more firmly, and paused.

And then he gave a great shout of laughter.

4. Eyes

I've got to admit, that dream scared the hell out of me.

But the thing with the eyes, when I noticed it, that unnerved me even more.

It was midnight and there were about fifteen of us in our home theater. The only light came from the screen, which was showing Hitchcock's *Vertigo*. But the sound wasn't on and we weren't watching. We'd turned the couches around, and we were talking and listening to blues on the stereo. Amelia and Riley slipped into the room along with a burst of party noise from upstairs. As usual, there was a subtle shift in the room when they walked in. Some people sat up who'd been slumped down, some slumped further. The girl beside me lifted her bare feet onto the couch and used her thumbnail to scrape at her toenail polish.

This was the day after the dream about Riley in the circus tent. I looked at him, remembered the dream, and uneasiness swept over me.

But then I turned back to my conversation. A few people left, others came in, and I found myself watching Amelia and Riley again.

I was watching their eyes.

At first I thought I was imagining something.

Then I looked at the eyes of others in the room — people were talking about Em's ghost and about the Ashbury-Brookfield Art Exhibition coming up — and I realized what I was seeing. With most people, focus shifts and fades. Usually you look at the face of the person who's speaking but now and then, you drift — lose focus, disappear into your own thoughts.

Amelia's and Riley's focus never broke.

I don't mean to say they were like Secret Service agents when the President's giving a speech. They didn't have their hands on their holsters all the time. (They didn't have holsters. If they did, I'd have mentioned it by now.)

I mean their eyes never stopped taking things in. They watched the faces of people who spoke until the person had stopped. And when nobody was talking directly to them, they looked around the room — their eyes took in its spaces: the couches, the screen, the entertainment unit, the shape of the furniture, the space between the furniture, the shadows and the light, the people in the room, the faces of the people, the thoughts behind the faces.

All this, their eyes did in a steady, mild way.

I don't believe I ever saw their eyes disappear inside their heads. And that's just weird.

5. Voices

One night, there was this whole hour when I found myself studying the air just in front of Riley and Amelia whenever they spoke. Because it suddenly occurred to me that their voices might be using different dimensions of the air than the rest of us.

But they weren't.

Their voices were perfectly normal. (I was totally ripped that night.)

That's the end of my first set of observations.

Lots of Love,
Lydia

❖

Oh!

I beg your pardon.

You've finished.

I think I must have dozed off for a moment.

Well, LYDIA! That is *quite* a catalogue! I can't help wondering if you had a moment to think a single thought, or dream a single dream, of your OWN, given all the attention you were paying to A and R.

OF course, everything you say is total ballycock.

The reason Amelia and Riley are popular is this:

They know how to hold a conversation.

With great respect to your friends, Lydia, their conversation is so dull it makes me want to stick a fish hook in the other eye.

But Riley and Amelia? A breath of fresh air.

Ever Yours,
The Ghost

❖

I'd been planning to ask why someone put a fish hook in your eye but now I know. You're obnoxious.

I have a second set of observations of Amelia and Riley.

These are the differences between them.

1. *Riley talks more than Amelia.*

2. *They get drunk in different ways.*

I guess you noticed that Amelia gets wild and wonderful when she's drunk.

But Riley talks fast, stays physically still, and watches Amelia.

3. *Amelia has a secret.*

In some ways, they're like the perfect couple. They glance at each other often, as if they like to confirm that the other still exists; or as if they can read the other's thoughts. They light up when the other person speaks, and smiles form on their faces even before the other reaches the punch line in a joke.

And I see them cross the road near our school. Let's say Riley is talking when they're about to cross. Amelia keeps watching his face as he talks. She watches his eyes check for traffic, then she steps onto the road when he does. The same thing happens in reverse. It's pure listening and pure trust between them.

But Amelia has a secret. I know because I see secrets just like you can see the air.

I think Riley senses something and it's breaking him apart. I saw this the first time I ever saw them at school — cobwebs in the space between their hands.

Saw it again the night a bunch of us were trapped in a closet.

We talked about shadows for three hours that night. It's a shame you weren't there. It might have helped you see the truth: Shadows and secrets are wrong.

Now this is where I want to go back to the secret I kept about Amelia and Riley — about seeing them in Castle Hill with a baby. It **Cannot resist interrupting here to say, ever so gently, DID YOU NOT *HEAR* ME EARLIER?!! STOP DISGRACING THE WORD BY CALLING SOMETHING SO MUNDANE AS THIS A SECRET!!**

(Also, about the "shadow conversation" — what makes you think I wasn't there?)

❖

Interrupt again and I swear I'll get a priest in to do an exorcism.

Okay, listen. I'm going to tell you about an incident.

The incident took place on a Thursday night, the night before the last day of term.

A group of us were in the Art Rooms.

We were there helping Em chase her ghost.

Some of us believed in the ghost. Some of us were there to laugh at Em.

Seb was there, and so were Amelia and Riley.

We'd been hanging for a while, joking around, and, so far, no ghost. The group started to splinter; people wandering. I heard Seb say he was going back to his car.

The Art Exhibition was happening in the Gallery the next day. Seb had a work in progress in it, and he said he had something to add to it in his car.

I saw the door to the auditorium close behind him.

I was vaguely aware of one or two other people leaving the room.

Decided I would follow Seb.

There was something important that I wanted to say to him.

I went to find him. The Gallery's just down the hall from the auditorium.

Someone was outside the door.

Thought it was Seb at first, but he heard my footstep, turned in my direction — and turned out it was Riley.

Riley's hands were pressed to the Gallery door, about to open it.

He saw me, gave his slow, warm smile, waited. I reached him. We were both about to speak, when someone screamed.

The scream was loud.

Instinctively, I reached for Riley, and he did the same to me. One of his hands held the side of my arm for a moment. Our eyes rushed into each other's eyes — he has this way of looking into eyes like he's diving right in — then we turned down the hall.

The scream faded — and I recognized it.

It was Em's scream. (I've known her a long time.)

Already, a crinkle had formed in the corners of Riley's eyes. Still, he tilted his head slightly, watching the empty corridor, listening, waiting.

The silence continued. We dropped our arms, and smiled.

"I guess the ghost is here," I said.

"Not anymore it's not," he said — meaning the scream would have scared it away.

I laughed and so did he. He pushed open the door.

One light was shining down the end of the Gallery, but otherwise the room had a dim, hushed feel.

Windows were black with night. Walls were hung with paintings, neatly labeled. There was something calm and expectant about the room.

I looked around for Seb's piece. I knew he was doing something multimedia but hadn't seen it yet. I'd never even been in the Gallery.

Then I realized Seb himself was not here. He must have been still out at his car.

Riley had moved across the room, and was standing by the window.

There was a small card fixed to the wall beside him — *Riley T. Smith*, it said — and a series of black-and-white photographs stretched beyond it.

The first photo was a young guy with a goatee, slouching along in the middle distance. The next was a close-up of the same guy's face, but now it had a huge, unexpected smile. Then an old woman in the same middle distance, eyes sad and lost — followed by a close-up of the woman, radiant with her smile. There was a series of similar pairs: a distant face, distracted or sullen; then a sudden, looming close-up — each with a smile that was lit with something vivid, fresh, and warm. The effect was strangely confronting — the transformation was so complete, it was as if an otherworldy switch had been at work.

I moved along the wall — and found myself looking at photos of me.

It was intensely embarrassing. I felt as if they were nude portraits. I moved on, passing more pairs, and then I came to a small card labeled *The Switch* – so that was the name of the series. I'd been thinking of that exact word. Beyond the card was a final photograph: this one a close-up of a baby in a carrier, asleep.

"That's my sister," Riley said. He'd been gazing out the window as I looked at his photos, but now he moved to my side. "Chloe. I had this idea that I'd walk around with her for a few weeks and photograph people's expressions before and after they saw her. There's something about her face. Not like other babies' faces."

I'd seen the baby, I knew what he meant. But I didn't want to mention that — it would draw attention to the photos of me and I wanted to pretend they weren't there.

Riley reached out a hand and touched the image of the baby with his fingertips.

"You should have seen her this morning," he said, smiling. "She'd got into the pantry and tipped a box of Cheerios all over the kitchen floor. I walk in and she's crawling around eating them as fast as she can. Mum's standing there, watching her — she got this embarrassed look when she saw me — she goes, 'I know, I know, but I can't bring myself to stop her. She thinks she's hit the jackpot.'"

I laughed but before I had a chance to speak, there were some freakish, loud noises from somewhere down the hall, followed by screams from our ghost-hunting friends — then footsteps pounding from the Art Rooms.

Riley and I looked at each other and laughed hard. We couldn't stop laughing. It was like we were laughing at everything — his beautiful photos, his funny little sister, the image of her crawling around eating Cheerios, the fact that we both knew there were photos of me on the wall but weren't mentioning them, the madness of our friends chasing terror — it all seemed connected. We were the observers, like Riley's mother. Standing apart, watching fondly, laughing at the weird happiness of the kids.

We waited a few moments, then went out into the corridor, chatted a bit, still laughing, and headed out into the night.

And that's the incident.
Do you understand why I told you about it?

Love,
Lydia

❖

To prove that I was right about your secret? That it was no secret? Simply, Riley out with his sister taking photos for an artwork? Well! That is generous of you, Lydia.

❖

No, I am proving that you're wrong.
When I saw Riley and Amelia with a baby last term, you know what I thought?
That it was *their* baby.
It explained their separateness. (And their sleepiness in classes.)
I didn't tell anyone 'cause I thought it was Amelia and Riley's secret to tell.
I wondered about their lives — seventeen years old with a kid. How scared and trapped they must feel. No wonder Amelia was up to something, I thought. But it made her secret — and the space between their hands — even sadder.
I thought about the knowledge they must have that we didn't — how to change a nappy, get a baby vaccinated. Where to buy a pram.
How much more grown-up they were than us. How childish we must seem.

Next thing, Riley's talking like an ordinary boy about his mum and his baby sister.

I felt like an idiot. I'd been thinking *I* was the only one at Ashbury who could see Riley and Amelia clearly. But I'd made an ordinary scene — two kids out with a baby sister — into something extraordinary.

I was just like everybody else: looking for a mystery, wanting a twist.

I also realized that those few sentences — Riley's cute story about the sister and the spilled breakfast cereal — was the most I'd learned about Riley all year.

There's no such thing as "Amelia and Riley" — I mean the *mysterious, amazing* Amelia-and-Riley; they don't actually exist.

Just like Em's ghost doesn't exist, because there's no such thing as ghosts.

❖

Hmm.

Something not quite right about your final thought there, but I can't get my head around what it is.

Oops. No head.

Well. You know. Amelia and Riley? Whatever.

I'm kind of "over them."

Much more interested to know what it was that you wanted to tell Seb that night. When you followed him to the Gallery, and found Riley there instead. Did you ever catch Seb? Did you tell him?

❖

Huh. I wondered when you'd get to that.

No, I haven't told him yet.

Term 2 ended, the Exhibition happened. Seb's artwork was a surprise. My parents came home, the parties stopped, and I didn't see Seb alone again. Now it's about to be Term 3 and the Trials. There'll still be drama rehearsals and I guess I'll see him there —

But what I wanted to tell Seb was that I lied to him on the first day of Term 2.

Here's my final story:

First day of Term 2, early morning, Blue Danish Café.

An all-night party at my place the night before.

A group of us have stopped for coffee on the way to school.

We're sitting by the window and the white light hurts my eyes. I close them. But a voice across the table hurts my brain. Pick up my latte with both hands, open my eyes, and study it. Such gentle twists and peaks in the foam. Such subtle swirls of caramel — and it's so creamy — so creamy. I put the coffee down and push it hard away, so it begins to tip.

Riley is beside me. He's talking to someone, but his hand reaches out and rights my coffee. He keeps on talking, doesn't look at me.

I close my eyes again but that voice across the table.

It's the same pitch as a fire alarm. She should take a vow of silence.

It's Astrid from our school. Em made friends with her last year. They're leaning close together now, their hair is entangled, and Astrid's telling a story that goes like this: *And he's, like, and I'm, like, and it's, like like like, so cold!*

I think suddenly of Christmas pudding so crowded with raisins that you can't find any cake.

I look at Em. How can she sit so close to Astrid and not throw up?

I can't even be in the same room.

I push back my chair and get out of the café. As I leave I notice Riley's hand reach out again — this time he's stopped my chair from toppling backward. Once again, he doesn't even look around to do it.

Nearly trip over Toby from my school on the way out — he's sitting near the door with some woman. Maybe his mum. He looks sad.

See myself reflected in the café door as I walk out.

I look sad too.

I think this childish thought: *What's to be sad about, Toby? You've got your mum. Where's mine?*

And then, just outside the door, lost inside my mind, there's suddenly a sense of something right.

A sense of something falling into place.

It's so soothing. I can't figure out — and then I can.

It's Seb. Standing in front of me. He's so close I can't see his face. It's the smell of him, the closeness, that's what's right. He's arriving at the café just as I'm leaving and his hand is reaching out toward the door. His arm has crossed right over my shoulder.

He stops, we step back, and I look into his face. The surprise of the meeting, the physical closeness, makes our eyes honest for a moment.

Then someone else is trying to get past us, and we step away, get shy again.

This is the first time I've seen Seb since I ran into him at a petrol station first term — the night he warned me to stay away from Riley and Amelia. This is before the drama rehearsals and the parties that he comes to all Term 2.

Now we step away from the door, stand together in the cold — talk about the cold. Talk about the fact that my parents are away in their Tuscan retreat. Seb's art and soccer, the computer course he's been taking in graphic design, how he's getting into programming. Our words are smooth as latte foam. They're tangling like hair. He's listening to every word I say, and then I see he's listening to more than that. Trying to hear the air between us, trying to hear my thoughts.

There's a shine in his eye as I tell a stupid-funny story about the party last night, but the shine outlasts the story and he says, "Lyd, I miss you bad."

He says, "Can we —?" Keeps looking into my eyes.

He means he's ready to end the break.

I turn cold as shadows.

I'm still smiling but I'm cold: "We can be friends, but that's all I want, okay?"

"If that's all I can get," he says, fast. He's still smiling too, and the shine's still there but fading.

"That's all you can get," I nod, and reach out to punch his shoulder like a "pal."

I want to touch him and hurt him both at once.

I don't expect to see him again, but he surprises me by signing up for the Ashbury-Brookfield Drama. He tells me he isn't stalking me; he just got invited to supervise set design. And when they all start coming to parties at my place, it makes sense for him to come too.

So Seb's my friend all term.

And then, on that last night, I tried to find him in the Gallery to tell him that I lied. That I've been pretending all term.

It's not all I want. It's never all I wanted.

Just to be friends. I want more than that.

❖

And you still haven't told him?!
Well, my child, you must!
Call him now!

❖

Ha-ha.
I could tell him at rehearsals now that school's going back.
Or he can call me now if he wants.

❖

"Ha-ha?" Whatever do you mean? You sure can be exasperating,
Lydia! Call him at once and let him know!
  We'll wrap up this assessment task so you can.
  If I may be so bold, I shall now retell your story of last term.
Here it is. Last term:

You were abandoned by your parents during the most stressful
  academic year of your life.
You felt abandoned by Seb at a time when you needed him most.
You were anxious about whether your parents' marriage would
  return in pieces or not.
You punished your parents by letting the house get trashed, and by
  siphoning money from their online bank accounts.
You punished Seb by pretending you no longer cared for him.
You punished yourself by pretending you no longer cared
  for Seb.
You distracted yourself from the sound of your own thoughts by
  holding party after party after party after party — and when the
  thoughts were still louder than the backbeat of the parties, you
  buried them with Riley and Amelia obsessing!
You did (I concede) consume enormous quantities of coffee,
  almonds, Magnums, and pecan cookies.

Ever Yours,
The Ghost

❖

Okay, now you're just weird and annoying.
Drop the ghost thing. Get out of my head. And call me.

Drop the ghost thing. Hmm. How exactly?
As to getting out of your head, why, I've only just got started!
Are you not delighted with my insights?!
Your obsession with secrets and shadows! While all the time
you're hiding from the truth! Now there's a rich seam to mine!
Which brings me to something that we haven't even mentioned!
The secret that your mother told you just before she left!!!

How do you know about that secret?

❖

Well, DUH! I haunt this house. You haven't noticed how much
I've noticed? I was *there* when she told you the secret.

❖

Seb, what the f. are you talking about?

❖

Okay, setting aside the curious fact that you just called me
"Seb" — a few nights before your parents flew away, your mother
was getting ready for a reception at Distressed Weasel Records, that
"hot, new independent label" that she recently acquired. (Oh, your
mother is transparent! Longs to be hot, new, and independent

herself!) (Or does she wish to be a distressed weasel? Hm. But why?) As I recall it, she had wandered into the living room to "take a break" from getting ready. She was wearing her white bathrobe but had already set her hair and donned her jewelry, so her bangles slid up and down her arm as she mixed herself a cocktail. She was chatting to you about the olive grove she would see from the window of her Tuscan villa — when you both heard the sound of your father's car in the driveway. And suddenly — in a warm, smiling, confiding voice — she told you her secret.

❖

[At this point, I stopped typing and picked up my phone. Here is probably the appropriate time for me to point out — if you have not already guessed this yourself — that I had believed, for almost the entire correspondence, that the "ghost" was in fact my friend Seb. I assumed it was Seb because I recalled that, following a course in computer graphics, he had developed an unexpected interest in programming. I thought he must have hacked into my computer. The ghost's praise of Seb — his soccer-playing abilities, etc. — seemed to confirm my assumption. I had revealed the truth about my feelings for Seb, thinking I was telling Seb himself.

However, I had not told a single person the "secret" that my mother revealed to me in the living room before she went to Tuscany. (Nor do I think it necessary, for the purposes of this narrative, to reveal that secret now — it's a family thing.) In fact, until this moment, I have not mentioned to anyone that she so much as told me a secret. Yet the details set out in the letter above are accurate: the robe, the bangles, and so on.

The only way anybody could know this was if they were spying on the room.

I picked up the phone and called Seb.

He did not answer. (The time was now close to 4 A.M., so this is not surprising.)

I left a fairly garbled and angry message. (He called me back eventually,

and left a message of his own — he seemed genuinely confused. In my expe-
rience with Seb, he has never [or rarely] been deceptive. I believe that, if the
"ghost" HAD been Seb he would have admitted it in the course of the cor-
respondence — or at the very least confessed when I challenged him on the
phone. But he insisted that he had not been talking with me online all night.
He asked if I was all right. He sounded concerned.)

Getting back to last night: Once I had left the message on Seb's phone, I
sat back in my desk chair, breathless for a few moments, and then, hesitantly,
I typed:]

Seb, you are seriously scaring me. You've been in the house?
You've been watching us? What the f. is going on? This isn't funny
at all. I just left you a message. Call me back.

❖

And most people think *I'm* the loony tune! Oh Ly-y-y-d-i-i-i-aaa
(singing tone)! Yoo-hoo! Earth to crazy one!

Why are you calling me Seb? Don't tell me you think *I'm* Seb!
He's not dead! Nowhere near the haunting phase!

And I'm much prettier than he is! Or I was. In my day. Less so
now with my head under my arm, the blood gushing from the
fish-hooked eye, the crumbling bones, etc., etc.

If only I could *show* myself to you! But I can't. Invisibility. It
can be a drag. Sigggggggh. (☺)

The main thing that you need to get clear is that

I

Am

Not

Seb.

I'm not Seb.

I'm not Seb.

I'm not Seb.

This is not Seb. This Is Not Seb.

I
Am
Not
Seb.

Anyhow, are we done now? Need any more ghostliness from me? Oh! Those icky parents of yours are home! That's their car, isn't it? (They do keep late hours for people of their age. I mean, they only got back from Tuscany a couple of weeks ago. May as well still be there!)

Yours,
The Ghost

❖

[Now I was both angry and frightened. The ghost was right — my parents had just arrived home. I ran downstairs to meet them and told them that someone had hacked into my computer and was talking to me. They were both drunk (and shouldn't have been driving). They found it wildly hilarious that I was frightened by the fact that someone was talking to me online. They could not seem to get their heads around the difference between an online conversation and one that occurs in a Word document. They did not find it at all disturbing that my correspondent must have been in my house. (For obvious reasons, I could not tell them that the "ghost" knew my mother's secret.) They made "joke" after "joke" to each other about the situation, got themselves more drinks, went downstairs to play billiards. . . . They were in fine spirits.

Feeling exhausted, I came back to my computer and saw this on the screen:]

❖

Dear Lydia,

Signing off now. It's been a pleasure and treat to talk to you at last. All the years I've been haunting you — that day when a relative visited and told you she'd seen a little chick being eaten by a fox, and you — such a feisty six-year-old! — pretended you had to get something from your room, so you could run up here and cry for the chick; the winter when you were eight, and secretly wore your sneakers to bed each night because you thought you had "foot and mouth disease" (strange child!); the time you hid that Easter egg for months and when you found it again it had gone mottled and stale so you gave it to your father for Easter the following year . . . ! — oh, so many sweet, pointless memories! — I never guessed we might get to chat!

We will never chat again, you know.

This is, after all, some kind of glitch in reality. Henceforward, little one, I will merely be a presence in your home. That odd chill you feel in the large games room — the chill that makes you look for open windows. The creak in the floorboards of the library. The strange, unsettled feeling you always get in the wine cellar.

Those, my dear, are me.

I'll leave you with some ghostly sounds to help you sleep:

SHRIEEEEK! SHRIEK. HOWL! SHRIEK! CLATTER CLATTER CLATTER! SIGGGGHHHHH! SHRIEK! SHRIEK! SHRIEK!
CLANG!
CLANG!
Moan.

Yours Evermore,
The Ghost

❖

[As you've no doubt guessed, the ghost's recollections of events from my child-
hood are accurate — and include details I don't think I've ever told friends.

I spent this morning asking all the "computer experts" I know for their views on how a hacker might infiltrate my Word document like this. They were mystified.

The above was the final "letter" I received from the ghost. I watched the screen for another half hour or so. I typed repeated (and increasingly manic/ angry/pleading) letters of my own. There is no need to include those here. The only response was silence and a relentlessly blank screen.

I sign off myself now — hopeful that my readers might offer an answer. And terrified, I am ashamed to admit, of typing at this computer. The ghost interrupting — keys falling away beneath my fingers — like slipping down a staircase in the dark.]

End of Transcript

3.

Emily Thompson
THE STORY OF TERM 2 AS A GHOST STORY

1.

Listen!

I have a story to tell!

Come closer and I will tell it! Closer! Closer, I say!

No. Seriously. Closer than that.

Okay, great.

My story is a ghost story! *And, by lucky chance, it is also the story of Term 2!!*

Every word in this story will be true. Oh, you will doubt me repeatedly. But then you will apologize for doubting! When you come face-to-face with a ghost! Along with categorical, documentary proof that this ghost not only exists, but is alive and well and living in the Art Rooms of my school, such documentary evidence to include a photograph that will make the hairs stand up on —

But I am getting ahead of you.

And so, without further manifestation, here it is!

The story begins early in the morning on the first day of the term. Close your eyes, picture a ghostly, shimmering effect, and then? Startle yourself with an image of me with a group of my friends. We are prancing along the frosty streets —

Excuse me. We were not prancing. In the spirit of honesty, I have to say that we'd been up all night and were nearly comatose, so, no, we were not prancing.

Never mind.

We reached our favorite café and the coffees were embalming to our souls.

It so happens that I was sitting beside my friend Astrid. She had broken up with a boyfriend the night before, so now we were lost in intensity. That is, she was listing the boyfriend's flaws.

Now, most details of this conversation mean nothing to my story — and I leave them on the table with our empty coffee cups. . . . However, this one detail. I will tell it.

Astrid told me that one of her boyfriend's flaws took place early in the year. It was the second day of the year, she said, and she and the boyfriend were in Geography in Room 27B of the Art Rooms.

As she uttered those words — Room 27B of the Art Rooms — a curious twinge hit me. I am deathly serious. The twinge hit the center of my upper lip. I touched my lip and the twinge went away. I remember that I thought to myself: *Huh.*

Astrid explained that she had been chatting quietly with the boyfriend when suddenly — *suddenly* — she had felt cold.

Not just cold, you understand, but freezing cold. As if icicles taken from the Danish Alps were spearing the back of her neck. (Those are Astrid's vivid words.)

She decided not to mention how cold she was to the boyfriend. She would keep talking and let her chilliness shine in her eyes. If he loved her, he would notice.

But did he? Did he say, tenderly, "Are you cold?" Or: "Why are your eyes shining so strangely?"

No. None of the above.

And that was a flaw.

At this point in my conversation with Astrid, I paused. Being a fair and reasonable girl, I wondered if Astrid was the same.

I took a thoughtful sip of my latte, looked up — and there was Seb.

(I give you a line, dear reader, to catch your breath.)

Seb is a Brookfield boy. He was standing at the counter waiting for coffee. I had not seen him for months — not since he broke up with Lydia — but now he was raising a finger in the air to say hello. He was grinning at me in his friendly Seb way, and yet — and *yet*, I thought I saw something complicated in that grin. My eyes flew to the seat opposite, where Lydia had been sitting. It was empty. Where was she? I looked around and found her through the window: She was standing alone on the footpath outside. I turned back to Seb. And suddenly all was clear to me.

Seb had just seen Lydia outside.

He had asked her to get back together with him.

And she had said no.

You may wonder how I knew all this.

I simply did.

I am a student of love.

"I *know*," I said to Astrid — taking a guess at what she'd been saying — and she continued speaking of her breakup. (Leaving a perfectly great guy was taking its toll.)

I'm sorry to say that I did not concentrate. All I could think was that the *true* tragedy was the breakup of Lydia and Seb.

Oh, Lydia, I thought, *it is great that you are Lydia, but must you always be?*

There she stood on the path outside, deep and proud in thought, but to me her shoulders looked vulnerable and cold.

Cold.

Something cold struck me in the face.

I realized what it was: Astrid had said she'd felt freezing cold on the second day of term. I remembered that day. It had been very, very hot. *But Astrid had felt freezing cold?!* How could this be?

One week later, I knew how it could be.
There was a ghost in the Art Rooms.

2.

"A ghost in the Art Rooms?!" you exclaim, and you look around nervously. (Especially if you happen to be reading this story in the Art Rooms, LOL.)

Be calm, gentle reader. We still have a little time before the terror begins. (We also have time before we see Astrid again — between us, that is a relief. It's great to have a friend like Astrid, but sometimes it's even greater to take a break from her.)

Come! Take my hand! We will trip through the term — and you will watch out for ghostly clues. . . .

That first week of term — well, what happened? We were getting our half-yearly exams back, so teachers kept pulling stacks of papers from their bags, and trying to make their faces solemn. They never succeed at the solemn at these times. I think they are just too proud of themselves for having got the marking done.

Why? Why so proud? I mean, *marking is their job.* (But this is an aside.)

Some of my marks made me ecstatic beyond reason, and some were like machine guns blasting black holes in my heart.

That is how it always is with exam results for me, and I think that you, sweet reader, of this ghost story, will agree that there is something *very wrong* with an educational institution that gives out inconsistent marks. Think about it. If I deserve good marks in *some* subjects then logically I deserve them in the rest. It's a mathematical equation and maths is always right. (Otherwise, what's the point of it.)

So, I was very busy that week. I had to have a series of mood swings because of my exam results, and the swings swung extra low when the following horrific event occurred.

An Economics class had just finished and I was talking to Mr. Ludovico about my exam result.

"Economics is not an exact science," I explained. "If it were, there would not be global financial meltdowns. Therefore, you can't actually judge that I was wrong in any of the questions, and you should increase my mark."

He laughed. "If we tried out some of *your* economic theories, Em," he said, "the meltdown would be more than just global."

Then he sauntered from the room.

I turned to Cass and pointed out that Mr. Ludovico made no sense. What else was there besides global? Global covered everything. That was its point.

People were packing up around me.

I said that Mr. Ludovico's laugh sounds like an espresso machine.

I said that *weeks ago now*, I had asked Mr. Ludovico to sign my application for Law at Sydney University, and he still hadn't done it. (It's a new requirement this year: The application has to be signed by your school principal.)

"It's supposed to be just a formality," I said. "But of course, Mr. L has to turn it into a kind of a power play. He's probably going to make me wait until the day it's due."

Cass said that Mr. Ludovico is on the K. L. Mason Patterson Trust Fund Committee with her mum, and her mum says he never comes to meetings because he's always too busy.

"He should not have taken on the job of principal," I said, "if he could not cope with the responsibilities."

Cass agreed.

"Don't forget, you should all be reading the *Financial Review*," said a voice.

It was Mr. Ludovico.

He was standing in the doorway, speaking to the room.

He hadn't left at all.

He must have heard every word I said.

3.

So. That happened.

What else?

Well, my mother collected my brother and me from school. This was unique. Mum is a busy lawyer but this year she has taken long service leave, to work on her master's and spend more time with us. She is excited by everything about being a mum as she's never actually done it before. She even gets excited by traffic jams.

"Who knew there'd be so much traffic at 3:30 in the afternoon?" she says. "I guess a *part* of me knew there was a *school rush hour* but was it a conscious part?"

And when we slow down for school speed zones she says, "It's great that the kids are safe, but do they really need to be *this* safe?"

She's just joking around, but it makes the drive almost like a party, since William and I catch her craziness.

4.

The second week of term began — and so did the rehearsals for the Ashbury-Brookfield Drama. Lyd, Cass, and I are in the English stream of the Drama which means we're on the team of scriptwriters. There's a complicated thing about us writing and rehearsing at the same time, which is too tedious to explain, so I will only say that it's a total disaster.

Never mind.

The first rehearsal was in the morning. (Morning rehearsals are ridiculous because people do not turn up, including me, I mean to say, I'm sleepy enough as it is.)

It was astonishing, that first rehearsal, and here is why:

Brookfielders came to our school.

I know: Why astonishing? It's an Ashbury-Brookfield production, so of course Brookfielders came.

And yet I was astonished. You see, even though I had *known* that the Brookfielders were coming, I think that a profound part of me had not *believed* it.

I never expected to see Brookfielders in my school except as an invading force.

And to be honest, they do look very strange here. Maybe their uniforms clash with the walls?

Anyway, there we were in the auditorium, watching the Brookfielders arrive. Ironically, they didn't seem to realize how strange they looked. They wandered around easygoingly, without even caring that their shirts were untucked or that their shoes were multiple and downtrodden. (Here at Ashbury our shoes are all the same: black, shiny, and reflective.)

A few of the Brookfielders looked at our audio system. It is the kind used by the UN General Assembly — and yet it only made the Brookfielders laugh.

Strange. Never mind.

More Brookfielders arrived — and one of them . . . was Seb!

He paused in the doorway, letting other Brookfielders push their way around him, and you could see he was relaxing his shoulders. It is most heartbreaking, I think, when a confident person like Seb has trouble relaxing his shoulders.

Then he noticed Lyd, Cass, and me, and grinned his Seb grin. It's a grin that makes his eyes as reflective as my shoes. He came straight toward us. I had strength of character and didn't turn to watch Lydia for her reaction. But even without turning, I could feel it.

She was brighter, warmer — and an electric force field flew up around her so that anyone who tried to touch her would have dropped dead on the spot.

I stepped away a little.

The force field hid the bright, warm Lydia, but being a student of love, I knew that she was there. Poor Seb is just a boy, however, and could only see the force field.

His grin broke in half.

Bravely, he joined us anyway, and Lydia raised an eyebrow at him.

Seb told us that Mr. Garcia, the director of the Drama, had sent him a letter, asking him to supervise set design. He did not say this to show off: He was letting Lydia know that he was not there just to chase her.

Her force field relaxed.

We wondered how news of Seb's artistry had reached Mr. Garcia — maybe the sweet picture books Seb and Lyd used to make together? They used to circulate at our school until the principal banned them because they were too violent — but then we were interrupted by the *next* astonishment!

Amelia and Riley walked in . . . !

Last term Mr. G had asked them to join and they'd been all: "No, no, not in a million years, thanks for asking."

This term they must have been all: "Okay."

A mystery!

Anyway, they smiled across at us in their uncanny way — they had come to a couple of Lyd's parties over the holidays. I quickly scanned the Brookfielders. But no reaction (apart from Seb, who blinked twice). So the rumors were true! Even though they used to go to Brookfield, nobody had ever seen them there!!!

I was lost in the intrigue of this thought when Mr. Garcia finally leapt through the door. He loves a dramatic entrance. But this was even more dramatic than usual, for just as he landed, there was a HUGE, CREAKING SOUND.

The creaking came from somewhere in the building.

You know when you're on an ancient ship in the middle of the ocean on a deep, dark night and the ship tips slowly sideways and there's a slow, spooky *cre-e-e-a-k?*

Sure you do. You've seen the movies.

Well, it was exactly like that.

Everybody stopped. Eyes opened wide. Mr. Garcia's eyebrows jumped to the top of his forehead, and that's a lot of eyebrow to be leaping.

Then, there was nothing. A long silence.

"It's an old building," Mr. Garcia shrugged.

And the rehearsal began.

5.

But where, you say, was the ghost?

Well, the ghost crept up on me slowly. This was creepy of it but I suppose that's the way with ghosts.

For a start, every time I had an English class in Room 27B I felt cold. Sometimes it was just mildly cold like when you fold your arms and go, "Brrr," but not in an openly distressed way. More a kind of sparkle-eyed way. But sometimes it was an EXTREME cold as if a giant frozen person was giving me a bear hug. At those times I felt hostile. I hate being cold. It hurts my feelings.

Lydia is also in that English class and she didn't know what I was talking about. She said she found the weather in Room 27B to be balmy.

Around this time I realized that whenever somebody mentioned Room 27B I would get a twitch in the center of my lip, like the one I first got with Astrid.

Lyd and Cass said I might be getting a cold sore and should start putting ointment on it, but that was false.

So, then there was the first drama rehearsal, and now, dear reader! Come with me directly from that creaking drama rehearsal straight to an English class in Room 27B. Hurry. We are running late.

As usual, I felt the twitch in my lip as I reached the classroom. It was getting annoying. And, as usual, I shivered as soon as I sat down. That made me sigh.

Anyway, I wrapped my scarf tightly around my neck, and made my hands into fists so I could blow warm air into them. Lydia, beside me, watched all this and breathed in slowly through her nose. Farther along I saw Amelia, who had come with us from the rehearsal. Her arms were bare, and she was leaning back and gazing at the teacher.

I sighed again. I picked up my pen and rolled it back and forth between my palms rapidly. Trying to start a fire with it. Useless. Not even a spark. I let it fall to my desk and stared at it, moodily. (I was very sleepy.)

The pen was lying on my desk.

I was thinking, *Why am I always so cold here?*

And, *What's this weird thing with my lip?*

And, *Why does this building creak so much? I mean, is it even safe?*

It seemed to me that something very strange was going on. I was thinking about taking it up with the teacher — he was talking about irrelevant things so it was a good time to interrupt — when suddenly a thought hit the side of my head.

It could be a ghost.

I was so shocked by the thought that I gasped. *Because it was so obvious.* It was like, say you'd been trying to figure out an answer to a crossword puzzle for weeks, then suddenly it comes to you — and it's such a simple word and fits so perfectly that you can't believe you didn't get it right away. The shock of your own stupidity! Sometimes it's the greatest shock of all.

(Not that I ever do crossword puzzles, but I know what I mean.)

And, listen, it fit so perfectly!

The Art Rooms is a very old building. It was once a mansion where people lived, and therefore they died, because people used to always die in those days. Then Ashbury bought it for boarders. Then, when they stopped taking boarders, it became the Art Rooms, and now it's been renovated.

Exactly the thing to wake a ghost! Noisy renovations! Or make a ghost angry!! Ghosts don't appreciate change.

Then there was the coldness. Well, everybody knows that you don't feel cold on a warm day unless you're in the presence of a ghost! Why had I not thought of this before?

Also, I'm a very intuitive girl so I realized that I must have been *sensing* the ghost in the middle of my lip.

And the creaking! That's what an angry ghost would do. Creak. It was probably trying to push down walls — leaning on beams, trying to make the place unstable.

See what I mean? It was very clear.

And we were in danger! *The ghost wanted to topple the building.*

So there I was, sitting at my desk, gasping at this thought — when my pen began to roll across the desk.

I am not kidding. I did not flick it with my fingernail or help it along with my elbow — nothing like that. It just moved.

Objects do not move on their own.

It's not possible. Everybody knows that.

The pen rolled slowly across the desk while I watched in heart-gasping terror.

What further proof could I need?

At that point, Mr. Botherit said, "Emily, are you hyper-ventilating?"

I looked at him witheringly for a second, and when I looked back at my desk, the pen had stopped.

"There is a ghost in this room," I announced. I was pleased because my voice had strength of character.

People turned and looked at me with interest. Many of them then looked up, as if the ghost was on the ceiling. Maybe they thought that ghosts rise, like hot air. That was a flaw, as ghosts are cold.

They looked back at me.

"There *is*," I said.

I hadn't planned to be defensive but if you had seen the way they looked . . .

Anyway, I explained my theory and some people seemed interested when I talked about how old the building is, and how people used to always, like, poison each other with darts, or cut each other's throats in closets, in the olden days — but then I got to the twitch in my lip and I lost everyone's respect.

It was a fatal error to include the twitch.

Yet, it was honest. I'm a very honest girl.

After that there was a lot of laughter at my expense, and people, especially boys, can be cruel.

But I can defend myself if I need to, and I did. In a way that used up a lot of the English class. And every time Mr. B tried to get back on track, somebody would veer him off again demanding to know if the renovations had disturbed a hidden cemetery, *and did they move the bodies, or did they JUST MOVE THE GRAVESTONES* (quoting from some old movie), or they would reach over to put icy cold hands on my neck (which I did not need), or slam a book down suddenly (so that people, especially me, screamed), or they'd laugh in a bloodcurdling, ghostly way.

Boys can be cruel but they can also do good impressions. Why are boys such good actors? A lot of them are, you know.

Anyway, it was funny. Or it would have been if I hadn't feared that we were all in mortal danger.

Let me tell you this, though, that at one point I sighed loudly and turned sideways for dramatic effect, and there was Amelia. She was sitting at her desk as usual, and she was gazing at me.

She never gazes at me. She always gazes at teachers.

But she was watching me, and when she saw me look, she gave the faintest, faintest smile, and turned away.

Later that day, I saw my friend Toby and I am pleased to say that he believed me about the ghost, *without even hearing my evidence.*

He is the unsung hero of the corners of my life, that Toby. As solid as wood, which is spooky actually, *because he's excellent at woodwork.*

6.

Speaking of corners, the next couple of weeks, the ghost retreated to the corners of my mind.

Isn't it strange that one day I could be fearing mortal danger, and the next I could be all like, *whatever*. But that is how it was. I blame the mysteries of the ghostly world and I also blame the HSC.

Whatever the reason, I kept going to rehearsals and to parties at Lydia's place, and doing (some of) my homework, and living my busy life. I *did* write a blog entry, which began:

> *I am about to say something that may surprise and possibly even terrify you. There is a ghost living in the Art Rooms. Specifically, the ghost resides in Room 27B of the Art Rooms, but it strolls around the building at its leisure.*

This was a tricky blog to write as Mr. B has continued to request that the blogs be entitled "My Journey Home" — which makes me question his teaching credentials, even as I applaud his stamina in the face of a growing underbelly of resentment. He might not know about that resentment and I mention it here in the spirit of letting him know —

Yes, so, what was I saying? When I wrote my blog about the ghost, I had to twist things around to make it relevant to my journey home. Who has the time for such twists?

Not me.

And nor did people appreciate my efforts. Most comments on the ghost blog went beyond the bounds of stupid.

Anyhow, as I said, the ghost retreated to the recesses of my mind, where no doubt it enjoyed fruit, chocolate, and conversation, in the international language of the recess.

But then, in Week 4, it got in touch.

7.

Not just once.

Three times that week it contacted me. To be honest, it was a bit like harassment.

The first thing that happened was the mandarin peels.

I expect you will laugh. Everybody else did. But I know in my heart it was not funny.

It was Monday, and another morning rehearsal. Winter mornings cause more sleepiness than other seasons, and, in addition, contain a disproportionate amount of the day's cold. It's like when you read on a cereal box that one serving of this cereal is 90% of your recommended daily intake of niacin. Each time I see this I think, *What, and you're PROUD of that? Aren't I going to be overloaded with niacin, whatever THAT is, if you're filling me up with it now?!* And so on.

But that is an aside.

The fact is, mornings are for sleeping, and in winter, sleep should be the law. (Another aside.)

This particular morning, the weather (or maybe the ghost?) was rattling our teeth as we waited outside the Art Rooms for the rehearsal to begin. By now, there had been a blending of Ashburians and Brookfielders. I mean, we were friends. Partly this was because working together on the Drama had made us bond, and partly it was because Mr. Garcia often brought Caramello Koalas to the rehearsals (which I applaud, in a teacher, the providing of chocolate), and *partly* it was because, at the third rehearsal, which had ended late in the afternoon, I had invited everyone to come to a party at Lydia's place for further bondage.

I was high on Amelia and Riley that day.

It was the first time I had seen them act.

Dear, sweet reader of this ghost story. Have you ever seen Amelia and Riley act? If so, you can skip the next paragraphs. For you will know, in your heart, what I mean.

They improvised a scene — and I nearly fell off the window ledge. I mean, I expected them to be great, but I had no idea they would illuminate the corners of my soul. That is not exaggeration. Their acting makes everything around them seem pointless. They immerse themselves so completely that it makes me want to dive right in and join them. (And that's saying a lot, considering how stupid the play is.)

So, I felt like crying, dancing, and having sex with strangers the first time I saw them act. (That part about sex, I mean it symbolically. I would never actually do that.)

Also, that day, I was in love with the Brookfielders. Maybe because Amelia and Riley's acting was making me see the world in a beautiful new light, or maybe there is actually something sexy about Brookfielders? I think there might be, you know. They're so wild. And Charlie, my Charlie, was a Brookfielder.

If all that is not enough justification for inviting a room full of people to somebody else's place for a party, I don't know what is.

Lydia raised an eyebrow at me — but she didn't mind. Everybody came and thus began the tradition of after-rehearsal parties at Lyd's.

So, as I said, we had blended, like pineapple and watermelon in my mother's juicer.

And now, on this Monday morning, we stood or sat on the wide front steps doing various things to warm ourselves: running up and down the steps, smoking cigarettes, and hugging each other. I used the traditional technique of shivering. Now and then, I watched hopefully, but Seb and Lydia did not hug flirtatiously: In fact, they did not hug at all. They were friends by now, and made each other laugh all the time — it seemed to me that their primary goal in life was to make the other one laugh. When either succeeded, you'd see proud little smiles.

But if Seb took a step closer or reached out a hand — Lydia would take a step away.

Cass and I sighed with our eyes. Lydia was making us crazy.

Eventually, Mr. Garcia arrived. Around me people were hiding their cigarettes; at the same time, Mr. Garcia was stamping out a cigarette in the car park, looking guiltily our way. Students love Mr. Garcia so they're always trying to make him quit smoking, for the sake of his longevity. Other teachers are welcome to smoke. It would not bother us, for example, to see Mr. Ludovico's lungs collapse in an Economics class. My only request would be that he face away from me when it happened as that might be disgusting to behold.

Anyway, so there was Mr. G, trying to smoke quickly before we saw him.

He joined us, full of excess energy, swiped his card to open the building, and we rushed inside to the warmth, and walked toward the auditorium.

I cannot say what happened first — whether the color orange caught the corner of my eye, or the twitch leapt onto my lip. I think maybe both at once. I looked sideways, saw the closed door of Room 27B, and there it was. On the floor. *A small pile of mandarin peels.*

I turned white as a glove.

There was something about them. The way they curled this way and that. Their orangeness. The way they *sat there looking up at me.*

And into my head rushed the thought: Cleaners would have been here on the weekend!

They would not have missed a pile of mandarin peels! So how did they get there?

The answer was clear as a ghost. It was the ghost.

Now, look, I am not a stupid girl.

I did not shout to all around me, "Hey! The ghost has left some mandarin peels!"

I knew that would not help my cause — both in relation to the ghost and as a human being generally.

And yet I also knew that the ghost had left those peels, *and it had done so to get my attention.* (Probably it had read about the drama rehearsal on the notice board and knew I'd be coming by this way.)

I continued on to rehearsal but my heart was curling and twirling like peels, and my lip was twitching so hard that I had to blow my nose.

I did tell Lydia and Cass about the mandarin peels when we were alone later that day. Their reactions were predictable. They are kind friends, but they can laugh hard.

8.

That day, Mum collected William and me from school. Everything was cheerful. William was excited because he thought he might have broken his toe. Mum was in her happy mood because that's her way these days. I think she really likes us (her children). She kept turning around in her belt to tell us that we're gorgeous. And then adding joyfully, "And you were such *ugly little babies!*"

That was harsh but fair. I've seen the photos. As babies, William and I both looked like profiteroles.

Anyway, then Mum told us she'd been thinking about baking cookies for us. She asked if we would mind discussing the pertinent issues in cookie baking.

We discussed cookies all the way home, and by the time we arrived, we had agreed that, instead of Mum baking cookies, William would make his *Chocolate Chestnut Torte with Cognac Mousse.*

So, William sat up on the kitchen bench, to give his broken toe a break (ha-ha), and Mum and I collected the ingredients and handed them to him.

I talked about the ghost, and William was especially interested by the mandarin peels. "The *peelings* gave you a *feeling*," he said, and pointed out that this rhymes.

I didn't know what he was trying to say but I was still impressed. For a thirteen-year-old boy, William can be very philosophical, and his mind works in various directions.

Mum, meanwhile, asked a lot of questions, and I began to notice that they were all focused on the Art Rooms. Once, years ago, my mother *lived* in the Art Rooms — back when our school was a boarding school — so I assumed her questions were nostalgic. But then I realized she was suggesting that the creaking might be connected with the renovations, and that the cold patches might be glitches with the new air-conditioning.

Not ghosts at all.

But just as William was putting his *torte* in the oven, Mum turned to me with a serious face and said, "But renovations can't explain the fruit peels."

The whole thing made me feel strangely lovely.

9.

The next day, Tuesday, my second message from the ghost.

This was the day of the Athletics Carnival and William and I were running late. Something to do with Dad needing to take his car in for a service. Anyway, we ended up walking to school.

My thoughts, as we walked, seemed somehow exciting. I couldn't figure out why. I was looking forward to something — but what? I knew I would see Cassie win some races that day, as she is a talented sprinter, but no, it was more than that.

Was I hoping for a message from the ghost?

Not really.

It was something else.

Then I remembered: Amelia and Riley were going to do something spectacular.

They have been spectacular, at regular intervals, since the day they arrived at our school, and it was time for the next dazzling.

But what would it be? Sprinting? No. That was unacceptable. If Amelia could sprint she might beat Cassie in a race. She would have to choose something else. Thanks all the same.

Maybe shot put? She seems very strong.

No. She's too beautiful for shot put. So, what? And what about Riley? Javelin? Like a hunter!

Anyway, these were my cheerful thoughts as William and I took the shortcut across Castle Hill Heritage Park.

And there they were.

That's the strange thing about Amelia and Riley — often, I'll be thinking or talking about them — and suddenly, there they are!

Spooky.

(Although, to be fair, I do think and talk about them a lot.)

They were in the Heritage Park. William and I were walking a winding path, and they were on the grass amidst the trees. Maybe the distance from me to my front door. Hm. But you don't know that distance. Never mind. Anyway, I could see them standing very close together. Amelia was talking. She was looking down at her feet as she talked, and Riley was watching her intently. They might have heard our footsteps on the path, but if so they did not look up. I walked the path, watching them openly, and they did not turn at all.

I did not call out. That would have been like calling to a television screen.

No, that's wrong: It was more like *they* were real life and *I* was the television screen.

Either way, calling seemed impossible. I left the park, looking back over my shoulder — and their intense conversation continued in the shadows of the trees.

Anyway, I carried on to school, and the Carnival. It was a relaxing day. Lyd and I sat on picnic blankets with various people, and Cass kept joining us after winning races. She'd lean over, holding on to her thighs, breathing quickly, her face pale pink. Then she'd turn into Cass again, smile, and help herself to my chips. I was honored to share them with her.

Afterward, I felt emotional because I knew it would be my last School Athletics Carnival ever.

Lyd pointed out that I'd never competed in a single event, and had sometimes skipped Athletics Carnivals altogether, but that was not the point. I saw Bindy Mackenzie taking photos for the yearbook and she was doing artistic shots of the bedraggled streamers on the grass, and it almost made me cry.

Anyway, we had a rehearsal that afternoon, so we walked over to the Art Rooms. On the way, Bindy took a photo of Lyd, Cass, and me — Lyd and I held Cass's trophies in the air, and pointed at her. That almost made me cry too.

"What if there's nowhere for Cassie to run when we finish school?" I said.

But Lyd said there would always be treadmills.

*   *   *

Anyway, we reached the Art Rooms and wandered toward the auditorium.

Then, just as I had calmed my emotions, it happened.

A feather landed on my shoulder.

This is not a joke.

I felt something — a very faint tickling sensation, and I looked down at my shoulder and there it was. A white feather.

I screamed. As you might also scream if someone dropped a feather on your shoulder.

Lyd and Cass stopped, and stared at me questioningly. I looked up and around, down and sideways — but there was no explanation for the feather. (I should make it abundantly clear that we were now *inside* a building, not outside where birds might fly by dropping feathers.)

The feather simply materialized. And there it was.

I looked quickly to see what room we were outside — would it be Room 27B?

No. It wasn't. It was Room 39M.

Cass said "Huh," and we looked at her, and she said, "No, nothing, it's just that 3 times 9 is 27, and M is a kind of a sideways B, so in a way 39M *is* 27B. Spiritually speaking."

I gasped.

Lyd and Cass practically murdered themselves with their laughing.

And then we were interrupted because others were arriving for the rehearsal. Some Brookfielders appeared first, and behind them Amelia and Riley.

I suddenly realized that they had not turned up to the Athletics Carnival at all.

I was openly astonished.

And yet, also, a part of me was not surprised at all. That morning at the Heritage Park, they'd seemed so intense, so *real* — how could two such *real* people come to a high school carnival?

You may not understand what I mean.

But, you should. For, you see, school and school carnivals are all about playing: They're not real. Whereas, reality is.

It suddenly seemed impossible that Amelia and Riley were even *here*.

I looked back over my shoulder to check that they weren't a hologram, but no, there they were. Two regular students, walking along to a drama rehearsal.

Impossible.

And then something else struck me: Something was different about Amelia and Riley.

Their faces were the same as usual — that watchful and expectant look, the faintest smiles.

But, for the first time, I could see the gap between them — the one that Lydia says she saw the day they first came to our school.

I looked away from them, and back to the feather in the palm of my hand.

Two impossibilities: Amelia and Riley at my school. A feather from a ghost in my hand.

And we all carried on to the rehearsal.

10.

Wednesday, no word from the ghost. It gave me a break. This was lucky as we got our report cards that day so I was very busy having mood swings.

On Thursday, the ghost was back with its third message.

The school was holding a Tertiary Information Day for Year 12, and it took place in the Assembly Hall in the Art Rooms. I was walking to the bathroom, taking a break from the excess information, when I saw an object lying on the ground.

It was a book.

It's true that the book was not outside Room 27B; however, it was ancient, or anyway old, with a hard cover. The cover was falling away, as if it did not want to have anything to do with the book anymore.

You couldn't blame it. The pages were flaking, spotty, and yellow, and more to the point, the book was called *The Complete History of Politics in Australia*.

There was a square of paper glued to the first page:

```
PRESENTED TO
SANDRA WILKINSON
FOR EXCELLENCE
IN PENMANSHIP,
1952
```

Clearly, the ghost had left the book here for me to find. It was old for a start, which was a clue. Ghosts are old. And the "penmanship" thing — well, that was the ghost's idea of a joke. It was referring to the way it made my pen roll across my desk earlier in the term.

Yes, I thought, *ha-ha, ghost. Funny.*

But as I stood there, alone in the corridor, my heart beating strangely, holding that old book, pinching my lip to make the twitching calm down — I suddenly looked behind me.

Why?

I don't know.

A whisper in the air.

A presence.

Something watching me.

Nothing was there so I looked back down at the book.

What was the ghost trying to say with this book?

I hoped it wasn't saying I should read it.

I now reach a point in the story that I wish I did not have to reach.

But I have to. It's part of it.

I think I said before that I am not a stupid girl?

Well, turns out, I am. Sometimes, anyway.

In particular, when alcohol has been consumed. (By me, I mean; I'm quite smart when other people drink.)

Well, I suppose I should just say it.

That very night, there was a party at Lydia's place. It was a HUGE party, a madness of a party. And I made one of those random decisions to go psycho. I mean, to drink everything my eye could see, and some things that my eye could not.

This is not my fault. My head was in a pattern of confusion. Stupid ghost throwing peelings and feathers and books at me! Stupid Amelia and Riley being too real and too impossible! (I know. That was unfair. But it confused me.)

And most of all: stupid school for holding a Tertiary Information Day.

See, the thing is, I have always known that I want to be a lawyer, just like my parents. And yet there I was at the Assembly Hall, surrounded by *other options*. Maybe I wanted to do Communications at UTS and become a journalist? Maybe I wanted to study crop rotation and become a farmer? Well, probably not, but you get the point, which is: *Maybe I was wrong about becoming a lawyer.* Who knew?

Life is confusing enough as it is.

I felt very angry.

And so, at the party — well, you don't need a list of what I drank. Let's just say that it seemed like a good idea at the time.

Actually, it was a good idea. I felt a *lot* better. I had a fantastic time. So many intense conversations! Laughed so hard! Danced and danced. Floated on the inflated dolphins in the indoor pool, watching the stars through the glass — it's so moody and steamy in Lydia's pool pyramid. At some point, Amelia climbed up one of Lydia's chimneys, climbed back down, went straight to the kitchen, and started getting ingredients from the cupboard. As if something in the chimney had told her what to do. We were following, watching, laughing. Turned out she was making a tiramisu! We laughed so hard at her serious, sooty face as she calmly reached for things around the kitchen. Next thing, she and Riley were dancing in the shadows — laughed some more — they are such cool, understated dancers — suddenly, I thought: Why am I upset about the ghost?! I love it. It has *chosen* me! And who cares that Amelia and Riley are impossible? I love them! And who cares what I become? I could be anything! Maybe I would be an astronomer! Such beautiful stars through the pyramid! Or maybe I'd get into swimming pool repair?

And so on. You get the point —

and then —

then, I don't know what happened.

All I can say is that by the next day, two new posts had appeared on my blog.

I mean, I had written them. When?

Well, I do have a vague memory of writing them. I was at home. I don't know how I got home. I remember typing at my computer with this mad, singing happiness in my head and feeling convinced that I was writing a masterpiece. I expected a billion comments. Exactly a billion. I worried the comments would crash the site.

Here is the first of the two entries I wrote that night:

My Journey Home
It is 3 A.M. and I just swam home from a party.
Stupid? No.
I have an important decision: I LOVE SEALS!
Yay! I feel so ☺ about it. I am going to be a SEAL TRAINER!
YAYA AYAYAY
And every day when I feel ☹ my seal will make me ☺ — clap your hands and splash me seal splash no not so much you're messing up my hair.
Oh, seal, stupid seal.
It's like a giant slug.

I hate it,

But salmon and El Salvador. Connection, please?

Seb and Lydia, when, oh when will your love be revealed to each other — I mean, GET BACK TOGETHER, ALREADY — THE UNIVERSE NEEDS YOUR LOVE —

I feel sideways.

oh. I fell asleep. Good night.

So, that was the first entry.

I think there is no need for you to comment on it.

Actually, the world didn't think so either. I didn't get a billion comments, I got two. They were:

CalypsoAngel said . . . Yeah, what's the story with Seb and Lydia? Cos if she doesn't want him a lot of girls at Brookfield'll take him, thanx. Incl. me.

Sasha345 said . . . Me 2.

Half an hour later, I must have woken up again. And I guess I'd had a mood swing in my sleep. Because this time, I'm sorry to say, I wrote:

My Journey Home

Look. If I had a dollar for every ghost I'd ever seen? I would not have any dollars. DON'T YOU GET IT! I've never even seen a ghost before this year. (And not even this year, actually, just got messages from it, but that is a point beside.) THE FACT IS, I AM NOT A GHOST GIRL!!!! I am alive! So ha-ha, no but DO I wander thru cemeteries at midnight making coffee for the dead people? NO. I do not. And do I dress like a goth? ARE YOU KIDDING ME? no way. Why are there EVEN GOTHS? i mean, sometimes IT HURTS MY EYES TO LOOK AT

THEM. They shld go on Extreme Makeover!! *they could be beautiful those goths*. If they just got some color in their cheeks. Why were they born with no blood? It's not fair.

It Makes me cry

But I am too ANGRY to cry!

Why? Thank you for asking. *I will tell you on my journey home!!!!!!!!!* no. I will not.

oh, why am I angry?

And tonight Amelia and Riley were talking about the taste of colors, and the flavor of weather, and we all started seeing things differently, including me, cos now I am thinking that the color of my anger is MAGENTA WITH BIG BLACK SPECKS, and they make us see everything different when they talk, Amelia and Riley, and that is ALL BECAUSE OF ME.

I MAKES NO SENSE AND THAT'S BECAUSE THERE'S A GHOST IN THE ART ROOMS AND I CAN FEEL IT IN MY LIP AND UNDERNEATH MY FINGERNAILS.

And sometimes in my belly button too. (I hate the word naval. what's the navy got to do with anything.)

k.

good night. have beautiful, beautiful dreams about swans and japan. love from emily.

I guess I phoned Lyd and Cass after I wrote that, and woke them, because these are the comments:

Lyd said . . . Ok, Em, here's the comment you want. I've read it and you're absolutely right. It's a masterpiece. Now delete it, and delete the post before it, and go to sleep.

Cass said . . . And drink a lot of water right now. You are going to feel like total shit in the morning.

Em said . . . Oh, Cass, you're so beautiful. You run so fast! When you run. And you sing so fast! No. That is incorrect. So are you, Lyd, you're a goddess. I love you guys. But, Lydia, I HATE you.

Lyd said . . . Ok.

Em said . . . Cos, when are you and Seb getting back together?

Lyd said . . . Delete that too. Can you cut out talking about my private life on your blog? I love you too, but I'm getting kinda mad too, and we need to do normal online talking and stop talking on your blog, and we need to go to sleep.

Em said . . . I can't delete comments, I don't know how, just as YOU cannot delete Seb from your heart! Can you? No. And I know he asked for a break last year and so normally I would want to TEAR HIM TO PIECES, doing that to you, but he kind of had a point. You were sometimes a difficult, distant girlfriend, and sometimes a bit sharp-edged, which is NOT your fault, it's just you have PASSION and DEPTH and I know you were ALSO a generous, sparkling, loving girlfriend cos that's who you are also, and otherwise Seb would. Um. I forget.

Lyd said . . . Cass, can you make her stop?

Cass said . . . Em, answer your phone.

Em said . . . Is it cos he's a Brookfield boy? So you want to kind of move up a notch? I didn't think you had class prejudices, Lyd. But do you think they ever get their hair cut? Brookfielders I mean.

Cass said . . . Em, quit while you're ahead.

Lyd said . . . What makes you think that she's ahead?

Em said . . . And their shoes? Why do they not floss their shoes.

Em said . . . Okay. Shhh. Great talking to you guys. I am SO going to sleep. You should too.

I slept in until after two the next afternoon, missing school (well, not actually *missing* it, like the way you miss your mum when she's away, but you know what I mean), and by the time I got up it was too late to delete the blogs. They'd been seen. There were already practically a billion new comments under the above exchange.

They were the comments of angry Brookfielders and angry goths (but I think goths might always be angry, or anyway despairing) and people from all over the world making fun of my ghost and my belly button.

11.

The next couple of weeks were difficult. Lyd and Cass forgave me because they are the best, but everybody else was laughing at me, including Lyd and Cass.

I was scared that the Brookfielders at drama would be hostile, but they were gentle and kind as if I had some kind of mental deficiency. That was worse.

And worst of all? This happened.

Well, you remember that Mr. Ludovico had to sign my application form for Law? The form was due at the end of the term, and I was worried because he still hadn't given it back to me. I knew other people whose forms *had* been signed by Mr. L, so why not mine? I couldn't sleep, I was so scared that he might be planning to refuse to sign it.

But I also couldn't ask him. The fact is, ever since the day when he was standing in the doorway while I talked about him, I had been finding it hard to look at him (harder than usual, I mean). Imagine overhearing someone say you had a laugh like an espresso machine! As deeply flawed as Mr. Ludovico is, I did not want him to hear that.

Eventually, though, I had to go and see him. Maybe he was waiting for an apology? Maybe he *hadn't* overheard anything in which case an apology would be a disaster? Maybe he had misplaced the form and had no idea I was waiting?

Time was running out.

I knocked on his office door.

"Em," he said, smiling his spectacles-glinting smile, and continuing to scribble on a random piece of paper. "You're here about your application form, I take it. Sit down."

I sat down. My heart thudded.

Eventually, he looked up from his scribbling. His smile turned upside down. It was sympathetic. My heart thudded more loudly.

He took out my application form, and held it up. The line for his signature was blank.

"You really think you have what it takes to be a lawyer?" he said.

Now my heart stopped still in its tracks. Before I could get it pumping enough to speak, he went on.

"Lawyers are adults." His voice was weirdly compassionate. "Let's take a look at what it means to be an adult, shall we? Adults are independent. You, Em, can't seem to take a step in any direction without Lydia and Cassie by your side. An adult would simply work hard to improve his marks. You, Em, make foolish requests for your marks to be altered. An adult is a rational being. *You* ran around last term obsessing over Amelia and Riley, and *this* term you're shouting to the world — including, I might add, on some childishly hysterical blogs — that there's a ghost living in the Art Rooms at this school!"

He paused to make his face look like an exclamation mark.

"You are every inch a child, Em," he said, sounding sad. "And I see no indications that you will ever grow up. Now, let me ask you this. Would I be doing my job — would I be *carrying out my responsibilities as principal of this school* — if I signed a form that allowed you to be a lawyer?"

My head was in a jumble. Angry sentences ran at me from every direction. They collided with pleading sentences, fell down, stood up, and turned into new sentences. They told me to grab Mr. Ludovico's stupid nose and twist it.

I didn't do that.

"There *is* a ghost living in the Art Rooms!" I cried. "And I can *prove* it."

Mr. Ludovico grinned. He looked happy.

"You go ahead and do that," he said. "Prove to me that there's a ghost in the Art Rooms, and I'll sign your form and get it to you in time. Deal?"

"Deal!" I cried, and marched out of the room.

I closed the door gently, like an adult.

I stopped in the corridor.

I was in serious trouble.

A twitch in my lip? Mandarin peels? A book and a feather?

Of course there wasn't a ghost.

I'm not as stupid as I sound, you know.

12.

Now you are confused.

If I didn't believe there was a ghost, why was I getting messages from ghosts? Telling everyone there was a ghost? Feeling angry with the ghost?

These are excellent questions, and your guess is as good as mine.

Or maybe not. What's your guess?

Here's mine.

A part of me *did* believe there was a ghost, even though I knew there wasn't one.

I can be a childish girl. That is honest of me to say, isn't it? I know I'm supposed to be an adult, and I guess I'll be one soon — but I feel like this is my last chance to be a child. So I'm kind of childish on purpose.

I miss being a child. Sometimes I'll be walking to a class and I'll feel a powerful need to play dress-up in Lydia's rec room. Or bake a cake in Cass's kitchen. Or get a "Secret Assignment" from Lyd in an envelope sealed with wax. I want these things so badly it almost makes me cry. I want to go to a slumber party, hold a torch up to my face, have a séance, tell a ghost story, have Cass creep up behind me and breathe on the back of my neck so I scream like a police siren.

I'm scared of the future and the adult world so I want that childish spookiness to return. Where you make yourself afraid, but all the time you know that it's just imaginary, and you're safe.

Maybe the reason I'd been *so* caught up with the ghost — and written that angry blog about it — was that nobody else was playing along.

I was alone in my childishness. Everyone else was being grown-up.

So when Mr. Ludovico accused me of being a child, it was like he had reached inside my heart to my most profound fears: that I *am* too childish; that I won't cope in the real world; that I can't be a lawyer, not without Lyd and Cass by my side.

That is why I lost my mind and declared I could prove there was a nonexistent ghost.

Now, if I wanted to study Law, I was going to have to do that.

Maybe I am as stupid as I sound.

13.

I couldn't tell Lyd and Cass about my dilemma. I had to do it on my own. Like an adult.

Ironically, just as I had acknowledged to myself that there was no ghost, ghostly things kept happening to me.

A faint smell of lilac talcum powder kept drifting by, and no one but a ghost would wear lilac talcum powder.

Once I smelled sausages burning. (Not sure if that was the ghost.)

One day, I was in the upstairs bathroom in the Art Rooms and felt something sting the side of my cheek. I looked up. A slow, steady drip . . . drip . . . drip of ice-cold water was falling from the ceiling above me.

The man at the Maintenance Office looked surprised when I told him about it.

"Water dripping from up there? But there's no reason why . . ." Then he lost interest and went back to studying his books. (The maintenance man plans to be an airline pilot.)

My childish mind exclaimed that all these things were mysterious, inexplicable phenomena, and therefore pointed directly to a ghost!

My realistic mind said, no, they don't, Em.

None of my minds believed that they would count as proof of a ghost for Mr. Ludovico.

I realized I'd have to set up some infrared recording equipment on 24-hour time delay in multiple locations around the Art Rooms and hope to catch some kind of ghostly activity on film.

But who even knows what I mean by that? Not me.

14.

I thought it might help if other people in my year believed in my ghost. Then I could point out to Mr. Ludovico that I was not unique in my childishness.

The best way to do this, I decided, was to give the ghost a more menacing image. So far, it had been innocuous — friendly, even. A fruit-eating ghost who reads history books? Why *would* anybody waste time believing in that?

So, I wrote a new blog entry.

My Journey Home

On my journey home today, I was looking at my shiny, black shoes, and they reminded me of cockroaches.

Moving on. More news on the Ashbury ghost. I was washing my hands in the third floor bathrooms today when I felt a thwack on the back of my head. A curious force propelled me across the room to the mirror where red writing began to appear, slowly, and with a dripping effect as if it were blood.

The writing said: *"HELP ME.*

HELP ME . . ."

I ran from the room as fast as I could, but when I returned, moments later, with the authorities . . . the writing had disappeared.

Thanks.
Signing off now,
Emily

1 Comment

Yowta772 said . . . Em, I love ya, but this entry is complete and total bull.

Yowta772 was correct.

It was all lies. Although, to be fair, shiny, black shoes do remind me of cockroaches sometimes.

Anyway. So. That didn't help.

15.

What if I tried a different strategy? Found a list of dead people with compelling reasons to haunt the Art Rooms and went to Mr. L with that?

I typed into Google: "Ashbury Art Rooms Used to Be Old House Who Died in It? Who Might Be Ghost Now?"

I got nothing.

I knew I was destined for that scene in the movies where the hero sits in a dark library, winding the handle on a clunky machine, scrolling through old newspapers and then suddenly! What's this? Report of fire in the Old Ashbury Mansion? Somebody *died* in the fire? Suspicious circumstances! And so on.

I knew that was my destiny, but I was (and am) a very busy girl.

I had no time for destiny.

Here is a blog entry I wrote around this time.

My Journey Home

My journey home, well, look, I have three assessment tasks, two exams, three essays, one folder of questions, one drama script (to help write), one haircut (to get from a hairdresser), one birthday afternoon tea at my Auntie June's in five minutes (to go to), one party at Lyd's place (to go to after that), and if that were not enough, I am consuming all my time trying to persuade my parents to buy me a car.

As for Auntie June's birthday party, don't get me started on that. Older people should stop celebrating birthdays. Don't they realize that they're already old? All they're achieving by having more birthdays is making themselves even older. What's to celebrate.

As for my parents' excuses for not buying me a car, don't get me started on THOSE either. Apparently, they're worried that I might not know the value of things. I know exactly how much things cost because I shop all the time. So. There goes that argument.

"I'm surprised you two are such successful lawyers when you make arguments like this," I said.

This caused Mum's and Dad's faces to distort as they tried

to imprison their laughter, and I have neither the time nor the inclination for distorted faces, thanks.

What was I talking about?

Yes! My journey home.

Look, there is just no time for journeying.

Thank you and good night.

I don't know if you can sense the anger in that blog entry, but trust me, it was there.

The fact is, Year 12 is stressful enough without the burden of Mr. Ludovico and a nonexistent ghost.

16.

Then something intriguing happened.

It happened during a party at Lyd's house.

It was a Wednesday and I remember thinking: *This is not much of a party.* People were talking and laughing too loudly, trying to force it into partyness. You can't force a party. I went into the kitchen and somebody had spilled a whole bag of rice onto the floor and just left it there. Someone else was sitting up on the bench, blowing cigarette smoke through an open window, and cold air was blowing back into the room, making the central heating pointless.

Back in the living room, I accidentally started talking to Astrid, and had to listen to a very boring story about some injustice to do with the kilt she is making for Textiles and Design. I looked around the room — Lyd and Seb were sitting side by side on a couch, their feet up on the coffee table, heads tipped back onto the top of the couch, both laughing. That seemed like a positive step but I wished they could shift it my way.

This was around midnight and I made a decision: As soon as Astrid reaches the final button on this kilt of hers, I'll call a taxi and go home.

And then the front door opened.

Amelia and Riley walked in.

The entire party changed. I am not kidding. Before they had even taken off their coats, it became a party.

Someone put on better music. A bunch of people who'd been out on the terrace spilled back inside, filling up the corners and the silences. Cassie wandered in from the games room and headed toward me. Toby Mazzerati (the solid wood boy) also headed toward me. Somebody, somewhere, started telling a story that was making people laugh hysterically. And Astrid's phone was ringing so she had to stop talking to me.

All this, just because Amelia and Riley arrived.

Well, look, I realize that's not why.

And yet, I think that it was.

Three hours later, I was trapped in a closet.

I'm not sure exactly how this happened. There was a point where I was talking with a Brookfield boy from the Drama, and thinking about hooking up with him. There was a point where I noticed he had sweat dripping down from his hair to his chin, and I said I had to go now, sorry. (When I got back he was already hitting on somebody else, which confirmed I had made the right decision.) There was a point where someone did a magic trick which involved setting something on fire. Then, right away, there was a point where people started screaming for a fire extinguisher. (Cass put the fire out with water from a flower vase.)

There was a point where I noticed Seb murmuring something to Lydia, and then Lydia stepped away — *always stepping away, she drives me mad* — and Seb's face fell and then turned cold and he walked out of the room. Then I heard Lyd speaking to people, in a voice with its own cold edge, and she was offering a tour of her mother's closets.

Now that was a surprise.

Lyd's mother has five interconnected closets. There are display cases for scarves and favorite gowns, and there are specially designed holders for underwear.

Cass raised her eyebrows at me: She was surprised too. One thing that Lyd's mum gets explosive about is Lyd letting friends into those closets. (We know this because the three of us used to spend a lot of time dressing up in there.)

And yet, next thing you knew, ten of us were in the shoe closet.

This is the smallest of the closets, and the central one.

A light went out, the sliding doors closed — and we were trapped.

It turned out to be strangely wonderful. Sometimes I am claustrophobic but I wasn't in the mood for hysterics so I decided not to be.

Some of my favorite people were there — Cass and Lyd (though, sadly, not Seb), and Toby Mazzerati, and Amelia and Riley, plus some other friendly nonentities from both Ashbury and Brookfield.

Once we had all tried the two doors (many times) and shouted, knocked, kicked, pounded, etc., then remembered our phones, and SMSed and phoned people at the party (but they'd turned the music so loud they couldn't hear anything, including their phones) and phoned people who were not at the party (but they just laughed — or got mad for being woken up) — and once we had tried more imaginative solutions such as climbing to the top of the shoe shelves and prying the ventilation cover loose — then we all just found places to sit and we relaxed.

One of the Brookfield boys had been wandering around all night with a bottle in each hand — I'd noticed him earlier — almost as if he knew he would soon be trapped in a shoe closet. So now he shared the vodka around, and that helped the mood. It was crowded enough that arms and legs brushed and touched, but I was next to Toby Mazzerati and he is a pleasure to brush.

It was not so crowded that I wanted to scream for personal space. Not at all.

It was dark but people kept splashing us with little bits of light, via their cigarette lighters and their mobile phones.

We talked about Lydia's mother, and how she had got famous as a soap star and then made some smart investments, and now directs many media entities and has many shoes.

We talked about the fact that Lydia's parents were not coming back until the end of the term, and *imagine if all our phone batteries went dead and we were trapped in the closet until then!* Lyd's mum would get back and say, "What's that terrible smell in my shoe closet? Do I really have such bad foot odor?" and then she'd open the door and *there'd be ten dead, rotting corpses* lying by her shoes!! She'd SCREAM and SCREAM and never wear another shoe again.

We all agreed that this would be a harsh but important lesson for Lydia's mum — she had valued her shoes so highly that she'd locked them up out of fear of losing them, and *ironically*, had ended up *losing* her most valuable possession, her daughter.

The closet would always be haunted, we said, by ten dead students — lost on the brink of our beautiful lives.

So then, of course, in the context of haunting, somebody mentioned my ghost.

There was some laughter at my expense.

I laughed too, but then I pointed out, forcefully, that every time I had English in Room 27B I ended up *covered* in goose bumps because it was so ghostly, icily cold in there and *how did they explain that?*

This was the point when Riley spoke.

He said, "You get goose bumps?"

Now, here I should say that both Riley and Amelia had joined in the earlier conversations — about Lyd's mum, and designer shoes, and starving corpses — now and then. Not much, but enough so they did not seem like silent presences. However, when Riley said, "You get goose bumps?" he said it in his Riley voice.

Amelia also has an "Amelia voice."

These are the voices they use in certain conversations. It's a voice that seems to tip from their mouths at an angle like a children's slide. A voice that has a strange sort of suspense in it so that people turn toward them quickly.

Often, the voice begins as here — with Riley or Amelia asking a simple question of the person talking. This makes the person feel strangely special. The person feels as if Riley or Amelia has caught onto something extraordinary about them. The person's heart stops for a moment, and the person thinks: *Yes, actually, I do get goose bumps! I do! Um. Doesn't everyone?*

And then the person thinks: *How do I answer this question?*

In the closet, the only answer I could think of was: "Yes."

But it didn't matter. Riley and Amelia were interested in my goose bumps. They wanted to know how often I got them, what they feel like, what they look like, where on my body they are.

Amelia, or maybe Riley, talked about why we get goose bumps. Not in a lecturing voice — just as an aside as if we probably already knew this. It turns out that in the very olden days, people used to be covered in long hair like orangutans. When it was cold, all the tiny muscles on their skin would make the hair stand up, so they'd get warm.

These days, as you may know, we don't have long hair on our bodies — if we did, we'd be spending a fortune on waxing — but our bodies still think that we do. So all the little muscles still stand up when it's cold, and that's goose bumps.

The way they talked about this made me feel strangely excited. As if getting goose bumps was a kind of time travel.

From there, Amelia and Riley navigated the conversation until we were talking about coldness itself. People told stories about being very cold — not just skiing in Canada (like I have, and trust me, it's COLD), but also about the coldness of fevers, and a sudden splash of water on the back of your neck. And the coldness you feel toward people you used to care about when they hurt you. And the cold things people do. Somebody remembered a story about a man whose wife was dying, and he got the funeral director to measure her up for her coffin — *even though she was still alive.* That was cold.

This was not just Amelia and Riley talking, by the way — it was everybody — but Amelia and Riley make people more amazing. People remember things they never knew they knew. If you get what I mean. Stories they'd forgotten. And all the time, Amelia and Riley listen so intently and ask questions like they really care. Everybody starts to *feel* intriguing.

And then, Amelia (or maybe Riley) asked questions about my ghost. They did not laugh. Their questions were serious. I admit they didn't seem very interested in the mandarin peels and feathers — but they were fascinated by the coldness.

Amelia said she never gets cold in Room 27B, but this didn't seem to make her doubt me. It seemed to make her *believe.*

Riley wondered why ghosts are cold.

"Maybe ghosts are shadows," he said. "Shadows are cold."

And then we talked about shadows.

I cannot remember what we said about shadows, although I do remember Toby Mazzerati being very intense about fetching, starving, black holes, and ships.

In his mind this was all connected to shadows. It made absolutely no sense, but at the time, with that alcoholic beverage in my bloodstream, Toby's words seemed profound. I remember I hugged him and promised that there is no such thing as black holes. (I don't think there is. Is there? Hmm. I might be wrong about that. Never mind.) Anyway, my friend Toby — sometimes he seems so sad. I wanted to cheer him up.

And then, suddenly, there was a knock on the closet door. It was Astrid — she must have finally got my text — and Lydia was calling out instructions on how to release us — and then we were free!

I went home feeling beautiful, in love with every person in the closet, and with a head that was brimful of shadows.

17.

After that, things began to change.

I didn't notice right away, but over the next few days I began to overhear people talking, quite seriously, about the Ashbury ghost. Once, two girls asked me if I'd felt the ghost lately.

They weren't being funny.

It was the strangest thing.

It was as if Amelia and Riley had made the ghost real. The way they had talked about it in the closet had been so serious and respectful — so now that respect was billowing out across the school.

It was not enough to go to Mr. Ludovico with, but it sure was soothing.

18.

One day, near the end of a drama rehearsal, somebody suggested that a plant would look good in a particular scene. The actor could water the plant as she talked, and this would be symbolic of her taking a shower or something else equally ridiculous. Anyway, I remembered the potted plant outside the lower photography lab, and ran to get it.

I felt like a break anyway.

It was very quiet in the corridors. Dusk was in the windows. I could hear my footsteps on the carpet. I could see the door to Room 27B just ahead of me, so there was the twitch in my lip, of course — but I also felt something else. Something new. As if the twitch was also in the center of my *chest*, but this twitch had a handle and somebody was turning, tightening it. Also — this will sound strange — I felt as if the dusk was creeping through the windows and shadowing my eyes.

I thought: *What's going on?*

Then I realized what it was.

It was fear. I felt frightened.

I slowed a little — and at that exact moment, something touched my ankle. It was a soft, gentle whisper of a touch. As if someone lying on the floor at my feet had reached out a hand and stroked my ankle.

I was too terrified to scream. (And that is really saying something. I like screaming.) I could only make this weird, gasping sound with an element of yelping in it. (I'm ashamed to say.)

Then I looked down. No scary stranger on the floor.

A white handkerchief.

It had got tangled around my shoe as my footsteps slowed and had somehow wrapped around my ankle.

I laughed but my cheeks were still weird from the terror so the laugh didn't come out right.

I picked up the handkerchief. I don't like people who use hand-kerchiefs. I mean, why not use a tissue to blow your nose? I think they want to carry snot around.

I held the hanky by the corner, but it seemed clean. Also, it seemed old — the white was not bright, and the lace was frayed. And there was some kind of swirlingness on it, which I believe is entitled "embroidery."

I put it in my pocket, but I'm sorry to say, I was too frightened to go on. I ran back to the rehearsal as fast as I could.

19.

This was real fear.

This was not my childish, imaginary spookiness.

Here was the difference: Amelia and Riley had believed in my ghost.

And they weren't playing.

A real ghost is a whole other thing.

20.

The next day, a window in Room 27B fell onto somebody's hand. It was somebody I don't like very much — Saxon Walker (he used to be okay but the last year or so he's turned into one of those guys who says mean things to girls, pretending to be funny) — and he was trying to force the window up even though I had specifically told him I was cold — and then suddenly a rope snapped and the window rushed down with a BANG onto his hand.

Wow. It must have hurt.

He tried to be brave but I think if he'd been alone he'd have cried. His face went white! And afterward, his hand was swollen and purple. (Then he got a bit annoying, talking about how the bones were probably broken, but I doubt it.)

I looked at his pale face, and the smell of lilac talcum powder drifted by. For some reason, that strange, sweet smell wafting by while windows crashed onto hands — that terrified me more than anything.

21.

Does all this terror mean that I now believed in the ghost?

I honestly don't know.

A part of me continued to think that there is no such thing — this part scared me, because I knew it meant I had to prove the impossible to Mr. L.

Another part kept thinking of Amelia and Riley talking ghosts and shadows in the closet — making the ghost real — and that part also scared me, because, you know, ghosts.

Basically, everywhere I turned in my mind I found terror.

It was exhausting. I tried to behave like an ordinary person but one day at lunch, Cass said, "What's going on with your face, Emily?" and Lyd said, "Yeah. What's up with the way your eyes keep opening wide like that?"

I guess that my terror was on display.

They looked at me with such kind, open interest, waiting for my reply, that I burst into tears and told them the whole story.

About Mr. Ludovico and everything he'd said.

They were so angry! There was a flurry of sentences from them:

"He can't *stop* you getting into Law!"

"He can't make you *prove* something *impossible!*"

"He's getting *revenge* for what he overheard you say, and he thinks *you're* the childish one?"

"Too *dependent* on us? Does he not know what *friendship* is?"

"No, he doesn't. Because he doesn't have any friends."

"He's probably *jealous* of you because you *do* have friends!"

"This is such an abuse of power."

"He has a *serious* God complex."

"You are *not* childish, you've just got an imagination."

"And imagination is *exactly* what a lawyer needs."

"Don't worry, we'll take care of it."

"We'll go see him."

"We're gonna fix this, Em."

So, that was fantastic.

But I said I wanted to resolve this issue on my own.

"Don't let him mess with your head with that thing about being dependent on us," said Lyd. "You're supposed to get help from your friends when you're in trouble."

I said thank you, but it felt important to me to do this alone.

"Maybe I'll actually prove there *is* a ghost," I said.

Hm. Well. (They said.) They glanced at each other. They looked at me closely.

If you change your mind, they said, we're here.

That night, I felt so much better that I wrote a new entry in my blog:

My Journey Home

Today I am feeling incandescent. I don't know exactly what that word means, but never mind. That's the word I'm using.

As you may know, there is a ghost living in the Art Rooms of my school (Ashbury High). But who is this ghost? And what does it want?

If you, dear readers of this blog, have any information about this ghost, please let me know as soon as possible.

Because I think it is time for the ghost to *begin its journey home*. Thank you and good night.

15 Comments

SunflowerSeed said . . . Didn't our Art Rooms used to be a mansion or something? So it'll be someone who kicked it back in the ole days.

Em said . . . Thanks, SunflowerSeed, but I was thinking we need to open our minds to other possibilities. People did not just die in the olden days. They continue to die up to the present.

DeannaG said . . . LOL

Em said . . . I don't get it. What's funny? You think that death is funny, do you, Deanna? Well, hm, maybe you should just try it sometime.

Yowta772 said . . . It could be some ex-Ashbury student still pissed about getting accused of cheating when it was actually the guy beside him who cheated off *him*. Injustice. It's a killer.

CarrieMW said . . . It could be a former teacher who used to get called names by students behind her/his back, and now she/he wants revenge on Ashbury students for all time? :(In which case, I don't think there's anything you can do about it, Em, except maybe watch your back?

Mark said . . . Or a student who got shafted/ignored by hot, popular girls like you, Em. So therefore I repeat CarrieMW's advice.

Billiej said . . . Em, have any students DIED at your school?!! I suggest you get a list of all students who have died in or near the Art Rooms, and that will help to narrow your search.

Sasha345 said . . . But it cld be sbdy who left schl then lived til old age then wanted to go BACK to schl cos schl days were the best days of their life eg me, cos I plan to haunt Ashbury for eternity cos I can't get enough of the place *ROTFL*

BenB said . . . Em, didja check whether any students from our school have gone missing recently? If someone's been murdered and bricked up behind a wall while the renovations were happening — *the perfect time for a crime* — then it'll be that particular student fo sho.

Em said . . . Ben, I feel like we would have heard about it if one of the students from our school was missing. And the smell of the corpse? Also, I think this is a ghost from a long time ago — e.g., it has old books and handkerchiefs and feathers and it likes history. But thanks. And thanks to everyone else for your comments.

FloralNightie said . . . Surely it is K. L. Mason Patterson, feeling angry about the way his money has been spent on "disadvantaged neighboring schools"?

Magicmustard said . . . Renovations always piss off ghosts. You need to tear them down (the renovations). Have you got the authority?

Yowta772 said . . . If the ghost wanted to tear the building down, wouldn't it have done it by now? Ghosts are just misty and floaty, right? It probably can't do more than creaking sounds and minor structural damage.

Shadowgirl said . . . Em, are you still the only person who has contact with the ghost? You must feel very alone.

These comments came through quickly, right after I posted the blog. So I was sitting there reading and responding as they arrived. I knew a lot of the people — they're from Ashbury as you might have noticed. But some were strangers to me. (Yowta772, for instance — who is *that*? Always around!)

And Shadowgirl . . .

I have no idea who that is. She's a blogger on Glasshouse — I clicked on her name — but *her blog can only be accessed by the blogger* (her). Which, I mean, go figure. What's the point? Keep a diary, already.

I ran down to the kitchen and found my parents making cinnamon toast, and after a while I started feeling warm and safe. I asked Mum if anybody had died while she was a student at Ashbury, and at first she misunderstood and started going through all the people who had died then including her grandmother and Elvis Presley — but when I got her to understand, she said no.

I was not disappointed.

I was glad to stop thinking about the ghost for the night. Maybe the mysterious Shadowgirl was just trying to be kind when she said *you must feel very alone*. But for some reason, her comment sent a chill right through me.

22.

The following event happened in Week 8 of the term.

(That's only two more weeks until the holidays, which, if you're getting tired of my story, cheer up, it's nearly over. Although, what's wrong with you? It's good.)

Anyhow, the event was this:

SOMEONE TOOK A PHOTO OF THE GHOST.

[Some space here to recover your balance.]

Yes. That is what I said. A photograph was taken of my ghost.

It was taken by the most reliable person in the history of the world, so there is no need to doubt, thank you very much: The person was Bindy Mackenzie.

That is: school captain, yearbook editor, smartest and most moral girl ever (also, coincidentally, almost-victim of a wicked murder plot last year) (but that is another story) (luckily not another *ghost* story) (as Bindy is still alive) (so therefore she is not a ghost).

Anyway, what happened was, Bindy had taken some photos for a two-page spread in the yearbook, about the renovations to the Art Rooms. Very fascinating, I'm sure. Early on the morning of this particular day, she and her friend Kee were sitting at a computer in the library, uploading the photos (which must have been extremely boring) (apparently, she'd taken over three hundred) (Bindy is a very thorough girl).

They were watching a slideshow of the photos when suddenly they both gasped aloud. (I don't know if it's possible to gasp un-aloud but never mind.)

They gasped. Their hearts careened and cantered like Kaimanawa wild horses. (That is a direct quote from Kee.)

They looked at each other — and then they both said: "Em."

(They were referring to me.)

They ran all over the school — they were pale and breathless when they found me — and rushed me back to the computer to show me . . .

A photograph of a face.

The face was behind the window.

The face had gleaming red eyes, a manic grin, and a bright, bright glow.

The face was not attached to a body.

There is more.

What window was the face behind? Guess.

A window in Room 27B.

Bindy remembers very clearly that this was where the window was. She also swears there was nobody there at the time. Certainly not a face without a body. She would have remembered that.

Plus, there were other photos of the same window, taken just before and after this one: *And the face is missing from those photographs.*

I looked at that photo and I felt cold with terror.

At the same time I felt fantastic.

Because, do you realize what this meant?

I had proof.

News of the photo rushed helter-skelter through the school.

Everyone who saw it blinked. At the very least, they blinked. It is not, I repeat, *not* a situation of: *Oh, yeah, maybe that's a face if I blur my eyes?* No. It is not. It is clearly, adamantly, undeniably, undoubtedly, unassuredly: A FACE.

I don't know if the ghost had hired a publicist and the campaign kicked off with that photo, or whether news of the photo opened eyes to its presence — either way, suddenly, everyone was having ghostly encounters in the Art Rooms.

By home room, five different people had told me they'd seen or felt something ghostly.

By lunchtime, it was at least twenty.

It was a wild and wonderful day. Everywhere I turned there was talk of the ghost. I think it would be correct to say that hysteria ran riot. Sudden noises made people gasp. Cold wind made them grasp the hand of the person beside them. You couldn't walk through the Art Rooms without hearing at least one shriek — followed by pounding footsteps or bursts of embarrassed laughter (because, for example, the person realizes they've just seen their own reflection in the glass of a classroom door and thought it was a ghost).

Now, this day happened to be the birthday of my friend Toby, and some people had organized a party for him. It was in the Student Recreation Room in the Art Rooms. We had balloons, streamers, party poppers, chocolate crackles, and cupcakes. (In other words, it was a "children's party" — people are holding a lot of "children's parties" this year, I've noticed — hmm, are others, like me, trying to "cling to a fading childhood"?)

Anyhow, we sang "Happy Birthday," and when Toby went to blow out the candles, Astrid stepped forward to help. I don't know why. I think she was overexcited. Anyway, she leaned forward to blow — and her hair caught on fire!

There was so much screaming!

Don't worry. It ended quickly. I just pressed the flames between my hands and they were gone.

But everyone was sure it was the ghost. People said the ghost was probably letting Astrid know she shouldn't blow out candles on another person's cake.

Toby was in a great mood, though, and couldn't stop laughing (once he knew that Astrid was safe).

I'm not certain that all of the ghost reports of that day were actually the ghost. The reports included:

- things going missing (including a school uniform from a locker!)
- things dropping from people's hands even though they were sure they were holding on to them tightly

- lockers that wouldn't open
- hair being unusually frizzy
- a toothache

I have to admit, a lot of these things can be explained as normal, day-to-day life rather than as paranormal activity.

However, there were *also* reports of:

- the dripping in the upstairs bathroom suddenly getting heavier and splattering the ground
- the distant sound of someone sobbing (and the people who heard that swear they could not find *anybody* sobbing even after looking very hard)
- doors banging suddenly even though there was no gust of wind
- a strange sensation of somebody breathing even though there was nobody there (a lot of people had this one)

So, that was more like it.

Over the next two weeks, I walked around feeling happy. I did not go directly to Mr. Ludovico with the photograph. I thought it best to let the ghost encounters multiply, so that, by the time I approached him, it would be incontrovertible.

He would probably apologize as he signed the form.

I smiled at him openly in Economics classes, and thought that I saw apology and/or respect behind his eyes. He must have heard about all the sightings! Everyone was talking about them.

I tried not to gloat.

The application form was due on the last day of term, so I continued gathering encounters, and recording them in a notebook, until the second to last day.

On that day — a Thursday — I would knock on the door to his office.

23.

The day arrived.

In the morning, my mother ran downstairs in her pajamas, just as Dad, William, and I were about to leave. (Mum sleeps in often now that she is not a frantic lawyer. It makes her even happier, if that's possible.)

"I remembered something," she called in a sleepy voice — and the three of us stopped at the front door and turned around. "Emily, you know how you asked me if someone had died when I was at Ashbury? Well, someone did."

"Are you saying," William interrupted, "Mum, are you saying you saw somebody die when you were at school and you have only just remembered this now? But where is the body?" My brother looked thoughtful.

Mum was stretching her arms like a sleepy child. "I was just lying there half-asleep and it came back to me," she said. "When I was at school, they used to *talk* about a girl who'd died back in the 1950s. She fell out of a window or something. People used to say she haunted the place."

A huge smile exploded onto Dad's face. "All this time Em's been talking about a ghost," he said to Mum, "and you didn't think it was relevant to mention that you'd heard about the ghost before?"

"There wasn't a shred of reliable evidence," said Mum. "As far as I was concerned, there was no ghost. Em's ghost is different."

"I was in the Art Rooms yesterday," murmured William. "I closed my eyes for a moment and the strangest pinpricks of light appeared behind my eyelids."

"There you go," said Mum, heading back upstairs. "That'll be Em's ghost."

At school, Lyd and Cass agreed to help me follow up on Mum's story. I was trembling with excitement: It was possible that my ghost had haunted here before! It was almost too much! I was very excited about going to see Mr. Ludovico.

But how do you find out about a dead girl from the 1950s?

The Internet was useless. Strange. How useless it is sometimes? And it gets so much acclaim.

Anyway, Cass suggested we try looking through old yearbooks. The librarian hunted them down for us.

It was genuine research! The three of us gathered around a table covered in piles of books, trying not to spend too much time saying, "ohhh," at the pictures of sweet historical people.

And then Lydia found it.

A two-page spread in a 1952 yearbook with the heading: *A Tribute to our Darling Sandy*. There was a blurred photo of a girl with a cute smile, a long fringe, a ponytail, and downcast eyes.

Cass started reading it out, and it was all about how much everyone adored Sandy, and how she herself adored vanilla ice cream and field hockey. (Hmm — selfish — should have adored the others back.) And what a tragedy it was, the tragic accident in which she tragically fell from a tragically dangerous window and tragically died. (The editor of that yearbook was no Bindy Mackenzie.)

I had a sudden thought: This was a two-page spread about a girl who died — and Bindy was doing a two-page spread about the Art Rooms when the ghost got itself into a photograph!!!! Coincidence? Surely not! (And even if it *was* a coincidence, well, what is a coincidence if not a sign of something awry? That's what my dad always says and it kind of makes sense.)

I felt chilled to the apple of my core.

And because I was busy chilling, I did not register at first that Cass had read out the girl's name:

Sandra Wilkinson.

"I've heard that name before," Lyd said.

And so had I.

It was the name in the old book I had found.

Presented to Sandra Wilkinson for Excellence in Penmanship, 1952

When I said this to Lyd and Cass — when I got the book from my locker and showed them — their faces changed.

Years ago, a girl had fallen and died. This year, her book had appeared in a corridor.

For the first time, they believed in the ghost.

24.

It was 3:30 P.M. on Thursday afternoon.

My mother had promised to personally deliver the signed application form the next morning. All I had to do was get it.

I knocked on Mr. Ludovico's office door.

I had a manila folder in my hands. It was labeled "The Ghost of Ashbury High — Evidence." Inside was: the photograph, twelve pages of notes recording ghostly encounters, and copies of the relevant pages from the old yearbook.

I smiled at Mr. Ludovico, sat down opposite him, and placed the file on his desk.

He glanced at it then back down at his work. He continued scribbling.

"Proof that the ghost exists," I said, in case the word "evidence" wasn't clear.

Mr. Ludovico kept writing.

"In the last few weeks," he said, still writing, "my school has been overrun with hysteria about your ghost. Students are refusing to enter the Art Rooms. Teachers can't get their classes to concentrate." Now he looked up at me. "You have infected my entire student body with your childishness."

He opened a drawer and took out my application form.

"There is no ghost," he said firmly, "and yet" — here, he laughed to himself — "if I didn't sign this form, your parents would be in my office in an instant. Taking some kind of legal action, no doubt. Not letting me get away with it! Protecting their precious little girl!"

He got out a pen, and scribbled his name on the blank line.

"I was always intending to sign it," he said, handing it over to me with another laugh. "Just thought I might try to teach you something about the real world first. Help you to grow up a little." He flicked the manila folder across the desk. "But it looks like you're a lost cause."

And he looked back down at his notes.

25.

The funny thing is that I'd gone into Mr. Ludovico's office expecting to walk out in tears. If he refused to sign the form, I thought, they would be tears of disappointment. If he signed the form, they would be tears of joy.

I did not walk out of his office in tears. I went straight to the bathrooms, locked the door, kept the form tightly folded in my pocket, and cried harder than I have in years.

26.

There was a party at Lyd's place that night.

By then, Lyd and Cass had retrieved their faces. I mean, they had stopped believing in my ghost. A short-lived belief, no?

It was a trick, they said. Someone must have found Sandra's book, and thought it would be funny to leave it lying around and see if we'd track down the story of her death and get spooked.

"Yeah, probably," I agreed.

Lyd and Cass looked surprised, and a little disappointed.

I did not tell them what had happened with Mr. Ludovico. I just said he'd signed the form (which was true), and they were happy.

There was a bunch of people in Lyd's living room — including Lyd, Cass, Seb, Astrid, Amelia, and Riley. (Not Toby, though. He'd stopped coming to parties. His absence was a small black hole in our lives, but of course, there's no such thing.)

So, it was around ten, and we were lying around on the couches, eating nachos. Everyone was talking about the ghost, and about Sandra Wilkinson, and about whether the ghost *was* Sandra.

Imagine falling out of a window and dying, people were saying. How sad! But also how stupid.

That kind of thing.

Some people agreed with Lyd and Cass — that it must be a hoax. But others were convinced of the ghostly connection.

"It's so *obvious*," Astrid said. "She died by falling out of a window?! Hell*o*? How much more *suss* do you guys need? And now she's trying to tell us she was murdered and we're not going to hear her cries for help?"

"There isn't a ghost," I said.

Astrid ignored me. She said she thought we should have a séance. (Sometimes Astrid is very "hands-on," as my mother would say. She's a "go-getter," as my father would say.)

We should sneak into the Art Rooms around midnight one day, she said, and bring a Ouija board, and call on Sandra.

"We'll ask who pushed her out the window, get that person put away if they're still even alive, which, who knows, they might be. And then poor Sandra can be at peace. It's so, like, effin' *simple*?" Astrid said.

Then Seb said, surprisingly, "Let's go now."

People turned to him with slow *why not?* expressions building on their faces.

I didn't think it was a good idea. "No," I said. "How could we even get in?"

Again Lyd and Cass looked at me with surprise. (We can get in anywhere.) (Cass has a talent with locks.)

So we tumbled into cars — I was pleased to see that Lyd got into Seb's car — and off we went.

27.

And now, here, in the final twist of this tale — a twist of epic proportions — on the very day that I lost all belief in the ghost — and in myself — well, the most terrifying event of them all took place.

You will be paralyzed with fear.

I suggest that you run to the bathroom now, before the paralysis sets in.

The hair will stand up on the back of your neck!

(But if you have hair on the back of your neck you should get dialysis. Is that the right word? Maybe not. Remove it anyway.)

Listen! Come closer! Closer!

Okay, not so close. Have a little respect for my personal space.

Close your eyes, picture a ghostly, shimmering effect, and then? Startle yourself with an image of me and my friends, filing into the Art Rooms auditorium late at night!

(We drifted straight there as it's where we usually go for rehearsals.)

At first, there were a lot of jokelike calls for Sandra, Sandy, Santa, Willski, and other terms of disrespect. Nobody had any candles to light, and not a Ouija board in sight, so conversation and people scattered around the room. Some people leaned against the window ledges, breathing mist onto the glass. Others climbed over rows of seats, or searched for lost treasure underneath the seats.

I overheard Seb say he was going to his car to get something.

Seb left the room.

I saw Lydia, across the room, follow him with her eyes. I felt my hope grow bright. I am a very intuitive girl and that moment, as I stood and watched Lyd's face — well, it became clear to me that she wanted Seb back. I also saw that she had decided to tell him this. (Do not doubt me. This is what I saw.)

I was feeling quietly pleased about this, and lost in my own thoughts — when I realized that Astrid was beside me.

I was surprised. It's uncommon to stand beside Astrid and not know she's there.

She breathed in slowly. It was clear she wanted to say something. I thought maybe she had another boy to talk about.

I was right.

She did.

I just didn't know it would be this boy . . .

"Em," she said in a very low voice. "Can I tell you a secret?"

Of course. I love secrets.

"I just, kind of like, can't stand keeping this a secret anymore?" she said, and then: "Well, you know, Seb? He and I are together. We hooked up at a party a while ago, and we're kind of like secretly together now."

[I leave you space to recover.]

[Maybe a bit more.]

I wished that I had some space like that of my own, actually, but Astrid was standing very close.

"You probably guessed already," she added.

Well. As I said a moment ago, I am a very intuitive girl, but no, I had not guessed.

The idea of Astrid and Seb together was as distant from my mind — as unrealistic — as a moon that revolves around a non-existent black hole.

It took all my strength of character not to take her by the shoulders, shake her like a rag doll, and scream, "ARE YOU *OUT OF YOUR MIND*?!!"

"Wow," I said, instead. "Um . . ."

Which is unlike me. I usually have a lot to say.

"But I can't seem to get him to commit," she murmured, in a sighing breeze of a voice. "And it's really ripping my heart apart." Then she looked around her.

"He's gone to his car, hasn't he?" she said. "You know what? I'm going to go find him now."

Her determined, go-getter look appeared, and she left the room.

I stood in a state of horror.

I watched the door close behind her.

I continued staring at the door.

I was vaguely aware of Riley approaching the same door, opening it, and leaving the room.

Still, I could not move my eyes. The sight of Astrid leaving to find Seb — to *hook up with Seb* — that image was still imprinted on the door. As if the door was now haunted by Astrid and her determined hair. It was too much for me. I considered hyperventilating.

But I was transfixed by the door.

Someone else approached, opened it, and left.

It was Lydia.

I stood in my trance, still thinking: *Astrid and Seb* —

And then a cascade of horror crashed upon me:

I just saw Lydia leave the room — I know exactly why she did — she is going to track down Seb — she plans to tell him she wants him back —

She is going to find Seb with Astrid.

There was nothing I could do.

I screamed.

It was my biggest, most powerful and magnificent scream, and I apologize to all those whose eardrums I destroyed.

The fact is, there was nothing else to do.

I had to stop Lydia somehow.

The scream had to reach her wherever she was, and divert her from her anguished destiny.

Of course, it was not necessarily the best plan, because it meant that people came rushing to my side, wanting to know what had happened, looking around in horror, and picking me up in protective bear hugs. I was trapped.

I could only hope that my scream had summonsed Lydia back, or at least stopped her in her tracks, because I couldn't run after her now.

* * *

I needed an explanation for my scream. Luckily, I can be inventive at times, so I said that I had just seen a girl in a white tennis dress crossing the stage of the auditorium. I said I had seen her jump, as if to hit a ball, and then she had faded away.

Now, maybe I was strangely convincing — or maybe it was the fact that it was late and dark — or maybe the ghost of my powerful scream was still sounding in everybody's ears — I don't know what it was . . . but everyone believed me.

There was a moment of complete, blinking silence as everybody turned to the stage and stared.

They were all seeing it — my imaginary ghost in a tennis dress —

And then it happened.

The building screamed right back at me.

I cannot explain it any other way.

It was the most anguished, terrible, furious shrieking sound you have ever heard — and it was coming from just down the hall.

There was something human in its emotional depth *but it was not human.*

There is no doubt — it was a ghost.

As one, we ran from the auditorium, and out into the car park. We ran — we pounded — away from that place of evil.

But as we ran, even in my horror, I felt a flicker of hope. Because Mr. Ludovico was *wrong* — there *was* a ghost in that building. And if he was wrong about that, then maybe he was wrong about me?

And here, I am sorry to say, my story ends.

We were safe — we all got home that night.

The next day was the last day of term, and we avoided the Art Rooms (including the Exhibition) if we could, and I avoided Mr. Ludovico's eyes. We did not say a word about the ghost. Partly because we couldn't admit to breaking into the Art Rooms, of course, but it also felt impossible to talk about. As if the anguish and anger of that scream was too much to contain in simple words.

Then it was holidays. Now I am writing this. And tomorrow Term 3 will begin.

I cannot promise that I will stay safe. I suppose, if you are reading this, I was safe for long enough to hand it in. That is a relief.

I do not know for certain whether the ghost is Sandra Wilkinson — that sweet girl who fell from the window — but I am now certain that there *is* a ghost.

Maybe Sandra was a gentle ghost, scattering memories like books, feathers, and handkerchiefs, as she wandered the building. Maybe my scream has awoken something darker within her? Or awoken *another* ghost? Her murderer, perhaps?

Come closer — for I am whispering now:

I have awoken an angry ghost.

4.

Riley T. Smith
THE STORY OF TERM 2 AS A GHOST STORY

In Term 2, this happens:

Two male residents of a local assisted-living facility for the mentally ill are out on a therapeutic exercise. One hacks another to pieces with an ax and heads home.

Blood and brain dripping from the ax. The resident is hungry. Puts the ax in the corner, asks for potatoes.

In Term 2, also, this happens:

A girl across the table says something like, *"Colder than the Danish Alps!"*

This is maybe the first day of the term. In a café, on the way to private school.

The girl across the table is named Astrid.

Funny thing is, the first time I saw Astrid she was hot. Clothes like cling wrap, eyes like lime zest.

There are no alps in Denmark. No mountains, no hills, no slopes, not even any angles. Just Danish children, sleds beneath their arms, looking sad.

The café is the Blue Danish. So that's what's happened — that word "Danish" — it's edged its way sideways into Astrid's brain.

The human brain is folded. Not so much folded. More like a towel that you've scrunched up to press into your backpack. If you pulled out your brain, shook it hard. If you spread it out to dry in the hot sun. It would be bigger than you realize. Look at me. I'm holding out my arms. I'm showing you the size of your brain.

That girl across the table named Astrid. I don't know that her brain is folded up.

Amelia beside me in the rain.

This is also in Term 2. A week or so after the café.

It's raining, but it's not. The sky, trees, path, road are slick and shocked with just-rain, edgy, strained with almost-rain — but this is the moment in between. We're walking in the now.

Bright and suspenseful, the now.

We're walking to her place. We'll talk and while we talk she'll stroke her long, fine hand along my inner thigh. We'll take that stroking pace awhile, the swimming, stroking pace. Rain will stroke the window. The words, our hands, the words, our hands, our legs entwine, our bodies. A braiding until words dissolve, and then I'll take things faster.

She'll cover her face with her hands.

Another day, early in Term 2: I'm waiting to pick something up from the office of our private school.

There's a leather couch to wait on, studded with bronzed gold. Carpet quiet. Behind the desk, a woman with gold loops in her ears. Her fingers softly, softly on computer keys. A swoop of white camellias in a vase.

A flat panel wall-mounted screen twists and turns discreetly between images of upcoming events: the Ashbury-Brookfield Art Exhibition, the Ashbury Athletics Carnival.

Antique pieces whisper. Original artwork on the walls.

Two women float from behind glass and wood.

"I've been burned a couple of times before, that's all," murmurs one.

"Mmm."

"Because the thing is," says the first, "people don't think. They just forward things. E-mails are so easy to forward."

On the polished wood of the table before me, *The Illustrated History of Ashbury*, two copies of the *Financial Review*, and the *Ashbury Collected Recipes*.

Smoked trout, strawberry ice, lemon meringue pie.

I laugh to myself, but silently.

There's a terrible silence in absence. The absence of a person. All the noise around you, all the clanging, words, rules, an elbow in your windpipe, manic laughter, flushing toilets, heavy feet on staircases, chairs scraping vinyl, all the noise is shadowed with a silence.

That's what a ghost is.

The silence of the one you want —

    sounds clash with the silence —

        there's your ghost.

One night, Term 2, a party at the home of a girl called Lydia.

Trapped inside a closet, people talking shadows.

Lydia says that shadows are the dark side of your soul.

A girl named Emily talks about the shadow games her parents played on walls when she was little. Peter Pan sewing his shadow to his feet. Chasing friends' shadows. I wonder when she'll stop. (Talking, I mean.)

A boy named Toby talks about approaching a black hole.

These people.

Sitting in a network of closets. In a house with a master suite that spans a single floor. Masterpieces hanging on the marble walls of bathrooms. A guest suite, home theater, library, billiards room, gym. Kitchens and swimming pools in pyramids of star-spangled glass. A tennis court, topiary gardens, outdoor swimming pool, plus lap pool and jacuzzi on the terrace.

These people talking shadows.

They've never even seen one.

Later, Amelia says to me: "I think the topiary gardens used to have shadows but the family got them steam cleaned."

What they don't know about Amelia:
She grew up fighting with her mother,
ran away from home the day she turned thirteen,
long hair flying as she ran
ran to a room behind a red door
in a hostel where she
still lives today. The same red door.

Also in Term 2 at the private school — there's birthday cake for someone.

The girl, Astrid — *cold as the Danish Alps* — blows out the candles on someone else's cake, and her hair catches alight.

I got burned, she tells us, walking out of Drama later that day. Shows us the singed ends of her hair. Her hair still has that acrid smell. Amelia blinks, once.

We're passing the room where they had the party. Glance through the glass.

I got burned, Astrid repeats, like maybe we didn't hear.

I make my face react and Astrid's happy.

But I'm thinking of the cleaner's face. Later tonight when he opens that door. Sees the torn streamers,

      cake crumbs,

         deflating balloons.

What they don't know about Amelia:

She closes her eyes at cinnamon.

Lights up at blueberries and gingerbread.

Loves fairy tales so much she sinks beneath their spell.

Tells stories from her own imagination that are wilder than wolves.

Covers her face with her hands when pleasure's too much — long, fine fingers, small, scarred knuckles, the tiny opal on her wrist.

The first time we met, when I knocked on her red door, we were both fourteen.

She introduced me to her giant stuffed cow. The stuffed cow and I had a long conversation about the height of the moon, and the taste of low-fat milk, while Amelia tried to change the subject. She jumped up and down on the bed in this cute T-shirt nightie and these sexy, thigh-high boots. Then she stopped, sat down, and strummed her guitar. We mixed drinks from the bottles she'd stolen when she ran away from home. She leaned out the window and knocked in a strange, blurred rhythm.

She said: *That's the sound the bandicoots make when they run along the roof.*

She knocked again — that rhythm, her concentrating face — turned away from me to get it right, turned back to check my reaction.

I said, *How do you know they're bandicoots, and not rats?*

She leaned even farther out the window, ignoring me, her eyes in the breeze.

Then she said: *Now we'll go to sleep for half an hour and when we wake we'll tell each other our dreams.*

She said, *Wait. No. Let's wear these.*

Her stepfather's gardening gloves. Her mother's silk scarf.

She stole these too, when she ran.

And we'll see how they affect our dreams.

We fell asleep on the single bed. Her boots against my jeans. Gardening gloves enormous on her hands. The silk scarf reached across my chest, across her hair, and kissed her cheek.

Her T-shirt was a soft, soft cotton.

We woke at the exact same moment, eyes in each other's eyes. The leather of her boots.

I couldn't remember my dreams.

Amelia said she'd dreamed about a girl with snail-shell eyes.

Term 2, we walk through dreams.

Ghost of a backbeat deep in our ears. Chlorine rimming our eyes.

Walking each other through drama lines. Essays at the kitchen table while my baby sister reaches up to taste the paper. Making art. Rubbing our eyes. Rubbing our eyes. Falling into bed together, slipping into each other's bodies, into sleep. (I spend a lot of time behind Amelia's red door.)

She has her own room in the hostel. Shares a bathroom with old men and schizophrenic women.

Her mother sends money to help her pay the rent. Social workers used to show up now and then, but Amelia and her mum always told the same story: It's an arrangement they've agreed on; they'll patch it up soon and she'll go home.

Social workers leave her alone now. So does her mum.

Parties at the home of the girl called Lydia. Some nights the music was surprisingly good.

You hear more with drowsy ears, see more with sleepy eyes.

We hear a girl say this: *You got me hooked, by the way, on vanilla lattes.*

(The friend says: *But have you tried a caramel macchiato?* and they both gasp.)

We hear a boy say this: *I told my dad, I said, look, get me a heavy-duty sleeping bag, and I'll sleep on the streets of Byron Bay. You'll save yourself five grand on accommodation.*

(He means the trip to Byron Bay after exams.)

And we see that the girl called Astrid (*burnt by birthday candles*) — we see she is hot for a Brookfield boy named Seb.

(A lot of girls want Seb. But Astrid's making plans. We see that in her eyes.)

Term 2, Emily finds an old book in the Art Rooms. It's inscribed to an ex-student.

Weeks go by before they realize who the ex-student is. Even then they have to scour through yearbooks. But it was there all along.

On a polished coffee table, front office of the school: *The Illustrated History of Ashbury.*

Chapter 4, page 57: "A Tragic Accident."

She fell from a window in the Art Rooms and died.

You only have to flick the pages once.

Who cares, right? These private-school kids and their hunt for a ghost, who cares?

But, you know, it's just. It was there all along.

You only have to flick the pages once.

All I'm trying to say is —

"They're a simple people," Amelia shrugs — and gives me her wicked grin.

Parties at the home of the girl called Lydia.

We hear a girl say this: *She prefers pencil eyeliner over liquid, but, you know what? She doesn't explain why.*

We hear a boy say this: *I'm in peak physical condition at the moment. It's amazing.*

And we see that the Brookfield boy named Seb is in love with Lydia. Lydia loves him back, *but she pretends to herself and to him and to the world that she does not.*

What they don't know about Amelia:
She prefers the shadows. Try to paint her, and she'll disappear in shadows. Photograph her and she'll slip out of the frame.
I call her my Shadowgirl. She smiles like this is soothing.

The night of the shadow conversation, we're touring closets of designer clothes and jewelry, and there's Astrid — *cold as the Danish Alps, burnt by birthday candles* — she's with us but she's silent. When we reach the inner closet — just for shoes and bigger than Amelia's room at the hostel — Astrid slips back into a shadow, watches us go in. She doesn't know I see her. The door slides closed; she's gone.
She's locked us in — locked Lydia in. She wants some time alone with the boy named Seb.
She comes back three hours later to set us free. Her eyes are gleaming victory.

The dark side of the soul.
In the shadow closet, Lydia says *the dark side of the soul.* She doesn't mention the Jungian shadow — the secrets we keep from ourselves. Passions stored in interlocking closets. Anger kicking the side of a chair. Monsters hanging in picture frames that we turn to face the wall.
All that Lydia says is: *A shadow is the dark side of the soul.*
In her mother's designer closet in the dark. While outside another girl moves in on the boy she loves. Her fingers know this. The way that they play with the buckles on her mother's shoes. But her eyes don't know a thing.

Playing shadow games.
Em talks of Peter Pan and shadow games. She doesn't want to grow up and her eyes sparkle with *cupcakes, party hats, white clouds.*

She's talking of taking a needle and thread to your heels.

Your shadow follows, watches, judges, knows you. If you could tear it off, why sew it back?

Approaching a black hole.

The boy named Toby says a shadow is a black hole. He's making connections between black holes, Irish history, Irish folklore. It almost makes sense. He's pissed out of his brain, but he's smarter than he knows.

I look at him and remember — he shows up at the Goose and Thistle some nights. And earlier this year, he drove Amelia home.

So he knows that she lives in a hostel, but he hasn't said a word to the others. If he had, we'd have heard them talk about it.

The boy named Toby.

He's the only one in this mansion, this school, this mad, mad world of wealth, of games — he's the only one that I respect.

In a Music class, also in Term 2, Amelia tells me she's made a new friend.

Amelia never makes friends.

"Here?" I say.

"No," she says. "Not here." And we both laugh.

The teacher, Ms. Wexford, is saying: *composition — third fret — violin — first fret.*

I don't know what she's saying. I never listen to her.

Amelia says she met this girl at a bus stop. "Her hair is the same color as mine," she says.

As if that's what she's been waiting for all along — a girl with the same color hair.

The girl is a few years older than us.

"She lives in some kind of a home," Amelia says, "for the mentally ill."

Oh.

"But I think it's just depression, not psychosis."

As if those are the only options.

"And she says she's only pretending to be mad."

"That's a psychosis."

"No, it's not."

Amelia's watching Ms. Wexford's face as she speaks.

Ms. Wexford is saying: *the long arm of the law.*

"She's funny. She's kind of ironic. She says crazy things, but ironically. Like she wants to meet King Louis of France. And she dresses really wild. Kind of unique, but simple. And she's allowed to — I see her at the bus stop. So, she's kind of free — I guess it's a kind of an assisted-living place."

I'm thinking: *Why is the music teacher talking about the long arm of the law?*

"It's just depression," Amelia repeats. "She's waiting for her boyfriend. He broke her heart but she's waiting for him to come get her. He's not coming."

"Delusional," I say.

Amelia shakes her head.

"If you think that the school is wealthy enough to do without a set of castanets," says Ms. Wexford.

A set of castanets is missing.

Amelia says, "She has this lovely, lyrical way of talking."

She means her new friend. She means the new friend's mad. "It's musical," she says.

The music teacher says, again, the *long arm of the law.*

The castanet thief.

Amelia, beside me, kicks the side of my chair. The beat of her kick is a good one. I let it thrum right through me.

One night at a party: Amelia standing alone. She's on the terrace, staring at the lap pool. I know what she's doing. She's staring back in time.

There are jets in the lap pool. You swim against the jets. Swim hard and you stay here in the now; do nothing and they'll swim you back in time.

What they don't know about Amelia:

When she was ten, she and her mother moved in with her mother's new boyfriend, an Irish guy named Patrick O'Doherty.

Let's call him her stepfather (although they didn't marry). The first few weeks he was friendly but reserved. Then one day he pointed out the horseshoe hanging on the door. Told her stories about lucky horseshoes. Moved on to four-leaf clovers. Had her listen out for fairy songs with him.

He's full of Irish fairy tales: direct route to her heart.

She fell in love with him, head over heels.

When she turned eleven, he made her a moonlight surprise. Paper lanterns in the back garden.

He took her swimming at the local pool one day, and noticed she had talent. Started coaching her himself because he used to be a swimmer.

He was the first father she ever had, and he was lovely.

But she kept right on fighting with her mother.

And one fight — over nothing, something burning in a pan — she got so mad, she ran away.

I know what she wanted when she ran.

She wanted the stepfather to come for her. She wanted him to bring her home.

When she stares into the nothing — when she looks for the past — she's looking for her stepfather.

When's he coming for me? is what her shoulders say.

It's been three years.

The castanets turn up the following day, caught in the back of a tambourine.

Amelia's crazy new friend turns up too; at the bus stop, Amelia tells me.

The next few weeks, they keep meeting at the bus stop.

The girl never catches the bus, Amelia says. She presses her hands into fists, presses her tongue into her cheek, frowns at the wind.

Everyone else ignores the girl, Amelia says.

"Like you do with crazy people," I suggest.

But Amelia asks the girl questions.

"So far, she won't tell me anything," Amelia says, "except her stories."

Not even her name.

Amelia's new friend is crazy, and she won't even share her name.

My heart hurts for Amelia.

The girl at the bus stop keeps the ex-boyfriend's letters in a secret pocket that she's sewn into a fold of her dress. She showed Amelia the pocket, tightly folded papers, but won't let her see any of the words.

She also has hallucinations. Amelia calls them stories. The girl hallucinates: elfin people, flutes and fiddles, silvery voices, windows ablaze with light, a little man with buckles on his shoes.

So big these buckles, these silver buckles, it's a wonder the little man can lift his feet at all.

"Your friend has a way with words," I say.

Amelia writes the hallucinations down in her diary.

Maybe the letters are hallucinations too. Tightly folded blank pieces of paper.

One morning, Term 2, Amelia arrives late at the pool and her face looks washed-over pale.

She says she just saw her friend at the bus stop.

The friend told Amelia she'd been attacked by a crowd of little people carrying a corpse.

"Turns out you were right," Amelia tries to laugh. "My new friend's nuts."

It's her broken laugh.

She'd wanted her new friend to be real. One real friend amongst these Ashbury half-people. These Ashbury shadows and ghosts.

Her friend also saw a "little person" falling down the chimney.

"There's a chimney in the home?" I say.

"I guess. I don't know. I guess it could be part of the story. Anyway, the little person scalded himself. In a pot of boiling water that was standing at the fire."

And now Amelia's eyes and voice are drifting. She tells the story like it's her own. "He let out a terrible squeal," she says, "and within minutes, the place was full of other little creatures, pulling him out of the pot.

"And they pointed to me" — here Amelia points to herself — "and they said, *Was it her? Did she scald you?* And the little one said, *No, no, it was me that did it, not her* — and the other creatures said, *Ah well, if it was yourself that scalded yourself, we'll say nothing.*"

Amelia pauses, looks at me, then continues in a deep and creeping voice: *"But if SHE had scalded you, we'd have made her pay."*

She looks into my eyes. A beat goes by.

I say, "You mean they pointed to your friend."

Amelia, sassy again: "I'm quoting. I'm telling it like she did." She grins and puts her goggles on. Then she repeats, in a weird little whisper: *"But if she had scalded you, we'd have made her pay."*

I say, "Let's get in the pool."

Another day, Amelia tells me that the crazy friend has invited her to see her vegetable garden.

I say, "Why don't you just keep chatting at the bus stop?"

Amelia says, "It's just a — I guess it's an assisted-living place."

She's said that before.

"Sometimes," Amelia adds, "she seems perfectly sane."

Now I'll tell you something that you don't know about me.

If you lock me up, if you padlock doors, if you close me in, I think of fire. I think my own brain is burning its way through my skull. I think about corpses collapsing into charcoal.

That's one thing. Another thing.

If you hurt Amelia —

If you keep me from Amelia —

What they don't know about Amelia:

She's light as a cloud to pick up.

Gather her into your arms when she's passed out on the floor and she's light as a leaf.

But the strength in her grip when she wants to stay out longer and I'm trying to take her home — the strength in her body when she's angry.

The strength in her shoulders when she swims —

I love that strength. I think that what I feel when I think about her strength is called elation.

Term 2: a lot of talk about ghosts around Ashbury.

They have a photo that they think is the ghost: image of a face as bright as fire.

A ghost is trapped. Can't get back to the past where it was somebody, can't get forward to the future on the other side. Trapped, locked up in the now.

"Or it just doesn't *want* to leave," Amelia points out.

She starts meeting her new friend near the home.

There's a vegetable garden, Amelia says. The friend turns the soil with a trowel, while Amelia sits on a cold stone wall and listens to her stories.

There are stories about roasting babies alive on griddles. Burning babies' noses off with red-hot tongs.

"So the medication's working," I say.

Amelia laughs. But she keeps visiting.

In Term 2, I fall asleep in daylight.

There's a drama rehearsal, late afternoon.

I'm watching from up high, and then I'm not.

It's one of those tricky dreams where everything's in shadow. Like a hat pulled low over my forehead — if I could tip the hat back I'd pool the dream with light.

In the dream, I'm talking to Amelia, trying to see her face.

"What would we want with castanets?" she says, and we both laugh hard.

Then she says she has to go do something. She gets her distracted expression, and we move to a new scene.

We're outside, by a highway, and I can see Amelia across a stretch of lanes. She's watching traffic, her head tilted, a tiny smile. The dream's shadow trick is getting worse — now it's a beekeeper's net over my face.

I keep losing Amelia, then there she is again.

I watch as the shadows billow around her.

I think, *Wait. That's not shadows, that's smoke.*

So then I'm shouting: *Amelia, Amelia —*

But her name gets tangled in the shadows and the smoke. It twists into ugly shapes.

Aymeelia. Armenia. A meal of you.

I'm hitting my own face, hard, trying to make it say her name, but my mouth is shouting:

A maze of you. Oh mania. Ah murder you —

The shadows shove against her now — I see her frown, push her hair behind her ears, her hands form fists —

And then her face assumes its lost and vacant look. The look that means she's heading to her past — searching, disappearing.

Not now —

Not with the shadows — the smoke coming to get you —

Then the shadows are so thick they turn to blackness and a new horror bursts at me — that's not shadows, that's not smoke, *that's a black hole —*

If the black hole gets you, Amelia, *you're more than dead.*

I'm shouting and shouting, but her name —

And all I can do is stand and watch as she moves in her trance toward the darkness.

I make myself wake from that dream.

Breathing hard.

Look around the auditorium, and the beautiful relief — there she is, safe, alive. She's by the stage, listening to Garcia. He's holding up some object — it's a table lamp, I think — he's holding it high as he talks.

It's while I'm watching her, breathing in her safe, sweet body, her concentrating head, she's listening so hard — that it comes to me.

Those stories the crazy friend is telling her?

They're fairy stories.

Flutes and fiddles, silver buckles, little people, fireplaces — those are fairy stories.

Just like her stepfather told her.

His were stories of horseshoes, four-leaf clovers, fairy songs.

But it's all the same weird, spooky Irish folklore.

That boy Toby — he connected Irish stories to black holes. I can't remember how.

But now I see, now it's clear: No wonder Amelia loves her crazy friend.

The day after that dream is the day that a resident of a local assisted-living facility hacks another resident to pieces with an ax.

Amelia misses swimming that morning.

I'm waiting for her, sitting on the edge of the pool. She never misses swimming. My eyes are on the entrance gate.

She turns up at the time that we normally leave. Her face has its distracted look. She comes right up and says there's been an ax murder.

Early that morning, she says. She stopped by to see her friend on the way here, and the friend told her about it.

I say, "It's one of her hallucinations."

No. Amelia shakes her head. "This was different."

Here's something else you don't know about me:

I never once told Amelia what to do.

Except for now. By the pool. The ax, the blood, the brains.

I said: "I want you to stop going there."

She looked startled.

She said: "It's okay, it's just — it's not an institution or anything — it's just some kind of assisted —"

I said: "Amelia, there are ax murders."

She looked over my shoulder, eyes getting vacant. I thought I'd lost her again, but her eyes flickered back.

She said: "Only the one ax murder. What if I take you there?

"We could skip the Athletics Carnival," she said. She could introduce me to her friend. Then I would say the friend's sane — and that she needs Amelia.

So that was the deal.

You might already know this about Amelia: Moods flicker across her face like fast animation. Like cloud shadows moving in hurricane winds.

She breaks the deal.

The day of the Athletics Carnival and we're walking. She's chatting, happy. We're walking through the Heritage Park. She's telling me I'll love her friend. She's always alone in the vegetable garden, Amelia says — she's never met any of the other residents. We'll be able to see the institution from the outside, she says — a beautiful, stone building — but we can't go in. The friend tells Amelia it's a dump: rats, fleas, bugs, lice, cracks in the stonework, mold on the floors. Not enough bed linen, and what there is is worn, filthy, ripped. Not enough clothes either, and everybody stinks.

Amelia wants to write a letter to the Department of Health.

"But you've never met anybody else, or seen it. How can you know she's not making all this up?"

Amelia walks silent for a while, flicks something out of the corner of her eye.

"You're going to love her," she repeats, as if I hadn't spoken. "She's got this — this musical voice. The way she speaks is so — and wait till you hear her fairy stories."

"Maybe she'll tell me her name," I say.

Then Amelia stops. I watch her.

Moods flicker across her face — she's startled, angry, dreamy. She's solemn, anxious, and something else.

She looks at me, defiant, smiling, and says, "I've changed my mind."

And there's nothing I can do to change it back.

We stand at the side of the path in that park and I talk and talk at her.

I keep saying her name. It feels good to me. Being able to say it. It feels like control.

But it's not. She's staring at her feet; staring at nothing.

I was thinking.

A ghost is a person who is there but not there. They look like they're there, but they're not.

Amelia staring at her past — there's your ghost.

Not much else to say about Term 2.

Amelia's an actor but she cannot lie to me. She's still going to meet the friend, but she doesn't always tell me. She doesn't want to see me mad. The last few weeks of term, she goes to the library, to the supermarket, to buy a Coke.

All the time she's lying. She's going back to see her crazy friend.

The second-to-last night of term, we're at another party at Lydia's. There's talk about a ghost. We end up at the school, in the auditorium.

I see the Brookfield boy, Seb, I see him leave. I see Astrid — *cold as the Danish Alps, burnt by birthday candles* — I watch her leave too.

I think about Astrid. How she locked us in that night.

I think about the story that Amelia's crazy friend told — a little person scalded in a boiling pot of water. And the other angry little people: *If she'd scalded you, she would have had to pay.*

I'm thinking — Astrid locked us in a wardrobe.

If she'd locked us someplace separate, she would have had to —

But Astrid glances back as she reaches the door. She's got her determined look. It gives her lines. She's seventeen years old, but in this light, with that frown, she could be seventy.

It was just a closet. She's just a stupid kid. They're all just stupid kids.

I'm thinking this, so I don't hear what Amelia's saying.

Then I hear. She's saying she wants to go look at the Gallery. We've both got pieces in the Exhibition the next day. She wants to go see what else is there.

I look at her. She's lying.

And it's after ten at night.

She knows I know that she's lying.

I say, "I'll come with you."

"No," she says, "they need you here."

We both smile.

She leaves the room.

I wait a beat. Follow her. I know where she's going but I hope maybe I'm wrong. So I check the Gallery first.

The girl Lydia turns up beside me.

We hear somebody screaming. I make myself joke with her, this half-person rich-kid named Lydia. I push open the Gallery door.

Amelia's not there.

Not much else to say about Term 2, like I said.

Except, I guess, something else they don't know about Amelia.

She was in juvenile detention last year. So was I.

We had to include it in our scholarship application. Brookfield knows we were there and would have passed it on.

Here's what happened: After we met behind the red door, Amelia and I went to Brookfield for maybe a couple of weeks. Then we ran away together. Lived on beaches, on the streets. That's why the kids at Brookfield don't know who we are.

They caught us stealing from a petrol station, and put us away for a year.

Locked up, apart from Amelia. Red-hot tongs pushing things around inside my chest.

Scholarship Committee believed us when we said we plan to change.

I saw her through the windows of the Gallery, watched her disappear.

Small talk with the girl named Lydia while I watched. She's got a good smile, Lydia. Wealthy parents must have picked it out for her. Or maybe Lydia herself is from a catalogue. We'll take the pretty one, the pretty smile. A soul? Now, why would she need that?

Small talk was cut through: the sound of something cutting wood. Woodwork down the hall.

Kids in the auditorium thought it was the ghost. We heard them run.

I laughed hard.

Because there was Amelia fading behind glass, my Amelia, my ghost, heading to a madhouse, and here were the private-school kids in a madhouse frenzy over an imaginary ghost.

Lydia laughed too. Who knows why. Wealthy people laugh all the time.

I didn't sleep that night. Went home, stared at the ceiling.

But in the morning, last day of term, there she was again.

Amelia, by the side of the pool. I couldn't touch her.

Later that day, I'm walking with Amelia.

We don't say a word about the night before: how she disappeared into the dark.

We pass classrooms. At each desk, a flat panel computer. Chairs are ergonomically designed. Lighting is curved so it won't distract the eyes. A SMART Board at the front of every room. We pass the library: a flat screen TV huge against the wall. *World News* all day. I once heard a librarian say, "You see, they're not cloistered here. At any point, they can pull up a cushion, watch the news, be part of the real world."

The real world.

And now I realize this: I've never once heard these people talk about the ax murder. It happened just down the road. A crazy person kills another crazy person with an ax, and they don't care. These shadow people sitting on their cushions and their ergonomic chairs.

I reach out and take Amelia's hand.

One last thing.

Juvenile records are sealed.

Ashbury knows what we put on the scholarship application — that we stole from a petrol station, got caught and put away.

The truth is sealed, bricked up.

You never know what ugly things decay behind brick walls.

PART THREE

Progress Meeting — The Committee for the Administration of the K. L. Mason Patterson Trust Fund — Minutes

6:00 P.M. – 10:35 P.M., Wednesday, July 16

Conference Room 2B, the K. L. Mason Patterson Center for the Arts

Chair Roberto Garcia (History Coordinator, Drama Teacher, Ashbury High)
Secretary Christopher Botherit (English Coordinator, Ashbury High)

Participants

Constance Milligan (Ashbury Alumni Association)
Patricia Aganovic (Parent Representative 1)
Jacob Mazzerati (Parent Representative 2)
Lucy Wexford (Music Coordinator, Ashbury High)

Apologies

Bill Ludovico (Ashbury School Principal/Economics Teacher)

AGENDA ITEMS

Agenda Item 1: Preliminaries
Welcome back, Constance

Once again, the group welcomed back Constance Milligan (Ashbury Alumni Association).

Constance did not attend the progress interviews of our scholarship winners, which took place at the end of Term 1, and was absent due to illness from the progress meeting at the end of Term 2. It is now Term 3, so we have not seen Constance for some time!

"Ahoy there, folks!" Constance beamed.

Minutes of the previous meeting

The minutes of the previous meeting were circulated for comment.

- Constance Milligan declared that we were a "pack of fools" who had all been "damned to hell" for we had "struck a deal with the devil — no, no, worse, with a pair of demons." She "bid adieu" to our souls.
- There was a startled silence.
- Eventually, Roberto Garcia (Chair) spoke: "Ah!" he said. "She means the agreement we made with Amelia and Riley. To overlook their absenteeism if they signed up for the Ashbury-Brookfield Drama."
- Everybody laughed with relief.
- No, no, we explained (laughingly) to Constance. That was in no way a deal with the devil! Nor was it blackmail . . . bribery . . . corruption (nor various other words that Constance threw at us). It was just a tactic. By getting Amelia and Riley to join in a school activity like the Drama, we would help them to integrate. And that would make them less likely to skip classes! It was pure genius (we explained).
- "I might point out that *I* was opposed to the idea," Lucy Wexford (Music Coordinator) told Constance, "but they shouted me down."
- "You should have shouted louder, then," Constance said tartly.

Agenda Item 2: Financial Report

Roberto Garcia (Chair) circulated the latest Financial and Audit Reports.

• Everybody looked at the Reports for a while.

• Jacob Mazzerati (Parent Rep 2) wondered why Bill Ludovico (Ashbury School Principal/Economics Teacher) never comes to any meetings.

Action points

• We will stop looking at the Financial Reports until Bill starts coming to meetings again.

Agenda Item 3: The K. L. Mason Patterson Center for the Arts: Progress Report

Chris Botherit (English Coordinator/Secretary/me) circulated the Structural Engineer's Report on the K. L. Mason Patterson Center for the Arts.

• Everyone was delighted to read that the building is "safe." It turns out that the distant cracking/creaking sounds are temperature changes affecting the wood. The cracks in the brickwork, meanwhile, are most likely a result of the foundations settling under the weight of the new additions.

• Chris Botherit said that the students would be disappointed. "They like to think that the sounds mean there's a ghost in the building," he said.

• Much laughter about the sweet simplicity of youth.

• Discussion of the fact that it seems to be mostly Year 12 students who believe in the ghost. They are not so sweet nor youthful as they once were. Aren't they practically grown-ups? Shouldn't they have moved beyond childish fears?

• Roberto Garcia shook his head slowly. "Year twelves? They are the most hysterical of them all," he said. "Blind with panic about the future, they run like the devil to the past."

• A thoughtful pause.

• Then, Lucy Wexford (Music Coordinator) joked that if the Fund were ever running short on cash we could hold "ghost walking tours" of the building!

• Patricia Aganovic (Parent Rep 1) said she'd heard (from her daughter, Cassie) that "word on the street is the ghost is a former student who fell to her death from a window back in the 1950s." Did we think this was true? Could that be the ghost?

• "I've heard it was a tennis player," Jacob Mazzerati (Parent Rep 2) said, "looking for a lost tennis ball." Patricia raised a single eyebrow at Jacob. He raised both eyebrows back. A dimple flashed in his cheek.

• "Oh, piffle," said Constance. "The ghost is undoubtedly Sir Kendall. He is distressed by the way we are spending his money on all these *joint* activities with that dreadful *Brookfield* school. He loathes poor people. And he rather suspects that the word *joint* has direct associations with the underworld."

• Everybody looked at Constance. "I said to him — I said, '*Kendall*, do you know you are right? I believe it's something to do with that marijuana?' And Kendall said, 'Not forgetting, Connie, it's another word for prison.'"

• Everybody looked harder at Constance. "This was in a dream," she explained. "Kendall and I converse quite often in our dreams."

Agenda Item 4: Scholarship Winners: Progress Report

Roberto Garcia said he believed he spoke for us all in expressing his "mind-exploding happiness" about our scholarship winners. Their schoolwork continues to impress their teachers. Their performances at rehearsals have been "astonishing beyond the point of human endurance." (Roberto has to lie down after rehearsals, to recover.) Riley's contribution to the Ashbury-Brookfield Art Exhibition was universally admired. (Opinion was divided on whether it was better than the other favorite, the controversial multimedia work by Brookfield student Seb Mantegna.) Amelia, meanwhile, had continued to swim her way up through the ranks.

"We have unleashed a pair of gods onto the world," Roberto concluded.

• A round of applause, cut through by —
• Constance murmuring, in chilling tones, "I see that the demons have cast spells of evil enchantment upon you all. That my glorious Ashbury should be so sullied! Is it safe to be in a room with such people as *you* who have —"
• But Constance's murmurs were cut through by —
• Lucy Wexford (Music Coordinator) announcing, in ringing tones, "I hereby move that Amelia and Riley be stripped of their scholarship immediately and expelled from the school."
• Sharp intakes of breath — a strangely beatific smile settled on Constance's face —
• "They stole a set of castanets," Lucy declared.
• Her words seemed to rebound around the room. They echoed for some time. (Lucy is a music teacher so perhaps she is trained to project her voice in this way.)
• Then, a clamor: Why haven't we heard anything about these stolen castanets before? (cried all the teachers in the room); Are you sure? (said the parent reps, looking concerned); Can you remind me what castanets are? (said somebody) (possibly me).
• "We knew we were taking a risk giving them the scholarships," Lucy continued. "We knew they had been locked up for stealing. We trusted them when they said they planned to stop. Why? That is what I cannot understand! How did they lull us into that false belief?"
• Everybody waited for her to go on.
• "One day the castanets were there," she said. "Amelia and Riley were in a class with me — I distinctly saw them standing very close to the musical instruments — the next day the castanets were gone."

• "It's not at all surprising," Constance chipped in. "They need to steal frequently, you see. It's in their nature. A sort of addiction. And they have to pay their dealers."

• Roberto Garcia pointed out that there had never been any suggestion that Amelia and Riley have drug abuse problems. Or dealers.

• "How far does a set of castanets take you with a dealer these days?" Jacob asked, mildly.

• "These were *very fine antique Spanish castanets!*" Lucy exclaimed — and with that she produced a set of castanets and *ca-clicked* them above her head like a triumphant flamenco dancer.

• "Ah," said somebody (possibly me), "that's right. Castanets."

• "How did you get them back?" Jacob asked.

• Lucy explained *that the castanets had turned up themselves, the following day, behind a tambourine.*

• There was another stunned silence — then Patricia Aganovic (Parent Rep 1) said, "Are you saying that you have no evidence that Amelia and Riley even *took* the castanets?" and Jacob Mazzerati (Parent Rep 2) added, "They might not have been stolen at all, just misplaced?"

• Lucy began to answer but —

• Roberto launched into a tirade about second chances, redemption, reform, and so on, leading (unexpectedly) to convict times — specifically, when Macquarie was Governor, and thousands of convicts re-created themselves as law-abiding citizens with bakeries of their own. "The bread they baked was the foundation of Australia," he said, fixing a fiery gaze on Lucy.

• "Some wouldn't even taste the bread!" he cried. "Some believed those people should be cursed forevermore!! That anyone who has a criminal record must surely be *demonic*!!" (Now the fiery gaze shifted to Constance.)

• Then he explained that the convicts did other things besides baking. Could not keep up with him but he said something about girls who'd been pickpockets or streetwalkers in England and Ireland ending up as landowners, dairy women, shopkeepers here — I think he might also have mentioned bonnet-making. He went on a lot.

• Lucy spoke through Roberto's rantings to say that it might *appear* that the castanets had just been misplaced, but that she herself had no doubt that Amelia and Riley had stolen them, and that her own speech about the "long arm of the law" had spooked them into returning them in secret, and —

• Roberto was suddenly silent. His silence silenced Lucy. He shifted his body toward her, tilted his head, smiled quizzically. (Tried to study the technique to use on difficult students in my own class, but I suspect you need to start by being Roberto.) Lucy tried to hold his gaze (as a difficult student would). Her eyes dropped. I believe her cheeks turned pale pink. She was silent for a moment, then —

• She complained: "Well, Amelia and Riley *do* still miss my Music classes sometimes, and I rather thought that . . ." — her voice wilted — she was quiet again —

• Roberto asked if there was any other business. If not, he said, it was time for us to go back to Jacob's.

Agenda Item 5: Any Other Business

• Jacob said that everyone was welcome at his place.
• Constance and Lucy declined.
• A rather tense pause then —
• A distant moaning sound drifted into the room — a sound uncannily like the sound of a young girl weeping — but which was, of course, the wind, and just as we were all frowning and blinking at that sound, the lights flickered, and —

Meeting Closed (abruptly): 10:35 P.M.

2

Board of Studies
New South Wales

HIGHER SCHOOL CERTIFICATE
EXAMINATION

English Extension 3

General Instructions

- Reading time — 5 minutes
- Writing time — 4 hours
- Write using black or blue pen

Elective: Gothic Fiction

Question 1

Write a personal memoir which explores the dynamics of first impressions. In your response, draw on your knowledge of gothic fiction.

[ANSWERS CONTINUED . . .]

February 2, 1803

'Tis as fine a night as a heart could wish — the moon round and bright in the sky — and "Phillip," says I to my friend, Phillip Cunningham. "Phillip," I says, "it's fond I've grown of the birdsong here, to be sure."

"Tom," says Phillip, and he takes a thoughtful drag on his pipe. "Tom," says he, and he squints through smoke, "the devil himself has taken up abode in the throats of the birds of this godforsaken land, and you say that you're fond of their song?"

He shifts his body to look at me, his eyes agleam in the moonlight, and we both laugh hard, to be sure.

Sure, but I tell you, it's the truth. I've grown fond of many sounds here in Castle Hill: the scuffle of creatures, slither of snakes, howling of native dogs. I'm fond of the colors too.

There's a deep red-gold in the soil, and in the bark of the trees after rain, and sure if it isn't the color of my Maggie's hair.

There's the pale blue of the mountains in the distance, a little like the color of her eyes.

The overseers say there's no crossing those mountains, but I hear that there's a paradise hidden just beyond. (Well, it's paradise or China. Depends who you're talking to. Either way it's just over the mountains.)

We talk often, Phillip and I. He could talk the teeth out of a saw on most things, but not a word of his wife and little ones anymore — like he's grown afraid to say their names. You can feel them in his stillness now and then, though. And sense them in his use of the word, *home*.

And speaking of *home*, there are plans. Not just talk. Not just sketches of ships in the mud — but real plans made by Phillip and other strong, bright men — to rise up against the English and go home.

Last year, two new ships arrived from Ireland — the *Atlas* and the *Hercules* — and it seems that their journeys were a pure hell. So crammed together were they, and only a drop of water a day, so that nearly half were dead before they landed. Most of the survivors so sick it was direct from the harbor to the hospital. Those that could walk — marks of the irons still clear around their ankles and necks — were sent to us here at Castle Hill. That's some angry, thirsty, desperate, wild-eyed men, I tell you, with a grim determination to join us in these plans.

(I hear that the *Atlas* also brought a load of wondrous things — beaver hats, cuckoo clocks, and satin shawls — and I plan to try to find some for Maggie.)

There's more anger too, for they've lost our indents — that's the papers that record the lengths of our sentences. So we've all got to stay here for life. That's neither here nor there for people like me who already had to stay for life, but it's here and there and more besides for people who were sent for seven years.

And everyone's been practicing, you know — like rehearsals. On every ship from Ireland here there's been at least one attempted uprising. Not long back, the women convicts ground up glass and hid it in the sailors' flour, hoping it would kill them. (It didn't.) And the Irish here have planned uprisings aplenty, but something has always gone wrong.

Not this one. Not with Phillip in charge. There's secret meetings, secret handshakes, secret codes. The plans inch forward at a slow, careful pace, and we'll not make a move until we're certain to succeed.

In the meantime, we're working the land and making the best of things.

On my birthday just the other day, I woke missing Maggie and my mother, but Phillip drank to my health, and drank to my health, and drank to my health once more, and everything was cheerful again.

He ruffled my hair, which I've cut very short — all the Irish have so they call us "croppies." "When you see your Maggie," Phillip said, "she'll fall knee over toes in love with you again, such a handsome young man as you've become."

I liked to hear that. The part about Maggie I mean.

The others joke and tell me she's forgotten me. They're not like that with the older men who've left wives and sweethearts at home. I'm young so they think my heart's for laughing at. Just because Maggie's letters are not so frequent as they were. She's busy, that's all, and her letters, when they come, are just as passionate and sweet.

Speaking of Maggie, would you kindly forget what I said earlier of the pretty girls in Sydney Town? I'm dead ashamed of my thoughts (and my deeds, I confess). There was a madness took me over, is all that I can say. But now I'm older, and wiser, and I see that the girls in Sydney Town, they've got sharp edges. They make me long for Maggie and her softness.

She can be angry, sure, when she wants to be, but she'd never grind up glass to put in flour.

But tonight, as I talk with Phillip in the moonlight, I'm not thinking of errors or sharp edges. There's a mad kind of flutter in my heart, like flags flying high in the wind

Phillip tells me they've ordered him to oversee the building of a grand stone barracks here in Castle Hill.

"A two-story barracks," says Phillip, looking about him in the darkness, measuring air with his eyes, "with a fireplace there" — he gestures with one hand — "the sleeping quarters there — and we'll store the grain here."

Sure, and my heart surges with pride.

Phillip will build his barracks, all the while making his plans. The plans will run smooth, and I'll sail home to Maggie with the gifts of cuckoo clocks and satin shawls.

I laugh aloud, and Phillip says, "What?" and I shake my head. I'm laughing at nothing but the smile in my chest, for whichever way I turn toward the future, I cannot see a thing that could go wrong.

RILEY T. SMITH
STUDENT No. 8233569

You should know our plan.

I know what you're thinking. Something demonic. It's not, it's just — calculated.

You should know the reason for the plan.

We lived on the streets for a year or two, detention for a year after that.

You can never know what it is to be apart from Amelia. So just imagine this: Every day, you want to take her hair, her long, long hair, and wind it tight around your wrist. Tighter, tighter. Knot the ends together. Never let her go again.

Every day you want that like a wrenching in your chest.

That year apart, we wrote to each other. Talked each night as we fell asleep — inside our heads, I mean. What a counselor there called a psychic connection — I told him he was nuts, but it's the truth. We held each other's souls.

And we looked around and saw that we were different. These kids with their track marks, suicide scars, hepatitis, couldn't finish sentences.

So we made plans. We'd never live on the streets again, never be apart. We knew we should Get An Education like the counselors said. But then what? Careers would split us down the middle, lock us up in corporate suits.

No. Amelia and I would be free and rich and we'd do it playing music. It's what we love, and it binds our souls even closer.

We're okay at music, nothing special — but we know how to deceive, and we know what you need to succeed.

You need rich people.

That's all it was. Our evil plan.

Convince the counselors at the detention center that we wanted to get honest.

Write a scholarship application that would shock them into meeting us.

Convince the committee that they held the power to save our evil souls.

Then, once we were in, pretend to be friends with these rich half-people. Trick them into thinking we were something. Use them, and manipulate them. Their money, their connections — their independent record labels.

Lydia was perfect.

Term 3, her parents were back, so the big parties shut down. They turned intimate instead. That was perfect too.

Blue Danish Café, late afternoon, early in Term 3. The number 15, white on black, propped on a metal stand, center of our table. Chairs and conversations scraping between tables. I happen to look sideways and there, at the next table, an Ashbury boy named Saxon. I've seen him around. I don't like him. He wears his hair long, in his eyes. He's always tilting his head forward, pausing, then throwing it back. Clears his eyes a moment, like a horse.

Also, he blinks slowly, as if he doesn't care how long his eyes stay closed.

Now I hear him talking to an Ashbury girl.

"Seriously," he's saying. "There's something simian about you. The disproportionate length of your arms."

He's saying it with his charming smile. She's trying not to look at her own arms. Trying to pretend she knows what *simian* means. Hoping that it might be complimentary.

He's saying that she looks like a monkey.

"You haven't noticed? It's in the structure of your jaw too."

He's making scientific observations in a fascinated voice. Some people at the table look bored, look out the window. Others say, "*Saxon!*" which only makes it worse. The girl is catching on that he's insulting her.

"I wouldn't worry," he says now. "It's your heritage."

Then he starts a monkey imitation: *Ha ha ha ha heee heee heee —* scratching under his arms. Looking at her all the time with a glint to let her know that she's supposed to laugh along.

I've had enough.

I'm getting up, I'm on my feet, my eyes on Saxon when —

Emily, who's at my table, is also standing up. She's finishing a conversation, but she's moving sideways behind the chairs, and now she's right behind Saxon. She takes a strand of his long hair and grips it in her fist.

"Yeah, Saxon, get a haircut," she says. "Chimpanzee."

And while the others at the table laugh, I notice Em's fist move. Taking the hair with it. Saxon tries to laugh, but his eyes panic. She lets go just as suddenly, looks across the table, says, "Oh, Briony" — so that's the girl's name — "Oh, Briony" — as if she only just noticed her — "I was just telling Lyd and them about how the ghost took your iPod? They're not believing me, so can you come and tell them yourself?"

Briony finds her smile. "I never actually said it was the ghost. I just lost it."

The table laughs at Em, who says, "Okay, come and lie for me," and Briony stands up.

I hadn't known that Em could hear the conversation at the next table. But I did know this: She had not been talking to the others about Briony's lost iPod or the ghost.

*   *   *

Later that night, we're at Lydia's place.

Her parents are inside. Lights in windows.

It's a mild night. So quiet we can hear the dog crossing the terrace. We're all on floating armchairs in the outdoor pool. We're separate, reclining, watching stars. There's lantern light around the pool, a turquoise glow inside it.

It's just a small group — Lydia, Emily, Cassie, Toby, Amelia, and me. Chocolates are being passed around. They're so good, these chocolates, that you don't need to check the chart to choose the best one. Any one you choose will be the best you ever ate. And the box seems endless.

Sometimes there's talking, sometimes just hands trailing the water. I won't lie to you. It's nice.

We're talking about time travel, ghosts. They're making fun of Em. Whether ghosts exist.

I say: "I think you can miss a person so much it's like a fatal wound. So your mind goes into panic, and projects an image of the person onto the air. Gives the person back to you, to fix the wound. That's a ghost."

There's a moment of quiet in the pool: *Who has Riley missed so much his mind went into panic?*

Now is the time to take the next step. I feel Amelia thinking the same thing.

Next step: Share a secret. Make them think that we're true friends.

So we tell them. Not much.

Just the fact that we've lived on the streets and in detention.

We stop.

They're thinking. We're waiting. Then something surprising happens.

Cassie says I'm right.

I don't know what she means.

About ghosts, she says.

She's gone back in time. To what I said before, about your mind giving a missing person back.

I think: *She's changing the subject. They don't know what to say about our past, so they're going to pretend that we never said a word.*

Then Cass explains to Amelia and me that her father died a few years ago. She says they were close. Then she says again that I'm right — you can miss someone so bad your mind goes mad.

It's not exactly what I said.

Floating armchairs brush one another, brush the side of the pool.

I realize: She wasn't changing the subject. She was giving something back. We gave her a secret; she gave one of her own.

Then something else surprising.

Em tells Cass she wants to hear one of Cass's new songs.

Cassie's in our Music class, but I've never heard her sing. Didn't know she could.

Amelia and I are thinking: *Please don't break into song.*

We're thinking: *Things were going fine here. But please don't make us hear this —*

And then she does. She sings.

And Jesus, she's good. The song is simple, nothing special, but her voice is beyond perfect.

I let my hands trail water, watch the stars.

That night, we sleep in Lydia's rec room. Couches are deeper and softer than any bed I ever slept on.

We end up at the Blue Danish again, for breakfast. Somebody mentions an essay due today. Lydia swears. It's a quiet, almost indifferent kind of swearing. She says, "Has someone got the question?" Takes out her laptop.

And she writes the essay. She talks, drinks her coffee, eats a pecan cookie (those are her favorite), and writes an essay in less than half an hour.

I read over her shoulder.

The question's about ghost stories. I remember some of the lines she wrote.

> *On either side of the ghost story's path is a dark, uncertain*
> *wilderness: the "supernatural" (in which ghosts are real) and*
> *the human psyche (in which they are imagined, symbolic,*
> *and possibly even more sinister).*

Something like that. I don't remember exactly. My point is that she wrote fast and well, without thinking. The girl is smart.

I know what *you're* thinking.

You're thinking that I'm falling for them.

You think that's where I'm headed here — the surprising complexity of a lesson in human life. Turns out our new friends are people after all.

I liked what I saw; I adjusted my vision of all three girls, a little — but on the way to the Blue Danish that morning, Emily called ahead, ordered coffees, reserved their favorite table. Asked for double chocolate in her caramel macchiato.

So, you see. Nothing changed.

These girls were who they were: rich kids, shadow people — and the plan was going fine.

EMILY MELISSA-ANNE THOMPSON
Student No. 8233521

I shall be frank as a boy named Frank.

When Term 3 began I was so despondent I was practically fainting senseless.

I had spent Term 2 trying to get Lydia back with Seb, and how did that plan go? It went at a rate of nots.

(For the nonsailors among you, rate of nots is an expression which I believe means *not* going. Or possibly going backward and crashing into the wharf.)

Of course, I was already gloomy about starting Term 3 because it was the Trials, and then Term 4 (the HSC), and then . . . Term 5: *the term of your natural life!*

That is, life in the real world. Not a school student. *Nevermore.* O Time, Time! I hate it! The way it rushes you along and spits you — a hopeless child, a lost cause — outside the school gates!!

Anyway, but getting back to Lydia and Seb.

My plan had been many-splendored. I did not deserve to fail, just as I did not deserve to fail Economics this year.

What was the plan? Well, first, I had persuaded Lyd and Cass to join the Drama with me. Next, I had written a letter to Seb — *pretending it was from Mr. Garcia* — asking Seb to supervise set design. So Seb had joined the Drama too!

Perfect! All going well, so far . . . I stepped back to watch the romance unfold.

And it *did* . . . slowly, Lyd and Seb headed toward one another, and then?

Astrid Bexonville.

I say no more.

Thus, as Term 3 began, I was depressed. I was especially tragic because everybody was talking about Seb's contribution to the Art Exhibition. He had glued or stapled or nailed a strange collection of objects onto a giant stretch of canvas. Somehow, they all seemed to be blowing sideways, as if in a hurricane. In the center of the hurricane: a portrait of a NAKED GIRL. (He hung it at the last moment, getting it from his car the night before the Exhibition to avoid controversy.) The naked girl is facing away from the picture so it's not as naked as it could be, but still. It's a scandal. Anyway, her hair is blowing around her wildly yet she is strangely calm in the midst of the storm.

Oh yeah. And she's Lydia.

SEB SHOULD BE WITH LYDIA. IT IS *SO CLEAR* FROM HIS ARTWORK THAT HE (A) SEES THAT LYDIA IS A WILD AND STORMY GIRL WITH A CALM AND BEAUTIFUL SOUL; AND (B) THINKS LYDIA IS HOT (which she is).

I mean to say, he *knows* Lydia. What was he doing with Astrid? (He couldn't possibly know Astrid.)

I did not blame Seb. I mean, I did. But Lydia had been telling him, over and over, that it was over. So. And Astrid is skinny as. So, you know, technically speaking, why should Seb not have a thing with her?

Nevertheless.

It was a disaster of magnetic proportions. It was a broken nose for destiny.

And there was Lyd, her heart ready to speak . . . ! !

Speaking gothically, I felt like a corpse.

All I could do was tell Lyd to ignore Seb for a while.

I said this to her on the first day of Term 3. She looked surprised and then there was a flash of hurt in her eyes.

Oh, when you see that flash in Lydia's eyes! It's as powerful as her smile (but in reverse, of course). She so rarely shows her hurt!

"Okay," she said, and raised her eyebrows at me.

She thought that Seb had told me he'd lost interest — that was clear.

But what else could I do?

On no possible stretch of reality could Lyd know that Seb and Astrid were together. It would kill her. (She is not fond of Astrid.)

So, I resolved that I would keep Seb-and-Astrid a secret from Lydia, *while* at the same time trying to break up Seb-and-Astrid *or*, alternatively, finding a new boy for Lyd.

This would all be tricky. My mind was agitated.

Meanwhile, everyone was talking about the Tennis Playing Ghost of the Art Rooms which was tedious because I had invented the tennis part. Now I had to play along. I didn't even know why I'd made her a tennis player. (I think I had it mixed up with hockey.) Tennis is okay but not when it's all in my own mind.

Also, I heard that Mr. Garcia had seen the letter I had written to Seb in his name. I knew Mr. G would forgive me — but I just didn't need it. The embarrassment. You know? And the forgery.

And so, I was gloomy.

But time is splendid!! Do you know what it can do? It can change things!

To explain: Moments go by (because time makes them) and just one moment makes a difference!

The relevant moment was a star-spangled one.

We were floating about in the pool at Lydia's place. It was a beautiful, moony night, and conversation splashed gently. People sharing jokes and secrets. Toby talking too much about his History Project, but never mind. Everyone else was interesting.

And now pay heed for I am about to share a truly interesting, gothic secret.

Amelia and Riley TOLD US OF THEIR DARK AND WICKED PAST!!!! Oh, it was wondrous!

It turned out that they had lived a wanton life of crime (stolen from a petrol station) and then been caught and thrown into the dungeons (more or less)!

I had to hide a gasp at first. THEY WERE GOTHIC VILLAINS!

But I quickly reminded myself that I am sophisticated.

Also, that people change. (There are intensive programs for reintegrating juvenile offenders into the community.)

And then I realized, with unexpected wisdom: Amelia and Riley trusted us. How vulnerable they were, voices talking into the night, telling tales of past misdeeds! It was proof that we were truly friends! I could not have loved them more if I had tried! I was *desperate* to help them, in any way I could, on their road to happiness and freedom!

Then Cassie sang and I thought that my heart would burst — such wonderful friends! A friend who can sing like an angel! A friend who is good at woodwork and is dedicated to his History Project! A friend who is smart and has many inflatable armchairs! And two new friends who are wild, wicked, dangerous, and totally reformed!

It was perfect.

And that was the moment when it came to me.

Those words — *it was perfect* — seemed to bring it all together.

Because right away I thought, sadly: *Well, it* would *be perfect if only one more friend was here.* That is, Seb.

I thought of his portrait of Lyd, and the flash of hurt in her eyes. Then I thought of the opposite flash — the flash of her beautiful smile — which led me to think of *Riley's* artwork. And how funny it was that Riley had *also* done a portrait of Lydia for his Major Work. Not really. His artwork was actually photographs, but Lydia's face is amongst them, and it is the starring one. He captured her two faces actually: moody, angry Lydia, and the Lydia that shines brighter than the moon.

And then it came to me like a comet in my brain: *If not Seb, then Riley.*

That is: *Riley should be with Lydia.*

But Riley is with Amelia, you protest.

I know, but listen: There was a crack between Riley and Amelia. Early on, Lydia had predicted they would soon break up (and Lydia is very smart). And *I'd* seen them fighting in the Heritage Park, and *I'd* seen that gap between their hands.

So! Any moment, they would break up.

And once they did, Riley would be free. And then?

A perfect substitute for Seb!

He was sexy like Seb, and an artist like Seb.

He recognized Lydia's beautiful smile.

He was smart. He was dangerous. (About Lyd: She loves danger.) So.

All I had to do was locate the crack between Riley and Amelia — and then gently, gently, gently . . . split them up.

LYDIA JAACKSON-OBERMAN
Student No. 8233410

You know the expression on the gothic villain's face?

The scene where he wants the heroine to sign away her fortune (plus her hand in marriage and the life of her favorite puppy dog)?

Villain's black cape is *casually* flung across the document so all that the heroine can see is the dotted line. She's sweet, trusting, prone to fainting fits, and happily agrees to sign — but just as she puts her pen to the paper, something makes her stop! A frown creases her brow! (Who knew she had a frown in her?)

"Sir," she says — hesitant, "might I trouble you to move your cape? Just so I can see what I am signing?"

And then, the expression on the villain's face!

He *needs* her fortune or he's ruined! All is lost! Now he won't get the signature, so his face —

Black as night. Ferocious as a wolf. Treacherous, thunderous, *murderous*.

That expression — that's what I'm talking about.

I saw it on Riley's face.

All Term 2, I'd watched his face, and every expression had been framed.

First week of Term 3, Riley and Amelia came to my place. Told us they had a criminal past. I wasn't concentrating. I was still thinking of earlier that day:

Blue Danish Café.

Guy at the next table making fun of a girl.

Riley is watching. Riley is drinking his espresso, eating his pecan pie (he always orders pecan pie) — and now the guy goes too far, gets cruel — and there it is: Riley's face.

Treacherous. Thunderous. Murderous.

Unplanned. Unframed. Real.

It only lasted a moment. He didn't know anyone was watching him.

I've gotta say, I liked it, but it kinda startled me.

www.myglasshouse.com/shadowgirl
Wednesday, July 30
My Journey Home
He said:
I keep ordering pecan pie.

A horseshoe was nailed
to the front door
of the house
and my stepfather said:

he said, I keep my luck hanging
on the door here, see, and
let's say you ever need
some luck, Amelia —
let's
say you're playing Monopoly one
day
all you've got is train stations
in a minefield of hotels —
well, you say to your friends,
you say,
hang ten, friends,
and you slip out the
door and
fetch some luck.

He showed me how
to scoop it from the horseshoe.

Okay, I said.

and when we go away,
he said,
on holiday, say?
we'll tell the neighbors
they should help themselves.

It'll just build up otherwise,
and go to waste,
or worse, it'll
tip over the edge,
and isn't it the truth,
doesn't everybody know,
that
luck overflow causes wood rot?

They seem so complete,
said Riley,
pecan pies.
they seem comprehensive,
the pastry, the nuts,
and what else —
is it brown sugar and eggs?
but they're not,
there's something
missing from a pecan pie.

The day we moved into
my stepfather's house,
all that he said was
welcome home.

Last night,

Riley's porch,
something missing from a pecan pie.
his mother laughs:
maybe you're just thinking of a lid.

0 comments

www.myglasshouse.com/emthompson
Wednesday, July 30
My Journey Home
Dear Readers of this Blog,
   Something TERRIBLE has happened and it's all my fault.
   Please forgive me in advance.
   Thank you.
   Okay, now I'll tell you.

Well, you know the Joint Ashbury-Brookfield Art Exhibition?
   You don't? Oh. Well, whatever. Trust me. There was one.
   It happened at the end of last term, and everyone was all:
Wow! So much talent! So much — you know — art! And so on.
The best ones —
   Wait. I just have to eat some coconut chocolate. I can't
stop eating it.
   Anyway, the best ones — wait. I need more.
   Okay, everyone agreed that the best ones were by Riley
(Ashbury) and Seb (Brookfield). There was a division of opin-
ion about which was number one, Riley's or Seb's. But a
lot of people, me included, think you can't put a number
on art. Art is pure, you see, whereas numbers are just, like,
maths.
   So.
   But Seb's was a bit better.
   Whatever, the main thing is, both were masterpieces, and
sophisticated grown-ups said so too. Some of the artworks

are still in the Gallery now. (Others have been taken down for people to keep working on them.)

Now, this morning I was in the Year 12 Common Room, pre-paring for my exams. For those not living in the universe, the Trials begin in one week. In fact, this is a stressful time for me and the last thing I need is for a terrible thing to happen to somebody else. But that's a selfish approach. I shouldn't have said that. Excuse me. I need more chocolate.

Anyhow, so there I was, googling "good memory." (An important first step in a study regime is to google advice on how to study.)

My friend Toby was reading a book nearby. He kept interrupting to tell me historical facts — Toby is great but obsessed with a convict who once lived right here in Castle Hill. Look. A lot of people live in Castle Hill. Toby needs to get over that.

Anyway, I was just saying, "Toby, this is quite interesting, but not so much to me," when there was a sound of rapid, high-pitched talk and gasping outside the door.

Toby and I leaned forward, hoping to hear the gossip with-out having to, you know, stand up.

(Am just having some more coconut chocolate.)

And sure enough, the news rushed into the room, and it was this:

SOMEONE HAD ATTACKED SEB'S ARTWORK.

This, so we can be clear, was his MAJOR WORK for the HIGHER SCHOOL CERTIFICATE. (Apart from being a windy master-piece in its own right.)

Toby and I ran to the Art Rooms and joined the crowd of people. And it was true. Seb's artwork had been slashed, ripped, and torn to pieces. There were also splashes of pink and red paint on it.

Somebody — *or something* — wanted to destroy it.

Why? Who would do such a thing?

I have not yet seen Seb — I'll see him at rehearsals tomorrow — but I have no doubt he is feeling slashed, ripped, and torn to pieces himself. (Emotionally speaking.) He will be suicidal and will need therapy.

This act of blatant terrorism goes to the heart of who Seb is. It will likely undermine his HSC, his artistic confidence, and his entire career. His life will be in tatters for eternity and a good while after that.

There are rumors that it was an Ashbury student who did this: either out of jealousy of Seb's talent or because we just don't like Brookfielders.

What?! No! No! No! We LOVE Brookfielders. (They're sexy.)

And anyway, an Ashbury student would NEVER do such a thing!!

Yet, that is the rumor. Let me say now. For once and for all. With no arguments accepted.

THIS WAS NOT AN ASHBURY STUDENT.

How can I be sure?

Because I know who it was.

It was the ghost.

Think about it. The ghost lives down the hall from the Gallery. The incident happened at night when the Art Rooms are locked. The incident was angry! The ghost is angry.

Why is it my fault?

I woke the angry ghost.

And so, it's all my fault.

(But please note that you began this blog by forgiving me.)

I felt very depressed all day, and also on my whole *journey home*. Now I can't stop eating chocolate.

The universe has lost something beautiful (Seb's artwork).

And I, personally, need more cho — oh. It's all gone. I ate it all. Can life get any worse?

6 comments

Yowta772 said . . . No.

DainaB said . . . That totally sux. ☹ Did you find anything good online about remembering things for exams? I SO need a better memory. LLOL

Em said . . . Well, I read that it's important to sleep. While you sleep, the hippopotamus in your brain replays things that happened during the day, e.g., what you studied. So therefore it remembers it for you.

DeannaG said . . . LOL, Em, I doubt there's a hippopotamus in my brain ☺

CalypsoAngel said . . . I think it's a hippocampus cos we did it in biology, and I also think it's disrespectful to talk about the brain while Seb's beautiful art is being destroyed.

Em said . . . It's not BEING destroyed, it WAS destroyed. It's happened. Get on top of the concept of TIME, CalypsoAngel. Also, I am sure that, even though Seb's artistic career is effectively over, he would not want us to mope around. He would want us to get on with our lives.

LYDIA JAACKSON-OBERMAN
STUDENT No. 8233410

Just like that, Amelia became our friend.

It started after rehearsal one day. A few of us had stayed back, talking.

Night was painting the windows fast. The auditorium was dark — seats heading up, up, up into the black — warm glow of light around the stage.

I was sitting on the edge of the stage between Riley and Seb. A group of people circled us. We were talking about Seb's artwork — vandalized the night before.

"I am so, so sorry," Em kept saying.

Seb was shrugging. "It needed work anyway." But he was also pale — something vicious in the vandalism. "I guess if someone hated it that much, it needed work," he joked. People laughed.

"I'm just so sorry," Em murmured.

"It won't take long to fix," Seb said. "Or I keep it how it is and change the name to *Slash and Burn*." They laughed again.

"Yes, but Seb," said Em. "I'm sorry."

"Okay." Riley spoke up, his voice mild and interested beside me. "What's with Em and the apologies?"

"The ghost did it," Em explained.

People turned to see Riley's reaction to this. His eyes squinted ever so slightly, then squinted more. He seemed to be rolling Em's words around in his mouth. People giggled, then laughed, the laughter faded into quiet — and a strange thing happened.

Into the quiet came distant sounds — a voice calling — someone laughing — footsteps — keys doing their *beep! beep!* thing — car doors — engines — then *brrrrrrm* (my impression of cars leaving the car park all at once).

Then, nothing.

Silence.

A powerful sense pooling over us, that we were the last ones in the building.

And the strangest sensation *that the building didn't know we were still here.*

Okay, it sounds weird, but that's exactly what it was.

The sensation seemed to grow all around us. Like the building was stretching, reaching its arms into the empty night, letting down its guard. I had this sudden, mad urge to call, "Wait! Don't do that yet. We're still here!"

I didn't.

But I won't lie to you. It was spooky.

I don't believe in ghosts, but I do believe in haunting, if you get what I mean, and this building was haunted — by a girl named Sandra Wilkinson, who had fallen to her death; and now by an anger so profound it had attacked a major work.

"Somebody's got a lot of anger," said Amelia, speaking calmly into the moment — "to do that to something as beautiful as Seb's art." She was plaiting her long hair as she spoke. "That's what's scary," she said.

I liked her. She was speaking my thoughts aloud.

I had some anger of my own, actually. Seb was on my left and my left side felt like ice. He had asked Em to let me know he wasn't interested. As if we were in primary school, passing around notes.

It pissed me off. I'd told him a few times I wasn't into him myself. He didn't need to do this childish "Guess what, I'm not into *you* anymore either! Ha ha ha." (Especially not via Em.)

I guess it was his pride that made him do it.

Well, I've got some pride myself, and the funny thing is, I'd been about to say to Seb, "Okay, I want you back." So that was something.

I'd been saved from that moment: saying those words while his face fell with pity.

I'd missed out, by seconds, from stepping off a cliff.

But now, in the big, empty, stretching building, our conversation changed. Faster, slower, louder, softer, and more intense all at once. Different ways of dealing with the spookiness, I guess. A kind of rush to fix it.

Our words wanted to fix things too. *We have to find out who did this to Seb. We have to find the true story about Sandra Wilkinson. Did she fall or did she jump or was she pushed. Who would hate Seb that much.* And so on.

Toby talked about time travel, and Cass talked about CCTV, but somehow they were talking about the same thing. Seb's art and the falling girl, braiding together like Amelia's hair.

I felt as if a shift was taking place.

We seemed to be falling together — but falling where? Into the silence. Into love. Out of love. Into the future. Take your pick.

It felt like: *Something's going to happen.*

"There's a section on Sandra Wilkinson in the *History of Ashbury*," Riley said.

Seb said, "Ashbury has a history?"

"In the front reception," Riley answered. "*Illustrated History.*"

Seb on my left; Riley on my right, talking across me. Left side, cold; right side, warm. I looked from one to the other and saw that they look alike — Seb is lean and Riley's broad, but same height, same dark hair, same smooth, strong profiles.

Em was excited. She was saying we should find *The Illustrated History of Ashbury* right now. Would the front office be open? She looked at her watch — and then she panicked. It was after nine. The Trials were next week, and Em, Cass, and I had planned to study at my place tonight.

"Should we still come back to your place?" Cass wondered.

"For sure we should," said Em. "There's time to get an entire subject done." And then she turned to Amelia, now unbraiding all her work, and said, "Do you want to come too?"

Amelia looked surprised, pale, pleased. It seemed real, the pleasure.

"Yeah, okay." She didn't look at Riley. The way some girlfriends do. I noticed that.

It was a few moments later, as we were packing up to go, that the building gave one of its distant, cracking sounds. This one was short and sharp, almost like a cry.

Riley's voice rose easily, somewhere just behind me.

"That'll be Sandra Wilkinson," he said, "letting us know she needs our help." And then he added, in the same easy tone: "Somebody has to catch her before she hits the ground."

It was the way he talked in present tense — not Sandra come back to tell us she had fallen, but Sandra, falling, now —

A slip in time.

It scared me and I liked it both at once.

EMILY MELISSA-ANNE THOMPSON
Student No. 8233521

Ah, Seb! Poor Seb!

We stayed back after rehearsal and gathered around him, beating our chests. The night was a deep and gloomy one, and there we were — alone! — in the great, gothic castle called the Art Rooms.

Seb sat on the edge of the stage alongside Lydia (his lost love — oh, Seb! why Astrid? you fool! and etc. — but that is a separate issue).

He was so distraught about his major work that now and then he had to fall senseless to the floor.

"Oh God!" he muttered (from the floor, when we roused him with drops of peppermint oil). "Why am I thus afflicted?" And then the voice tore from his throat: "Be calm, be calm, my soul!"

Or, anyway, that is not exactly how it happened, but, gothically speaking, it could have.

In fact, we did gather around Seb after rehearsal, but he was quite easygoing about the art attack thing (ha-ha, that sounds like heart attack), and he was already talking about ideas for a new major work.

But it was a strangely agitating night for me. I could hardly concentrate on the conversation. However, I do remember some of it.

Cass said she'd seen people installing security cameras in the Music Rooms that morning. "If they're doing secret surveillance," she said, "they should do it in the Gallery. You can always buy a new trombone or whatever but you can't replace art."

"They need retrospective cameras," Amelia said. "To see back in time. To see who did it."

Toby glanced at Amelia. She stood up on her toes, in this way she has, like a ballet dancer, or like she wants to be taller for a moment, and then her feet fell back to the floor. As soon as her feet hit the floor, Toby spoke. He said that time travel was possible.

He is an honest boy, Toby, but I know for a fact that time travel is *not* possible. (It would have been on the news if it was.) So I looked pointedly at him — however, it turned out to be true! Not exactly *travel*, but listen:

"You put a mirror on a planet way across the universe," Toby explained, "and make sure the mirror's facing you. Then you get a super powerful telescope, and point it at the mirror. You know what you'll see?"

"What?" said Amelia.

"The past. Not yourself looking into the telescope, but the past."

"When in the past?"

"It depends how far away the mirror is. The farther away, the farther back in time."

People started talking about distance and time in a confusing way. I did not pay too much heed because it somehow reminded me of Economics. HOWEVER, it turned out that scientifically speaking, what Toby said was *absolutely true*!

So then I went a bit mad. I was like, "Okay, already! — let's get the mirror set up!"

Because I wanted to see!

To see who had destroyed Seb's painting!

To look farther back and see what happened when Sandra Wilkinson fell from that window! To see if she really is the ghost!!

(I knew that Toby would want to go even *farther* back, to convict times, to see his friend Tom — but I myself can live without Tom.)

Then Lydia, who was sitting between Seb and Riley, and slowly kicking her heels against the side of the stage, spoke up. "Em," she said, "there might be a few technical hitches."

"Like how to get the mirror far enough away," Riley said.

"And I don't think there's a powerful enough telescope yet," Cass told me.

"Even if there was, I think there'd be too much space noise or interference in between. You couldn't get a clear picture," Toby apologized.

"And does Ashbury have an observatory?" Seb smiled.

Why do other people have to be so *knowledgeable* sometimes?

And why use their knowledge to stamp all over sparks of hope?

To be honest, the whole thing agitated me beyond belief.

I was tired of not knowing, you see.

We left the building soon after this, and as we did there was a distant, cracking sound — and I trembled violently. But *I did not feel like trembling*! Always with the trembling: the HSC, the future, the ghost!

293

If I was tired of not knowing, I was even *more* tired of being scared!

Those two issues are related, I think. The not knowing and the being scared? You're scared of the things that you don't know. That's my wisdom for today.

And now, a final confession. A terrible secret.

That night? *I felt annoyed with Riley and Amelia.*

Sacrilege, I know! But suddenly, out of nowhere, I'd had enough of my own fascination. Enough of yearning to see them and feeling excited when I did. Enough of pondering: *Why are they so amazing? When will they ever notice me?*

It was exhausting.

All year they'd been twitching out of my reach. They came to parties — great! But they arrived at strange hours. Mysterious. They came to coffee with us — great! But they didn't talk about themselves. Mysterious. They told us about their past — great! *But look at that past!* The streets! Juvenile detention! A whole new can of mysteries!

And kind of scary mysteries too. I'm very sorry, but crime scares me. I try hard to be "modern" — compassionate like Cass, or cynical like Lyd — but I can't be.

Therefore, I was scared. Scared of Amelia and Riley.

I invited Amelia to come and study with us at Lyd's place. And she did. And the next few weeks, she spent a lot of time with Lyd, Cass, and me, especially Lyd.

But do you know why I invited her to study?

Because I was scared of her. And I didn't want to be. It made me mad.

Different ways of being absent, Amelia collects them.

Dreaming of her stepfather — she's gone.

Slipping away to spend time with a madwoman who speaks in fairy tales.

And now, check it out, she's hangin' with the richgirls.

It's a trick, she says, but I taste something like fear.

TOBIAS GEORGE MAZZERATI
STUDENT No. 8233555

February 1, 1804

A blast of rain like a sudden loss of temper. Thunderclaps that feel personal. Hailstones the size of sheep.

I feel the darkness looming, and taste fear.

My final letter to Maggie is shredded in the mud. I'll not write again. I've not heard from her for almost a year; she's forgotten me.

So she should have, for I am doomed.

It's true there are nights when I talk to Phillip, look at the grand stone barracks that he built, and the stars light up my heart and make me think his plans will succeed.

But mostly I think they will shoot us down like dogs.

The signs are everywhere. Here's three that come to mind:

1. Not a single uprising has ever succeeded here. There was one planned a couple of years back now. They captured two men, thinking they might know who the ringleaders were. Three hundred lashes each, just to make them say.

   "You'll not get any music from me," said one, "for other men to dance on air."

The floggers shook their cat-o'-nine-tails, so that the blood, skin, and flesh flew fast in the wind, and carried on counting the strokes.

2. Not long ago, some men escaped from the barracks, visited a nearby farm, made themselves hot dumplings, and headed back out into the night to sleep under stars. They were captured. We assembled to watch the execution. Then the sound of galloping hooves and a soldier, breathless, announced that straws were to be drawn.

   The first man drew the long straw, and the noose was lifted up off his head. The other two got short straws and were hanged. One kept laughing 'til the pain twisted his smile into a shriek.

3. They've swept the natives away like so many dying bats before a hot wind. Because the natives fight back, the governor has issued a proclamation: Any native west of Parramatta must be shot on sight.

The signs are clear. Failure and death are everywhere. We will fail.

Knowing this, a secret terror stirs in me each night, and it is this: What if Maggie has *not* forgotten me? What if the reason she's not writing is that she's carried out her foolish plan to steal something? And she's on her way here, a convict too?

Do you know what happens to female convicts when they arrive? As soon as the ship's in anchor, the decks are crowded with gentleman settlers and male convicts, come to choose servants or wives. They look about them, rub their chins, squint at women's waistlines. Take wrists between their hands and turn them to the light.

In my nightmares I see Maggie's wrist in the light. She laughs and then her laugh becomes a shriek. Then Maggie's own voice speaks to me: "Never look at a cat that's washing its face," she says, and my blood turns cold. "The first to look at such a cat will die."

I remember her telling me this years ago at home, and I laughed. But here, in this place, I fear it may be true.

Eat hot dumplings. Draw a short straw. Look a cat in the face. Or just be seen west of Parramatta.

This place is a vortex with death at every curve.

Sure, and I never knew that fear could be this vast.

RILEY T. SMITH
Student No. 8233569

We overhear them talking in the courtyard.

This is August, the coldest month. Amelia and I walking a balcony — voices drifting up from below.

"There's a whole section on her, like Riley said. Photos and everything."

"Have you got the book?"

"They wouldn't let me take it away from the front office. But it was nothing new anyway — just, she fell out of a window and, you know, died. Tragedy, tragedy, blah blah."

Emily, Lydia, and Cassie, sheltered from the wind by the angle of the courtyard. Legs stretched out to the winter sun. Hair catching sunlight.

We can't see their faces.

"Does it say why she fell? Because who falls out a window. What, was she leaning out to see a bird? Was she a bird-watcher?" That's Lydia's voice, dry, ironic, impatient all at once. Also sleepy. As if her eyes are closed.

"Maybe she was trying to get away from someone," Emily says. "Or there could have been a fire. She was trying to run away from a fire, and the school hid the evidence so they wouldn't be liable."

"Maybe she was sleepwalking," says Cass.

A slow sigh from Emily.

Silence. Vague rustle of papers.

*   *   *

It's the first week of the Trials. They're looking over study notes. About to go into an exam.

We wait. Lean against the railings. Amelia beside me.

"Lyd, do you seriously know all this already?" Em's voice.

"She's reading through her eyelids," Cass says.

"There's only five minutes to go, and I've still got, oh my God, thirty pages to learn, so, what is that, like, five pages a minute? That's physically impossible, right?"

"If you shut up and let me sleep," says Lyd, "it's not."

Low, slow giggles. Laughing just because it feels good to laugh.

Something shifts beside me. Amelia tensing.

Then Emily speaks again. "Oh, there was this one thing, though. In the history book? After she died, they went and carved on this tree. There used to be this tree where people carved, like, S.B. loves N.W. or whatever, so, after Sandra Wilkinson fell out of the window they did this ceremony where they wrote W.A. loves S.W. on the tree."

"Why?"

"The W.A. stood for *we all*. Like, we *all* love Sandra Wilkinson."

Another sleepy, sultry giggle from Lydia.

Cass says, "They were kind of nauseating back then, weren't they?"

"They decided to stop carving any other names on the tree after that," Em continues. "So it would be, you know, sacred to Sandra's memory."

Silence, more flipping of pages.

Emily speaks again: "I was thinking. After this exam do you want to see if we can find the tree? And look at the initials? Just for, you know, fun?"

A pause.

"Where's the tree?"

"The book says it's a Moreton Bay Fig. Behind the Music Rooms. It might still be there."

"It is," says Cassie. "I know that tree."

The bell rings out. Emily swears. Papers fall. More laughter from below.

Amelia and I step back. We look into each other's eyes. I'm thinking that she's thinking what I'm thinking: The timing could be perfect.

Then complicated clouds blow across Amelia's face.

She doesn't want to do it — She wants to see her crazy friend — She likes the richgirls too much now — She's hoping that they'll ask her to join them in their ghost hunt. . . .

All of these. Or none.

But then the clouds clear and Amelia laughs.

EMILY MELISSA-ANNE THOMPSON
STUDENT No. 8233521

The plot thickens!

(Which is very gothic of it.)

It was late afternoon and we'd just had an exam.

Lyd, Cass, and I tramped through the cold afternoon, down to the Music Rooms, and around the corner.

And there it was — plain as day, a big, old tree carved with initials!

All three of us stopped suddenly.

Strange, strange! that this tree had been here all along and I had not known! *Oh, Ashbury,* I thought, *you still have some secrets in you, don't you, old girl?*

(I was going quietly mad, I suppose. The stress of exams.)

Then, as I approached, the tree seemed to me to be angry!

It was wrinkled and twisted like an old person, and the old often *are* cranky — but was this the anger of the forgotten? Once, the tree had been popular — the place young romantics declared their love.

Now, a nobody. Who amongst us likes to be famous when young only to become a wrinkled old tree in later years? (Not Lydia's mother, certainly.)

We looked closely but initials and hearts swarmed all over that tree. *There were too many!* A jumble of foolish little letters. Young love *itself* began to seem foolish to me (sacrilege).

No wonder the tree is angry! I thought. *Carvings all over its bark!*

The sun was sinking fast, and the chill was in my shoulder blades. I began to wonder, with gothic horror, what I was doing here. Why was I studying this tree when I should be studying for tomorrow's exam?! There could be snakes in this grass! And what would happen to my eyes if I kept peering at tiny, faded letters in this gloomy light?! I would go blind! And what if I put a crick in my neck from leaning forward like this?!

And so on.

I was just about to shriek to the others, "LET US FLY FROM THIS PLACE! LET US FLY TO THE BLUE DANISH CAFÉ!" — when Lyd and Cass both said: "Here."

They were looking at separate parts of the tree — Cass crouching down to read near the ground, and Lyd stretching up high — I wondered, briefly, how they could both say, "Here," at the same time.

Cass stood up. Lydia pointed to a heart shape. Inside it:

Just as *The Illustrated History of Ashbury* had promised.

"We All Heart Sandra Wilkinson," I whispered.

"Not so much me," Lyd said.

"Me neither," Cass agreed.

But, you know, they were just being funny? I felt at that moment a gust of something warm and I believe all three of us felt it. The tender sadness of the past stood before us — people our own age had lost their friend and had wanted to tell the world they loved her. And here we were, the *future*, hearing their words. A shiver of goose bumps struck me — the thrill of a message from nowhere. The joy of an impossible connection. A bit like being able to make a mobile phone call in a tunnel.

The three of us stood in the gathering dark for a few moments. Just staring at the heart shape.

Then I remembered something. "What was it you found, Cass?" I asked. "You said 'here' at the same time as Lyd."

"It was nothing. I saw an S.W. down there so I thought I'd found it, but it was just S.W. loves someone. Probably a different S.W."

We breathed in the cold air. We sighed quietly, and straightened up, ready to go home —

And then?

Then something happened.

It was the plot thickening, I guess.

LYDIA JAACKSON-OBERMAN
STUDENT No. 8233410

You want gothic?

Stand by a gnarled old tree in the deepening dusk. Music Rooms hulking on one side. The reserve — or the *woods* if you prefer — a rustling darkness on the other.

Faded initials of a dead girl on the tree.

And then?

Music.

Otherworldly music. First, an impossibly beautiful girl's voice, sweet and husky both at once. And then, the tremble of a drumbeat — a beat that builds, twists, grows, braids itself with the voice, and thrums to the essence of your soul.

Unexpected. And *totally* gothic.

6

**The Committee for the Administration of the
K. L. Mason Patterson Trust Fund
THE K. L. MASON PATTERSON SCHOLARSHIP FILE**

Memo

To: All Members of the K. L. Mason Patterson
Trust Fund Committee
From: Lucy Wexford
Re: Amelia and Riley

URGENT! URGENT! URGENT!

Dear Committee Members,
   I hereby demand an urgent meeting of the
Committee.
   Pronto!
   Or whatever the technical words are.
   Something remarkable has happened!
   Background: In the last couple of weeks, I've had
security cameras installed in the Music Rooms.
Nothing to do with suspicions about Amelia and
Riley, of course. No, no. Just — you know —
castanets missing one day, cellos the next?
Couldn't afford to lose our string section, could
we? No. So, I persuaded the powers that be . . .
   Anyhow, I looked over the footage last night and
you will not believe what I saw . . .

*Amelia and Riley breaking into the Music Rooms —
after school hours!!!*

They rifled amongst the musical equipment; Amelia began to sing; Riley played the drums; and . . .

Their talent is extraordinary.

Forget swimming, acting, art — all piffle, I say, compared to their sheer, musical genius.

Their performance gave me chills. I am not the crying type but I literally sobbed my heart out as I watched.

The Ashbury Musical Concert is next week. Obviously, Riley and Amelia must participate. For Ashbury's sake.

I propose an "arrangement" be made, similar to the deal we struck with them about the Drama. Usefully, they entered the Music Rooms after hours — clear violation of school rules, and thus a threat to their scholarships. Could this be used to "persuade" them to "volunteer" to "participate" in the Concert?

So — a meeting please. Let me remind you, people, that *valuable time has already been lost.* If it is already too late, *let that be upon your heads.*

Sincerely,
Lucy Wexford

EMILY MELISSA-ANNE THOMPSON
STUDENT No. 8233521

I have an Auntie June.

Last year she got cancer. We were all so frightened and sad for her. Going through chemotherapy. Turns out, it sucks. It seemed to work, however, phew. But then, not long after, she got kidney stones. Those were even more painful than childbirth, she said, and that kills (I hear). Poor Auntie June! Anyway, then her washing machine malfunctioned and flooded the living room! Poor Auntie June. And *then* her car got stolen and, oh, for crying out loud, enough already.

Do you see what I mean?

I know it sounds harsh but when too many bad things happen to a person, it's just, like, I have to feel sorry for you again?!! Couldn't you let someone else have a turn at bad luck for once? Aren't you being a bit greedy with it? And well, could some of this be your own fault? Are you taking care to *avoid* things like kidney stones and laundry floods?

I tell you this cautionary tale, first to discourage you from too many misfortunes, but mainly for the gothic purpose of explaining my own emotions as per the following:

The night we saw the ghost's initials on the tree? Just as we were leaving? There was the sound of music from the Music Rooms.

At first, I was transfigured. The music was the opposite of kidney stones.

But then we went in, and saw who it was. Amelia and Riley.

And seriously.

Wasn't swimming, art, drama, and essay-writing *enough* for them? They had to go and have *another* talent? It was ridiculous. Plain unrealistic. It was like Auntie June and the stolen car — enough already, you guys. Now you're just being greedy.

More importantly, their greed had stolen CASSIE'S TALENT. Singing belongs to Cass, and I had the terrible feeling that Amelia's singing might be better than Cass's. All Cass *has* is singing and running, and she doesn't have a dad since he's dead, so, you know, *leave Cass's talents alone, Amelia!*

That was the angry thought that leapt to my head when I saw them.

(At the same time I had this strange thought: *So you two just HAPPENED to be practicing here while we were right outside at the tree?* I knew this was unfair. They could not have known we were at the tree so it WAS a coincidence. And yet I had this unpleasant suspicion. It felt supernatural.)

Lyd and Cass did not seem to be sharing my angry/suspicious thoughts, and were full of praise and queries. Riley and Amelia said they were working on something to play at the Goose and Thistle — they play the dawn shift there sometimes, apparently. It was all — *amazing* —

And yet, I just wanted to go home.

Anyhow, that happened, and then the weeks went by.

The weather grew warmer and we plummeted toward our final days of school. The Music teacher was going wild about R and A's music, but they just laughed when she asked them to be in the school concert.

I still watched them sometimes. Looking for the crack, so I could get Lyd together with Riley. She seemed especially mesmerized by his drumming, so that was a step.

But there was so much else!

The HSC was lurching toward us like a monstrous antelope. Bindy Mackenzie, Yearbook Editor, was demanding we write profiles of our friends. We had to plan the Formal (which is after the HSC), the Muck-up Day (banned, but whatever), and the Final Assembly. We had to finalize the Drama. We had to wonder who would be top student of the school (not really — it would be Bindy Mackenzie).

Also, much emotion to experience. Everywhere I turned: a beautiful memory from earlier days at Ashbury. Every moment: a memory slipping out of my grasp. I realized I loved everybody — or most of them — and all my teachers — or some of them. Teachers are so sweet and dedicated sometimes! They look so old when they take off their glasses! And they're uncannily human when they want to be.

In those weeks, I couldn't stop taking photos on my mobile. I even went down to the old tree behind the Music Rooms, and photographed it — I thought that might cheer it up, remind it of its celebrity days.

And this brings me to the final, busy thing.

The ghost.

Oh, it was still there. Don't worry about that. There were cracking sounds, doors banging, distant sobbing. You name it.

But people either ignored all this, or they joked, "There goes the ghost!"

As with the tree. Once famous. Now, just any old ghost.

I realized that eventually people would forget her altogether.

Hadn't that happened before? When my mother was at Ashbury, they had talked about the ghost — and then she had faded out of memory.

So, I made a decision. I'd find out the truth about Sandra Wilkinson — reveal the ghost to the world. My gift to the ghost. My legacy at Ashbury.

All right, I admit it, my "bite me, Mr. L," to Mr. Ludovico.

But how?

This, I wondered as I stood photographing the old tree. I'd have to find out more about Sandra and why she fell. Was she known for being clumsy around windows? Had she had her heart broken and jumped? Witnessed a crime and been pushed? Maybe there was something in the archives? Student files, police reports, academic rec — and then, I stopped.

Had she had her heart broken?

Here I was taking photos of a tree covered in hearts. Maybe one of them had Sandra's name in it?

And then — of *course*! One did! Or maybe anyway. Cass had found the initials S.W. — it could be a different S.W. of course, but what if it was *our* Sandra?

I crouched down to where Cass had been looking, and found it quickly —

So. Was it our S.W.? If so, who was K.P.?

Was there a K.P. at the school at the same time as our S.W.?

I would look up class records!

Like an overexcited detective, I ran straight to the Art Rooms, and up, up, up the stairs to the archives room. It was empty. The window ledges were dusty, and there were splatters of red paint (which should be cleaned with methylated spirits) on the floor, and the compacting files were overflowing.

I pulled the files apart, one at a time, *whirrrr-THUNK, whirrr-THUNK*, until I reached the 1950s. I raced through those files! Like the lawyer I will one day be! Like television!

I found a thin manila folder labeled *Student Roll, 1952*! Sandra's year!

I went to open it, then noticed — nearby, *Student Records, 1952, Vol. 1*. There were five Vols! All bulging! I ran my eyes along the other files — suddenly, it seemed quite likely that there'd be a file labeled: *Reason Sandra Is Haunting the Art Rooms*.

I was alone in the room. My heart thudded madly in the silence as my eyes raced over the files.

And then?

clicketyclacketyclicketyclacketyclicketyclacketyclack

A rush of strange, sharp, clicketing sounds from *just behind the shelf that I was standing at*! Like a tiny machine gun! A toy train speeding toward me!

I screamed.

Spun around, skidded, and *flew from that room.*

Files slipped from my arms as I ran!

I tripped down a flight of steps — and then I stopped. I looked back up at the closed door of the archives room. It seemed to breathe quietly to itself, then glance up and give me a look like, "*what?*"

I was stern with myself.

"Courage, Emily!" I said, or words to that effect. "There is no doubt a perfectly innocent explanation for that noise!"

There was only one file left in my hands — *Student Records, 1952, Vol. 3.*

What if the important information was in a different file?

Besides, it was irresponsible studenting, leaving spilled files all over the floor. Even if there were already paint stains there.

I breathed in and out for a while. Walked bravely back upstairs, opened the door to the archives room —

And then, no, no! Help me, somebody! The shock of it!

The compacting files had been firmly closed up *and all my dropped files were gone.*

I ran again.

This time I did not stop until I was outside the front door of the building.

And as I leaned against the brick wall, my heart thundering, I thought again of those red splatters on the floor. . . . Were they paint . . .

. . . or blood stains?

Nothing — not the sneer on Mr. Ludovico's face, not even a lifetime of Toblerones — would ever get me back into that room.

LYDIA JAACKSON-OBERMAN
STUDENT NO. 8233410

An empty room, Riley at a window.

This is the middle of the day. I'm in the Art Rooms, walking a corridor of closed classroom doors, and then —

An open door, an empty room, Riley at a window.

Reminds me of the first time I saw them. Amelia looking out, Riley in.

Now he's looking out. He hears me, glances back. Smiles his eyes at me to say hello. Turns back to the window and I join him.

This is a classroom at the front of the building so it overlooks the oval. Beyond the oval, you can see the main school buildings. Look left, and there's a brick wall cutting the oval off from the road.

It's a spring blue sky. Passing cars flash sun.

A single figure crosses the oval. Long hair in a ponytail. Amelia.

"She's going to see a friend," Riley says. He pauses, then adds: "The friend lives in a mental institution. I've never met her, Amelia doesn't know her name, but she goes to see her all the time. Strange, no?"

He raises his eyebrows for humorous effect.

It's not like him: to talk about Amelia. Make clumsy jokes. Be afraid.

I want to say: "Strange? Are you kidding? Here it is — what I've known all along. Some mysterious friend she's gotta visit all the time? The mental institution is a nice twist, sure, but she's cheatin' on you, buddy. Open your eyes."

But what I say is: "Could be strange. Could be she's got a friend in a mental institution who doesn't want to say her own name."

Riley's smile is sudden and brief. He's still watching the window. Amelia's close to the edge.

It makes me sad, his smile.

He's drumming softly on the window ledge. Left hand swerving back and forth, right hand resting but its forefinger taps, quick and steady.

I look down at his hands and he stops.

We both look up and Amelia's gone.

So I ask about his drumming. How he got started.

As long as he remembers, he says, he's liked finding the sounds in surfaces. Tables, bowls, garage doors, his dad's bald head.

His earliest memory is sitting in a high chair, thunking a banana with a spoon. He remembers loving the deep, warm sound it made.

"Just never grew up, I guess," he says.

But you are grown up. His hands are big, brown, sinewed, veined, scarred.

It comes to me that all his other talents are just role-playing — but the music, this is who he is.

But he's changed the subject. He's talking about his little sister. The banana story reminded him. She put a handful of mashed banana in his hair this morning. Concentrating fiercely as she did it, like that was her job.

The baby makes him real too — makes his face light up.

"She likes it when I blow up a balloon and then release the air against her cheek," he says. "She gets so tense, waiting, and then, when I let go, it's like I'm releasing a burst of giggles along with the burst of air."

Telling pointless baby stories, proud, and he can't help his smile and nor can I.

We're sitting on top of desks now, just by the window. Still watching the empty oval, but not seeing it. I want to ask more about the drumming. I want to see them play again.

But I feel shy. It's not like me. I try a different angle.

"The night we heard you guys in the Music Rooms," I say, "we were looking at a tree, looking for Em's ghost."

"The falling girl," he says, then glances back toward the door. "This is Room 27B. Where the ghost lives. Where Em gets cold."

He does that a lot: remembers details.

I watch his face. He's looking around.

"Not here now," he says.

"Nope."

"Em gets a twitch in her lip, doesn't she?" he says. More details.

He looks directly at my mouth as if the answer's there. In my own lips. He's playing — but you know, come on.

So I say, challenging: "Do you believe in ghosts?"

"Don't know if there's a ghost in this building," he says. "But ghosts. Why not?"

"There's an explanation," I say, "for every single sighting of a ghost."

"Could be," he says, "that some experiences are so emotionally charged — something like murder or betrayal — they get imprinted on the air. We see glimpses in the air years later."

"Not that kind of explanation." I shake my head. "Something physical, I mean, like earth tremors. Or shadows. Or someone left the TV on in another room. Or something in the person who sees the ghost — some psychological flaw."

"Could be that there's a kind of collective memory," he says, as if I haven't spoken — but his smile knows that I have and I smile back — "like the collective consciousness. And a ghost is just a fragment from the collective memory."

"There's no such thing as a collective memory," I say, "or consciousness either." I'm still smiling, and my voice feels oddly free. "It's hallucination. Or a seizure. It makes you think you see a ghost."

"Or could be," he says, "a dead person come back."

"Now we're getting somewhere," I say.

He laughs.

Turns to the window again.

"Em does have a photo of her ghost," I say, playing along with ghost-boy here.

"The crazed red face in the window," he agrees.

We're both smiling again. We're quiet a few moments.

Then he raises a hand, points toward the window. "See that?" he says.

I look, but the oval's empty.

"The gap in the brick wall," he says.

I stand up, find the gap. He stands too.

"See the cross street through the gap," he says. "The stop sign there?"

I can't see it.

He moves closer to me, points. "There," he says. Puts an arm around my shoulder, leans his face close to mine so he can see my line of vision. Lifts my hand, his arm along mine, presses my finger to the glass. Waits.

"Okay," I say.

He shifts away again.

"There's your ghost," he says.

I squint at the stop sign.

"You're saying that's the red face in the photo?" I say, and laugh. "That stop sign? It's too far away."

"It's a trick of the light," he says. "Stop signs are designed to be super reflective. Right time of the day, the sun shines on it, it'll light up and jump right into frame."

I'm staring, silent, still not sure. I remember that he's a photographer.

The bell is ringing. We both look back toward the open door. Sounds of footsteps, talking.

"You'll see what I mean if you look at the photo again," he says. "The flash makes the blurs for the features on the face. The face is the stop sign."

"You knew that all along?"

He smiles, raises his eyebrows, turns to go.

RILEY T. SMITH
STUDENT No. 8233569

It's called pareidolia.

A pattern, a shape, in an unexpected place, and your brain turns it into something real. Makes it familiar. Animals in clouds or in a cliff face. Jesus in a tortilla shell; the Virgin Mary etched into your soap. A face in a photograph of smoke or of a stop sign through a window.

Your brain wants the world to be familiar so it sees familiar things like faces. At the same time, *you* want things to be remarkable — so you grab on to that familiar image: Yes, I'm not mistaken, that *is* a giraffe etched in the cliff face! A miracle!

But it's just the way that things are arranged.

The school was alight — how could Amelia and I be so multi-talented?!

Let me set it out for you. Watch.

We're okay at acting. Had a lot of practice in police interviews, courtrooms, detention, with youth workers — practice being the people they wanted us to be.

We're okay at essays and art. We both like to read and sketch. Write letters to each other — and Amelia writes poetry and songs. Living on the streets, we spent a lot of time in libraries. They're warm, and people trust readers — wallets in coat pockets hanging on the backs of chairs.

Music, we love. We connect through it. Okay, we've got some basic musical talent, but so does every second other person. Amelia's voice is sweet to me, but I'm biased.

Anyhow, noticing something here?

Our "talents" are all in the arts.

No Maths or Science. Nothing you can judge with precision or accurately grade. (For the record, we couldn't do Maths or Science to save our lives.)

Okay, there's swimming. That's precise enough. You can't fake that. And it's true: Amelia can swim. But whenever she reaches higher levels — the nationals, even the states — she starts to fall behind. She won't be coached, that's why.

As for my own swimming: Swim every day and you get faster. Give it a shot.

So, take away Amelia's swimming and think about what's left.

Drama, essays, music: It's all about how you frame them. Tell someone they're about to see the greatest actor of all time — or read a prizewinning novel — or hear a critically acclaimed musician — they'll see, read, and hear in a whole different way. They'll transform something good into genius.

So. This is how we arranged it.

We started with mystery. Stayed behind the scenes. Made them wonder. Made them think that we were nobody. Then we swam fast. Got their attention, but now they think we're scholarship kids who know nothing except sport. Stayed silent in classes. Didn't do any work.

Then chose the right moment, and surprise!

We could act! Write an essay! The crowd goes wild.

Might not have worked at a different school. But these rich people are bored and like a show. They like to be surprised.

It's all tricks. It's all in the way things are arranged.

Then a pause. New aura of mystery: refuse invitations, then suddenly accept. Drift in and out at unexpected times. It was Amelia's idea to sometimes leave a party after just three minutes — no explanation, no attitude, just turn, say good-bye, and go. The hardest part was keeping a straight face.

Be friendly, listen but never let the conversation touch us. Stay unknown. Keep them guessing. At the same time, make them our friends. Share something intimate, so they'd feel close to us. A fine balance. And then — when the time was right — the music.

They'd get us in. They were the richgirls. Sexy, beautiful, gleams in their eyes. They'd unfurl a path for us right to the door of Distressed Weasel Records, and they'd make the producers believe.

Like I said, we're average musicians. But guess what. So are half the rock stars making millions today. They got lucky or they played the game right.

The key for us: Make the richgirls think our music was extraordinary.

So, a cold and darkening night. Edge of woods, an ancient tree, our music.

It was perfect. It worked. They were transfixed. Em was so stunned she was silenced.

We forgot the new security cameras, though. Now the Music teacher was in raptures. That was an unplanned illusion, but you can see how it worked. She hates us — thinks we're musically retarded criminals — then catches us unexpectedly on grainy security footage, and we're not bad?

Imagine the effect.

But we didn't want her praise. A high school teacher raving. Only dilutes things. School concert would have been disastrous. Comparisons with other students, for a start — and there are talented kids at that school.

Cass herself is a better singer than Amelia.

That scared us for a while — the first time we heard her sing at Lyd's place. But it didn't seem to matter. They saw our music as a kind of phenomenon — a team — Riley-and-Amelia, the drummer-and-the-singer.

My point is, it was working.

I saw Lyd in a classroom one day, near the end of the term. She can be disarming. Her voice has this sexy combination of dryness and spark. Rake up some autumn leaves, throw in a match, it's just about to catch — there's her voice. She's smart too, but I've never seen her patronize. She's passionate but shrugs and stays indifferent. She's hurting, you can glimpse it in her eyes sometimes, but she hides it fast.

I see all this, and, like I said, she can be disarming.

That day in the classroom, I told her about Amelia's mystery mad-friend — that friendship was scaring me. The ax murders. The madness. Amelia, so small.

It was a betrayal of Amelia, sharing this with Lyd, but it also felt good. Lydia has this calm confidence: Nothing to be scared of, Amelia is safe.

Also, I told Lyd something about my drumming — how I've always loved it.

Didn't think that could hurt.

One other thing I told Lydia? That the photo of Em's ghost was an illusion — pareidolia. Stop sign in the distance.

It was nothing, but somehow it felt dangerous — another betrayal, even to hint at the concept of illusions. That concept is our secret, Amelia's and mine.

Something about Lydia, though.

The way she arranges her face when she listens, the way she arranges her words.

TOBIAS GEORGE MAZZERATI
STUDENT NO. 8233555

February 26, 1804

They've moved the garrison of soldiers back to Sydney Town, the fools, and there's nobody here to watch us but a handful of constables.

Messages have flown around the colony. Not on paper but in flying words, and the words they fly direct from Phillip's head.

Four lines only has he written down — the fine bones of the plan — and sent with a trusted man to trusted men.

It's to happen, then, on a signal a week from today.

<u>www.myglasshouse.com/emthompson</u>
Friday, September 19
My Journey Home
You will not believe it but I finally have a journey home worth writing home about. (Ha-ha.)

It happened just now. Here I am. Just home.

This is what happened.

Okay, I'm driving along IN MY NEW CAR!!!

(It's new in the sense that it's new to me. Don't think that my parents saw sense and bought it for me. No. Auntie June's car got stolen so she bought herself a new one, but the stolen one turned up, so she gave that to me. Which was nice of her although not *that* nice cos it's been battered by the thieves.)

Let me go on.

I was driving along, feeling emotional. The Final Week is next week! After that, nothing but the HSC will stand between me and the real world!

So, anyway, I had a manila folder on the passenger seat beside me. The folder was entitled *STUDENT RECORDS, VOL. 3, 1952.*

Why? Because I was recently informed, by a tree, that S.W. loved K.P.

Was S.W. Sandra Wilkinson? Who was K.P.?

Perhaps the answer was in the file beside me? And so I flicked through it as I drove.

Which reminds me. Why are car horns so limited? All they do is *BEEP BEEP*. They should have different sounds depending on what you want to say to other cars.

For example, there should be a sound to say, "Sorry, I was reading the papers beside me so I didn't see the lights change, but you don't need to be so cranky about it. See? I'm going now."

Also: "Sorry, I didn't mean to honk my horn at you just then, I bumped the steering wheel in shock because I just found something EXCITING in the papers beside me."

Also: "Thanks for letting me get in front of you just then even though I know you didn't actually realize I was going to, but thanks for braking fast enough to stop you crashing into the back of me, which you came SO CLOSE to doing, and I guess that was my fault. It was because I wasn't concentrating because I JUST THOUGHT OF SOMETHING *AMAZING* ABOUT THESE PAPERS!!"

And so on.

But, yes.

You heard me right.

I found something EXCITING and then I thought of something *AMAZING* to do with the papers beside me.

I was reading a section where they talk about a boy named Kenny playing a "prank" on some girls. (These are high school students! But so childish! Even their names!) I had read this before, but I hadn't noticed that the teacher sometimes refers to the boy named Kenny as "Young Patterson."

Kenny Patterson!

So! That was the exciting thing. I'd found a possible K.P. for S.W. to love.

Then?

As I drove onward, thinking — I realized this.

Kenny could be short for Kendall.

KENDALL PATTERSON.

DO YOU REALIZE WHO THAT IS???

K. L. Mason Patterson!!!

The rich man who died and left money to our school.

The money that was used to renovate and extend our Art Rooms.

The Art Rooms that are now actually called the *K. L. Mason Patterson Center for the Arts*!!!!!

And if that's not *AMAZING* I don't know what planet you inhabit.

It is now very clear to me that Sandra Wilkinson loved Kendall Patterson, and she has come back to haunt the Art Rooms now that it is named after her lost love.

It makes me tremble with fear, having the ghost so real, but that's all right, because trembling is good exercise.

The only thing still to be cleared up is whether (a) Kendall murdered Sandra by pushing her out the window after a "lover's quarrel," or (b) Sandra jumped because Kendall broke her heart, or (c) Sandra fell by accident and Kendall was sad, and in fact maybe there are *two* ghosts in the Art Rooms now — Sandra *and* Kendall, together evermore!

I hope it is option (c).

PLEASE! Share your thoughts! Which option do YOU think it is?

Thanks.

1 Comment

Yowta772 said . . . Em, I love ya, but remind me never to get in a car with you.

Sunday, September 21
My Journey Home
walking home
from the
Goose and Thistle
after rain
in early light

trying
not to think
about thursday.

square of white
on the mud-wet
grass
labeled in black marker
with
a smudged and running
word
the word is
lost.

He says,
I spent an hour
with a torch
yesterday.

It's a CD case
it's the tv series
lost
lost on the dew-green
grass beside the path.

Hit the
wall,
the floor
the nappy box
the wheels of the cot.

Or it's a lost
lost poster
its own lost poster
lost on the boot-crushed
grass beside the path.

She never gives
up,
he says,
chases hard
reaching little hands
for the
circle of light

Riley talking
his little sister
— playing
flashlight
games with his sister

you can't
stop,
he says,
if you stop . . .
you have to
keep the light
twitching

out of
reach.
if you stop,
let her catch it
then she'll
see that it's
nothing

nothing but
the carpet or the wall

he means
us

can't stay
still
or they'll see
what we are —

you end the game
he says
by switching off the torch.

or he might mean
himself —
can't stay
still
or he'll
have to see
thursday.

thursday's
too big

when I try to
hold it for him —
put my arms
around
him
can't get
my arms
around
both.

riley,
I say,
let's stop.

label ourselves
with a smudged and running
word, and
lie down by the
side of the road.

0 Comments

9

LYDIA JAACKSON-OBERMAN
Student No. 8233410

Story's winding up.

Guessed what happens? Are you even concentrating?

WAKE UP!

Too much herbal tea.

It's the final week, then a two-week break, and the HSC begins.

See any contradictions there? Endings and beginnings. Festive and tragic. Coming to school at strange hours in regular clothes. Saying good-bye to people you've seen every day for the last six years. Knowing that, in a couple of weeks, you'll be back in uniform, sitting behind them in exams. Contradictions everywhere you turn. Opposites clashing and turning —

Okay, maybe I'm overdoing this a bit.

But, seriously, that week was weird.

And it seems to me that Young People Today are neither Designed nor Equipped to cope with Confusion of this kind.

The people in my year were strung out, doped up, and/or drunk.

They were hysterical, weeping, and wild-eyed.

(Em was a combination of most of the above.)

I saw one guy throw an egg at a teacher's head, do a kind of victory yodel when it hit, then *run up to that teacher and ask, in serious, polite-boy voice, for some extra revision notes.* (The teacher couldn't see him for the egg yolk in his eyes.)

I saw a girl write *Love u 4-ever* in green ink on another girl's thigh. The second girl promised that she'd never wash it off but *worried that it could look like cheat notes in an exam.*

Ah, humanity. It lets you down sometimes.

So. Here we are in the middle of that week.

It's Wednesday night.

Tomorrow's the last day — there'll be a final assembly, and then tomorrow night, a once-only performance of the Drama.

Tonight, an Ashbury tradition, a farewell reception in the teachers' gardens.

They open the gates, let us in, and we gasp in awe! Paradise! Hiding behind those gates all this time! (We used to break in here a lot, so we're more: Huh, tulips looking fine. Like what you've done with the hydrangeas.)

Girls in tight dresses, boys in suits, teachers wearing makeup. It's Ashbury saying: "Welcome to the grown-up world! Turns out, it's lantern-lit with floating silver trays. Isn't it the best?"

The kids are impressed. They're controlling their madness. But it quivers in the hands that take the pastries from the trays.

I find Amelia on a garden bench. A dark corner. Blue mosquito zapper just behind her.

She looks sane.

We're friends now, Amelia and I. We've spent some time together. But our friendship is just joking around. We've talked about — what? Spiders. TV. Sausages. Shared some stories too — turns out we both like telling stories. She tells me fairy tales she's heard, and makes some up herself. Her imagination is wild.

I like Amelia, but I don't trust her yet. All along, I've wondered if she's cheating on Riley, and I don't like cheats.

I don't want to know, but no point being friends unless it's real.

*   *   *

So tonight I've decided to find out. I'm thinking about what Riley told me the other day. That Amelia has a friend in a mental institution down the road.

If it's a cover, it's a strange one, but Amelia's a strange girl.

She's never mentioned a mentally ill friend to me. But then, why would she? I didn't even know there was an institution nearby. But then why would I?

The story could be true. I want it to be true.

The way to get a friend to share, is share a secret of your own.

I surprise myself: I tell Amelia something that I've never even told Em and Cass.

It's boring but I'll tell it for the record:

My dad moved out last year, when he discovered my mother had been having an affair. She promised it was over, so he moved back in. Therapy and Tuscany saved their marriage. (That's what my mother tells her friends. Ho ho!) These days Mum and Dad are so sweet together it makes me want to rip out my own tonsils. (Or theirs.)

But just before Tuscany, my mother told me a secret. In her bathrobe, diamond bangles sliding up and down her arm — she said that her affair isn't over at all. It's with some TV star — which is probably why she told me ("See, Lyd, I'm still a star!"). It's not over, she said. It's too beautiful. But the TV guy is married. So is she, and —

Then my dad arrived home, and Mum shut up.

My house is a lie. I hate lies. I hate affairs. I hate cheats.

Let me know if I can make myself clearer.

Moving on.

I tell Amelia the family secret on the bench at the garden party.

She listens with her eyes and says, "That's not fair."

She says: "Your mum should never have told you that. You shouldn't have to live with that."

She's so emphatic, I feel confused. Try to laugh but panic I might cry.

I want to say: *This is not about me, I want to know YOU.*

328

So I say, in a tumble: "But people have affairs. Sometimes they can't help it. Is there something that you're keeping from Riley?"

I hadn't meant to be so direct. It's Amelia's fault — she's too nice. We're silent a few moments. Look around.

Across the gardens. There's Riley, talking to Mr. Garcia. As we watch, they both laugh.

Amelia says, "Yes."

RILEY T. SMITH
STUDENT No. 8233569

I'm talking to Garcia and we're laughing.

Something about tomorrow — thursday — the drama.

He's a funny guy, Garcia, good director, good guy, but what's so funny about thursday.

So, I'm laughing but I'm looking for Amelia.

And there she is.

On a seat across the garden,

talking to Lydia.

And it comes to me, it hits me all at once. it's so much all at once, that the only way I could make you understand would be to crowd the words together, in red ink on my knuckle, and punch you once, hard, in the face.

what I'm trying to say is these thoughts were not in sequence, they were one, big, chaotic black hole of a truth.

here they are.

that:

every time I see her she's talking to Lydia — or lost in thoughts about her stepdad, or somewhere with her crazy friend

so she's never there, she's never here for —

that:
too much time with ghosts and you turn into a ghost, too much time with richgirls, and you —

that:
she is one. she's a richgirl.

that:
she and lydia look alike — on that seat, facing each other, facing forward, talking — they're the same — different hair but something in their bright eyes and intensity

that:
she's always been a richgirl when you think about it, which now,

in the teachers' garden, while Garcia laughs, and I laugh along, keep right on talking, while, for the first time ever, I do

think about it,
she's always been a richgirl — you think about it too —

that:
when she ran away from home, she brought along the following:
guitar, stuffed toy, liquor, gardening gloves, silk scarf
your typical streetkid right there, ha-ha.

that:
she ran away from home because she had a fight, on her birthday, with her mother — have I told you what the fight was all about?

the dress she wanted to wear to her party, and
something burning in the fry pan while her mother said, no, you can't wear it

have I told you that?

her mother was cooking for the party, *and she ran away from home*

Spoiled brat.

That thought — spoiled brat.

That was separate. That one I can write on the knuckles of my other fist, and hit you with it separately. Under the chin maybe, snap your chin up. Moving on —

that:

all this time, *she could have gone home* — but she's been waiting for her stepdad — refusing swimming coaching even, loyal to her stepdad — but have I told you this? That her family home is ten minutes from here? We drove by once, saw the horseshoe on the door, she looked at it then slipped down in her seat. Her mother sends money to help her pay the rent, and have I told you this? She used to write her letters? When I first knew Amelia, now and then, her mum would write something like this:

> We both said some hurtful things, so let's make a deal?
> I forgive you, if you forgive me?
> Come home and we'll figure it out!

but Amelia stayed, then we ran away, and after that the letters stopped (but she *still* sends money).

that:

even the flavors she likes — cinnamon, ginger, blueberries — those are richgirl flavors.

that:

all this time she's been living in that hostel with the old men and their hacking coughs, the bandicoots, the mold-rimmed showers, fungal infections waiting to get her pretty toes on the tiles. The rats, cockroaches, dust-stained lights — all this time

she's a fake.

I say something to Garcia, and he laughs again — my voice comes out in the same smooth tone — and I look at Amelia and Lydia — they've stopped talking now — they're looking toward me, they're standing up, I smile at them and they float my way — past lanterns, waiters, boys in suits. Lydia's wearing something tight and white that glows in moonlight, Amelia looks hot in a dress black as night —

and
Lydia's the real one.
Amelia's the fake, the reflection, the —

I've known it all along.
She's the shadow.

EMILY MELISSA-ANNE THOMPSON
Student No. 8233521

Plunge with me into the teachers' gardens in the middle of the final week of school!

It is lantern lit, and highly enchanting, and . . . listen to what befell —

Amelia and Lydia were talking on a bench.

Just behind me, Riley was chatting with Mr. Garcia. Their conversation leapt back and forth like an antelope across a laughing brook.

Amelia and Lydia stood up from their bench, and walked toward us. Amelia looked pale. Lydia had an odd gleam — her eyes like silver coins.

Some other students began to prattle at Mr. Garcia, and he moved slightly to join their circle.

Lydia switched directions. She crossed the gardens, away from us. Amelia continued toward us, and joined Riley.

"I have to go see my friend," she said.

Riley was silent a moment. "Now?"

"She seemed kind of crazy when I saw her yesterday."

"That'll happen," said Riley, "with a crazy person."

Amelia smiled. Riley smiled back.

At that moment, they both sensed that I was watching them. They glanced toward me, smiled quickly, then turned away and their serious faces resumed.

Amelia touched Riley's cheek.

I had never seen Amelia touch Riley's face before. They were not that kind of couple. But this? This brief, trembling, tender touch — I can honestly say that it felt like the most loving touch I'd ever seen. (And I am a student of love.) My heart swooned.

And then Amelia walked away.

Riley watched the gate close behind her.

At which moment the strangest thing happened. It happened to Riley's face. Imagine hitting a cymbal so hard that it vibrates violently, clashes and flashes with light. That was Riley's face.

Within a fraction of a second, however, it was Riley again.

I was understandably bewildered.

I saw Lydia and Cassie chatting across the garden. I joined them.

Lydia was telling Cassie something: "She pretends she's going to see a crazy friend," she was saying. "But I don't think she is. She's cheating on him."

Amelia was cheating on Riley? The crazy friend she just mentioned was not real?!

But that loving, gentle stroke . . . ?

I made a decision.

I turned and walked through the garden gate.

I was not too late. There was Amelia — a shadow in the distance — and I followed her into the night.

TOBIAS GEORGE MAZZERATI
Student No. 8233555

March 4, 1804

It's a darkening Sunday eve, the moon slipping upward of the trees — and it begins.

Fire is set to a hut. I smell the smoke before I see the flames, and the bell rings out sure and true.

Phillip steps from the shadows, watches the smoke rise in a column. "Well, Tom Kincaid," he says, solemn-like. "You'll be coming home to Ireland with me on the morrow?"

"Aye," says I, "that I will." And we both smile sudden, frightened smiles.

The bell and the smoke bring a constable running, but there's some, as planned, who surround him, and he's under control without fuss. Others come, likewise, and it's all so easy it takes the breath from me. They're our prisoners at once. Now our men run from every direction, eyes alight, all afire themselves.

Phillip speaks to the constables under our guard.

"Join us and we'll play you fair," he says, and there's a moment of stillness. The crackle of the hut burning. Its heat on my cheek. Constables white with fear. The shadow of the barracks that Phillip built, casting its darkness over all.

"Whatever you choose," says Phillip, voice ringing out into the night, "by first light tomorrow we'll be sailing toward home."

Now a great roar of cheering, native dogs howling, another hut catches the flame, and we're running, stumbling along — over a hundred of us convicts, and most of the constables too — to the nearest farm. We're fast and strong, we're men, and we are free. For the first time in four years, I taste the truth of that.

The farmer stands to fight then sees our numbers, curses, and stands back. There's convicts who work his farm, and I hear their shouts outside as they join us.

It's weapons we're after — the shout flies about — and I run from room to room. Catch sight of myself in a mirror, face determined, eyes agleam, like a child in a game. The mirror's above a fireplace, and if it isn't a poker beside it! A weapon, sure! — I grab for it. But it's flimsy in my hands and ashamed, I put it back. A moment later, another man pounces on the poker. I feel cast down, as if I've lost points in the game.

Then I'm in the kitchen, and there's men up on the table, and standing on chairs, singing, eating, and drinking. It seems wrong — and then it swells inside me. The joy of it. There's meat and gravy, cinnamon cakes, apples, grapes, and someone has a keg.

There's the sound of Phillip calling us outside.

I'm ashamed of the crumbs on my chin, but if it isn't an ax leaning up against that wall! A weapon, sure, and I'm back in the game, and my vision blurs with tears of home and rum.

We head to a hill behind the farmhouse, and Phillip's eyes, they gleam like stars on a frosty night, and his voice catches us all in its glow.

Aye, and it's proud I am of my friend, to be sure.

"No violence," Phillip is saying. "It's weapons and men that we're after, not a bloodbath."

We've friends all over the colony, he says, and as we stand here now, they're out collecting friends and weapons too. (Shouting and laughter.)

The rum fans out in my chest as he speaks, and I feel the force of his words — how we're fanning out across this colony, how the hills about us will be ours.

"Once they've secured Parramatta," Phillip says, "they'll set a thatched cottage alight" — he throws his arm and we follow its line with our eyes — "and the flame will be our signal. Then we know it's time to meet at Constitution Hill."

We'll fan out and snap together as one.

"From there, we march on Sydney. Plant a tree of liberty at Government House. Head to the harbor, and home."

More cheers — and the sweat of men around me — and, "Now, my boys," says Phillip, "it's death or liberty, and a ship to take us home!" — and the hair stands up on the back of my neck and my forearms.

They're splitting us into groups, but my eyes, they're fixed on the distance — the darkness where Phillip just pointed. The signal flame will rise up red, and red-gold is the color of my Maggie's hair, and it's the color of soil in this land. It's the color of magic too, for sure, and don't fairies choose red for their caps as often as not? That's what Maggie used to say with the dream in her eye.

So I look to that darkness, and in my mind's eye, it lights up with a red-gold flame. Shouting and singing and laughter, and we head to the night.

**The Committee for the Administration of the
K. L. Mason Patterson Trust Fund
THE K. L. MASON PATTERSON SCHOLARSHIP FILE**

Memo

To: K. L. Mason Patterson Scholarship Committee
From: Stephen Latimer (Ashbury English Teacher)
Re: Riley T. Smith and Amelia Damaski

Dear Committee Members,

I hope you will not find it odd, me — a non-Committee member — writing to you. I'm just home from the Year 12 Reception in the teachers' gardens. A fine night was had by all, me included, and I would now like to get some sleep — but I find myself moved to write this note.

To begin, some background. A couple of months back, Year 12 English wrote an assignment — "the true story of Term 2 as a ghost story." (Mr. Botherit will fill you in.) Riley Smith is in my English class. His ghost story disturbed me.

I hasten to point out that a *lot* of the students' ghost stories disturbed me. Let's just say that some had trouble with the concept of a "true" ghost story: hence, severed limbs and massacres aplenty (and I must assume that these were false).

Thus, I put Riley's story out of my head.

But it kept coming back. You see, Riley is bright. Not the type to be confused by the fiction/nonfiction divide. And much of his story *did* ring of "truth." He talked of Amelia. People in his year. His criminal record.

Two things in particular disturbed me about his story. The first was the tone with which he referred to his "friends" at Ashbury — it was one of dismissive contempt. They were "stupid kids" and "half-people."

More disturbing, however, was the second thing — a hint that he and Amelia had concealed the true nature of their criminal record from the Scholarship Committee. The truth, he suggested, was "sealed up" — and ugly.

Of course, this could be "creative nonfiction" — Riley making his memoir more "ghostly" — giving it an edge. And that is what I assumed. And yet, tonight, at the Reception, I saw something in Riley's face that brought his story back to me. I do not mean to be melodramatic. He laughed and talked as charmingly as ever. But now and then, when he thought no one was watching — an expression crossed Riley's face that chilled me to the bone. Something primitive — something howling and ferocious. A pure rage and violence seemed to lurk beneath the surface of his smile.

And so, I came home, had a glass of red — and wrote this.

Of course, the school year is almost over — final assembly is tomorrow. But they'll be back for the HSC exams. More to the point, it appears that they are still "friends" with the people mentioned in the story — including, I might say, Lydia, Cassie, and Emily.

Now, if this friendship should continue outside school — if it should be as false as Riley's story suggests — if Riley looks upon Lyd, Cass, and Em with such contempt — if, as he hints, his criminal record is uglier than we know — and if, finally, I truly did see rage in his face tonight — well, perhaps some action should be taken? Even if only to look into the question of the record — or to warn Lyd, Cass, and Em?

I apologize if this is all the product of a feverish imagination (and the second glass of red I just drank). Please know, however, that I have not taken up my pen lightly.

Kind regards,
Stephen Latimer

P.S. I have a nagging feeling that Cass's mother might be one of the parent reps on this committee — if so, I apologize if I've caused any hurt to you by passing all this on.

11.

The final day of school, Thursday, and how did I feel? *Totally* agitated.

"I do not want this secret! Get away from me, secret! Jump overboard!"

Those were my harried thoughts. Could I concentrate? No. Will I ever forgive the universe for making me decide to follow Amelia into the night so that I saw something that made my head spin like a Mixmaster on high speed *for the duration of my final day of school?*

No.

I will not.

What was it that I saw?

Wait a moment. I will draw out the suspense.

For now, let's just say I was so agitated *I forgot to take any photographs of the Final Assembly!!*

My heart still aches about this.

Instead, my eyes darted around like goldfish, looking for Riley and Amelia. They arrived together, late — and slipped into seats up the back. Riley looked as if he had just walked into the side of a refrigerator (I mean, he looked shocked, not flat). Amelia was so pale that I thought she needed replacement toner. Or that someone should take her toner out and shake it around.

My brain leapt around in its head (that is, my head), like a goldfish (sorry for repetition). How could I keep being friends with Riley and Amelia now that I knew this secret?!

The secret of what I had seen!!

What had I seen?

I saw Amelia in the arms of another man!!!

(A man who was not Riley.) (Just to be clear.)

Thinking of this at the assembly, I was so overcome that I swooned. Or thought about it anyway.

Then I paid heed for a moment. My name was being called. I'd won the Legal Studies prize.

So that filled me with joy beyond belief.

But next thing I was back in my seat and agitated again! And the Assembly was all just *Prize to Bindy Mackenzie, Prize to Bindy Mackenzie* — so no suspense. Nothing to distract me from the vision of Amelia under dark, wind-swept trees, running across open grass — running toward the open arms of —

Prize to Tobias Mazzerati for Design and Technology.

Much applause and cheering — partly because everyone likes Toby and we're proud of his woodwork, and partly because it was good to have a break from Bindy.

But was it any help to me? NO. IT WAS NOT.

It was the opposite of help.

Because guess whose arms Amelia ran toward?

Toby's.

I rest my case.

The day staggered onward. *Oh, stop saying good-bye and that you love me! I'll see you in a couple of weeks at the exams! And you were always kind of annoying!* Those were my harried and dastardly thoughts as people ran up to give me hugs. And thus were the beautiful, final moments of school swept from my grasp . . . I did not even cry!

After the Assembly, we had to run over to the Art Rooms to set up for the Drama that night. I was fascinated to see how it would turn out, but was there any room in my head for fascination? NO! Not really. I was too fretful.

I was so disappointed in Toby!!! I thought he was upstanding!! And my friend!

And here he was lurking in parks with Amelia.

More than that, I was disappointed in LOVE. You know how I had been looking for the crack between Riley and Amelia? Well, between us, I'd kind of hoped not to find one. Even as they annoyed me for being too talented, still I had admired their great love. In my heart, I had hoped Lyd had been wrong about them. But no. *Sigh* Of course not.

And now, a dilemma. Should I let Riley know that Amelia was cheating? Force open the crack now I had found it? So that Riley and Lyd could get together?

It had seemed a good idea when I planned it, but in reality? It terrified me! I did not want to hurt Riley! Maybe Lydia's heart was healing on its own? We hadn't seen Seb for a while, and she'd never found out about Seb and Astrid, so that was something. Maybe they were over now anyway? Astrid hadn't said anything for a while. Maybe —

And so my thoughts whirred onward. . . .

In the auditorium, there was mild chaos, mainly caused by Mr. Garcia having a new idea about colored lighting. Students were telling him to be reasonable. Artists were painting final details on the set, and actors were bumping into one another. Cassie went to help with the sound.

And then — here were the Brookfielders arriving, and here was Seb.

Lydia tensed beside me. Seb headed toward us, and Lydia picked up a cardboard box, dumped it in my arms, grabbed another for herself, and headed out the door. I followed.

It seemed that Lydia was not healed yet at all.

We went into a classroom and began folding the programs in the box.

My turmoil continued. *And I'm* tired *of secrets!* I thought. *Seb and Astrid. That's one secret I've had enough of! Now I've got a new one! It's not fair!*

I slammed the programs down noisily.

After half an hour or so, Lydia asked what was wrong.

Here's a funny thing — I did not want to tell her. Partly because saying it aloud would make it gossip: It was too grown-up, too sad for gossiping schoolgirls. Also because Lyd was already upset by Amelia's hints that she was cheating. She did not need me to give her the facts that confirmed it.

So I made up an answer on the spot. "It's the last day," I said, "and I still haven't found out the truth about the ghost. I'm just annoyed with myself because I'm too scared of the archives room to go and find out more. I . . ."

I talked on recklessly — and what I was saying was *true*, but it was not, of course, what was agitating me — but then I realized that Lydia had fallen into a reverie.

Or, anyway, that she wasn't concentrating on what I was saying.

She looked at her watch. "We've got time," she said, and she stood up.

She had a spark in her eye. She looked almost like the old Lydia — excited, wild.

"Come on," she said.

And then we were running up flights of stairs toward the archives room. My heart was drumming with fear, but it was an elated sort of fear.

Suddenly, wonderfully — I was a child again! Who cared really that Amelia and Toby were embracing in dark parks?! We would leave all that behind and go out in the world — but here, now, we were young, racing up the stairs, faster, faster, faster —

And the door of the archives room opened.

Two people came out.

They paused on the landing.

We were close, just a step down from them.

It was Seb and Astrid.

And Astrid was buttoning her shirt.

I looked swiftly at Lydia. She was staring, confused.

Then her childish joy fled as understanding hit — and, for a fleeting moment, there was anguish in her eyes.

At once, she gathered her courage, raised her eyebrows, turned, and walked back down the stairs.

In that moment, I knew what I must do.

I would do it at once.

Enough of Lydia's anguish. Enough of my fear.

LYDIA JAACKSON-OBERMAN
Student No. 8233410

Last day of school, funniest thing happens.

You'll get a laugh out of this.

I'm heading up a flight of stairs, a door opens, and there's Seb — my Seb.

With Astrid.

You remember Astrid? Sure you do. Skinny girl. Says the word "like" like she doesn't know there's other words available.

She's half-undressed.

And even though she's half-undressed, I still think nothing.

Almost make a joke about how this looks.

But then I see Em's face — and it hits me. This *is* how it looks.

I remember Em telling me to give up on Seb. This is why? Seb and Astrid?!

Seb and Astrid.

This is the guy my heart's been hurting for this whole year? This is the guy whose face I see when I close my eyes at night. And he's gettin' it on with *Astrid* all this time?

I stand on the stairs and I laugh so hard I knock myself unconscious.

You know — that laughter where you howl and accidentally slam your head against the wall and knock yourself out? So that's what happens. I'm unconscious on the floor, wake up, and see them around me — Seb, Astrid, and Em — looking concerned. I laugh even harder. Get up off the floor. "You won't be needing *that* anymore!" I say, reaching out to take my heart back from underneath Seb's arm. "You've had it long enough. It was a stupid place to keep it anyway. Underneath your sweaty arm!"

Ah, no.
That doesn't happen.
The laughing bit.
What, are you as stupid as my mother?
But I've gotta say, I laughed on the inside. Headed back down-stairs. Laughed my way through the rest of setting up for the play. Through the speech about what a success the play has been — Ashbury and Brookfield are the best of buddies now! Ha-ha. My Brookfield boy and his new Ashbury girl — ha-ha.

The play itself does distract me for a while. It's okay. The writing works, mostly. Astrid has the role of a fat and stupid snowman, so that's fun. Amelia and Riley are stunning — get standing ovations at the end. Seb's set design is beautiful. People talk about it as they leave, and I feel proud a moment — then remember, and laugh again.

It's later that night. The audience gone. We're cleaning up, clearing out, there's talk of moving on to someone's house. Not mine. I haven't offered, and Em hasn't offered for me either. Em and Cass are careful, kind, so now I know Em's told Cass. I'm laughing at Em for not tell-ing me sooner. I'm laughing that she's known all along.

I've run upstairs, to get a practice exam that I left behind in German today, and now I'm laughing my way along a corridor, thinking I might head home.

And there it is again.

Another open doorway. Riley at a window. A pattern repeating.

It's the room where I have my German classes. One of the upstairs conference rooms.

It's dark. He's looking out into the night.

He sees me.

Sits up on a table near the window. Like an invitation. I sit beside him. Our legs in a row. Shaft of light from the corridor, dim moonlight from outside. I notice that Riley has a piece of paper in his hand.

"There she goes again," he says, nods at the window.

I stand so I can see. You can see the car park from up here, Drama people spilling into it — little voices calling to one another. Curve of the brick wall, headlights on the road. The oval, an empty darkness.

But he's right. There she is. Amelia. Tiny, moving figure crossing the oval fast.

Now I laugh aloud. And behind me, Riley laughs too, surprised. The paper in his hand rustles. He puts it down, still laughing. I sit back on the table beside him, and we ride on that laughter for a while.

Then we pause. We're side by side, facing the window. From this angle, you can only see the stars.

There's movement from his hand, the one closest to me. He gathers his fingers together, places them lightly on my knee, and spreads them out. For a moment they rest there. Then he gathers them together again and away. It's so quick and light it almost hasn't happened. His fingernails fanning out, snapping together again. It's like a game you might play with a child, something affectionate and quick. You could say, "spider" as you did it.

But it feels like he's found something inside me. Like a chime — or a wail or a cry — all in that quick spread of his hand.

I don't know what to do. There's nothing to do but —

And then we're kissing, his hands on my body like fire, his arms like the comfort of shade.

Here's something.

It's Thursday and my family's an illusion. Ghosts, a simulation. Not real.

Same goes for my private school, but you already knew that.

Thursday, my mum gives me a ride to school. I sit in the back so I can sing and do the finger-puppet thing to my little sister, Chloe. The round-the-garden thing too, her little hand wanting it, not wanting it, her desperate giggles.

Look out the window once, and that hand touches my neck, the back of my neck, the trust in the touch, her little hand.

Mum in the front seat talking, trying to keep things bright — at traffic lights, behind a white van, she says, "I don't like vans."

"Why not?" I say, and Chloe leans forward in her car seat straps, in the same way as me, a slight lean forward — just as interested — *why?*

"They're always the bad guys in the movies."

I swear to you, we break up with laughter at the exact same time: Chloe, like she knows why she is laughing.

Pull up at the school, and I see her through the window. Her little face lost in thought. I tap the window. She giggles with delight at the surprise of me through glass.

I can't hear the giggle, I just see it.

I role-play my way through an assembly, prizes, good-byes, the play.

Then — how about this.

Someone's left a note on my backpack. Open it and read it.

Now here's Amelia, jeans but still in stage makeup. She says she has to go and see her crazy friend again.

"She was really bad last night," she says. "It gets worse at night."

Amelia talks again about her friend's broken heart. She's waiting for someone. Someone isn't coming. It's all in the crazy friend's head.

"Just for half an hour," Amelia says. "Then I'll track you down."

I smile at her. Sure. Why not.

She asks if I'm okay, and if I'm sure. And she's gone.

A few moments of working, dismantling the set — then I can't take it anymore.

I just want to see her.

I run upstairs. Up another flight of stairs.

To see her from above. See her cross the oval. The truth of her walking away.

It's the conference room — the place they interview us for our scholarships. I don't switch on the light. Cross to the windows and look out.

There she is. So small. Walking fast. Away from me.

Press my forehead to the glass, say her name. It comes out right. It's a beautiful name. I want to hold it to my heart but there it goes.

The note is in my hand.

Dear Riley,

I am very sorry to have to ask you this, but have you ever actually SEEN the mental institution that Amelia visits to see her "friend"? Are you sure it even exists? Are you sure that Amelia is being honest with you? Could there be another person (male) involved?

Anyway, perhaps you should think about letting Amelia go? I know this might hurt right now but I promise that things will feel better.

A Friend

I say her name again. It comes out as a whisper and a cry. Amelia — come here-ya — who cares if she's spoiled, rich, or a ghost. I want her here, but there she goes.

Then Lydia's beside me. I can feel her in the room, and she's real. Her laughter. Her lips, her skin, her body. She's warm and she's real and she's here.

TOBIAS GEORGE MAZZERATI
Student No. 8233555

Well, folks, me again. Toby. Back to finish up the tale.

That's the last you'll hear from Tom, which kind of breaks my heart, but also, between us, is a relief. Couldn't keep that Irish accent up.

Sorry about it. Did my best.

So, let me wind it up for you. Without in any way intending on showing off, I have read myself some historical books. So. I'm your man.

Last you heard from Tom, things had just got going here in Castle Hill. He's all drunk and emotional, watching the darkness for the red light of the flame.

What happens next? Just like they planned. Running around the countryside with two hundred buddies or so, like a high school Muck-up Day.

Breaking into farms, grabbing guns and pitchforks, telling other convicts, "Join in! You'll have a blast!" and the other convicts are all, "You totally rock! We will!" (But in olden-day accents, of course.)

As we stand here now, they're out collecting friends and weapons too!
That's what Phillip had shouted on the hill, and he'd believed it to be true, but it was not.

His message had not got through.

Fine bones of the plan on a single piece of paper, sent out with a trusted man — but the guy got arrested before he'd gone half a mile.

They have now invented SMS and Facebook, etc., to prevent mishaps of this kind. But too late to save Tom and his buddies — running wild, collecting guns, eating, drinking, eyes on the darkness, looking for the signal in the hills.

The signal never came.

Meantime, all over the colony, news that the Castle Hill convicts had gone wild was spreading. Sound of drums found its way into everybody's dreams — beating on and on, calling the soldiers out to fight.

In Castle Hill, no signal fire and not enough men to take down Sydney. But Phillip's no quitter. *Here's the new plan*, he says. *We'll head to the Hawkesbury. Get more men and try again.*

So they're on their way. They're wasted now, too much fun last night. But they've got themselves a whole pile of muskets, pistols, pitchforks — and they're running west.

Meanwhile, a battalion of soldiers, led by a guy named Major Johnston, is chasing them down. Half of the battalion splits away to cut them off.

The convicts gather at the top of a hill, surrounded.

The major and another soldier ride up flying white flags.

Picture this.

Two or three hundred convicts with ratty clothes, sleepy eyes, and pitchforks at the top of a hill.

Soldiers in red coats and breeches, guns at the ready at the foot of the hill.

In the middle — halfway up the slope — the major and a soldier facing up to Phillip Cunningham.

"Tell your men to surrender, and we'll treat you nice," the major says.

Phillip looks around at the faces of his boys. He sees they're not buying this.

He shakes his head. "Death or liberty," he says, that old phrase.

He's ready to fight. Looks into the eyes of the major. It has come to this. The major and soldier will head back to their ranks, and the battle will begin.

Then — *wham!* — the major's got his pistol out, pressing it hard against Phillip's head, saying, "I'll blow your soul to hell!"

Shoves Phil down the hill, gun pressed to his back, down to the soldiers who are lined up, ready, and he shouts, "ATTACK!"

I kid you not.

Convicts think it's real. Rules of war. White flags. But the major's only playing.

So now the convicts in their ratty clothes are going: What the f. just happened?

While the soldiers in formation go: READY, AIM, FIRE.

Rebels try fighting back, but leader's gone and gunshot raining down — so they run.

The soldiers chase them, cut them down, shoot them at close range. Dead and injured bodies on the road, and in the woods.

Phillip C. is still a captive. A soldier slices him with a sword and he falls to the ground.

He gets up. Tries to run. Streams of blood behind him. Stumbles, falls to the side of the road. He's half-dead but still breathing.

The soldiers pick him up. Carry him with them while they chase the convicts all the way to the Hawkesbury.

When they get there, they hang Phillip from the staircase of the public store.

www.myglasshouse.com/emthompson

Tuesday, October 14

My Journey Home

Hello.

This is the last you shall ever hear from me.

I hope you will miss me.

I think you will.

It is late and I have an exam tomorrow morning, so I should not be blogging. But I can't study any more because my head is already full and I can't sleep because there's no room on the pillow for my head.

And I have something important to tell you.

But first I'll just get some of the maple-chocolate cake that William made yesterday.

Okay. I'm back.

I wonder if some of you have been crying softly, knowing that this is my last blog? If so, cut it out. It wasn't that good a blog. How could it be with the repeated title of "My Journey Home"?

Actually, at our last English class, I demanded to know what was up with that, and Mr. B said, "If you keep coming at the same topic, over and over, from as many different angles as you can, you will find yourself close to the truth."

Then he smiled and said, "You, of all people, should know that."

I think he meant that I talk a lot, but so does he, so that's just an example of the pot calling the kettle up and asking it out on a date. I don't want to date Mr. B.

"You seriously meant us to get to the *truth* about our journey home?" I said.

Mr. B looked at me with teacherly silence.

"You might have mentioned that in the first place," I said.

"But part of the journey, Em," he said, "is finding things out for yourself."

I hate it when people talk about journeys, other than in the context of return flights to New York, Paris, Vancouver, or any other destination of choice.

THIS CAKE IS FANTASTIC! MY BROTHER SURE CAN COOK. WAIT WHILE I GET ANOTHER PIECE.

Anyway, I suppose you are wondering about my HSC exams? Yes. They have begun. I am in their midst. After the Dramatic Production (which was actually fantastic, huh, surprising), there was a two-week study break, during which I discovered that it is biologically and chemically impossible to study for two weeks (again — surprising). Oh well. Never mind.

I've had three exams so far, and here is my wisdom for the younger folk: *It's all about getting through the first exam.* It's like when you go into the ocean. At first it seems impossible — the water is freezing! But then you just dive right in — and waves start dumping you face-first on the sand, seaweed tangles your legs, blue bottles sting, and here comes a shark's fin to get you. . . .

Ha-ha.

No, look, don't even worry about it. People have been doing the HSC since Queen Victoria was raining, and, as far as I know, they're still alive. Not Queen Victoria, though. She's dead. But I don't think you can blame the HSC.

However, you will be waiting to hear my important news. Well, I arrived at school for the first exam, and there on my locker? A mysterious envelope.

I turned the envelope over and this was scribbled on the back:

i'M lÍkE: W#A+?!! YoU wÍll Bɛ +oo.
LoVɛ, AȘtRÍᴅ

This made no sense. And to be honest, I was suddenly afraid of what the envelope might hold. I considered throwing it away and disinfecting my hands.

But I didn't. I opened it.

And what was in the envelope?

A document *about my ghost*!! (Sorry for doubting you, Astrid, if you read this blog.)

It was a Highly Confidential Letter relating to Sandra Wilkinson's accident.

Where had Astrid got it from? And why? These are questions only Astrid can answer, and if she doesn't, they'll haunt your sleep forevermore since this is my last blog, and —

"Yes, yes!" you cry. "But what did the document say?"

Let me type out the important bits for you. Why not? It's only 11:30 P.M. Ha-ha. Wait, I'll get it. It's a letter from a housemaster to the principal of the school at that time.

Dear Mr. Spender,

At your request, I have been up until dawn interviewing the boarders about last night's distressing incident. I have spoken extensively with Kendall Patterson, of course, and also to his family.

As far as I can piece together, it seems that Sandra had been having intimate relations with Kendall for some time. (It goes without saying that I had no knowledge of this.) Last night, she had slipped into his room, as was their custom. It was a hot night and so the window was open. It seems they had *both* been imbibing

Scotch whisky, and Sandra was sitting on the window ledge, and had fallen asleep when she fell.

In other words, the fall was an accident brought on by the hijinks of an infatuated young couple in a highly intoxicated state.

Kendall is very upset by having seen Sandra — the love of his life (his words) — fall to her death. Meanwhile, Kendall's family is, understandably, anxious to keep the sordid details from official reports.

They have intimated that their family will remember Ashbury, very generously, in perpetuity, if we agree to keep this quiet. . . .

I see no reason why Ashbury (and indeed, Sandra's own family) would want the "sordid details" reaching the public domain, and rather think we ought to be amenable to Kendall's family's wishes.

Yours sincerely,
Mr. Clarkeson

So, my dear readers!

It turns out that Sandra Wilkinson *was* involved with Kendall Patterson! And they were getting it on in ways that I didn't think were possible in the olden days. (The document does not exactly say this but it tries to.) And she fell because she was ripped on whisky and passed out!

Now we know why Kendall Mason Patterson left so much money to our school!

Well, I feel both tragic and annoyed.

Readers of this blog, remember this: It is perfectly possible to be young, wild, free, drunk, stupid, happy, and in love *without plunging from a window to a hideous and blood-splattered death*!!

I myself am living proof of that.

Sandra and Kendall could have grown old together! Got married, had twins, traveled the world, swam in oceans, danced the Hokey Pokey (not because it's a good dance or anything, just because this was the olden days). But no. They did not.

YOUNG LOVE GETS THWARTED OFTEN ENOUGH (e.g., when people move to Singapore, or through certain people not recognizing that they are in love until it is too late) WITHOUT THROWING IT OUT OF A WINDOW!!!

I suppose they might be together right now, if they are both haunting the Ashbury Art Rooms, but, seriously, is that fun?

Anyway, the mystery of the ghost (or ghosts) has been revealed. I leave you to ponder and learn from it.

Now, I must wish you farewell, but first I am just getting some more cake.

Okay. Back again.

My mother's phone is ringing. She has the theme song from *Boston Legal* as her ringtone. (She's totally in love with James Spader, which intrigues my dad.) Who's calling Mum so late? James Spader? Ha-ha. No. Oh, she's answered it. I thought she was asleep.

Anyway, tomorrow's exam will be English Extension 3, so after that, the subject will no longer exist. It will be nevermore. And therefore so will this blog.

I hope you understand. All things must end. Even school! Which makes me so emotional, because we are such a close-knit year, it's amazing!

This cake is so moist! It's amazing. It's making me a little crazy, I think. All the chocolate. I feel like waking my brother up and hugging him. Maybe I should get some more. You are thinking, "What? Hasn't she already had three pieces?" Well, you are wrong. I had two before I started writing this so that means I've now had five. Ha-ha. But seriously, you could go into a café and order cake and they might give you a really HUGE slice, which would equal —

Huh.

Now my mother's calling me. Strange.

I'd better go! BYE, EVERYONE. THANKS FOR READING! HAVE GREAT LIVES! ☺ ☺ ☺

Love,

Emily

4 Comments

Yowta772 said . . . Em, you will always rain over my heart, or reign even, and I promise not to put up an umbrella.

FloralNightie said . . . You certainly *are* a "close-knit" year. As an example, on the night of the Dramatic Production, I saw Riley kissing Lydia in a conference room!! And isn't he supposed to be "with" Amelia??

Shadowgirl said . . . I think you probably imagined that kiss.

FloralNightie said . . . No, Shadowgirl, I did not.

Tuesday, October 14

My Journey Home

sometimes
people say the strangest things.

*That looks like something a
snake left behind.*

*What are you,
an extra in the
Rocky Horror Show?*

my mother
frying onions
and
the dress
i
found in
St Vinnie's
on the way home
from school,
it was only 2 dollars.

it's my birthday
I get to choose.

*I'm not in the mood for an
argument*

take it off and put it in the bin

well, *he* likes it.

Trust me
he also wants
that dress taken off.

Which struck me
as funny.
You're not
wrong there.

What's so funny.

You realize that
he likes to take photos
of me
when I get changed?

I mean
before
I get —
when I'm not —

after the pool
early in the morning
after training?

which struck my mother
as funny.

You're suggesting he
takes nude photographs of you

it's not suggesting
if it's true

the last couple of years —
used to be he'd promise
a new story about
fairies
or
four-leaf clovers
but now
it's just what we do.
it started —

Sometimes
people say
the strangest things

my mother
winding a tea towel —
eyes over my head
voice winding slowly
around the room

They say
hurtful
spiteful
untrue things
but we both know
it's just
they have a wild imagination
and
they want to wear a dress
a very
stupid dress
to their
party

turning
back to the stove

And now that stupid dress
has burned the onions!

like I said,
people say the strangest
things
and usually
they're
just
not
true.

   0 comments

EMILY MELISSA-ANNE THOMPSON
STUDENT NO. 8233521

Now, I don't know about you, but an evil monster has fallen into my lap.

Speaking gothically, this is great news.

But get a life outside the gothic, already. If you did, you'd realize that I don't actually *want* an evil monster in my lap, thanks all the same.

Sigh This exam is almost over — a final gothic blast concludes my tale. . . .

Today, I arrived at school in distress. Somebody had phoned my mother last night, and told her something that made me fall senseless to the floor.

I will not tell you what, just yet. You may live in suspense.

Mum and I talked electrifyingly for some time about her news, and then I went upstairs to bed.

I spent the night tossing and turning.

I had Special K and the last of the maple-chocolate cake for breakfast, and came to school for this exam — in a state, as I said, of distress.

The sky was gloomy (in all honesty), and behold! this exam was to take place in the Art Rooms.

I walked across the oval to the Art Rooms in a storm cloud of personal chaos. Through the entry door, along the corridors (muttering crankily to the ghosts, "Could you not have been more careful?") — and toward the room where I am now.

A collection of people stood there — and my heart plummeted to my feet.

For there, amidst these people, were: Lydia, leaning against the wall, eyes closed; Amelia, lost in the middle of the corridor; Riley, against the facing wall, frowning deeply to himself — the three of them eerily silent —

. . . and here came Toby, approaching from the opposite direction.

As Toby and I closed in on the trio, they shifted, looked up, changed position — and I observed this:

Toby's face lit up at the sight of Amelia —

while Amelia turned toward Riley —

and Riley, pointedly, looked instead at Lydia —

who, having opened her eyes, gave Riley a powerful, extraordinary glance, before closing them again.

At this moment, the door to the exam room flew open from the inside, and a woman leaned out and blinked at us.

This caused a bigger stir. People picked up pencil cases, water bottles, talked loudly to one another.

In the stir, Toby leaned toward Amelia, *slipped a folded note into her hand*, and then walked into this exam room, without a backward glance.

Amelia pressed the note into her pocket, and moved to Riley's side. She spoke to him intensely. Riley watched her as she spoke, and his eyes glinted fiercely like a chain saw in the sun. Then he stood and walked farther down the corridor. She followed him and they continued talking with their backs to us. From behind, Amelia looked as fragile as an anorexic movie star.

All this time, Lydia's eyes stayed closed.

Then we had to go into the exam. As I walked through the door, I could see that Riley and Amelia were still talking.

I am sorry to say, I could not hear the words of their intense conversation.

Neither do I know what was in Toby's note (I don't have X-ray vision). And, speaking generally, I cannot explain what on earth *all* these flashing looks and moments meant.

However, there is one thing I *can* say. . . .

Something romantic has happened between Riley and Lydia.

How do I know this?

The look that they exchanged. It said it all. Trust me. I am a student of love.

Riley must have got my note suggesting that Amelia was cheating, and moved straight on to Lyd.

But oh, oh, woe and betide me! Horrors! Oh horrors! *That it were not so!* Even now, little shrieks assail my ears from within my troubled brain. As if banditti were lurking in the woods!

You do not know why it is so horrifying, do you?

Trust me. It is.

Speaking gothically, the end is nigh, and I would quickly like to point out that the **dynamics of first impressions** have been very significant to this **personal memoir** and that I have drawn on my **extensive knowledge of gothic fiction** and you will recall that there has been plentiful gothicnesses! I have used words like **agitated**, and **moat**, and I have done a lot of **senseless fainting**. With a little more time I might have found some **femmes fatales** and **family curses**, yet still there have been **ghosts**, and **doppelgangers** (e.g., Lydia has both a big games room and a small games room), and **gloomy weather** and so this is a very valuable HSC exam — and now, finally,

there is a **monster**.

A GOTHIC MONSTER.

Who is it?

. . . . . .

. . . . . .

It is Riley.

You recall the suspenseful phone call that my mother got last night?

It was from Cassie's mother. She is on the Scholarship Committee. Apparently, a teacher had suggested to the Committee that maybe Riley's and Amelia's criminal record was worse than they had thought? So the Committee spent the last couple of weeks making inquiries. And yesterday they found out the truth.

AND IT *WAS* WORSE!! MUCH WORSE!

The reason Riley and Amelia were put in detention was not just because they stole money from a petrol station. No.

It was because, when a man tried to *stop* them stealing, Riley beat him up so badly — with his bare hands — that the guy ended up unconscious, his arm fractured in three different places, and his spinal cord damaged in such a way that he'll never walk again.

Cassie's mother was calling to warn us to stay away from Riley.

Too late!

The monster has ensnared one of us —

And, oh, it is *Lydia* — who would have thought it would be she?

Worse, worse, it is *all because of me* that Lydia has been so ensnared!! I made it happen!!

Here are my final words:

Inside, careless ghosts are haunting. Outside, thunder is rumbling. And the future? What does the future hold — what HELL does the future hold with a MONSTER in our midst???

This I cannot tell you. . . .

The bell is clanking gloomily — PENS DOWN, PLEASE! —

Alas! Oh, woe! Oh, nevermore! Mercy! Help me! Help us!

And so on . . . .

THE END

Okay, life, enough with the lessons.

Lesson 1: You think you're one kind of a person — smart, kind, loyal — turns out you're the opposite.

Thanks. Great. Really glad to hear it.

Things are winding up here. A whispering around me. Not words, exactly. Just sighing, stretching, yawning, clearing throats. Someone drops a pen, shakes out a hand. It's been a long exam. Thunder outside, so people giggle — thunder being gothic, and all. The supervisors frown but they can't catch the giggles in their outstretched hands.

That night with Riley. We didn't go far, but far enough to send me home fast. Heartbeat pounding as I got into my car: noneedtofeelguilty, noneedtofeelguilty — Amelia is cheating on *him*, so it cancels out! — noneedtofeelguilty. Foot on the accelerator, revving at the lights: but she must neverneverneverfindout.

A two-week study break, and I hid at home.

Kept my eyes half-closed, even closed when I could. Tried to look at myself in the mirror through my eyelids once. (You can't do it.)

Shrugging too — I did a lot of that. Reach for a pecan cookie, shrug. Get myself a coffee, shrug. Open up a book. Yeah, whatever.

If you haven't figured it out, I was trying not to see and not to care. (I'm so transparent.)

A funny thing happened one night, a few days before the HSC started. I was in my window seat with a Maths textbook. It was making me uneasy, this book: The level of mathematical detail was kind of surprising. Maybe I should have started reading a few months back? That's what I was thinking.

Huh. Shrug.

I needed a break. Thought I might call Em or Cass. Or maybe they'd be online.

You know what I did?

Sat at my computer and went straight to a folder of old e-mails between me and Seb. Found some archives of our IMing. Read through fragments, laughed at some, thinking as I did: *I'm so over Seb, I can look at our past and just laugh fondly.*

I felt grown-up.

Then I found an exchange about the first mix Seb ever made for me. Found the mix in my music files. Drums and thrash, then something softer — lyrics and acoustic guitar. A chorus that repeats, "Remember me."

So, this night, I left my Maths book on the window seat and played the song. Thought of the sunflower Seb gave me the first time we met. How we used to go quiet when we listened to each other's music: concentrating, giving it a chance. How nervous we'd get around each other early on, and we'd cover it up by being stupid. Shout at each other about irrelevant things, make dumb jokes, fall down laughing. Get serious suddenly, about our plan to make kids' books together. Or about our secret fears — he used to be a bad boy and got into fights, but he'd got it under control — so his fear was that his temper would come back. We'd call each other up in the middle of the night with ideas or crazy thoughts.

I played the song again. And it crept up on me —

Lesson 2: You're not honest with yourself.

You want the truth? In our last few months together, I'd started messing with his mind. Not on purpose. I think my own secret fear was that I liked him too much. I was afraid he'd see that in my eyes and laugh or run away. And it made me crazy. I'd ask for the impossible one day, and turn cold and sharp the next.

When he asked me for a break, he deserved it.

And then, when he asked me back, I'd been too proud to take him. So now he had Astrid, and whose fault was that?

I played the song again. Found YouTube covers, and played those too. "Remember me," the song said, over and over, like a ghost — like someone gone, or someone left behind.

And it draped itself over me like fabric —

Lesson 3: You've lost him.

Sat at my desk — kept right on playing that song, exactly like a freakin' teenager.

Close your eyes all you like, the tears find a way to get out.

The HSC started. I've been slipping in and out of exams like a ghost. Apart from one conversation yesterday, I haven't talked to anybody much.

Not even my parents, but that's nothing new. When they're home, they don't quite see me — I'm not in focus. And here's something funny. This morning, I'm heading down the driveway on my way to this exam — and there's my mother's voice.

She's in her robe, hand against the sun, framed by the front door — movie star pose — calling my name.

I pause, look back. In a flash I think of her affair — I think of *femmes fatales* and *family curses* — I think, that's *me*, framed by that door —

I close my eyes and listen to her voice.

"There's a message on my phone," she calls, "from Cass's mum — from late last night. There's someone at school you should avoid! A boy who was in juvenile detention! Do you know him?! His name is *Riley*!"

I laugh, and drive away.

Five minutes to go! the supervisor says. Thunder, gasps, giggles, faster writing.

I have one last thing to say.

My conversation yesterday was with Amelia.

I was crossing the oval after an exam. Amelia crossing toward me. Bloodshot eyes, she must have come from the pool.

We stopped, chatted about nothing. Then something changed. Her hand flew sideways, oddly, and her bloodshot eyes found mine.

I noticed something: Her hair was dry. She hadn't been swimming, she'd been crying. *She knows.*

"Riley's not talking to me," she said. Her voice was like a series of blocks that she had to take out one at a time. She never shares herself. My heart hurt to see how hard she found it.

"He hasn't — he doesn't call me back," she said.

"Since when?"

"Since the last day of school. The Thursday. The day of the final assembly, and the play."

That was the night I'd kissed him.

I tried to focus. *She's cheating on him*, I reminded myself, and then a surge of anger: *What, Amelia, you cheat on Riley and he stops returning calls? You don't think the two things are connected?*

It felt great, the anger.

"Maybe," I said, "maybe he found out your secret."

Her eyes widened. Then she shook her head. "But if he knew — I don't think he'd . . ."

And then — standing in the middle of the oval, sounds of traffic, student voices in the distance — she told me.

She fixed her eyes to the collar of my shirt, and told me what she hasn't told Riley.

It's to do with her stepfather.

"I've never told anyone that before," she said with a small smile — "except my mum, and it made her burn the onions."

She laughed. I was breathing hard.

"It's nothing. It's not a big deal."

It is a big deal.

"I've never told Riley because — I guess I didn't trust him not to go kill my stepfather. Plus, I liked telling him the good things about Patrick. That way Patrick stayed special, and the other stuff kind of never happened. I always meant to tell Riley, one day, I mean. He's my, Riley's my . . . I think he knows I'm keeping something from him, and it hurts him. But you think he'd stop talking to me if he found out?"

She was actually checking.

"No," I said. "He would not stop talking to you."

She smiled sadly, and said she had to go. Her face was so thin, her bones were casting shadows.

So, just summing up for you. A few weeks ago, I kissed Amelia's soul mate (*he's my, Riley's my . . .*). Yesterday, she trusted me with a secret she hadn't even told him yet. Last night, the kiss was there for all the world to see on Em's blog.

Today, before this exam, Amelia sat alone and wouldn't look at me.

I closed my eyes, and —

Lesson 4: I don't deserve to live —

That's it. That's my story.

RILEY T. SMITH
STUDENT No. 8233569

My last look at her was a desk.

Polished, curved, and pushed against a window.

A fly crosses the window.

Before this exam, Amelia's silent. Then sudden fast talk. Who knows what she's saying. Something about how I haven't called her the last few weeks. I lead her down a corridor, and we turn our backs.

She changes the subject — "Heard you kissed Lydia" — and gives her wicked grin.

"Where'd you hear that?"

"Read it on a blog last night. People say the strangest things."

That cracking grin. She's holding it. She's waiting.

All I can do is hold her gaze — "Didn't know you read blogs," I say — and now she knows it's true.

Time was, I used to kick the faces in on garden gnomes. That crumpled, broken shock.

Never found a sound that could catch my love for her, and now, look at that, I've gone and broken her.

"Ame," I say.

Some things you can't ever mend.

"After this," I say, meaning this exam —

She's shaking her head. The pride so fast, it makes me proud. The strength in her.

"After this exam," she says, "I have to go see my friend."

Ah. The friend in the institution.

Me kissing Lydia — Amelia knowing that — none of that counts, because Amelia's already gone.

Amelia crossing away from me. Clean, diagonal cut.

I am very sorry to have to ask you this, but have you ever actually SEEN the mental institution that Amelia visits to see her "friend"?

Now there's a white flash of truth in my eyes like a migraine: a folded square of paper.

Toby slipped it into her hand just a moment ago, and Amelia put it in her pocket. I saw this and I didn't think a thing.

But the folded paper.

It's a place to meet.

It's Toby.

There he is.

Toby.

In the Goose and Thistle. His hand hits the exit door above Amelia's shoulder. He looks sideways at Amelia, and she smiles her eyes.

There he is.

Toby.

On the street with us. Asking where she lives. Saying that's on his way.

There he is.

Eyes in the rearview mirror as he drives her away.

There he is.

Toby. Running up a staircase. "I think he's in my History class," Amelia says.

There he is.

Toby. Talking to people at parties. Taking control of the music, making it better.

Trapped in a closet, talking Irish folklore and black holes.

Irish folklore. Of course. The folklore, the fairy tales, the path to her heart. I could never compete with the stepfather. Now I can't compete with this —

Toby.

There's no such person as the crazy friend. That's her cover story. Her wild imagination gone mad.

It's all a story, all code for Toby.

And there he is.

Toby. Floating in Lyd's swimming pool, talking Irish convicts, while the others laugh, ignore him, tell him to shut up.

There he is — Toby. In the auditorium, talking about time travel with mirrors.

At the final assembly, heading up to get his woodwork prize.

Toby — the Irish folklore boy, playing tricks with time.

Toby —

he's been there all along.

You just haven't seen him.

I see him now.

Three desks to the right, two up.

Leaning over, writing fast.

His woodworking hands.

Just beyond him, the empty desk. The fly still walks the window.
A clean, diagonal cross.

Its wings flutter, flutter, buzz — those wings don't work. That fly
can't fly.

Imagine that.

A fly that can't fly.

A man who can't walk.

Woodworking hands that don't.

But let's head back to the corridor, just before this exam — Amelia
and I unblinking. Amelia's face. Telling me she has to go to see her
crazy friend.

Don't ever push me.

"Your crazy friend tells you Irish fairy tales," I say. "Like your stepfather used to tell." Now Amelia blinks, and I add, "Like you're telling
me now."

She stares.

My voice turns soft — cold as the freakin' Danish Alps — "I've
given up on you, Amelia."

She turns,

    and just like that,

        she's gone.

Toby's been taking her away all year — but I just made her disappear for good.

My last look at her is that desk.

Polished, curved, and pushed against a window.

Empty chair lit by thunderclouds.

I always knew my Amelia was a ghost. Never knew I'd be the one
to make her so.

*　　*　　*

There he is.

Toby — just put down his pen and stretched his arms.

TOBIAS GEORGE MAZZERATI
STUDENT No. 8233555

What can I tell ya?

The only real convict uprising in our history, and it almost worked.

If only the message had got through.

Just to round things up, then — you've got a few rebels dead from the battle, a few more dead on the side of the road.

A bunch hide in the woods, and some disappear.

Redneck locals round them up and play this sick (in the old-fashioned sense) game where they get them to line up in a row. "Every third man, step forward!" Drumroll. "Congratulations! Men out the front get executed!"

And they hang them.

I kid you not. Maybe it's where *Idol* got the idea for their show.

Governor goes, "Cut it out, boys. We'll do this proper now." Had a trial of a few more rebels: guilty, guilty, guilty, death by hanging, death by hanging, death by hanging in chains.

Some were flogged, some sent to chain gangs, the rest went back to Castle Hill.

Not for long, though. The crops all went to hell. History reckons it was a disease called rust, but I reckon the crops just up and died on account of all the blood and death.

So they closed down the farm. And that stone barracks that Phillip C. built?

Guess what they did with that?

Ah, you'll never get it. But check it out. It's gothic.

They turned it into a lunatic asylum — Australia's first. There was even an ax murder there — more gothic — they let a couple of the inmates out to chop firewood, and one hacked the other to death. Shifted the asylum somewhere else in 1826.

Stone crumbles — they tear it down — and all around the building starts: houses, roads, shops. Ashbury High. Brookfield High. Castle Towers Shopping Center, cinemas, and mobile phone retailers. A sweeping stretch of grass and trees where the barracks once stood, and these days they call that the Castle Hill Heritage Park.

So, that's the story, and I've gotta say, it kind of gets to me.

Maybe because it's the first time I ever really thought about history, you know, historically speaking? Or maybe because it happened down the road.

If I had a mirror and a telescope, I could sit right here and watch.

As it is, I can drive ten minutes to the place where the battle took place — where the major clapped the pistol to Phillip's head. (It's a graveyard now, which is gothic.)

I can *walk* to the Heritage Park from where I'm sitting. I can show you the spot where Phillip's barracks stood.

The foundations are still there. Shadow of a building. Getting darker and thicker where the fireplace once was.

"Yeah, but what about Tom?" you go.

I told you some guys hid in the woods, and disappeared? That included Tom. They never caught him.

Turned up dead about eight years later. He and another guy lived in the bush all that time, natives helped them survive. A year or two of drought, and they tried to cross the mountains — find that hidden paradise (or China). Couldn't make it, of course. Ended up starving, crazy, sick as dogs. They were on their way back, to give themselves up. The other guy made it (and wrote to Tom's mum to let her know the story) — not Tom.

Almost, though — he fell down dead just moments from those old stone barracks.

And there you have it.

The final gothic moment, in my very gothic tale, which might not in fact be gothic at all, but give a guy a break, I wrote a lot.

As for what the dynamics of first impressions have to do with anything, who knows. Ah well.

Might as well head home and shoot some pool. Stop by the Heritage Park on the way, say g'day to my ole buddy Tom.

Thanks for your time.

PART FOUR

1.

Hills Shire News, Thursday, October 16
Ambulance Called to Brutal Beating; Possible Lightning Strike

Three people are in the hospital, one in a critical condition, following two apparently unrelated incidents in Castle Hill yesterday.

In the first incident, an ambulance was called to a Castle Hill residence. Witnesses say they saw two cars arrive separately at the residence in the early afternoon. Approximately ten minutes later, both cars were seen speeding away in opposite directions. An ambulance arrived shortly afterward and paramedics discovered an unconscious man in the doorway of the home.

Police have arrested a youth in connection with the incident. The youth, who cannot be named for legal reasons, was treated for fractures to both hands.

In an unrelated incident, a second ambulance was called to Castle Hill Heritage Park. A girl had apparently collapsed in the Park during yesterday's electric storm. Earlier reports that she had been struck by lightning have not been confirmed. The girl was taken to Baulkham Hills Hospital by ambulance and is fighting for her life.

Both incidents allegedly involved students from exclusive local private school Ashbury High. Ashbury School Principal Bill Ludovico declined to comment.

❖

From: Bill.Ludovico@ashburyhigh.com.au
Sent: Thursday, October 16
To: Roberto.Garcia@ashburyhigh.com.au;
Chris.Botherit@ashburyhigh.com.au
Subject: CONFIDENTIAL — URGENT — *NOT FOR INCLUSION IN SCHOLARSHIP FILE*

Rob and Chris,

Can you two put together a solid answer to this question for me:

Why the hell were Riley and Amelia chosen for the scholarships in the first place?

I need to know exactly what happened yesterday. Get the Committee together and find out. Tonight, if possible. (And find out if we're going to be liable for any of this.)

Cheers,
Bill Ludovico
Principal, Ashbury High

Inquiry into Events of Wednesday, October 15
Transcript of Interviews — Thursday, October 16 — 6 P.M.

EVIDENCE OF LYDIA JAACKSON-OBERMAN

Mr. Botherit: Lydia. Can you tell us what happened after your English exam yesterday? In your own words.

Lydia: Whose words did you think I was going to use?

Mr. Botherit: Forgive me, Lydia. I have no doubt that you will never use anybody else's words but your own.

Lydia: After the exam, I spoke to Riley.

[Long pause.]

Mr. Botherit: Maybe you could be a little more — detailed.

Lydia: Like how?

Mr. Botherit: Like — what did Riley say?

Lydia: If I told you that, it wouldn't be my own words.

EVIDENCE OF EMILY THOMPSON

Emily: Well, after the exam I was exhausted and I was thinking of going to the Blue Danish to recover, and I was calling out to Lyd but she couldn't hear me, and I was texting Cass at the same time because her exams had finished and I was missing her and I thought she could come and meet us too.

Mr. Botherit: Okay. And — can you get to something relevant, Em?

Emily: I am an extremely relevant girl, as I think you know, but I am understandably distressed at the moment. So, I'm calling Lyd, and texting Cass, and out of the corner of my eye I see Toby walking out the front gate of the school. And behind him was Riley.

That made me stop texting because I knew that Toby had been having a thing with Amelia and I'd just found out about Riley's violent past the night before, when you called my mum, Mrs. A, and so when I saw Riley following Toby, I was frightened for Toby's life, so —

Several people speak at once: What is she talking about?/Can someone tell her to slow down?/Did she just say that *Toby* was "having a thing" with *Amelia*?

Emily: Yes.

Jacob Mazzerati: *Toby* has been — dating Amelia?

Constance Milligan: Could somebody remind me who Toby is? And tell this girl to speak *slowly*.

Jacob Mazzerati: Toby is my son, Constance.

Emily: Okay. And he and Amelia had a secret romance, but nobody knew except me. And then Riley found out because I told him in a letter. I didn't tell him it was Toby, just that something was going on.

However, at this point in time, after the exam yesterday, I began to think that maybe Riley *did* know it was Toby, because he was walking toward Toby with very intentional footsteps.

Mr. Botherit: Let me get this clear. You recently wrote a letter to Riley telling him Amelia was cheating on him?

Emily: Kind of. Anyway, Riley was walking toward Toby and I was in extreme trepidation, but then I saw Lydia stop Riley, to speak to him.

Constance Milligan: And now we have Lydia?! It's too much!

Mr. Botherit: We just heard from Lydia, Constance. She was right here — sitting in that seat.

Constance Milligan: [*frostily*] I am perfectly aware of who Lydia is, thank you. I was just having a little trouble keeping up —

Emily: Anyhow, Toby continued out the gate and got away safely while Lydia talked to Riley, so I was relieved. Only then I realized that Lyd and Riley were walking toward the car park. I was petrified. They got into Lyd's car so I dropped to my hands and knees and crawled across the gravel to my own car, ready to follow.

Constance Milligan: Did she just say she dropped to her hands and knees and crawled across the gravel? Whatever is the matter with this girl?

Mr. Botherit: Emily, why were you petrified?

Emily: Because of the thing between Riley and Lyd. Did I mention that Riley and Lydia had a thing?

EVIDENCE OF TOBIAS MAZZERATI

Toby: After the exam I went to the Heritage Park.

Mr. Botherit: Why?

Toby: Well, I've gotta start by saying what my exam was about. It was about this convict named Tom, who was living in this stone barracks that his friend Phillip C. built, and Tom's girl, Maggie, was back in Ireland, and —

Constance Milligan: Slow down, fellow! Now, Maggie. Who's that? She's the one we just spoke to? The girl who also talked too fast?

Mr. Botherit: No, Constance. That was Emily. I think Toby might be referring to imaginary people.

Toby: Not imaginary, historical. Anyhow, the story ends with Tom's best friend dead, and same with most of his buddies, and Tom himself half-dead and starving, and then he ends up fully dead right by the old stone barracks where he used to live. Never got to see his

Maggie again. It's just your basic happy story of everything going to hell.

Mr. Botherit: You've cheered me up, anyway.

Toby: Sorry, Mr. B, but that's my point — I wrote the story out for my exam and while I was writing, it was like someone else gradually took over. Like Tom was there writing it for me, and I just let him, or maybe I *became* him some of the time, and I realize that doesn't make sense so you can get that expression off your face, Dad, but I've gotta say, *something* was going on, cos I never wrote so much in an exam in all my life.

Jacob Mazzerati: Expression? This is just admiration, Tobes. Never heard so much sense in all my life.

Toby: Anyhow, so, after the exam I decided to go to the Heritage Park — that's where Tom used to live. I don't know why, but maybe there was still a bit of Tom inside me and he wanted to head back? Or maybe I just wanted to say thanks for his help.

Mr. Botherit: Wasn't there a thunderstorm threatening? You went to the park in a storm — to say thanks to — to the ghost of Tom?

Toby: Tom would have done the same for me.

EVIDENCE OF LYDIA JAACKSON-OBERMAN

Mr. Botherit: Okay, Lydia, you should know that Riley has told us the nature of your conversation with him after the exam so we just want to make sure you have the same version.

Lydia: [*a faint, distant smile*] Nice try.

Mr. Botherit: All right, *after* the conversation, what happened?

Lydia: Riley asked me to drive him somewhere.

Mr. Botherit: Where?

Lydia: I have no idea.

[Long pause.]

Mr. Botherit: Maybe someone else should ask the questions.

Mr. Garcia: Let's get Emily back.

EVIDENCE OF EMILY THOMPSON

Emily: Anyhow, I was terrified because I had just found out about Riley's violent past, and it seemed to me to be a very dangerous combination, a violent person in a car with his secret lover. What if Lyd ended the romance while they were driving? Violent people always strike again.

Riley got in the car with Lydia, and he was looking ferocious.

And so I followed.

I stayed a couple of cars behind so they wouldn't notice me. It was early afternoon but stormily dark. There were distant, ominous sounds of thunder, which seemed to me to echo my own terror.

We drove for about ten minutes. The rain had just started — it was really pouring — when I saw Lyd's car stop outside a house. I pulled over a short distance away. My heart was beating like horses' hooves.

The passenger door opened and Riley got out.

It was raining so hard that water splashed into his hair, and down his face. He walked toward the house.

Lydia's car stayed where it was.

Nothing happened.

I sat in my car while the rain clattered on my car roof and crashed against my windows.

I wondered whose house that was — and then a terrible thought occurred to me.

What if it was Toby's house?

What if Riley had decided that, instead of following Toby out of the school gates, he should drive to Toby's house and wait for him there? Like a trap.

I knew Lydia would not sit in her car and let this happen, but maybe he had tricked her?

I got out, and started to run. My shoes were instantly soaked through. The rain was like an angry, moving shower with excellent water pressure.

I reached Lyd's car and saw her sitting at the wheel with her eyes closed.

I ran down the driveway and stopped. There was a horseshoe knocker and I was reaching up to bang it, when the door suddenly opened.

Riley came out.

He hardly glanced at me.

His shirt was rumpled, and he was still dripping from the rain. His face looked calm.

He walked up the driveway, and stopped at the side of Lydia's car.

I turned back to the open door before me.

A man was lying in the hallway. He was covered in blood.

EVIDENCE OF TOBIAS MAZZERATI

Toby: So I walked to the Heritage Park. It's only ten minutes from the school. I went up the path to the spot where the barracks used to be. Sat down on the grass and said, "'Tsup, Tom?" It started raining just at that moment. I'll be honest with you, people. I felt like a right fool.

EVIDENCE OF EMILY THOMPSON

Emily: Maybe not covered in blood. But there *was* blood, and a lot of it. Mostly in the area below the man's nose, across his mouth, down his chin, and dripping onto his shirt. His eyes were closed. He was lying in a very peculiar way, with his legs kind of tangled around sideways.

He was a man I'd never seen before, and yet I knew I had to save his life.

I did not know how to save a life, and had no access to the Internet to find out. Therefore, I'm sorry to say, my primary emotion was annoyance.

I crouched down to see if he was breathing. I knew this was important to life.

I put my ear very close to his nose. At first, all I could hear was the rain outside — but then? I can't tell you how happy I was to hear that tiny airy sound. This strange, grown-up man with whiskers and blood all over his chin was breathing. And therefore, I didn't have to give him mouth-to-mouth resuscitation.

My phone was in the car, but I could see a wall phone just inside the door. I stepped over the breathing man, and called an ambulance. I have never dialed triple 0 before so I was nervous, but then I found I couldn't concentrate on the conversation because I suddenly realized the amazement around me. That place was *trashed*. Bookshelves tipped over. A table upside down, with one leg snapped in half. An open magazine with a muddy footprint tearing a page in half. Two holes in the wall right beside me.

The scary thing was, it was like the fight was still happening. I was in the room with it. *Things were still moving.* A bottle of tomato sauce was slowly rolling across a coffee table. The shadow of a light shade swayed back and forth across the floor. A desk chair was lying on its side, and the wheels were spinning. There was a *THUNK* and I saw that a block of cheese had fallen to the floor — from where? I don't know. I screamed. And then a piece of plaster slowly crumbled from the hole beside me — I screamed louder, hung up the phone, and got out of there.

I had to jump over the man to get to the front porch, and I looked up just in time to see Lydia's car speed away.

I almost screamed a third time — but then I saw her — Lydia — standing at the top of the driveway in the rain. She waited until I reached her, then walked toward my car. I guess she'd noticed it.

She got into my car and told me she had a message to get to Amelia right away.

"Okay," I said. "Amelia's place." And I stepped on the gas.

Lydia put her seat belt on, and closed her eyes.

EVIDENCE OF LYDIA JAACKSON-OBERMAN

Mr. Botherit: Lydia, let me get this straight. You waited outside a stranger's house for Riley, then he came out and asked for your car?

Lydia: Yes.

Mr. Botherit: So you just got out of your car and gave him the keys?

Lydia: Right.

[Long pause.]

Mr. Botherit: [*sighing*] And he asked you to pass on a message for Amelia?

Lydia: Yes.

Mr. Botherit: I suppose it would be pointless for me to ask what the message was.

Lydia: Right.

EVIDENCE OF EMILY THOMPSON

Emily: It was difficult driving. My socks were extremely soggy. And the rain turned the windshield into one big blur. The wipers were going so fast they were like annoying puppies.

Also, I realized we didn't know where Amelia lived. And no phone number for her. She never had a mobile.

So I was driving along at high speed, leaning forward, trying to see through the blur, all without having a clue where I was going.

Then I got a flash of inspiration.

I remembered Toby had given a secret note to Amelia earlier that day. Maybe the note was telling Amelia to meet him after the exam? Maybe they were meeting now?

The place I'd seen them meeting once before was the Heritage Park. It seemed unlikely in this rain but it was all I had.

I skidded around a corner, and the tires sent water spraying.

I did not crash.

Just as I was speeding up that small laneway — the one that leads to the back gate of the Heritage Park — well, suddenly, Lydia's eyes opened wide. She peered through her window — and then she opened the door. We were still moving fast, so I shouted and braked at the same time, but she was jumping — she was jumping from the speeding car. She hit the road running, and kept on running into the park.

EVIDENCE OF TOBIAS MAZZERATI

Toby: I'm sitting in the rain, feeling kinda dumb, and I sense something — turn around and there's a girl running. I recognize her. It's Lydia. She was coming from the gate and it seemed like she was heading straight for me at first, but then I realized she was cutting across the grass — toward the dense trees farther in.

I couldn't figure out what she was running toward — all I could see in that direction was trees and rain. But there was something urgent in the way she was running — like someone was in trouble, or something was seriously wrong. She was flying toward it, so I started running too.

EVIDENCE OF EMILY THOMPSON

Emily: I stopped the car with a screech of brakes and a crash of mud-splattered water, got out into the rain, opened my umbrella, and tried to see what was going on. I could see Lydia running toward the trees. And there was Toby, running after Lydia — he'd come from another direction.

But whatever it was that Lydia had seen — well, I had no idea how she could have seen it. The rain was so heavy it was like looking into a wave.

I started running anyway.

EVIDENCE OF LYDIA JAACKSON-OBERMAN

Mr. Botherit: Lydia. What was it you saw from the car window?

Lydia: Amelia.

Mr. Botherit: And you ran toward her?

Lydia: She was in trouble.

Mr. Botherit: Trouble?

Lydia: Right.

EVIDENCE OF EMILY THOMPSON

Emily: As I got closer, there was a huge blast of thunder — the kind you feel deep inside you, the kind that makes everything shake — and an instant flash of lightning. And in that moment, I saw everything. Lydia was still running — Toby was overtaking her — and they were both screaming and shouting. I couldn't hear what they were saying over the thunder and rain — I could just see their mouths.

But the person they were running toward — was Amelia. In that flash of bright light, I could see the color of her hair. She was facing away from us — standing on a log — with a white stretch of rope above her.

EVIDENCE OF TOBIAS MAZZERATI

Toby: I could hear Lydia screaming Amelia's name — but Amelia wasn't turning. Then Lydia started shouting that she had a message — and shouting the message itself. It felt important that Amelia hear it, so I shouted it too.

Mr. Botherit: What was the message?

Toby: *I haven't given up on you. Please don't give up on me.*

[Long pause.]

Mr. Botherit: But by then it was too late.

EVIDENCE OF EMILY THOMPSON

Emily: They were so close to Amelia, and she still wasn't moving — turning around — anything — Toby got there first and his arms were reaching up to her. And he was shouting something — and then something strange happened.

EVIDENCE OF LYDIA JAACKSON-OBERMAN

Lydia: I don't know what happened. I was running and running, but it felt like I couldn't get any closer. It was panic, I guess — my body wasn't going as fast as my mind wanted. I saw that Toby was almost at her side — and then — well, is it possible for rain to literally fill the air? Because that's what happened. For a few seconds, there was a whitewash.

I couldn't see or hear or breathe or move. It was terrifying.

EVIDENCE OF EMILY THOMPSON

Emily: It was like drowning. Like I wasn't looking at a wave anymore, I was *in* the wave. Everything went white and the noise was like exploding static.

Then there was another violent clap of thunder and the rain was just heavy again — more lightning, and I got a glimpse of Toby standing close to Amelia, holding her — and then Toby was walking toward me, and Amelia was in his arms.

Her eyes were closed.

This time I knew that I wouldn't be able to save a life, even if I tried.

I went and put my umbrella over them, and we all walked together to the entrance to the park.

EVIDENCE OF TOBIAS MAZZERATI

Toby: I don't know. It's gone. That memory's gone, I mean. One moment I'm running and shouting; the next I'm walking in the rain and she's in my arms. Lydia called an ambulance. People came running out of houses near the park. Somebody asked if it was lightning.

EVIDENCE OF LYDIA JAACKSON-OBERMAN

Lydia: Riley turned up at the hospital eventually. He said he'd heard on the car radio — on the news, I mean — that Amelia had been struck by lightning.

Mr. Botherit: You realize that late last night, Riley turned himself in to the police and was arrested and charged with assault, amongst other things?

Lydia: Okay.

Mr. Botherit: Lydia, we know that the man you and Riley went to see was Patrick O'Doherty, Amelia's stepfather. We know that Riley left him unconscious on the floor. And that he then drove away in your car, presumably intending to flee.

Lydia: Okay.

Mr. Botherit: Look, I realize this is a very difficult time. But you helped Riley commit a crime — it seems he hasn't mentioned your role to the police, or you might be under arrest yourself. Is there anything you can say to explain this? Any of this?

Lydia: No.

Mr. Botherit: [*quietly*] Lydia, why do *you* think Amelia . . . Why do you think she went to the Heritage Park yesterday, instead of to her English exam?

Lydia: Because of me. I was her friend. The day before the exam, she told me a secret she'd never told anyone before. She trusted me. And then she found out that I'd already betrayed her.

EVIDENCE OF EMILY THOMPSON

Emily: It was my fault. She was having that secret romance with Toby, and I let Riley know about it. I could tell that Riley was angry with her yesterday, and I could see she was heartbroken. And that's why it happened. Most things this year have been my fault, but this is the worst of them. Obviously.

EVIDENCE OF TOBIAS MAZZERATI

Mr. Botherit: I suppose it's your fault that Amelia went to the park yesterday.

Toby: [*brief pause*] Why would it be my fault?

Mr. Botherit: [*gently*] Toby, we know you were having a secret romance with Amelia.

Toby: A secret romance with Amelia. [*Laughs softly.*] In my dreams.

The Committee for the Administration of the
K. L. Mason Patterson Trust Fund
THE K. L. MASON PATTERSON SCHOLARSHIP FILE

From: Chris.Botherit@ashburyhigh.com.au
Sent: Friday, October 17
To: Bill.Ludovico@ashburyhigh.com.au
CC: Roberto.Garcia@ashburyhigh.com.au
Subject: Amelia and Riley

Dear Bill,

You asked us to find out what happened on Wednesday.

There is simply no clear answer to that question. We have done our best to piece it together — using a lot of guesswork — and, with that qualification in mind, I will tell you what we think.

First: Riley.

It seems that, directly after the exam, Riley learned something about Amelia's stepfather that made him angry. Lydia most likely shared this information with him. Riley went straight to the stepfather and attacked him. He intended to flee in Lydia's car, but news of Amelia's accident reached him, and he returned and turned himself in.

Now, I assume you got my message the other day, letting you know of a recent disturbing discovery: We had been asking around (discreetly) about Riley's criminal history for a couple of weeks, and a Brookfield sports teacher let me know the truth — that Riley had, in fact, committed a very violent offense.

That sports teacher was ready to tell me the truth when I asked — he'd been keeping it confidential these last years — and just as quick to declare that Riley is a "lost cause." Yet we wanted to trust Riley, to believe his claims that he has reformed. Thus, the only steps we took were to warn Riley's close friends (Patricia Aganovic called around on Tuesday night), and, of course, to notify you.

It now seems tragically clear that we were wrong: Riley is violent and dangerous — as that sports teacher said, a "lost cause."

Riley has been released into the care of his foster mother, pending trial. Here I might point out that the foster mother has always seemed to us a decent, honest person — and she spoke in Riley's defense last night.

Apparently (the foster mother said), Riley has been very upset lately by the departure of the other foster child in his household. A baby girl, Chloe, was moved back to her biological parents on the last Thursday of term. Obviously, this does not excuse his outburst, and, given his record, he is almost certainly facing prison time.

Which brings me to Amelia — this is difficult to write about.

All that we know for sure is that she missed her exam to go to the Heritage Park. While she was there, something happened which caused her heart to stop. Her system went into multiple organ failure — essentially, it shut down. It seems she was already in a weak, malnourished, and exhausted state, so she did not have the strength to fight.

The hospital confirms that they do not expect her to recover. Even if she regains consciousness, the brain damage will most likely be substantial.

What the hospital *cannot* tell us, however, is exactly what happened. You will have heard the rumors that she was struck by lightning — witnesses near the Heritage Park apparently drew this conclusion when they saw a girl being carried out of the park in the midst of an electrical storm. Also, Emily and Lydia both refer to a strange sensation as of a "whitewash," and perhaps this is consistent with a lightning strike?

The hospital, however, can find no evidence of any such thing.

The alternative, and more likely, explanation is that Amelia went to the park with the intention of harming herself. This is obviously very upsetting, but I think we need to face it. It seems that she may have felt betrayed by friends, and that her troubled relationship with Riley was disturbing her. Her physical condition suggests she had been suffering from profound depression — and Em, at least, recalls glimpsing a rope.

Again, however, and to be blunt: The hospital says there is no evidence of attempted suicide by hanging.

Our conclusion is that Amelia did intend to take her own life, and most likely suffered some kind of depressive breakdown.

We are all profoundly saddened by the way things have turned out for our first scholarship winners.

We hope that this account is helpful.

Yours,
Chris Botherit

From: Bill.Ludovico@ashburyhigh.com.au
Sent: Friday, October 17
To: Roberto.Garcia@ashburyhigh.com.au;
Chris.Botherit@ashburyhigh.com.au
Subject: *NOT FOR INCLUSION IN SCHOLARSHIP FILE*

Rob and Chris,

How exactly did we not know the truth about Riley's violent past? I did get your memo on this, and was livid. Too busy to follow up, though — all this might have been avoided if I had.

Also, this is the first I've heard that Riley lives with a foster family — what else do we not know about this boy?

As for Amelia — the "breakdown" theory is flimsy, and frankly, not my preference. Depressed and suicidal? Then why did nobody at Ashbury notice and take appropriate preemptive action? If you get my drift, we'd end up taking the fall. (Although, I take it she lives in some kind of a hostel? So presumably her family is not making trouble?)

Official line will be: struck by lightning.

Cheers,
Bill Ludovico
Principal, Ashbury High

P.S. Delete this e-mail.

Dear Amelia,

I hear there are giant jellyfish in the Arctic, tentacles longer than train carriages.

Haystacks fly over cities in whirlwinds, and fish, frogs, and turtles rain on towns.

There are spaces of perfect nothing that they call black holes.

Nothing's impossible — that's what you think I'm trying to say. But I'm not.

There are things that *are* impossible — unimaginable, even — and here they are: that I broke you. Betrayed you. Said I'd given up on you. Sent you flying to a park in a thunderstorm.

That I've been wrong about you all along — saw something in your face each time you faded to your past, when the opposite was true.

That all this time you've been lost and that I won't get a second chance to find you.

Amelia, your name is a song. It's a name that can't be spoken without smiling or crying, without casting both shadows and light. But there are too many places to hide or get lost in a name like Amelia.

So this is me shouting that name. They say nobody ever escapes from a black hole. They don't know the strength in my Amelia. The strength in your grip when you want to stay out dancing — the strength in your wicked smile.

Riley

The Committee for the Administration of the
K. L. Mason Patterson Trust Fund
THE K. L. MASON PATTERSON SCHOLARSHIP FILE

From: Bill.Ludovico@ashburyhigh.com.au
Sent: Monday, November 3
To: Roberto.Garcia@ashburyhigh.com.au;
Chris.Botherit@ashburyhigh.com.au
Subject: *NOT FOR INCLUSION IN SCHOLARSHIP FILE*

Rob and Chris,

Just got off the phone with the hospital and you should be the first to know: In a "miraculous turn of events," it seems that Amelia's awake and lucid.

Cheers all around.

My concern now is this: Riley might find a way to slip out of the charges against him — seems these kids know how to land on their feet. Next thing, they'll be running back wanting that scholarship bonus. Technically, they're entitled to it since they completed their final year of high school (although *did* Amelia complete it if she didn't come to her exams?).

Whatever, we need to shut down the possibility, right away.

Set things in motion to strip them of their scholarships.

Backdate it so they won't get the bonus.
Make it like they were never here.

Cheers,
Bill Ludovico
Principal, Ashbury High

❖

From: Bill.Ludovico@ashburyhigh.com.au
Sent: Monday, November 3
To: Roberto.Garcia@ashburyhigh.com.au;
Chris.Botherit@ashburyhigh.com.au
Subject: *NOT FOR INCLUSION IN SCHOLARSHIP FILE*

Just following on from my last e-mail —
I assume I don't need to tell you what the "grounds" are for termination of the scholarships — but I'm thinking we should throw in as many as we can.
So: Now that we know Riley's true colors, we should look back over "unsolved crimes" for the last year. What about that Brookfielder's artwork that got attacked while it was here in the Exhibition? I seem to remember Riley's art was in the same Exhibition? Look at him for that.

Cheers,
Bill Ludovico
Principal, Ashbury High

❖

From: Bill.Ludovico@ashburyhigh.com.au
Sent: Monday, November 3
To: Roberto.Garcia@ashburyhigh.com.au;
Chris.Botherit@ashburyhigh.com.au
Subject: *NOT FOR INCLUSION IN SCHOLARSHIP FILE*

Still thinking aloud . . . but wasn't there some question of them stealing castanets from the Music Rooms? Isn't that why we got security cameras?

Cheers,
Bill Ludovico
Principal, Ashbury High

P.S. And no offense, Chris, but you can be a bit of a pompous ass, and your e-mails are overwritten. Keep the next one to bullet points! Cheers.

❖

TERMINATION OF SCHOLARSHIP

• In accordance with Article 19(a)(i) of the Scholarship Charter, the K. L. Mason Patterson Scholarship Committee hereby moves that the scholarships granted to:

Amelia Grace Damaski
Riley Terence Smith

be terminated, with retrospective effect.

• Grounds for termination are as follows:

1. That, without reasonable justification, Amelia failed to attend her HSC English Extension 3 exam.

2. That Riley has been charged with assault occasioning actual bodily harm.

3. That Amelia and Riley engaged in misleading and deceptive conduct in the course of their original Scholarship Interviews, in that they did not disclose the true nature of their criminal record.

4. That Amelia and Riley broke into the Music Rooms after school hours.

5. That Riley may have destroyed the artwork of a Brookfield student (Sebastian Mantegna) while it was on display as part of the Ashbury-Brookfield Art Exhibition.

6. That Amelia and/or Riley may have stolen a set of castanets.

7. That Amelia and Riley deceived their fellow students by pretending to be friends with them although they did not, in fact, like or respect them.

• In accordance with Article 20(a) of the Scholarship Charter, the K. L. Mason Patterson Committee will hear the response of the scholarship holders to the above grounds before termination is confirmed.

Extracts from Transcript of Hearing — Friday, December 12

Absent: *Bill Ludovico and Constance Milligan*

EVIDENCE OF AMELIA DAMASKI

Mr. Botherit: Amelia, can I begin by saying how happy we are to see that you've recovered so well. Also, we assume you know that the Board of Studies has accepted estimates from each of your subject teachers for exams you missed while in the hospital, so you'll still get your HSC. We care about you and wish you the best, no matter how things might turn out here. . . .

[Amelia gazes steadily.]

Mr. Botherit: Let's get started right away. This is a formal hearing during which you and Riley will have the opportunity to persuade us that the grounds for termination of your scholarships are without foundation. Do you understand that?

[Amelia blinks, which we take to be a nod.]

Mr. Botherit: In effect, if the scholarship is terminated, you will miss out on the bonus.

[Another blink.]

Mr. Botherit: Right. Can you tell us why you failed to attend your English exam?

Amelia: Okay. Earlier this year I met a girl who lives in a mental institution in Castle Hill. She has serious depression. We got to be friends and I met up with her a lot. I missed the exam because I went to see her; I thought she was going to kill herself.

[Long pause.]

Mr. Botherit: Why — why did you think that?

Amelia: Not long before this she told me her heart was broken. And then she started falling apart — not eating, not sleeping — fading away.

Mr. Botherit: . . . Okay, but you came to the exam that morning — people saw you arrive. And then you suddenly left?

Amelia: Yes.

Mr. Botherit: You suddenly became convinced this — friend — was going to kill herself?

Amelia: Right.

Mr. Botherit: Amelia, you say that your friend was in an institution. Presumably they would have had safeguards in place to stop patients from killing themselves.

Amelia: They didn't have safeguards in place to stop a patient killing another patient with an ax earlier this year.

[Some murmurs of shock around the table — another long pause — then:]

Mr. Botherit: All right. And it was more important to you to — save this girl's life than to attend an HSC exam?

Amelia: Ah. Yeah.

Mr. Botherit: Forgive me, Amelia. You see, this is all rather — out of left field, is the expression I think. We had no idea about your friend in the — mental institution.

[Silence.]

Mr. Botherit: Amelia, where is this mental institution?

Amelia: It's near the Heritage Park.

Mr. Botherit: [*voice softening*] Okay. So that's why you went there. A friend — a friend had a broken heart — and she wanted to kill herself. So you went to — stop her.

Amelia: Right.

Mr. Botherit: And what happened when you got there?

Amelia: She wasn't there — where I usually meet her. In the vegetable garden. I spent a couple of hours searching around the park and the neighborhood. I was heading back to see if I could speak to the people at the institution itself — she's always told me to stay away from there, but I was too scared by now. I wanted to make sure. And that's when the storm started — and when I saw her. There was a rope — a tree — I started running — and then I woke up in the hospital. And two weeks had gone by.

Mr. Botherit: Did you tell the people at the hospital about this friend?

Amelia: Of course. I wanted them to find out for me if she was okay.

Mr. Botherit: What did they say?

Amelia: They said there is no mental institution in Castle Hill.

EVIDENCE OF RILEY T. SMITH

Mr. Botherit: Riley, have you ever seen the mental institution that Amelia refers to?

Riley: No.

Mr. Botherit: Why do *you* think Amelia went to the Heritage Park instead of to her English exam?

Riley: Because of me. I betrayed her. And I told her I'd given up on her.

Mr. Botherit: Okay. And do you have anything to say to explain the criminal charges against you?

Riley: No.

[Long pause.]

Mr. Botherit: All right. We'll move on to the next gr —

Mr. Garcia: Can I interrupt? — Riley, you turned yourself in to the police. Why did you do that?

Riley: I couldn't have stayed with Amelia in the hospital if I was running.

Patricia Aganovic: Can I ask when you realized that your hands were fractured?

Riley: When they tried to take my fingerprints.

EVIDENCE OF AMELIA DAMASKI

Mr. Botherit: Amelia, did your mother ever come to the hospital when you were there?

Amelia: How is that relevant? [*a pause during which Amelia thinks and then laughs to herself and says:*] Well, my stepfather was in the hospital while I was, and Mum would have come to see him, so, yeah, I guess my mother did come to the hospital while I was there.

Mr. Botherit: To see your stepfather. Okay. Do you have anything to say about the criminal charges against Riley?

Amelia: They're excessive. My stepfather was only in the hospital overnight.

Mr. Botherit: Excessive? But Riley's hands were broken. You have to hit somebody pretty hard to break your own hands.

Amelia: I don't think that's how Riley broke his hands. I think he punched the wall.

Mr. Botherit: So he swung at your stepdad and got the wall, it's not really rel —

Amelia: Riley doesn't miss.

Mr. Botherit: You're saying he just randomly, deliberately hit the wall.

Amelia: Yes.

Mr. Botherit: Why would . . . Oh, perhaps we should leave this for now.

EVIDENCE OF RILEY T. SMITH

Riley: Why did I not tell you in the scholarship interview that I once beat a guy so badly I snapped his spine? Well, I didn't plan to do it again.

EVIDENCE OF AMELIA DAMASKI

Amelia: Why would we tell anybody that?

Mr. Botherit: You didn't think we deserved to hear the full tr —

Amelia: [*calmly*] If you want the full truth, you should know this about Riley. From the age of two, he drummed on everything — garbage bin lids, walls, the TV. It gave his dad a headache. He used to punch Riley in the head, so the kid would know what a headache felt like. Sometimes he'd press Riley's hands against the hot element of the stove, hoping it would stop him from drumming.

They put him in five different foster homes — he ran away from all of them, ended up in the hostel where I live, and that's how I met him.

Mr. Botherit: [*quietly*] It's not surprising that Riley became a violent person.

Amelia: [*slowly, calmly*] Riley is not a violent person. That time he attacked the guy in the petrol station? It was the manager. He had my arm twisted so hard behind my back I was about to pass out. Riley went wild — he was protecting me.

Mr. Botherit: But how could you know he wouldn't go wild again? When another occasion came up to — protect you?

Amelia: He promised he wouldn't.

Mr. Botherit: Amelia, a promise —

Amelia: Do you know what he promised? That if he ever felt that angry again he'd punch a wall with both fists. My stepdad got off easy. Look at the wall, and look at Riley's hands, and then give me a lecture about promises.

Ms. Wexford: What's that noise? That banging?

Mr. Botherit: The Ashbury ghost.

Mr. Garcia: It's Amelia. She's kicking the table leg. This is what she does when she is angry.

[The kicking stops, abruptly.]

EVIDENCE OF RILEY T. SMITH

Riley: We used the Music Rooms after hours to practice. Amelia has an old guitar but that's the only instrument we have.

Ms. Wexford: But you could have used the school's resources anytime! You just needed to ask.

[Riley gazes at her steadily.]

EVIDENCE OF AMELIA DAMASKI

Mr. Botherit: Amelia, did you or Riley steal a set of castanets?

Amelia: *[laughs — keeps laughing]*

EVIDENCE OF RILEY T. SMITH

Riley: [*laughs — keeps laughing*]

Ms. Wexford: Riley, the fractures to your hands. Do you think the agility — the flexibility — of your hands might be affected? Permanently, I mean?

Riley: [*stops laughing*]

EVIDENCE OF RILEY T. SMITH

Mr. Botherit: Did you attack Seb Mantegna's major work?

Riley: Why would I have done that?

Mr. Botherit: I seem to recall that everyone who went to that exhibition said that yours and Seb's were the best. So. Destroy Seb's and your work is the best.

Riley: Seb's was better. Destroying it wouldn't have changed that.

Mr. Botherit: Maybe you had an emotional motive? We know there's romance between you and Lydia. We also know — everyone knows — that Lydia and Seb were once together. Perhaps in a jealous rage . . . ?

Riley: There's no romance between Lydia and me. Ask Lydia.

EVIDENCE OF AMELIA DAMASKI

Mr. Botherit: Amelia, do you think Riley might have attacked Seb's major work?

Amelia: No.

Mr. Botherit: It's just that — he's obviously an angry person. And that attack was an angry one.

Amelia: [*laughs*] That's the best you've got?

Mr. Botherit: All right. Let's move on to the final ground — it's been suggested that you may have deceived people — that you had some ulterior motive for your friendships here at Ashbury. Perhaps you could help us figure out the nature of those friendships? Did you genuinely like anybody? Was there, for example, a secret romance between you and Toby? Were you and Riley —

Amelia: Are you asking these questions because they're relevant or because you want the gossip?

Mr. Botherit: Can I be frank with you, Amelia? You are not helping yourself here. The grounds for termination are — well, let's go back to your friend in the mental institution. Would you —

Amelia: It's okay, Mr. B. I get it. You think I made her up — you think I projected my own heartbreak onto an imaginary friend. You think the fact that my mum and I don't talk — that she didn't bother to come see me at the hospital — means I'm a sad little abandoned girl, and that I went to the park to kill myself. Don't worry about it. I'm used to people telling me the truth is my imagination.

Mr. Botherit: You seem very angry, Amelia.

Amelia: [*laughs*] Maybe *I* attacked Seb's major work.

EVIDENCE OF RILEY T. SMITH

Mr. Botherit: We've all read your ghost story, Riley. And, well, we just want to know *why* you were friends with these people if you didn't like them?

Riley: [*steady, inscrutable gaze*]

[long pause]

Mr. Botherit: Riley, you do understand that if these scholarships are terminated with retrospective effect, not only will you not get the bonus money, you'll also, technically, be required to pay everything else back?

Riley: [*a brief breath of laughter*] Okay.

Mr. Botherit: And you have nothing else to say in your defense?

Riley: [*slowly shakes his head, the same ironic glint in his eye*]

Mr. Botherit: Well, that concludes our interviews. The Committee will meet next Friday to — finalize the decision, and we'll let you and Amelia know the outcome.

MONDAY

Dear Amelia,

If I were you, I wouldn't want to see me either. Fair enough. I'll stop stalking you with phone calls.

But I'll be at the Blue Danish at three this afternoon. I'll wear one of those Freddy masks from the *Nightmare* movies so you won't have to look at me.

Not really. I haven't got one.

I'd like to say I'm sorry and try to explain. I know: Who cares what I'd like, so you can tell me where to go on that issue. But I've also got an idea that you might want to hear.

I hope to see you there.

Lydia

❖

From: Emily.Thompson@ashburyhigh.com.au
Sent: Monday, December 15
To: Chris.Botherit@ashburyhigh.com.au
Subject: The Scholarship Committee Meeting

Dear Mr. Botherit,

I understand that the Committee is having a meeting this Friday night, to finalize the termination of the scholarships of Amelia Damaski and Riley T. Smith. I have read the transcript of interviews and the grounds for termination.

I hereby propose to attend this meeting.

Even though Friday is the day of the HSC results and I was planning to have a party at Lyd's to celebrate/ distract myself from misery that night.

Nevertheless, I will be at your meeting.

Until then
I remain
Your former student,
Emily Thompson
(and afterward, well, I will still be her.)

❖

TUESDAY

Dear Mrs. Damaski and Mr. O'Doherty,

I am a concerned resident of the Hills District, and have followed the news of the attack upon you, Mr. O'Doherty, with great sympathy.

I hope that you are well on the road to recovery.

I am writing now because I have some important information concerning your daughter, Amelia, and her boyfriend, Riley T. Smith. (*You will recognize his name as he is the person who attacked you.*)

I believe that my information may be relevant in the police prosecution of Riley. It also pertains to a very large sum of money that Amelia and Riley may soon receive as part of their Ashbury scholarships.

Of course, I know that your daughter's welfare is your primary concern — however, I would imagine that you would certainly be entitled — legally, ethically, and morally — to this money, as compensation for the damage that Riley has done to your home and your health.

May I be so bold as to suggest a meeting with you both at the Blue Danish Café at 6 P.M. tonight?

Yours,
A Friend

❖

Dear Mr. O'Doherty,

You might have noticed that this letter is sitting exactly where your laptop computer was when you set out tonight.

Where could your laptop be?

And what might be on that laptop? Could there be files that would be of great interest to the police?

I am a fair person, so let's make a deal. It's a one-night-only offer. I need you to do one very simple thing for me.

I will call you at 9 P.M. to tell you what it is.

Once I know you have done as I ask, I will simply return the computer to you (with the photos deleted – I hope you understand I feel compelled to do that).

I give you my word that matters will end there.

I am a person who can be trusted and, as they say on television, what choice do you have but to trust me?

Cheers,
A Stranger

❖

WEDNESDAY

From: Chris.Botherit@ashburyhigh.com.au
Sent: Wednesday, December 17
To: Emily.Thompson@ashburyhigh.com.au
Subject: RE: The Scholarship Committee Meeting

Dear Emily,
Thank you for your e-mail.

I'm sure that anything you have to say at the meeting this Friday would be most enlightening, and in all honesty, I'd like to have you there very much.

However, I'm afraid that the meeting is only open to Committee members. If you have anything you'd like me to share with the Committee, perhaps you could put it in writing and I will pass it on to them?

Good luck with the results on Friday! Hope you're enjoying the real world!

Your affectionate (former) teacher,
Chris Botherit

P.S. I wonder how you got access to those grounds for termination and that interview transcript? I rather believed that those were highly confidential! (No mention will be made here of your friend Cassie and the fact that her mother is on the Committee. . . .)

❖

Dear Mrs. Damaski and Mr. O'Doherty,
  I'm so sorry to have wasted your time at the Blue Danish last night! Upon closer reflection, it occurred to me that I should speak to the police

417

about the information I had about Riley — and they had the audacity to say it wasn't relevant!

Also, I've spoken to a lawyer friend who says you couldn't get access to the scholarship bonus after all. And I hear that they probably won't get it! (The Scholarship Committee is meeting this Friday and everybody says they are going to terminate the scholarship retrospectively, which would mean that Amelia and Riley miss out on the money.)

Apologies again,
and hoping for a safer future for us all,
A Friend

❖

Castle Hill Police Records
STATEMENT OF PATRICK SEAN O'DOHERTY

Wednesday, December 17

I would like to withdraw my previous statement about the incident in my home on Wednesday, October 15.

I have now remembered that what actually happened was that Riley Smith knocked on my door and introduced himself. He said that he was my stepdaughter's boyfriend. My wife and I have not had any contact with my stepdaughter since she ran away when she was thirteen, so it was a real shock to me to meet her boyfriend.

Riley said he was there to try to patch things up with my stepdaughter and me.

I suggested to him that this was none of his business, and our conversation then turned heated.

I am sorry to say that I shoved at him, as I was feeling not a little angry. Now that I reflect on it, he was probably only trying to defend himself when he punched me back. It is true that we fought for a few minutes but I don't think it would be right to say it was anybody's fault.

I think that I got a bump on the head and that's why I was confused when I spoke to the police before.

I have now got this clear, and I am very sorry for wasting police time.

Patrick Sean O'Doherty

❖

THURSDAY

From: Tobias.Mazzerati@ashburyhigh.com.au
Sent: Thursday, December 18
To: Chris.Botherit@ashburyhigh.com.au
Subject: Meetings

Dear Mr. Botherit,
I hear that Em is planning to come to the Committee meeting about Amelia and Riley tomorrow night.
Can you put my name down for that too?
There's something I should probably tell you people.

See you then,
Toby Mazzerati

❖

From: Chris.Botherit@ashburyhigh.com.au
Sent: Thursday, December 18

To: Tobias.Mazzerati@ashburyhigh.com.au
Subject: RE: Meetings

Dear Toby,

As I mentioned to Emily, I'm afraid this Committee meeting is only open to members of the Committee itself.

If you have something you want us to know, why don't you tell your dad and he'll pass it on at the meeting?

Hope you're well, and enjoying "life on the other side."

Best wishes,
Chris Botherit

❖

Dear Mr. O'Doherty,

I've been doing a lot of thinking about promises this year – and turns out, there are certain times when betraying someone's trust is exactly the right thing to do.

Cheers,
A Stranger

❖

Castle Hill Police Records
STATEMENT OF AMELIA GRACE DAMASKI

Thursday, December 18

My name is Amelia Grace Damaski.

My mother and I moved into Patrick O'Doherty's home when I was ten.

Not long after we moved in, Patrick became my swimming coach. He used to take me to the pool on weekday mornings. The house was close to the pool, so we walked home after training so I could get changed for school.

Just after I turned eleven, Patrick asked if he could take a photo of me while I was getting changed. After that, he would often take photos of me while I was getting changed. Maybe once every week or two. At first, I didn't mind because I used to like getting my photo taken. I thought it meant I was pretty. I did poses for him like I'd seen in magazines, and sometimes he suggested how I should pose. I even thought it was fun.

But after a while I started to think it was embarrassing, especially as I got older. I asked him to stop. He laughed and said he couldn't stop now that he'd started. Then I felt stupid because I thought I should have said no in the first place. I thought it was my fault for thinking I was pretty and posing and so on.

I didn't tell anyone because I felt so embarrassed.

But then I did tell my mother, on my thirteenth birthday. She didn't believe me, and I ran away.

I didn't mean to run away forever. I thought my mum would come and find me and bring me home.

Since then I've never let anybody else be a swimming coach.

Also, I never let anybody take photos of me.

In the last year I've started to wonder what Patrick was doing with the photos. I started to get scared that he might have let other people see them.

Two days ago, I went to my stepfather's house, about six o'clock in the evening. There was nobody home, but I still have my house key so I let myself in.

Patrick's computer was on his desk. I looked at his e-mails and files for a while. It wasn't too difficult to find the old photographs of me. I also found that he had e-mailed some of the photos to a lot of different addresses.

I unplugged the computer and took it home with me.

I kept it in my drawer the last two days. I didn't want anybody else to see the photos, so I was just going to delete them. But then I started worrying that they might be on a website or something.

So I decided to bring the computer to the police. The photos of me are in a file called AGD. They were taken between the ages of eleven and thirteen. I hope that the police have experts who can find out if Patrick has the photos on a website, and if so, shut it down.

I am prepared to give a more detailed statement, but for now I would like to stop.

Amelia G. Damaski

The Committee for the Administration of the
K. L. Mason Patterson Trust Fund
THE K. L. MASON PATTERSON SCHOLARSHIP FILE

FRIDAY, DECEMBER 19 — 7 A.M.

To the Members of the K. L. Mason Patterson Scholarship Committee,

Toby here.

Mr. B suggested that I say what I have to say to my dad and get him to pass it on, but I'm putting it in writing instead. You'll see why.

I hear that you're making a decision about Amelia and Riley tonight, and I know you've got an issue about Amelia and her exam.

Some people think she didn't go to that exam 'cause she felt too depressed. If that's the reason, it's harsh of you to be calling her on it.

But I hear it's complicated because Amelia's got her own excuse for not going. She told you she had to see a buddy in a mental institution, and you're not buying that, on account of, there is no mental institution.

I have two main points to make in this letter.

First, Amelia is telling the truth.

Second, I myself did not tell the truth when I talked to you earlier. You might recall I said I had no memory of what happened when I ran toward Amelia in the park?

That was a lie. I did have a memory. Still do.

*   *   *

If I could have your patience please, I need to go back in time to the start of the year.

That was the point I started hanging out in the Heritage Park.

I told you about the convict Tom? Seems I got a bit obsessed with him. I had some low moments, this last year, what with my future heading down the drain, and it kinda cheered me up, hangin' with my buddy Tom. His story was sadder than mine — you know, dead without ever seeing Maggie again — so sitting there, where Tom once sat, was kind of like heavy metal music. It felt so dark it got ahold of my darkness for me.

Anyhow, I started running into Amelia in the park.

I know there's a story around that Amelia and I had something going. It breaks my heart to say this but that's not true. We got to be buddies. That was it.

I first saw Amelia and Riley play at the Goose and Thistle last year. The manager lets them do late shows sometimes. They're good — they're very good. But people are past it by the time they come on, so nobody notices their talent.

I knew they were a couple, the first time I saw them. Their connection is more than just music. So I never would have tried to make a play for her. You don't take another man's girl.

Anyway, she's out of my league.

I drove her home one night earlier this year. She needed some air on the way, and we happened to be near Castlebrook Cemetery, so I pulled over. It's where the battle happened, that Tom was in, and I told Amelia about it.

I don't think she heard a word. She was trashed. Still, it felt like we had a moment: We're both looking out over that moonlit graveyard, Amelia's red-gold hair flying sideways in the wind — an ant crawled onto her arm, I remember, and she crushed it as I talked. I felt like I *saw* that battle that night. The shock on Tom's face, watching his friend Phillip, betrayed by that

424

soldier, a gun pressed to his back. Soldiers on horseback all in red.

I think she'd forgotten the whole thing by the next day. She looked at me like she didn't recognize me.

But then, like I said, I started seeing her in the park. Used to go at night sometimes, 'cause it seemed like I could get closer to the darkness in the dark. And Amelia would be there too.

So, we started chatting. Told her the story of Tom all over again.

She'd tell me she was on her way to meet a friend. A girl who lived in a mental institution by the park. And she'd tell me stories about that friend.

I can't remember when this idea occurred to me: I think it crept up slowly.

Amelia would tell me about the institution, and the things she said washed over me. It was an old stone building, she said, with a vegetable garden where they grew cabbages and potatoes. Also, the friend said they only got clean clothes once a week, and that the other residents were stealing from her — that made Amelia mad, she wanted to write to the authorities. The friend said she was only pretending to be mad. And so on.

And then one day Amelia said there'd been a murder — one of the patients had killed another one with an ax.

If the other facts were slowly washing over me, well, that bit — the ax murder — that was like a splash of hot water in my face. I looked back at her other facts, and realized that they'd formed a pool of truth.

This is the bit where I'm going to lose you.

See, I did a lot of reading about Tom and his life. I read about what the land was like before Tom and the convicts got there — the Darug Aboriginal people, and how they got smallpox from the invaders. I read about the convict farm, and the stone barracks that Phillip built. How the crops went to hell and they shut down the farm. I read about how, while Tom was hiding out in the bush, a new governor came to the colony — nice guy named Macquarie, who wanted to make this country great. He built hospitals, orphanages, roads.

This is all to get to my point — that when Tom did come back, he got as far as the old stone barracks, but by then, Macquarie had turned it into a lunatic asylum. The first one in this country.

I had read a bit about this asylum.

I read that it had a vegetable garden. They grew potatoes and cabbages. They got clean clothes once a week. Stole rations from one another. That some convicts there had pretended to be mad, 'cause it was a better option, or easier to escape.

I also read that they used to send the residents out to chop firewood. And one day, one resident hacked another to death with the ax.

So. Like I said. That was the splash of hot water.

Amelia tells me there'd been an ax murder, and the pool of truth shines up.

I'll be straight with you, folks.

It's my belief that Amelia spent the last year making friends with a girl who lived in a lunatic asylum around 1812.

Okay, if you can stop laughing for a moment, I'll wrap this up.

I never told Amelia my theory. Didn't want her writing me off the way you have now.

The last few weeks before the exam, I'd see Amelia there sometimes and she was upset. She was worried about her friend, so I'd try to comfort her. Might have even given her a hug one night, which maybe somebody saw and that's why the misunderstanding? Anyhow, the night before the exam, she told me she thought her friend was seriously ill — wasn't eating, getting depressed, losing hope.

There's Amelia in the moonlight — pale and thin, purple shadows under her eyes — and I think she's describing herself.

"She says she's going to dance on air tomorrow," Amelia said. "That's a good thing, right? I don't get it."

I didn't get it either, and we both went home.

But I kept thinking — *dance on air* — and there was something familiar about it. I was almost asleep when it came to me. An Irish convict had used those words in a story I once read — *you'll not get any music from me, for others to dance on air.*

Dance on air means to hang.

I thought Amelia should know that.

I wrote it on a piece of paper, slipped it to her just before the exam.

Could be that's why she left. She read my note, realized what her friend was planning, and so she ran.

Later that day — when I'm running across the park in the rain — well, like I said, I do know what I saw.

A flash of white, like a rush of water or light — and behind that light, I saw this: A girl was standing on a log, a rope around her neck, like a noose. It looked like Amelia from behind, her red-gold hair.

I felt something behind me, made me turn around a second — and everything had changed.

Lydia was gone. So was Emily. The trees had changed. They were bigger, taller, different shapes, more shrubs, longer grass. It was still pouring rain, but through the rain I could see a big stone building.

Next moment things were back — the building gone, Lyd and Em running — and Amelia was in my arms.

*   *   *

427

You know, this last year of high school, it's what you might call a crazy time. It's like we're charged-up, revved-up, emotional freaks. It feels like we're all on the brink of something — we're standing on some fine, fine line between our future and our past.

Could be that standing on that line makes us more susceptible to slipping back and forward in time?

Maybe that's why Amelia's been visiting the past? Why I got that glimpse of it that moment in the rain?

If that's not scientific enough for you, please recall that black holes can bend time.

And that's a technical truth.

So, in conclusion, don't take Amelia's scholarship away on account of her not having an excuse. She did have one. She was chillin' with a ghost.

Thanks for your time.

Toby Mazzerati

P.S. You will now see why I didn't just get my dad to pass this on to you. He'd have laughed at me for the next few years and the message would not have got across.

7

Termination Meeting — The Committee for the Administration of the K. L. Mason Patterson Trust Fund — Minutes

6:00 P.M. – 9:00 P.M., Friday, December 19

Conference Room 2B, the K. L. Mason Patterson Center for the Arts

Chair Roberto Garcia (History Coordinator, Drama Teacher, Ashbury High)
Secretary Christopher Botherit (English Coordinator, Ashbury High)

Participants

Constance Milligan (Ashbury Alumni Association)
Patricia Aganovic (Parent Representative 1)
Jacob Mazzerati (Parent Representative 2)
Lucy Wexford (Music Coordinator, Ashbury High)
Bill Ludovico (Ashbury School Principal/Economics Teacher)

AGENDA ITEMS

Roberto Garcia (Chair) welcomed Bill Ludovico, explaining that Bill had been too busy with his duties as headmaster to attend meetings for most of the year. "Yes," said Bill. "Seems that if you want to get something done right, you've got to do it yourself." A loaded silence. Roberto then explained that the only agenda item for today was the termination of Amelia's and Riley's scholarships. Bill cleared his throat sharply. Roberto turned the floor over to Bill, who, he said, had some news for us.

• Last night (Bill said), the police had notified him that all criminal charges against Riley have been dropped. The stepfather had withdrawn his complaint.

• "What?!" "Really?!" and so on. That is, everyone was surprised and mystified. Much discussion about what might have happened — maybe Amelia's parents had realized Riley's connection with their daughter and withdrew the complaint as a gesture of goodwill toward Amelia? Or maybe —

• Here, Constance made a noise like a snuffling pig. "Why are we wasting our time?" she cried. "I have *read* the transcript of the interviews! They did not have an answer to *any* of the grounds for termination! Let's get this thing signed and stamped and put the whole sorry fiasco behind us. I'll make a point of not saying *I told you so*, and we'll all go home to bed!"

• There was a subdued silence. Some sighs. Everyone was aware that Constance was right — not so much about going home to bed, it was only 6 P.M. — but clearly, termination *was* the only option. Nevertheless, it was very depressing. Our first scholarship winners: They had shone like stars, and now, oh, how had they fallen.

• Bill said that he agreed 100% with Constance, and was glad there was at least one other person with some sense on this Committee.

• "We have to at least talk through each ground," Jacob Mazzerati (Parent Rep 2) said, firmly.

• "What about your Toby's letter?" Patricia Aganovic (Parent Rep 1) looked at Jacob. "It was kind of — interesting. The time travel theory."

• "The time travel theory," agreed Jacob, deadpan, meeting Patricia's eye. She tried to maintain a thoughtful expression, but could not resist her own smile — at which Jacob also smiled. General laughter and joking at Toby's expense.

• I noted that Roberto Garcia did not laugh. Neither did Constance — and Bill's laughter had an unpleasant edge. I'm afraid that Chris Botherit (me) did laugh (but kindly, I hope).

• "Well, I'll lead the charge, then!" said Constance, cutting through the talk again. "Right, ground 1 — well, if your only excuse for not attending an exam is that you were visiting a *ghost*, you *don't* have an excuse! So, yes, tick! Ground 2, well, the police might have gone soft on Riley but it's clear as the dew that he's guilty, so that's another tick! Moving on! Yes, ground —"

• Here, Patricia Aganovic suggested, politely, that maybe Constance was not the right person to be leading this discussion since, "after all, you didn't come to any of the interviews with Amelia and Riley, and have never even met them." Bill said he considered that irrelevant, and thought that Constance was doing fine. Constance herself drew in a breath ready to continue, when —

• A voice exclaimed, "I hereby address this meeting!" and we all turned as one and realized, to our shock, that Emily Thompson was standing in the open doorway. How long had she been there? Her eyes were flashing. She strode across the room, stood at the head of the table, straightened her back, narrowed her eyes, and glared at us each in turn.

• Chris Botherit (me) spoke up in gentle confusion to say, "Em, did you not get my e-mail? I'm afraid I said you couldn't come to the meeting."

• "If I wasn't obedient when I was a student here," said Emily, "what makes you think I would be now?"

• "Oh, it's this girl again," muttered Constance.

• Roberto Garcia, who had cheered considerably since Emily walked in, flung out his arms and announced, "I hand the meeting over to Emily!"

• "Can he do that?" Lucy Wexford wondered.

• "No." Bill Ludovico smiled. "He can't. On the road, Emily." He gestured with a thumb, meaning that Emily should leave.

• Roberto cast a dark look in Bill's direction. "I can do what I want. I am Chair!" And turned his moody gaze back onto Emily.

• Emily paused suspensefully, then, "BEHOLD!" she cried (unexpectedly).

• "Behold! Here you all sit" — her arms swept the room — "in the grandeur of your own incompetence!"

• Startled murmurs; some smiles; an amused, rather patronizing eye-rolling from Bill.

• "Imagine!" Her voice dropped to a whisper. "Imagine taking a scholarship away from a beautiful, innocent waif who has only just clawed her way back from the jaws of death!" (Guilty, defensive looks around the table.) "And from a handsome, charming young man who has just been in trouble with the police!" (Confused murmurs of, "Well, but, um . . .")

• "But let us set aside the extensiveness of your immortality!" (I think she meant *immorality* but I was glad to be immortal.) "I set before you — your seven grounds for termination!" At this, she took seven brightly colored, uninflated balloons from her pocket, and placed them on the table before her.

• "Ground 1!" Emily blew up a balloon, her eyes large and round, her cheeks swelling out, her face turning pale pink. "That Amelia did not go to her HSC exam and she didn't have an excuse!" This, a little breathless, pointing to the now inflated balloon.

• "Didn't have an excuse!? Why, I have read the transcript! She had an excellent excuse! She had to go to see a friend in a mental institution who was going to take her own life! Oh, I know what you're going to say! That there *is* no mental institution in Castle Hill! Well, but I've spoken to Toby, and he tells me that there *was* one. In another century! It was a lunatic asylum! Is there a better excuse than that? Having to visit the past because a ghost was going to take her own life?! NO! There is not! *Who amongst you has ever had to save the life of a ghost?*"

• And she took a pen from Lucy Wexford's hand and popped the balloon.

• "Ground 2!" She blew up another balloon. "That Riley has been charged with assault. This one's easy. No, he hasn't. The charge is gone. All that is left is a fight. Boys are always fighting. They are children." And she popped that balloon.

• "Ground 3!" A third balloon. "They didn't tell you the exact wickedness of their criminal records. My dear people, they would not have got the scholarships if they had! So, of *course* they didn't tell you."

• Here, she went to pop the balloon, but there was a clearing of throats around the table — "You are not convinced! Well, convince this! Juvenile records are sealed for a reason! Young people are *allowed* to make mistakes — yes, even serious mistakes — and then *leave those mistakes behind* and *re-create themselves*! It's the foundation of the law! Who amongst you dares to shake the foundations of the law!"

• And she popped the balloon. Now she was getting really breathless. She picked up a fourth balloon, handed it to Jacob Mazzerati, and said, "Can you blow this up?"

• While Jacob blew up this balloon, Emily's voice changed completely. It took on a conversational tone. "Oh, this one. They broke into the Music Rooms after hours. Are you guys serious? Do you know how often Lyd, Cass, and I broke into various aspects of this school after hours? And within hours. What, are you going to retrospectively expel all three of us?" And, just as casually, she reached over with her pen and popped the fourth balloon (which was still, at this point, being blown up by Jacob. He blinked, disconcerted, but then, good-naturedly, picked up another balloon and began to inflate it).

• "Five!" cried Emily — back in dramatic stride, "That Riley *may* have destroyed the artwork of Seb Mantegna! Need I go on? Did you hear that word — *may*? Are you people quite mad? Let's choose a few more random crimes and say that Riley *may* have done them! Evidence, my friends! Have you *any* evidence? Red paint splatters on Riley's clothes?" Here, Emily paused suddenly — a little frown crumpled her brow. Then she continued, "Anybody *see* him at the scene of the crime! Any witnesses! What have you *got*, guys? Come on? Give it to me."

• "She's right about that," Patricia Aganovic said. "I meant to say something myself." And *Patricia* leaned over and popped the balloon for Emily. "You're doing great, Em," she added. "But maybe don't share Cass's former crimes with the room?"

• "Thank you," said Emily, while Jacob obligingly blew up the next balloon. Now Em's voice became contemptuous: "A *set of castanets*! Well, I would repeat my previous arguments about proving people guilty, and I would add that the castanets were returned so it's technically not stealing, just a loan, but *I can't be bothered*. Who even *cares* about *castanets*? I mean, what even *are* they?"

• Here, Lucy Wexford interrupted in a small, irritable voice to say, "Yes, well, flamenco dancers — oh, forget it, Emily, I don't really think they stole them anyway. Let's kill this ground, shall we?" We waited for Lucy to pop the balloon but I think that was below her dignity, so Emily did.

• "One more ground!" Emily cried. Jacob had the balloon ready to hand over. "They pretended to like us even though they didn't! I have *so many things to say to that*! Of course they liked us! Are you mad? What's not to like? Oh, yes, yes, I know, I heard that Riley wrote a ghost story in which he said he didn't like us. Well, hello? It was a *ghost story*. Yes, yes, I know it was supposed to be *true*, but Lydia asked me to point out here that her own "true" ghost story had an actual *ghost* in it, and she wants to know if Mr. Botherit really believed that a ghost lives inside her computer?"

• Here Mr. Botherit (me) interrupted thoughtfully: "I remember Lydia's story. I did wonder whether that whole thing was an invention or whether — no, no, not that there *was* a ghost, but that somebody might have hacked into her computer somehow and pretended to be a ghost?"

• "No," said Emily, apologetically. "It was a fictional framing device for her nonfiction memoir. Those are Lydia's words. She told me to tell you. But you've interfered with my train of thought. Let me get back on the wagon. Yes! Friendship! Okay, so, Riley's story said he didn't like us but if there's one thing I've learned this year it's that you can't believe a word of things in writing! Everything has shades of dark and light! Even history! It's all slanted and biased and exaggerated! Do you think *my* ghost story about Term 2 was completely true?

I mean it was based on truth, but did I include all the illegal, sordid, sex, drug, drinking details about the parties in Term 2? Of course not! That was private. And did I mention, in my story, that the reason Seb joined the Drama was because I'd forged a letter to him in Mr. Garcia's name? No! I pretended that I was *surprised* by the letter! Because I didn't want to get expelled! And Toby has been telling me that nothing ever happened between him and Amelia, even though he had a serious crush on her, but do you think *he* mentioned that crush in *his* ghost story about Term 2?! No! And those are just the deliberate twists of the truth. Don't get me started about self-delusion! I mean, seriously, who can believe a *ghost story*?!"

• "Whatever is this girl talking about?" sniffed Constance. "And what's going on with the balloons?"

• "I'm so glad to know who wrote that letter," murmured Roberto Garcia.

• "And even if Amelia and Riley *didn't* like us!" Emily continued, ignoring Constance and Roberto. "Well, they were *right* not to! Lydia kissed Riley, which was not exactly being a good friend to Amelia. But I was a terrible friend! I tried to break them up! *I* made a mistake and told Riley that Amelia was cheating! And you think *they* were the bad friends?" Pause again — and she popped the last balloon.

• Before anybody had a chance to respond, Constance cried, "This girl talks a lot of nonsense! Blow those balloons up again! All seven of them, Jacob!" Jacob smiled at Constance, politely, but did not blow up any balloons. "Ah, never mind the balloons! Why are we listening to this loop-de-loop. She thinks Amelia went to see a ghost on the day of her exam!"

• Emily seemed to grow taller. "Why should Amelia *not* have visited a ghost! Everybody knows there are ghosts in this very building! I can sense their presence right this moment! I can smell the lilac talcum powder that they wear!"

• "Just watch your credibility there, Em," murmured Patricia Aganovic.

• But Constance was flashing back at Em: "If there *is* a ghost here," she cried, "it is surely the ghost of Kendall Mason Patterson, angry at the way his money is being spent on the likes of such young demons as Amelia and Riley!"

• Here, Emily paused a moment — another slight frown — then her face cleared and she cried, "Just because they have made mistakes before does not make them demons! People are *often* violent just once and then never again!"

• Here Mr. Botherit (me) could not help interjecting, hesitantly, "I feel like you once said the opposite, Em?" but Emily was in her stride: "That's why there's a law against similar fact evidence! It's more prejudicial than probative! I would never say anything like that, Mr. B, and if I did, it was a mistake, and I am very open to change in my own opinions, just not in other people's —"

• She was interrupted by Constance, who quavered, "You mark my words, girl, if they are not demons, I'm a monkey's uncle. Oh, they are wicked young miscreants! I do not doubt that they engage in all manner of wild, youthful ways — alcoholic beverages and drugs, looking at pictures of nude young women, vandalism, the works! They're always *laughing*! It's demonic! And they gaze with such unnerving intensity! Do not tell me that they have changed! A leopard cannot change its spots! Do not . . ."

• Constance's clichés accumulated, as various people tried to interrupt, but the frown was deepening on Emily's brow. She grew quiet. She looked at the door of the conference room, and at the window. She looked up at the ceiling. She scratched her ear.

• Then, suddenly — unexpectedly — she ran from the room.

• There was a long silence. Bill Ludovico was frowning deeply. People watched the open door, listened to the sound of Emily's footsteps — a pitter-patter along the corridor, then, unexpectedly, a pitter-patter running up, up, up steps. The pitter-patter faded. We raised our eyebrows at one another. Another long pause . . . then . . .

·BANG!

• It came from the ceiling. We all looked up. Quite distinctly, we heard Em's voice calling, "HEY, YOU! DOWN THERE!" It seemed to be coming from the air vent in the corner of the ceiling.

• We looked at one another, bewildered. Silence. Then from the distance — *pitter-patter pitter* — and along a corridor, getting louder, *pitter-patter pitter-PATTER PITTER* — and there was Em, breathless at the door.

• "Come with me," she ordered.

• Mystified, we followed her. Along the corridor. Up the stairs. Into the archives room. Past the compacting shelves to the far wall where there was an inconspicuous, low, gray door. She opened it, stood back — and waved her hands so we could look in.

• It was a small room — a large closet, really — with sloping ceilings, various mechanical units along the walls . . . and crowded onto the floor in there: a mattress piled with bedding, a floral nightdress, a portable stove, a basin holding a sponge and soap, a pile of books, a box of dominoes, a basket of fruit, a small radio, a tin of paint . . .

• "Somebody lives in there?" wondered Jacob Mazzerati.

• "She does," said Emily, triumphant, and pointed at Constance Milligan. "*She's* the Ashbury ghost! And *she* attacked Seb Mantegna's painting!"

• And then, to everyone's surprise, Constance Milligan fainted.

• "Maybe we should postpone this meeting," murmured Chris Botherit, to himself — and —

Meeting Closed: 9 P.M.

www.myglasshouse.com/emthompson
Friday, December 19
My Journey Home
My Dear and Wonderful Readers of This Blog,

I have a surprise.

It is me!

I am back.

Even though I said that this blog was complete, and therefore you have already grieved for me . . . well, you never know when someone might return . . . (e.g., ghosts!)

Do not be too excited, though, as it is a once-only encore performance.

My dear friends, I cannot blog! It is the time of summer and freedom, the HSC is done, I am no longer a student compelled to write blogs about "My Journey Home," I am a citizen of reality! Soon to be a student of the law!

(Yes, I modestly say that my HSC marks were somewhat great to me, and I think I have enough to get into Arts/Law at Sydney, in accordance with my lifelong dream. Also, please note that Lydia, Amelia, and Riley, amongst others in my year, were top ranked in the state in certain subjects, and Cass was happy with her result. Therefore, life is on track.)

However, I am not here to talk about life! I am here to tell you something astonishing.

I have spoken to the Ashbury ghost.

She is alive and well and living in a closet in the archives.

(At least, she *has* been living there — the school will expel her now — ha-ha.)

Her name is Constance Milligan.

Well, I can guess what you are all saying: *What? I thought the ghosts' names were Sandra and Kendall!*

Or maybe you are saying: *Huh. Interesting, but we need more information?*

Very well. I will tell the story.

Earlier tonight I went to a meeting that was in a conference room in the Art Rooms of Ashbury. Constance Milligan, former Ashbury student and profoundly old person, was at the meeting. Many things were said, including by me — but I will only tell you the relevant ones. Here! Come with me to the key moments that night . . .

. . . As I arrived, I overheard somebody saying that Constance had *never* met or spoken with Amelia and Riley.

. . . I was talking about the attack on Seb's artwork, and I mentioned *splatters of red paint.* As I said those words, a memory splashed into my mind. Red paint. Where had I seen it before?

. . . Constance said that wicked young people *look at nude pictures of young women.* Another thought splashed into my mind: Seb's artwork had a nude picture in it. Hmmm.

. . . Constance said that Amelia and Riley were always laughing, and had a penetrating gaze — nobody else seemed to notice this, but it smacked me in the face: *If she never met Amelia and Riley, how did she know this?*

My mind raced. Could Constance have spied on the interviews somehow? Climbed the side of the building and looked through the window? (Unlikely.) Somehow seen from above? What was above this room anyway? I looked up.

The archives room.

And that's where I'd seen red splatters of paint!

So I ran up the stairs — and there, at the end of the archives room, behind the compacting files, was a door.

I opened the door, and found . . . a large closet.

Inside that large closet?

Evidence that someone had been hiding in it! — an old person! There was a floral nightgown! a pile of bedding! a stack of books! a bowl of water! an electric cooker! a little rose jug holding a toothbrush and toothpaste! a box of dominoes! — and an air vent that looked down on the conference room!!!

Dear Readers — I hope you are keeping up with me!

It was an astonishing night.

I made them all come upstairs with me, threw open the door to the closet, and Constance fainted.

But she woke up when we called her name.

"I am undone," she cried, trembling with excitement, flinging her hands in the air.

So everyone gathered around her there in the archives room, and she sat on a crocheted cushion (someone got it out of her closet-room for her) and confessed.

She said that she first hid in there the night before the progress interviews with Amelia and Riley. They must never lay eyes on *her*, she said, but it was essential that she see *them*.

"To find out just how they cast their evil spells of enchantment on you," she explained matter-of-factly, looking around at the members of the committee. "It was for your own protection."

She had such fun, she said, staying overnight and watching the conference room — so she had decided she might come back now and then.

And that's what happened. Over the year, she spent more and more time in the building. She wandered the corridors by night, and hid in the closet during the day, watching the classes below.

"I belong here," she said, blushing. "I'm an Ashbury girl, through and through."

She was truly a ghost! A spirit from the past returned to haunt the place she had once cherished!

And also, truly, she *was* the ghost.

I admit, I do not think she was responsible for *all* our ghostly encounters — some of those are just day-to-day life — I am older and wiser now and have realized, for example, that pens *do* roll across desks sometimes, just of their own accord, and that mandarin peels may simply be left behind by cleaners, and that feathers can float long distances, and that distant sounds of traffic might *resemble* the sound of someone sobbing — and perhaps a person might *imagine* the smell of sausages frying just because the person is hungry . . . so I wisely admit that these things were probably not the ghost . . . but listen . . .

The book that once belonged to Sandra Wilkinson, *The Complete History of Politics in Australia* — Constance had brought in a pile of her old schoolbooks to help her feel like a schoolgirl. She had accidentally dropped that one in a corridor! She admitted it when I asked her! (Turns out Constance got Sandra's old textbooks after Sandra died.)

The handkerchief? Her schoolgirl handkerchief! (She had a pile of them in the closet!)

The lilac talcum powder? Constance wears it! (I had smelled it on her in the meeting, actually.)

The faint music — Constance listening to the radio!

The dripping in the ceiling of the bathroom? Constance admitted she had been bathing in a bucket and now and then the water spilled. It had leaked through to the bathroom next door to the conference room!

Even the attack on Seb's painting!!! IT HAD BEEN CONSTANCE!

She had to admit this — there was paint in her closet-room, and splatters on the floor of the archives room. But she had no remorse: She had saved the world from wicked pornography, she said. (She is quite mad.)

And, do you know what I have realized? The clattering sound that I once heard when I was in the archives room, that terrified me so much? Well, that must have been her! She must have been there in the closet at that time! (I wonder what she was doing.)

As for the creaking and cracking that everybody thought was the ghost, it turns out that those are just the building settling under the weight of the extensions.

(But cracking sounds are also caused by changes in temperature . . . and guess what was in the closet with Constance? A control panel for the air-conditioning! Maybe she had been switching buttons on and off? *Which brings me to the cold drafts in Room 27B . . .* I say no more!!!)

But I always do say more, don't I? Before I go, I want to personally thank Astrid. I am thinking about my value as a "friend" these days — as I was not a very good friend to Amelia and Riley — and I have not always been that great to Astrid. She has annoyed me, a bit. Sorry, Astrid. And despite that, she went to the effort of finding that report about Sandra and Kendall's accident!!

Thank you, Astrid.

A round of applause for Astrid!

Even if you did get the ghosts wrong.

Never mind.

You know, I must admit, I feel strangely sad that the ghosts are not Sandra and Kendall anymore. They seemed like part of the theme of the year — true love torn asunder. Me and Charlie. (Singapore! Of all places.) (Setting aside the fact that I tore us asunder to begin with. That was an error.) Lydia and Seb. Amelia and Riley . . .

But no. It is not so . . .

Oh, there is one thing more.

You have met the ghost before.

Her name is not just Constance Milligan.

It is also *FloralNightie*.

She is a reader of this blog.

This came to me while Constance was gathering her things from the closet-room, and we were all watching, and pretending not to. She had said something earlier that sounded strangely familiar: that the ghost was "surely Kendall Mason Patterson, angry at the way his money is being spent" — and I couldn't figure out why it was familiar. But, then, as Constance folded a floral nightdress, I remembered — a comment on my blog!

"Surely it is K. L. Mason Patterson, feeling angry about the way his money has been spent," the comment had said!

FloralNightie was the person commenting!

I asked her right then, and she was proud to admit that she had been using the school's computers at night!

Which means *she's* the one who saw Lydia kissing Riley in Conference Room 2B! And wrote about it on my blog!

As to which: Why did Constance/FloralNightie do that?

Well, that is the final mystery I suppose.

Anyhow, we all trudged from the building tonight — weary but sparkle-eyed with amazement — some of us helping Constance to carry her things. I found myself walking between Mr. Ludovico and Cassie's mum, Patricia.

Patricia congratulated me on getting into Law at Sydney Uni. "After your performance in the conference room tonight," she said, "you're seriously going to knock them dead in the courtrooms one day soon." Patricia is a lawyer herself, so that was praise indeed.

I glanced sideways at Mr. Ludovico. Was he smirking at me? Laughing his nasty laugh? Saying something sarcastic about my chances as a lawyer? No! His face was actually *sulky*.

"How about that, eh?" I said, turning to him, innocently. "There *was* a ghost in the Art Rooms all this time! You owe me a *huge* apology, Bill!"

The others laughed, Bill scowled like a child, and, for the first time in my life, I thought I might like being an adult.

The great tragedy for *you*, my readers, is that this really is my final blog. It is time for me to go and greet my future. This last year has been the storm. Life, from now on, will be the calm.

Now, I will fly into the arms of my family downstairs. William is baking something that smells *fantastic* and *full of chocolate*, and I can hear Mum and Dad arguing about who will get to taste it first. (It will be me.) And even as my heart is alive with the knowledge that soon I will leap into the world of the grown-ups, still, I will always have this family. Even as I grow old and ugly and crazy myself, like Constance, still, even then I will have the *memories* of this beautiful family. . . .

I'm a very lucky girl.

And I am home.

(Huh. How about that. *My journey* . . .)

And now: *Fly, Emily! To the chocolate!* (Bye.)

2 comments

Yowta772 said . . . Or you could fly to Singapore to see me, Em.

Astrid said . . . You are totally sweet saying *thank you* to me, Em!,,,, And I'm, like, I have to tell you this now . . . remember I once said that Seb and I were together?

That was not totally true. We DID get together that *1* night at the party (when u guys were locked in the closet,,,) but S. told me he didn't want to keep it going. ☹

I kind of, like, told you it WAS going b/c my dad said if you really want sthing you shld act like u've got it, and then it will b/come real. But it didn't. (b/come real.) Even when I asked S. to come up to the archives to help me look 4 info about your ghost [and S is actually the 1 who found that, cos he likes you and Lyd so much] & even when I asked him 2 help me try on my drama costume while we were there in the archives!!! *** He was just like totally sweet, and like, sorry, but it's not happening for me. And now my mum says I shld never listen to dad, and that <<honesty>> is the best. So, now I am totally honest, and totally sorry ☹ that I kind of, like, <<lied>> to you, and we're still BFF 4eva, yeah?

9

SATURDAY, DECEMBER 20

Dear Ghost.

Hey, it's Lyd.

I know you said we'd "never chat again" — but I didn't believe you. I think you only said that 'cause you've got a taste for high drama and sweeping declarations. Right? So. 'Tsup? How's the afterlife been treating you?

Not talking, eh? Ah, well. Whatever. I'll tell you, anyway.

Just headed out to the 7-Eleven to get myself a Magnum Classic.

Or maybe a Magnum Almond. It was going to be a toss-up.

Hot, sultry night. Stars out. Bare arms swinging. I had this mad, crazy feeling something good was going to happen.

Things have been good the last few days.

I did okay in the HSC, and Mum and Dad were proud. Their marriage, as you might have noticed, is settling back into its familiar patterns — they both have affairs but pretend not to notice, and most of the time they ignore each other. Everybody's happier.

So I've been messing with their minds. I told them I plan to dig trenches on the roads the next few years. Need to get some mud under my fingernails, I said. Been too sheltered all my life.

I don't want to dig up roads, but it's true that I've been too sheltered.

The things I didn't know about Amelia and Riley. I never even knew that Riley lived with a foster family. They're foster parents he lived with once when he was a kid, and ran away from. He used to run away all the time, wanting to get back to his mother, not realizing she refused to leave his abusive dad so the state would never let him back with her.

These foster parents kept their eye on him over the years, and offered to take him back again when he got released from detention.

I never thought what it must be like to live with a foster family. It's a family that doesn't stay still. That baby sister that Riley loved so much? They took her away. Imagine loving a baby for a year and then a social worker drives away with her.

He never gets to see her again.

He showed me her photo the other day. He keeps it in his wallet all the time. That tiny picture in the palm of his strong, scarred hands. The twist of his mouth as he looked at it, the smile in his eyes. It made me think of those before-and-after photos from his artwork — both expressions on his face at the same time. He pressed his fingers over the photo, and changed the subject fast.

I've been talking with Amelia and Riley a lot lately.

I got Amelia to meet with me eventually, after she got out of the hospital. We had coffee at the Blue Danish. She was cold and remote while I told her my story about what happened between me and Riley.

Then she stared at the ceiling, and a slow smile formed on her face.

"I get why it happened," she said. "Forget about it. It's nothing." She smiled again, ironically, and I saw what she meant — it was nothing compared to what else was going on.

That was back when Riley was being charged for assaulting her stepfather.

When you thought about what her stepfather had done to her, and what the assault charge meant for Riley, she was right — the thing between Riley and me was nothing.

"There's another reason I wanted to meet with you today," I said.

I told her my idea about blackmailing the stepfather, and getting him charged for what he'd done to her instead.

She half-laughed. She said she'd think about it. Our coffees were finished. We were standing up to go.

"It wasn't nothing, though," I said. "I was your friend and I betrayed you. That's not nothing, and I'm sorry."

Amelia stopped, looked me straight in the eye. She pulled on her lower lip, smiling again, watching me.

"Let's get another coffee," she said, and sat down.

That's when she told me the truth about what she and Riley had been planning. How they were only pretending to be friends with us, so they could get in with my mother's record company. How they were manipulating us to make us think they were musically gifted.

"But I *was* kind of liking you in the end," she shrugged. "And I guess Riley was too." Another sad smile.

It was beautiful.

I was happier than I had been in months. I could stop feeling so guilty about Riley, but it was more than that. It was the truth. Now the year made sense. Riley and Amelia made sense.

One thing didn't make sense.

"But you *are*," I said. "Musically gifted."

Amelia laughed. "See?" she said. "It worked."

Anyhow, the blackmail plan was successful — Riley got off, the stepfather got charged — and now Amelia and Riley are our friends. They think it's weird that we want to be, but we just think it's funny.

"You guys and your evil, secret plans," said Em. "You're even more dramatic than me."

These last few weeks, feels like I've opened my eyes for the first time in a year. I've been drifting around like a freakin' ghost, haunting the shadows of my life. (Not that there's anything wrong with haunting. Just remembered you're a ghost. Sorry.)

Now I feel alive (sorry, again), and tonight, like I said, I felt happy.

Em called earlier, and told me to look at her blog. There was a comment there from Astrid, and turns out the Seb-and-Astrid thing was an illusion. (Almost.)

As soon as I saw it, I knew that I was going to see Seb tonight.

I actually turned around, expecting him to be in the doorway of my room.

Walked to the kitchen, opened the fridge, thinking he'd be crouched down in the salad crisper, waiting to spring up like a jack-in-the-box.

I had to get out into the night, swing my arms, walk fast.

Summer cicadas, cars driving by with their windows down. People walking dogs, slapping mosquitoes, making jokes with strangers.

Hand against the glass of the shop door, and there he is.

I'm not even surprised.

He's coming out of there, a Magnum in his hand. He sees me, his eyes light up, and I smile back.

We stand in the doorway, his Magnum wrapper glinting in the fluorescent light, and I can't shift this smile.

I didn't frame my face, or plan my expression — I just smiled, and it felt like I *had* been digging in those trenches on the roads, but now I was taking a shower and letting the mud wash away.

*   *   *

Someone was trying to get into the shop and we were blocking the door.

We moved out together, along past the buckets of wilting flowers, stacks of newspapers, to the corner of the shop, out of the light.

We were kind of leaning, side by side, against the brick wall. Sharing his Magnum. (It was a Classic.) Talking about HSC results. Em and Cass. Amelia and Riley.

I said, "Why'd you tell me to stay away from Amelia and Riley that time?"

He told me again about how he overheard them talk to his soccer coach.

"They were asking for a favor," he said. "They wanted him to be a character witness at their criminal hearing. Sounded like they didn't have many friends, and they'd remembered he used to like them back when they swam for him for a week or something."

So the coach asked them what it was about. They asked him to keep it confidential. They explained the charges — the stealing and the grievous bodily harm — and he asked for more details.

After they'd told him, he laughed, said there was no way in hell he'd stand up in court on their behalf, and turned his back on them. They walked away.

"I didn't like the way he acted," said Seb. "He knew he wasn't going to be a witness for them, but he still made them tell the story. Like he wanted to make them feel like shit. But I didn't like the sound of what Riley did to that guy either."

"So why not just tell me?"

"They wanted a second chance. It wasn't up to me to mess with that."

"You still told me to stay away from them."

"Well, who knows if there's any such thing as a second chance?"

"You could have trusted me not to tell anyone."

"If we'd been together," he says and looks me in the eye, "I would have."

He looks down at the footpath. There's an old juice box there, half-squashed. He touches it with the side of his sneaker, turns it over on its side. Like he's thinking of kicking it somewhere.

Stops, looks up, gives me his Seb grin — I touch his arm, swing around so I'm facing him, then our arms are around each other, his hand's on the back of my neck, his mouth's on my mouth, and I can taste my favorite ice cream.

Turns out there is such a thing as a second chance.

See ya,
Lydia

❖

Oh, yes, and I liked the moment when he was driving you home, his elbow resting on the open window — a line of traffic blocking him — the way his hand slipped out the window, meaning, "Will you let me in?" and then he switched the open hand to the thumbs-up signal as he pulled into the traffic — all the while talking to you. . . . And another moment, his sideways glance — you had turned away, you were looking out the window — there was a sideways glance at the back of your head, the warmth of his secret smile as he watched you, the light never leaving his eyes.

(You thought that my haunting was restricted to this house? I like an occasional Coke from the 7-Eleven myself, you know. . . .)

The Ghost xxx

The Committee for the Administration of the
K. L. Mason Patterson Trust Fund
THE K. L. MASON PATTERSON SCHOLARSHIP FILE

From: Chris.Botherit@ashburyhigh.com.au
Sent: Friday, January 16
To: Bill.Ludovico@ashburyhigh.com.au
CC: Roberto.Garcia@ashburyhigh.com.au
Subject: Amelia and Riley: Termination of Scholarship

Dear Bill,

Last night, the Committee reconvened to finalize the termination of the scholarships of Amelia Damaski and Riley T. Smith.

As you know, the previous meeting fell apart when it emerged that Constance Milligan was a ghost.

Roberto and I met with Constance the other day, and she told us she was very sorry about having been a ghost, and could she please attend Saturday detention for as long as it took to wipe her record clear?

The woman has lost her marbles.

Roberto has suspended her from Ashbury until she gets them back.

Between us, it's a fascinating psychological case study. Constance had a pile of letters in her "closet-space," tied with a pink ribbon — and I noticed that one, dated not long ago, was to Kendall. Kendall Mason Patterson. She has been *writing* to a ghost. I'd kill to get a look at some of those letters (not literally, of course). They might help to explain what's been going on? As it is, I can only speculate.

It seems that Constance was deeply affected by her Ashbury days, and life has never lived up to them for her. Hence, her passionate involvement in all things relating to the Alumni Association — but that was not enough. She wanted Ashbury itself.

It also seems that part of the thrill of her Ashbury days was her fascination with a young couple: Kendall Patterson and Sandra Wilkinson. She clearly hero-worshipped them, even as she envied and resented their celebrity status. I cannot imagine what Sandra's death did to her psyche — perhaps it terrified her? Perhaps she felt somehow responsible for it, as a result of her resentment? But I may be overanalyzing.

What I had not realized was that she her*self* was a poor scholarship girl — poor as a church mouse! — so that the wealth and beauty of Kendall and Sandra had a complicated effect on her. She was also a "good girl" while Kendall and Sandra were "wild and wicked" ones — representing her own "shadow" side? (Again, I may be overanalyzing.)

Perhaps Constance has been grappling with these conflicts (these ghosts!) all her life — wanting to leave behind the stigma of her own poverty (so she resented our efforts to help out Brookfield), at the same time as wanting to re*live* those heady Ashbury days?

Forgive my musings. On to Amelia and Riley.

Not long ago, you asked me *why* they were chosen for their scholarships in the first place. We chose them because they wrote superb application essays and had excellent references (admittedly from their counselors

453

and teachers at juvenile detention facilities). They were remarkably bright, motivated, engaging, and articulate at the interviews. They had enormous potential as swimmers and we strongly suspected, on the basis of their essays and their interview answers, that they were very well-read and had a great deal of untapped academic potential too. Most of all, they were in desperate need of a second chance at life — a last chance, even.

They were very frank at their interviews. They told us they wanted to start their lives afresh. They wanted to focus on schoolwork for the first time ever — play music, try drama, behave, get into university. They knew how their records looked and knew they were asking us to take a big chance. As far as they were concerned, however, Ashbury was their *only* chance at making something of their lives.

It seemed to us on the committee — those who bothered to attend the meeting, anyway — that these were precisely the kind of people a scholarship like this is designed to help.

Picture, if you will, a fine line.

It is the line between the past and the future. Amelia's and Riley's past was terrible — they have both felt betrayed, hurt, alone. Their future, however, may be golden — their extraordinary talents, their own strength and compassion should guarantee that . . . unless, of course, they fall over the line into the past.

I am not a fool. I know that there is anger, violence, and deception in both of them — indeed, Riley unleashed that side of himself a few years ago, and a man will never walk again. It is clear to me that Riley suffers deeply from guilt and self-loathing as a result of that.

More recently, he turned his violence on himself. He wanted to attack Amelia's stepfather — but instead, he broke his own hands.

Hands that are the essence of his being.

It is not going to be easy for Amelia and Riley. They will fall, many times, onto the wrong side of the line — and hopefully somebody will catch them, and help them back toward the good.

Interestingly, in the course of last night's meeting, Lucy Wexford said *she* believed that the real problem was that they have no idea just how musically talented they are. She thinks that the most important step will be convincing them of their talent — otherwise, they'll think they have to use subterfuge to succeed. She said — and here I'm quoting from my notes — that Amelia's voice is divine, and that Riley, as drummer, could take on the combined talents of Lars Ulrich of Metallica, Jimmy Sullivan of Avenged Sevenfold, and Chris Adler of Lamb of God.

I have no idea who these people are, but they are apparently favorites of Lucy, and when I passed this on to Riley today, I think I caught the glimmer of a smile.

At any rate, the meeting last night was a good one. Constance was not there, of course, and neither were you (too busy, again) —

Do you know, I have suddenly recalled that you specifically said you find my e-mails to be overwritten?! And you requested that, in future, I use "bullet points"? And listen to me going on!

I beg your pardon. I will start over.

Dear Bill,
Last night, the Committee resolved:

• that the scholarships of Amelia Damaski and Riley T. Smith will not be terminated.
• that the membership of Bill Ludovico on the K. L. Mason Patterson Trust Fund Committee is terminated. (Grounds: He never comes to meetings and he's a bit of an arrogant ass [no offense].)

Cheers,
Chris Botherit

11.

Constance's Letters to a Ghost (extracts)

TERM 1

My dear Kendall,

I tremble to tell you this. They have given the scholarships to the young thieves.

If only I had gone to the interviews! I would have stopped this happening. But, of course, I could not. I am elderly, and live alone — it would have been the height of foolishness to risk them knowing me.

They have been in prison! That Ashbury should be sullied with the likes of them!

It is worse, too, than we knew, Kendall. The Committee tells me that the thieves *spent a year living on the streets* before they were caught and put in prison. Street urchins! In the corridors of Ashbury!

I cannot imagine how they will smell.

Apart from being horrified, I am bewildered. What could they possibly have done in their interviews to so blind the Committee members to their nature?

Yours with profound regret,
Constance

P.S. Still having dreadful nightmares about them. Last night they scuttled into my kitchen in the form of little werewolves, and helped themselves to my leftover lemon pudding.

❖

Kendall,

It is becoming ever more clear to me what the problem is.

Mr. Botherit and Mr. Garcia are what are known as "bleeding hearts."

They would sooner rescue a drowning kitten than practically anything. They do not believe in the principles that you and I hold so dear, Kendall — that a leopard never changes its spots, that certain people have forfeited their rights to live in society. And etcetera.

No, indeed, they seem to think that they can save the world one delinquent at a time. They are desperate to spend your money on that dreadful "poor" school, Brookfield. The fact that Riley lives in a foster home, and Amelia in a hostel, seems to make them *exactly* the right people for the scholarships, in their perverse minds. "They're the very people who need this kind of help the most," Mr. B was saying to me today.

The others on the Committee had seemed sensible to me, but Amelia and Riley must have cast a "spell" on them at the interview. (Lucy appears to have broken the spell, but nobody else.) You would think that Patricia and Jacob, having *children* of their own at Ashbury, would not have been so foolish. But no, they were telling me after the meeting today how extraordinary it was that Amelia and Riley had found ways to practice their "swimming" even while they lived on the streets — they swam on beaches in cold winter mornings.

As if this proved that the thieves had "character" and "resolve."

When all it shows is that they do not feel the cold as I do. No wonder — being the children of the devil.

What did they *do*? That's what perplexes me. What did they do at the interview to so "enchant" everybody?

I long to see them for myself, but how can I? Too dangerous.

Yours in consternation,
Constance

❖

Oh, Kendall,

I am agog at my own daring! Shall I tell you what I have done? I have stowed away to watch!

I could not bear it anymore — the mystery of Amelia and Riley. Do you know where the Scholarship Committee hearings are held? In a "conference room" at the top of your building — of our dear old building.

There is to be a "progress interview" today, and last night I was in such a state — I wanted so much to see these young thieves for myself!

Suddenly, I recalled that cubbyhole off the attic.

Did you know about it? Perhaps not. But in my Ashbury days I used sometimes to hide there. It gave me a little peace and privacy — the students were not always kind to me, in the early days, you know. My uniform was secondhand, and did not fit well, and my shoes were worn and tattered.

At any rate, there used to be an air vent in my cubbyhole that looked onto a room below. Sometimes I would amuse myself, in my schooldays, watching the goings-on.

What if my cubbyhole was still there? What if it looked down onto the very conference room where the Committee meetings are held?

No sooner had the questions occurred to me than I found myself hurrying to Ashbury late last night. I let myself into the building — I have a guest security pass, as president of the Alumni Association — and found my way up to the attic.

459

It's not an attic anymore — it's some kind of a filing room. Shelves full of archives. But my cubbyhole is still here! (They've turned it into some kind of utility closet/room — switches all over the walls.)

And so is the air vent! And, as I had hoped, it looks straight down onto the conference room!!!

So, here I sit — cold, uncomfortable, tired, but very, very happy.

I slept fitfully last night — should have thought to bring in some bedding — but have had a pleasant morning watching various classes and exams in the conference room. My view through the vent is excellent. Just saw a German Listening exam, and the progress interview is about to begin. . . .

More soon,
Constance!

❖

Dear Kendall,

It is as I suspected.

They are beautiful, charming, poised, and eloquent. They smile and laugh so *delightfully*, it chills me to the core. They make little jokes — they have startling eyes. You feel the room warm to them — drawn to them — the moment that they enter.

They put me in mind of a certain couple I once knew. . . .

But, of course, Amelia and Riley are not that couple. They are a sort of *mirror* image of that couple — *that* couple sprang from the glorious realms of society. Amelia and Riley come from the gutters. They should return there.

Do you know who I mean, Kendall? When I speak of a certain couple? I mean you and Sandra, of course. The shining king and queen of the kingdom that was once Ashbury.

It is late now. I have stayed here through the afternoon as the day grew cold and darkness fell. I suppose I must go home.

Yours,
Constance

❖

TERM 2

Kendall,
    You will laugh.
    I am back! In my cubbyhole.
    I had such a jolly time of it that day when I was spying on the progress interview last term — watching the ebb and flow of students below, feeling good old Ashbury seeping back into my old bones. I decided to do it again.
    I crept in last night and wandered the corridors eating fruit — left my mandarin peels right where they were, as I recall Sandra used to do! — so naughty! But fun.
    I think I might bring in a little fryer, for my cubbyhole, so I can make myself midnight feasts.
    Spent today watching classes again. Getting to know people slowly.
    All in all, a very nice day.

Yours in mischief,
Constance

❖

Dearest Kendall,
    Oh, dear, my nose is very stuffy today. It's so cold! I keep trying

to adjust the switches here but I think they affect the heating/cooling of the building *as a whole* rather than just this room.

I have been back here so many times now I've lost count. I'm getting to know all the students — that Lydia is quite a card! Very good at her German, and mine is coming along too. And a fellow named Saxon, he's very dashing. Wish he'd look at me.

Although, I suppose he'd have to look up. And through the vent.

I brought in my feather quilt last night — left a trail of feathers like a swan!

❖

Kendall,

You were so amusing last night. Let us talk more often in our dreams.

Well, a lovely day, and my goodness, didn't we have a ball in German! That song was so amusing! Everyone singing along! (I remembered myself just in time, and did so in a whisper.)

Yours,
affectionately,
Constance

❖

Kendall,

A very bleak, cold day.

I fried sausages and chips on my little cooker, and certainly don't feel so good now.

Had my hair permed by the other one today — Jan — wish I could show myself in the corridors. I look grand.

❖

Kendall,

I have been so daring! As you know, I like to wander the corridors at night, and I have been figuring out the computers. I'm even reading the Ashbury blogs — and contributing to them! I do wonder at myself.

But it gets better! I have been slipping out of my cubbyhole during the day sometimes. I know the back stairs and shadows of this building, so I can whisk around the building out of sight. It makes me feel like so much more a part of things, do you see? I wish I could get a uniform. That would help me blend in. Will look out for one — they leave them in lockers when they do sports.

It is all such a lark. Do you remember how we used to enjoy our games of croquet, and our picnics with strawberries and cream? Do you remember our school trip to Seal Rocks, and how we walked right along the beach? I found quite a lot of pippies that day.

Kendall,

Could I sit in on a class, do you think? Slip in at the back of the room and just stay very quiet and mouse-like? (I remember Sandra once joked that I was a mouse. Amusing, but it gave me quite a pang.)

No. Too risky. I'll stay in the shadows.

Your friend,
Constance

Kendall,

Trying to keep my spirits up, but today my closet feels small. So do I.

I listened to my little wireless, and thought of you. Could not help weeping. I do miss you, Kendall.

Constance

❖

My dear Kendall,

I sometimes wish we had met after high school. Apart from that one reunion dinner where you seemed to have forgotten my name. I know you were only jesting — you were always such a card — but it did hurt a little.

Never mind, I used always to read about you in the financial papers and so on, so I know you ever so well.

Now, of course, we get on like a house on fire! Isn't it a shame we didn't meet sooner and, I don't know, have a family?

Yours, thoughtfully,
Constance

❖

TERM 3

Kendall,

You will be proud of me.

I have been *assertive* — as they call it today. I have rid the world of a dreadful, evil, wicked, cursed painting. A naked girl! Despicable!

I used red paint, to indicate that it was the devil's work, as well as pink. I find that pink makes everything better.

Still trembling, though. And my head does ache today.

Kendall,

Do you ever wonder why we hold the Committee meetings way up in the conference room on the third floor?

It was me who suggested it. I specifically requested that room. Shall I tell you why?

It used to be *your* bedroom. I wanted to be close to you. Do you feel close to me? You were rather nasty in my dream last night. I suppose you were just being amusing.

Yours,
tenderly,
Constance

❖

Kendall,

A near miss today!

I was in my cubbyhole, setting up a row of dominoes. Do you know that marvelous game where you line them up on their sides and then flick one and watch them all trickle?

Any rate, I was almost done when I heard somebody enter the archives room. I stayed ever so still and quiet. There was some ruffling around in the files — I moved slightly — a cramp in my leg — and accidentally hit one of the dominoes! The whole row went! *Clatter-clatter-clatter* like a set of tiny fireworks!

Whoever was in the archives room took fright and ran from the room. Once it was quiet, I peeked out, and saw that they'd dropped files all over the floor. I brought them into my cubby-hole, closed the door — just in time! She was back again! This time, for some reason, she *screamed* and ran from the room!

Some excitement, anyway.

And the strangest thing. The files were from *our* year. There they all were. The records of our times together.

Yours,
in something of a state,
Constance

Dear Kendall,

I am reading through the files, and I cannot stop weeping.

Oh, we were so happy! Those were such glory days! It is bringing it all back. . . .

And I feel so dreadful. Oh, I feel so dreadful. Kendall, I have a confession to make. This cubbyhole is above your old bedroom — I used to watch you. Have you guessed? I used to spy on you.

You and Sandra. You were so happy. Oh, you *laughed and laughed and laughed*. You loved her so! And she, you.

Oh, I cannot stop the weeping.

Your
loving
Constance

I could have loved you, Kendall. You could have loved me. If you'd only stopped and looked.

It was preposterous, really, how much you and Sandra laughed.

You and I could have laughed, but more moderately. We could have read books. And so forth.

My heart won't stop its mad, mad beating!

What have I just seen?

Shall you guess? No! You will never.

I saw *Riley* kissing *Lydia*! In the conference room — in your own bedroom. Oh, Kendall, who knew you would ever betray Sandra in that way!

She must know! It will hurt you, of course, when she leaves you — but you will quickly recover and I will help you on that path.

I will be there, for you to weep onto my shoulder.

How can I let Sandra know?

Amelia, I mean, of course. How can I let Amelia know that you have betrayed her with Lydia!

Riley, I mean, of course.

I will put it on that girl's blog. Yes.

And then, soon, you will be mine. My darling.

TERM 4

Dear Kendall,

Well, the HSC has commenced, and it is just as we suspected. Very wearing.

But more to the point, the Committee has been making inquiries — and again, it is just as we suspected! Amelia and Riley are truly evil. They are not merely thieves, they are savages. They beat a man near to his death at the time they stole from the petrol station.

Chris Botherit got the information from a sports teacher at Brookfield.

It is rather satisfying, you know, to have been so right.

Now at last we can be rid of "Amelia and Riley" and move on with our lives.

Your loving Constance

❖

Good news. It's all falling apart. They will be stripped of their scholarships! They've made quite a mess of things, the silly ninnies. They have to defend themselves — but they won't be able to. I'll watch from up here. I'll bring popcorn. Shall you join me? Yes. Do.

❖

Kendall,

Have you guessed?

I was there — the night that Sandra fell. I was watching.

I could have warned you, you know.

You were turned away from her, looking through your records — choosing a new one to play. She was on the window ledge and had fallen asleep.

I saw her — I saw her beginning to slip.

I could have called down, you know — warned you.

But then you would have known that I was there. How you would have laughed at me — the pair of you. You would not have been angry. You were not that sort. You were so jolly. Oh, you would have laughed, and laughed, and laughed.

So, I stayed quiet — quiet as a mouse — and when you did turn back, it was too late — she was already falling.

Yours
forevermore,
Constance

12

Toby at his mum's place
Brisbane
Sunday, January 18

Mr. Roberto Garcia
c/o Ashbury High
Castle Hill

Dear Roberto,
You recall I once asked you if my dad was a black hole?

And it turned out to be a stupid question coz you made it into a homework assignment that ripped the heart out of my last year?

Nah. Just kidding. You didn't rip the heart out of my last year, I did that myself — you *gave* it a heart, if I'm going to be honest (and sentimental) when you gave me Tom.

Plus, I didn't spend much time researching black holes, if you want the truth. I googled them for twenty minutes. And I kinda liked them. Not as much as I liked Tom, but you know. Black holes. What's not to love?

Anyhow, that's all an aside.

I'm chillin' with my mum in Brisbane here — back in a coupla weeks to start that Certificate in Music Industry (Technical Production) I told you about — and you know I'm going to produce Amelia and Riley's first album one day? — make myself a fortune and spend my life doing woodwork and kicking your arse at pool.

Mum's chasing a blowfly around the room right this moment, so she's not chillin' I guess, but, you know. She was. Her kid,

Polly, is having an afternoon nap, and Mum's got these banana-chair lounges that flip right back, and we've been sitting in those, drinking ginger beer, looking through the windows at her over-grown, overgreen backyard.

There goes Mum now — she just jumped over my legs, flapping a tea towel, trying to direct that blowfly out the open window.

What was I saying?

Yeah, I wanted to tell you that he's not anymore.

My dad, I mean. A black hole.

Or anyway, seems to me he's got his head out of the hole, and he's taking some good, deep breaths of a sky full of stars.

I spoke to him on the phone this morning, and he's cleaning out the house. He had that excited, proud voice of someone who has never even picked up a duster, explaining exactly how you wash a window to avoid streaks. And turns out he's throwing away Mum's stuff. He was thinking of shipping it to her but he couldn't be bothered. He actually said those words. Then he sounded guilty and asked if that was wrong, and I said, no sir, it is exactly right.

He wanted to know about the giant wooden M, though. *M* for Megan. *M* for Mum. I made it for her to hang her keys on when I was ten. She left it behind when she left. Dad said he didn't want to throw *that* away, as it's pure genius, that. He still can't figure out how I got the angles so right.

And something came to me right then.

What was I thinking, planning to give my cabinet to Mum?

That's what I was planning. I told you that, didn't I? My prize-winning Major Work, which I am sorry to show off here, but I think it's almost as beautiful as I intended it to be — I was going to give it to Mum. I thought she deserved it coz she didn't get me. I mean, coz I didn't come with her to Brisbane when she left.

She left behind her giant M, she's not getting my cabinet.

Anyhow, there's Dad talking about how black the water was in the bucket after he cleaned the skirting boards. He was so excited about the color of that water. He also told me that the other parent rep from the Committee is coming over for dinner tonight and asked which of his pastas he should make.

"You think Patricia would like my *boscaiolo*?" he said — and I thought, *Damn me, he's remembered her name.*

Anyway, I've decided Dad can have the cabinet.

Funny to be writing this now while Mum's in the room. She's given up on the blowfly. She's back on her banana-chair, reading a novel. Right beside me.

Look. It's not complicated. She's nice, my mum, but she shouldn't have left the wooden M behind.

While I'm here I might even tell her that, and she'll say something like, "But I left it there *because* it was so wonderful — you and Dad deserved it more than me." Something like that, is what she'll say. She always does that. Twists things around so I feel bad for her again, and want to make her feel better.

But not this time. Whatever she says, I'll say, You bet, but you shouldn't have left it.

Just chillin' here, and it's not so bad. I've still got her, she made some mistakes, but here she is beside me and she loves me. Whereas, other people's mums are not so great. I'm thinking here of what I've heard lately about Amelia's and Riley's mothers.

Anyhow, speaking of mothers, that brings me to the real reason I'm writing to you. I couldn't wait until I got back.

Just before I came here, I went to the Mitchell Library, and looked up the originals of Tom's letters home.

Not just the photocopies that you gave me. Suddenly wanted to see his actual handwriting.

And there was one more letter.

I'm not kidding.

The last letter in *my* collection was the one that Tom's friend wrote — the guy Tom was hiding out with in the bush for all those years. He made it back and he wrote to Tom's mother to tell her that Tom did not.

But in the collection at the library? That's not the last letter at all.

There's another one, written two years later. I've enclosed it.

I guess I must have lost it, or it never got copied, but there's something keeps waking me at night — and it's this. Maybe it was never there at all.

Anyhow, whatever the explanation — sure, and isn't it the strangest tale you ever heard?

Love,
Toby

❖

My Dear and Beloved Mam,

I've learned today that, two years hence, you'd a letter from my dear but restless friend, James, telling you that I was dead!

You may now be pleased to hear that I am not.

But for a little scratch in my throat, sure my health is grand all together.

I'll tell you the story of what has befallen me, and sure, if it isn't the strangest and most wondrous tale you ever heard.

Now, James, as I think you know, was my companion in the bush, and didn't we have a rough time of it, year after year, foraging for what we could. And many's the cold night we'd lie under the stars, and didn't I long to be safe by the fireside in your own home?

So, and there came a time when there'd been drought for upward of three years, and nothing to eat but the skin of our own knuckles, and we bethought ourselves that we'd best take our chances with the soldiers back here or be dead within the week.

So it was that we found our way back one hot afternoon, just as a furious storm was coming on, and there were the old stone barracks. So weary was I that I fell to the ground, and I knew in my heart that I was done for.

"James," I whispers, "go on without me — but tell my poor mam that I loved her." Or somesuch, as I wish I hadn't now, for it seems that James set to work at once, soon as he'd had a good meal, and wrote you that I was dead.

Then he promptly sets out to make his fortune up north, being as he always was, a restless fellow. He's back again today, and wasn't he surprised to see me alive? He gave me a copy of the letter he sent to you (he kept it about him all this time, as a record of our time in the bush), and so it is that I learned that you took me to be dead.

But ah, never mind, back to my story.

What happened next is a wonder to me, and it will be to you as well.

There I lay on the dirt while the rain pummeled my face, and the thunder roared out the world's despair. Or so it seemed to me, anyways, at the time. The spirit seemed to ebb right out of me, I could feel it leave via my fingertips, when a voice spoke soft in my ear.

Ah, *says I to myself*, that's an angel with the voice of my Maggie.

Then the angel grabbed ahold of the ear and twisted hard, which *I thought to myself*, now that's not the way of an angel. *I found my voice to ask it to stop*, when the angel slapped me hard across the face!

Sure, and if it wasn't my Maggie.

I opened my eyes and there she is kneeling beside me, ready to slap me again.

It'd been years since I'd seen her but there she was, more beautiful than ever I remembered, bedraggled by rain which beat on her head, and rushed down her eyelids, and dripped from her chin as she leaned over me, that fury in her eyes!

She saw that my eyes were open and she gave me a mighty severe look and, "I was thinking you were dead," says she, and then the fury flew from her, and it was my soft, sweet Maggie again.

My Maggie in my arms, and me in hers.

I could hardly speak, what with the wonder and with being half-dead from starvation.

She dragged me into shelter, gets me dry and warm by the fire, and feeds me, bathes me, brings me food, and sure if it wasn't a week before I believed that I was not dead and in heaven.

Then one day I came to my senses, and there was Maggie, her tongue pressed in the side of her cheek the way she does, and I knew that it was not a dream, and the tears came, my heart up in my throat ready to choke me.

But I looked around and saw, so far from being in heaven were we that in fact we were in a sort of hell. The long and short of it was, we were in a lunatic asylum.

The barracks, you see, Phillip's barracks, had been made into a place for those of feeble minds, and them that had lost their wits. It had fallen into the worst sort of disrepair, with maggoty food, and damp everywhere, vermin of every description, bedclothes black with mold, and clothes patched together out of nothing but thin air.

But still and all, we were in heaven, because we were together.

And here is where Maggie told her story to me.

How she tried to carry out her plan, but couldn't bring herself to steal. In the end, she joined up with the Rebels, thinking she'd change the world and then bring me home. But they arrested her and shipped her here, so the result was the same.

Then, when she got here, and I was nowhere to be seen, and the men of the colony were sniffing around her like dogs, she'd a notion to pretend the passage here had sent her mad.

So she ended up here in the asylum.

It's years she waited, hoping I'd return, reading and rereading the letters I'd sent her — she always kept them close, says she, to give her courage. But all the time, says she, her courage was fraying at the edges. If it was not for a strange new friend she met, a girl who used to sit in the garden by her side, with a curious manner of speech and dress, she might have given up that much sooner. Even with her friend, though, in those last few hot, dry weeks — weeks of oppressive, wearing weather — she found that her heart had worn right through. She'd given up on hope, you see. No way home, and it seemed that I wasn't coming for her after all. And I suppose if you spend your days with lunatics, it might be like to get your spirits down.

The long and short of it is, the day that I was crawling my way back to the colony was the very day that our Maggie decided she wanted to find her own way home.

She'd run from the asylum, and thought she would take her own life.

Sure, and you'll recall that Maggie has a dreamy way about her, but she swears that the story you're about to hear is true.

As she tells it, she'd the rope, and the tree chosen, and the rain was pounding down, and her heart, she said, was dead, and she'd only to take that one step, that final step — when she saw me running toward her.

Through the rain, she swears, there I was.

I was running with the rain streaming from my hair, and I was calling to her. She swears it. She says that I was calling, "Don't give up on me, I've not given up on you," over and over, and her heart woke up again, and she sobbed with joy, and took the noose from around her neck, and ran into my arms. She said that I held her, and lifted her up off the ground, and we looked into each other's eyes —

And then she says, she was alone in the rain and I was nowhere to be seen.

But across the way she caught a glimpse of color, in the storm shadow just beyond the barracks. Something made her run to that color — and there I was on the ground near dead.

That's when she shouted my name, and pinched my ear, and slapped my face.

And if that's not the most wonderful tale you ever heard, I don't know what you've been listening to.

We made the best of a bad case, and we petitioned the governor, and he gave us our pardons, and a plot of land of our own, and sure if Maggie and I haven't got a farm under way?

She's seen some terrible things has my Maggie, as have I, and she's suffered things she's not even shared with me yet. Sometimes the weight of her suffering stops her in her track, and her movements are those of an old woman. We're broken a little, the pair of us, is what I'm trying to say, but at least we're broken together.

And there's nights when we're warm and snug at home, a good fire blazing in the hearth, and Maggie's young again, and moves about the room as nimbly as a cocksparrow. Then we talk of that strange, strange day, when she saw me running toward her through the rain. She's thought and thought about the matter, she says, and has begun to fancy she had only been dreaming. But I remind her how we used to believe in the future — it's a great unfolding set of mysteries, I say, with chasms of wonder between. Then her eyes, they twinkle as keenly as the stars on a frosty night.

So there's an end to this letter, trusting it might cheer you to know that Maggie sends her love, as do I, and that your son, Tom, has a heart so full of joy it can hardly bear the weight of it.

With love,
Tom

<u>www.myglasshouse.com/shadowgirl</u>
Thursday, February 5
My Journey Home
behind the red door,
blue glow
of dusk,
sharp rise
of telegraph poles,
and a splinter of
moon.

Three planes
fly
in uneasy formation,
they seem too fragile
to be up so high,
tentative
delicate —
the moon.

Had coffee
with
Toby
earlier.

He told us
a crazy story
about:

me
a ghost
a lunatic asylum
and
a letter.

We laughed
at him
and he laughed back,
it's a fine, fine splinter
of moon up
there
blowing shadows away
with
the planes.

Riley on his back
on my bed
studies a schedule
of surgery,
physio,
his broken hands.

the things you can repair
the things you can't.

my mother on the phone
today
now that the truth
is the truth.

the things you can forgive
the things you can't.

Riley says:
She should have come for you,
she should have put up
lost posters.

I'm still by the window
but when I hear those
words I feel
the sadness and
elation of
truth.

Riley keeps reading.

I think about Toby
and his theory.
The lunatic asylum
that's gone now,
the day that I tried to show
Riley and it wasn't
where it was,
the girl with the same
color hair as my own.
I think, what
if I was talking
to a girl from the past,
what if I became her,
the girl from the past,
what if
Toby became Tom.

What if
we got a message across?

What if,
between us
Toby
Riley
Emily
Lydia
and I
changed history that day?

then I'm laughing
hard
because
I think we did.

and if we can change
things that have
already happened

if those planes can fly in
uneasy formation

if that splinter moon
can blow away the shadows

then anything,
anything at all.

Riley sits up,
puts the schedule down,
and he laughs too.

the end

Although Tom is an invented character, he might have been any one of the young Irish men who were transported to Australia for stealing sheep (or cattle or pigs) in times of great poverty in Ireland.

The story of the Castle Hill Rebellion is based on actual historical events. Phillip Cunningham, a stonemason and Irish Rebel, was transported to Australia in a ship called the *Anne* in 1800. Tom's narration of the voyage of the *Anne* is based in part on actual events that took place on that voyage (including the attempted mutiny and punishments that followed), and in part on events that took place on other voyages to Australia from around that time.

Phillip Cunningham was sent out to the government farm at Castle Hill, and oversaw the building of a stone barracks in 1803. The barracks housed mainly Irish convicts, many of them political prisoners (or Rebels) who had been involved in insurgencies, or associated with "rebel groups," back home.

Along with another Irish convict, William Johnston, Phillip secretly planned an uprising, writing nothing down until the note that was intercepted. The uprising then proceeded in Castle Hill, more or less as Toby describes, culminating in the battle at which Phillip (and William) were tricked into coming forward, thinking that the rules of engagement would apply. The consequences, including the hanging of Phillip at the public store, and the random executions of every third man, were as Toby describes.

The history of the troubles in Ireland is very complicated, and both sides have been guilty of inflicting atrocities on innocent civilians. In the Castle Hill Rebellion, however, the only civilian injured was the flogging man — a couple of convicts beat him up. There was almost no property damage, and there were no casualties amongst the soldiers.

In 1811, the stone barracks became Australia's first "lunatic asylum" — and there *was* an incident where inmates were sent out to chop wood, one using the opportunity to kill another. Like Tom, Maggie is an invented character — but there are stories of the wives and girlfriends of convicts getting themselves arrested so that they will be transported too; and one of the inhabitants of the Castle Hill Lunatic Asylum was a female Irish Rebel who was "sent mad" by her journey here.

In 1866, the barracks were demolished. Over time, buildings came and went from the site, and the exact location of the barracks was lost.

In 2006, I was staying with my parents at Castle Hill. Their house overlooks Castle Hill Heritage Park and, while I was there, archaeologists uncovered the foundations of the lost stone barracks.

I toured the foundations, realized that Castle Hill was haunted, and decided to write this book.

❖

Some of the books that Toby found most helpful in researching for his assignment (and that would give a more balanced and comprehensive account than he does) included: Lynette Ramsay Silver, *The Battle of Vinegar Hill: Australia's Irish Rebellion, 1804* (Doubleday, 1989); James G. Symes, *The Castle Hill Rebellion of 1804* (Hills District Historical Society, 1979, reprinted with additions 1981, supplement added 1982, revised with further additions June 1990); Watkin Tench, *1788: Comprising a Narrative of the Expedition to Botany Bay and a Complete Account of the Settlement at Port Jackson,* edited and introduced by Tim Flannery (The Text Publishing Company, 1996) (first published 1789 and 1793); Frank Crowley, *A Documentary History of Australia, Volume 1, Colonial Australia, 1788–1840* (Thomas Nelson, 1980); Trevor McClaughlin (editor), *Irish Women in Colonial Australia* (Allen & Unwin, 1998); Patricia Clarke and Dale Spender (editors), *Life Lines: Australian women's letters and diaries 1788–1840* (Allen & Unwin, 1992); Bill Wannan, *The Folklore of the Irish in Australia*, (Currey O'Neil, 1980); *Journal of George Hall, 1802* (Journal kept by George Hall on board the ship *Coromandel*, London to Sydney, departing on 12 February 1802, arriving 13 June); *Memoirs of Joseph Holt, General of the Irish Rebels in 1798* (edited by T. Crofton Croker), (Henry Colburn, Publisher, London, 1838); William Noah, *Voyage to Sydney in the Ship Hillsborough, 1798–1799, and a Description of the Colony* (Library of Australian History, 1978).

Any errors are, of course, Toby's.

Acknowledgments

Special thanks to Liane, Natalie, Erin, Elizabeth, and, of course, Charlie, for making my days so bright while I was writing this book.

Thank you, also, to: Arthur Levine, Cheryl Klein, Emily Clement, and Elizabeth Parisi for superb and delightful editing and publishing; to Jill Grinberg, for being a wonderful agent and friend; to Liane Moriarty, Nicola Moriarty, and Rachel Cohn, for generous reading of early drafts; to John Wright for the leads on Irish convict history; to Erin Shields for answering all my questions and keeping Charlie laughing; to Tom Reichel for Distressed Weasel Records; to Maisy's Café in Neutral Bay and Avenue Road Café in Mosman, for the chocolate; to Rachel Cohn (again) for more chocolate; to Michael McCabe for the e-mails; to Corrie, Kristin, and Clara for the music; and to all the others who have brightened my days, especially the readers who write such lovely letters.

This book was designed by Elizabeth B. Parisi and Kristina Iulo.

The text was set in Adobe Caslon, a typeface designed by

Carol Twombly, based on William Caslon's original designs.

The display type was set in Bickham Script Pro

and Gill Sans Bold.

The book was printed and bound at R. R. Donnelley in

Crawfordsville, Indiana.

Production was supervised by Cheryl Weisman,

and the manufacturing was supervised by Jess White.